PENGUIN CRIME FICTION

THE GREAT CALIFORNIA GAME

Jonathan Gash's previous novels include *The Very Last Gambado*, *Jade Woman*, *Moonspender*, and *The Tartan Shell*. He lives in England.

THE GREAT CALIFORNIA GAME

JONATHAN GASH

PENGUIN BOOKS

PENGUIN BOOKS
Published by the Penguin Group
Viking Penguin, a division of Penguin Books USA Inc.,
375 Hudson Street, New York, New York 10014, U.S.A.
Penguin Books Ltd, 27 Wrights Lane,
London W8 5TZ, England
Penguin Books Australia Ltd, Ringwood,
Victoria, Australia
Penguin Books Canada Ltd, 10 Alcorn Avenue, Suite 300,
Toronto, Ontario, Canada M4V 3B2
Penguin Books (N.Z.) Ltd, 182–190 Wairau Road,
Auckland 10, New Zealand

Penguin Books Ltd, Registered Offices:
Harmondsworth, Middlesex, England

First published in the United States of America by
St. Martin's Press 1991
Reprinted by arrangement with St. Martin's Press
Published in Penguin Books 1992

1 3 5 7 9 10 8 6 4 2

PUBLISHER'S NOTE
This is a work of fiction. Names, characters, places, and incidents either
are the product of the author's imagination or are used fictitiously, and
any resemblance to actual persons, living or dead, events, or locales is
entirely coincidental.

THE LIBRARY OF CONGRESS HAS CATALOGUED THE HARDCOVER
AS FOLLOWS:
Gash, Jonathan.
The great California game / Jonathan Gash.
p. cm.
ISBN 0-312-06363-6 (hc.)
ISBN 0 14 01.7224 6 (pbk.)
I. Title.
PR6057.A728G74 1991
813'.914—dc20 91-20653

Printed in the United States of America
Designed by Lucy Albanese

FOR

Joan Kahn, with love

This book is respectfully dedicated to the Chinese god Kuan Ti, patron saint of wandering antique dealers far from home.

—LOVEJOY

1

IN ANTIQUES, everything is women.

Everything else is America.

I'm a convert to America. Like a nerk, I'd always assumed the Olde World was a cut above the Yanks. Now? Now, I can't honestly see why they bother with the rest of us. They've got everything. Like beauty. Antiques. Wealth. And, strangely, innocence. So if you're a confirmed Ami-hater, better swap this quick for some improving literature, because this story's how I fell in love with the place through the genteel world of antiques—meaning the hard way, via murder, robbery, fraud, larceny.

Antiques make you live that way. I'm an antique dealer, every breath I breathe.

I'd been in New York three days, and seen nothing but hurrying crowds. I worked in a bar eatery. From nothing, I'd already worked myself up to the lowest of the low.

THE Benidormo Hotel was as cheap as dinge could make it. The dozy bloke at the reception desk—a couple of planks flaking paint—made me pay a night's advance. His job was watching quiz shows. I tried to sound American, wrote my name as R. E. Lee, didn't tell him I'd just arrived from Hong Kong with nearly nowt, and found the right floor by trudging because I mistrust lifts.

A bird saw me in the gloomy corridor, a place for assassins. She was pleasantly laconic, overpainted. A little lad trailed her. I'm hopeless about kids' ages. Seven, eight?

"Can I help?"

"No, thank you." The key tag said this was it.

She followed, stood looking from the doorway. "I mean can I . . . *help*. Twenty dollars' worth."

I gauged her. This young, they should be at home worrying about term exams. "Unless you know where a job's going."

1

She appraised me more frankly than I had her. I felt weighed. "What can you do?"

"Anything."

"That means you can do shit," she said elegantly. I was trying to appear cool and streetwise, but women can always suss me. "How long're you here?"

"Until I get enough to travel. I'm from California, studying in England."

"Don't give me shit." She made up her mind. "I'm Magda, next door. No banging the walls when I'm working, okay?"

"Wouldn't dream of it." That didn't sound slick New Yorkese. "Sure," I amended quickly. "Lovejoy."

She nodded. "Whatever you say, Mr. Lee. You're weird, y'know that? Try Fredo. Manfredi's. He kicked a counterman."

"Fo' crackin' 'n' smackin'." The little lad rolled his eyes to show drug dementia.

How had a kid this young learned about ecstasy? Magda saw my shock and said, "Zole, meet Lovejoy. Short for Zola."

"He's soft sheet," Zole said with scorn. "So's Zola."

Maybe her brother? "Howdy, Zole. What time does Mr. Fredo open?"

Her eyes widened. "Where you say you're from?" She gave me one of those number sequences that are pinpoint addresses in this extraordinary country. "Get over there, Lovejoy. People'll be standing in line."

I thanked her, locked my door, and left. She too was leaving, would have held back but I dithered so we left together, Zole trailing and bouncing a worn tennis ball. I warmed to her. Considerate. I just didn't like the way she had me down as a prude. We walked a little way, then she stepped into a doorway and wished me luck with the job. It might have hurt her feelings had I wished her luck with hers, so I merely said so long.

"So long, Rube," Zole called with derision. What did Zole do while Magda took her clients upstairs? A New York problem. Unsolvable.

"LOVEJOY? Take the bar."

"Right, Fredo."

2

"And that jerk's a chiseler. Watch the bucks."

"Right, guv." He meant a man at the end might try to evade paying. I didn't know quite what a jerk meant, but it isn't praise.

Manfredi's was as crowded as I'd yet seen it. I'd been lucky: Magda's name had counted; Fredo gave me a chance because some employee had Monday bottle sickness. That first night I'd worked until closing time, frightened by the sense of this big city. I'd got myself hired, and threatened about behavior.

The drinks were a difficulty, contents I'd never encountered before, but at least I could clear tables and wash the bar counter. Fredo watched all dozen of us workers like a hawk. The first day I'd seen him fire two of the blokes for fiddling money and general slowness. It taught me New York's message: Earn your pay, or else. By the evening of the second day I'd memorized every drink, their prices, was hired on a daily basis.

"Guv? What's with this guv?" Fredo asked.

Fredo often looked at me, amused by my strange speech.

"Ah, it means boss, Fredo. Picked it up from the, er, Limeys."

He chuckled, an amiable man. "Sir yesterday, guv this. We'll talk English, yet!"

I chuckled along, groveling being my strong suit when poverty's trumps. I'd stuck to the story I'd told Magda: I was heading back to California after years of studies in London. Lies come naturally to an antique dealer. I hinted I had a girl in New York, which was why I wanted his job.

The other bar hand was late this third evening and the rush about to begin, so I tidied things and got started. I couldn't help looking for the girl with the antique amber brooch.

Tonight she was in early, eightish. Theatergoer? Meeting her bloke from work? She always—in N.Y. three consecutive nights count always—placed herself away from the door. I gave her a smile. That amber Agnus Dei brooch again. I tore my eyes away and started my job, saying, "Coming ride up!" and "Awl ridee" like I thought everybody else was doing. Mr. Manfredi had this complex system of double in-

3

voicing, which caused me a deal of trouble. But I'd mastered it, because I'd seen what happened to waiters who didn't. The idea in these American bars is there's a counter where customers perch on stools, while elsewhere floor space has tables for waitress service. It sounds a rum arrangement, but it works. A dozen tables, swing doors onto Eighth Avenue so you could glimpse those fantastically long motors everybody drives, a score of customers, and that was Manfredi's Manhattan Style Eatery. Oh, I forgot to mention the talk—God, but Americans chat. And they do it to anyone, even though they've not been properly introduced, or have any reason. I'd never heard so many opinions—weather, politics, sports, traffic, the Middle East. That you might disagree counts nil. Strangely, I was starting to like it. You could say anything to anyone about anything any time. Surprising.

The chiseler proved no problem this particular evening. He was three parts sloshed and gradually slumped to a fetal posture less than three drinks and an hour after the boss had left. Josephus, our giant waiter who sang the livelong day, threw him out toward nine.

"Hey, Josephus," I said soon after that interlude. "What time's Mr. Manfredi back?" At this social level, you start everything with Hey or Say-my-man. I was blending in.

"Doo any second, Lovejoy ma man."

A bit odd. I remembered Fredo's words, thirty minutes. He never missed checking the till money. I clocked the time. Two whole hours, and no sign.

But it was a normal evening otherwise. The punters came and went. I served the vodkas, learned two more drink recipes for my armory. People from work, offices, the shops disgorging folk into Manfredi's. I can't help looking at people, wondering why they're in a nosh bar instead of home. The trouble was, three days and I'd seen nothing of America except that taxi ride from the airport, my grotty little pad with Magda plying her trade in the next room. And here.

"New Yorkers live on the hoof," a woman's voice explained.

"I was just wondering." My words were out before I saw who'd spoken.

She'd finished her meal, an enormous salady thing of avocado and chicken in deep crisp-heart lettuce foliage. That's another American thing, the meals. I'd never seen so much on a plate.

"Nobody home-cooks."

Her Agnus Dei wasn't as ancient as some, but brooches like hers are unusual. Once, new popes issued wax Lambs for wearing in silver disks. This wasn't one, but could easily have been except for the amber. My chest bonged faintly the nearer I moved. Genuine antique. Norwegian? Swedish? She saw me looking. I went quickly to serve a lady's martini in that fearsome high-gin New York formula.

"You like my brooch?" Persistent.

"The Scandinavians' Agnus Dei pendants were usually silver. Amber's such a Baltic thing."

She was mid-twenties, shrouded against the autumn cool, and pale-featured. Long hair, nothing spectacularly fashionable. Slight, quiet, always reading.

"You know about such things?" Her gray blue gaze took in my lapel badge. "Lovejoy's some kinda name."

"It's all I have, miss."

She rocked with silent laughter and mouthed, miss? I went a bit red, stepped down the counter to punish a suited gent with a treble bourbon. I'd quickly learned that Americans drink booze through shovelfuls of ice, God knows why. Even their beer has to be freezing. No, honest. It's quite true. Go and see for yourself.

"Sorry, Lovejoy," she said when I drifted past her end. "I'm a New Yorker. Rose Hawkins. Can you price it?"

See what I mean? Straight to essentials. In sleepy old East Anglia getting down to a valuation would take a fortnight.

"I'd need a good light. But it'll keep you a month. Around 1800 A.D."

"That fits."

She looked at me curiously. For a few minutes I had to hear about baseball from three geezers, regulars in for the bar telly. Baseball—an unknowable ritual resembling our women's rounders—is as baffling as American rugby, which is all I ever hope to say about them for ever and ever. These fans kept explaining the ins and outs of the damned thing since they'd spotted my ignorance. Every religion craves converts.

"It was my great-grandmother's," she told me next pass.

"Don't give me provenance, love, not without documenta-tion. I've ..." I caught myself.

"You've ... ?"

"I've heard it's safer. Never mind what dealers and auc-tioneers tell you."

"Been to the exhibition, Lovejoy?"

"Exhibition?" I was casual, doing the mystique with ice and gin for a newspaper vendor. He called every second hour.

"Antiques. It's only two blocks, if you're interested."

Interested? I'd give almost anything. "I haven't time off. I'm new here ... I mean, I'm new back."

For a second I was proud of my vernacular, shortening my adverb; or whatever it is, American fashion. She began to ask me where I was from, all that. I gave her the Califor-nian back from England, desultory patter between hurtling orders for drinks.

Then I noticed the kitchen was being closed. Last orders for grub. Lil the elderly boss waitress was collecting the in-voice chits. Ten o'clock? Only nearby Apple Jack's stayed open later than us. No Mr. Manfredi.

"Hey, Josephus," I asked the big bloke. "Fredo back?"

"Dunno, man. I'm zoomin', Lovejoy."

"Doan look at me, honey," Lil called.

A couple of customers gave amused advice. A lass left the kitchen, calling goodnights. The mousey-haired brooch girl stayed, said she was from some place called Greenwich Village. Like a nerk I asked politely how often she went home to visit. She seemed puzzled. I hoped it wasn't any-where near California. Being merely one more illegal immi-grant working for the almighty dollar makes you edgy. Fredo had twice asked for my social security number. Not having any idea what that was, I'd told him I'd bring it in tomorrow and tomorrow and tomorrow.

Outside the traffic was still hard at it, zooming to and fro. Police sirens were a standard feature, I knew by now. The first night I'd twice got up from my pit to see what was happening, but by my second night I was impervious, by today oblivious. New York's siren song, always there.

Josephus had called closing several times. Finally the brooch made to leave, smiling.

"Goodnight, Lovejoy."

I was wiping the counter, washing glasses, keeping an anxious eye on the door for Fredo, not knowing what to do. Della, our cash-check lady, was locking up her pedestal and handing me the keys and donning her coat. I told Rose goodnight.

She left in the same door-swing as Della. Everybody was yelling goodnights to me, people giving me keys. Josephus was singing his folksy way out. I was desperate. He declined Della's keys.

"Dowan tra me, Lovejoy. I'm singin' in ma club tonight."

"Oh, aye." I'd forgotten. His big chance, some melody he'd written.

Which left worried me, the customers all departed, the greasy keys from the kitchen's street entrance on the counter. And Manfredi's Manhattan Style Eatery empty. Except for two cash registers loaded with money. Waiting. Gulp. Hurry back, Fredo.

Outside, sirens whooped. I stood there by my clean bar, wondering what to do. I went and turned off the lights in the kitchen. Only one story, thank God, so no upstairs to worry about. I called a feeble enquiry into the ladies' loos, checked the gents' for lurking figures. I was alone.

With all that money.

Fredo's home number? I hunted high and low. I tried the New York telephone book, my first experience. Its size took my breath away. There was a Greenwich Village actually here in New York. And a Bronx! No wonder Rose stared when I'd asked her what state she hailed from ... well, might as well look for an Italian name in a haystack. I gave up, took off my apron, stood there like a spare tool, thinking worried thoughts.

My doss house hotel was a couple of miles southwest, so no chance of popping round to ask guidance from the dozy old bloke. Magda I'd hardly glimpsed since my arrival. Lock up? Last night Fredo'd winkled out some tipsy customer with vigorous expletives and mucho muscle. Bums had to be slung out no matter what, and everybody was a threatening bum until proved otherwise. This morning I'd heard Della telling Josephus how she'd been mugged in broad daylight, her purse stolen with its credit cards. Danger land.

I bolted the door, but its lock was electronic—tap its buttons in the right sequence or it doesn't obey—so I achieved nothing more.

Money, though.

All American money looks alike—hundred dollar notes look like ones, fifties look like the rest. Weird. All decimal, of course, so my trick of translating into the simpler old predecimal guineas, pounds, crowns, florins, shillings, tanners, threepenny joeys, pence, and farthings, which everybody could understand, wouldn't work here.

Homesick and forlorn, I made myself some coffee, putting a coin on the till for it, and sat wondering about the U.S.A., with its enormous meals and streets all numbered in order so you couldn't get lost and everybody so cheery and . . . like Rose, for instance. So direct, so willing to smile and talk. Most odd. So unlike us. I mean, as recently as 1989 Lord Dacre threatened to resign because his Savile Club decided to allow members to talk during breakfast, the bounders.

Somebody shoved the door. I leapt a mile, bawled a terrified, "Hey, go home, ya bum!" and switched lights on round the place. Silence, or what passes for silence in New York. That is, traffic, sounds of people speed-walking, talk, sirens, motor horns, occasional yells.

The bar now seemed cold and uninviting, even stark. There's something unnerving about tidiness, isn't there? I'm always lost when some woman comes to stay, tidies me into her pattern, washes sheets and gets grub by the clock. I like a little disorder. Manfredi's, all prepped for the morning, was an uncomfortable oasis.

Nothing to read, so I switched the telly on for company just as a policeman pounded on the outer glass panel, frightening me to death. His silhouette seemed convincing. I went to let him in.

"What's going on here?" he said, eyes everywhere.

"Evening, constable. I'm still waiting for Mr. Manfredi."

He gazed around. He was all dark leather pouches. The gun made me swallow a couple of times.

"New, huh?"

"Yes, constable. Barman."

He walked about for a few moments, eyed me in what can only be called a threatening manner, strolled out without another word. I was relieved to see him go.

An hour on, I surrendered all hope and got some cold grub from the kitchen fridges. I made more coffee, though by now I was sick of the bloody stuff. The great survival trick is to avoid cinnamon. America must float on a sea of the wretched spice. They put it in rolls, things called muffins which aren't, in tea bags, in anything edible. Midnight came and went and the telly shows went on and on. I barricaded the front entrance with chairs and a trough filled with giant greenery, tested the windows, listened horrified to somebody fighting outside, pulled out plugs, generally lessened the electricity bill for the dark hours . . . except there are no dark hours in New York, that insomniac's paradise.

A bench seat would do me. Toward two o'clock I unfastened a window, peering out. Motors still about, pedestrians, somebody falling over, neons blinking multicolor into faces, somebody running down a side street. And the grids steaming as if hell were somewhere immediately below. I couldn't get used to the great funnels they stick into the roadway to pipe the gases high into the air. I latched the window, baffled. Grub finished, I washed the crockery in case the kitchen people went mental in the morning, and put the lights out.

The telly I left on, sound lowered. I dozed fitfully on the bench. Three or four times during the night I roused, thinking I heard people trying windows, doors, but there was no one and I slept on.

2

SEVEN o'clock, and I was dismantling my barricade when Fredo came. He was there breathing hard, with the same bobby from the previous night. Fredo looked distraught, a piece of sticking plaster on his forehead and his wrists bandaged.

"Morning, guv. You okay?"

"That's him, Fredo," the policeman said.

They pushed in. The law stood by while Fredo attacked the cash registers. I got fed up just standing about while they exchanged meaningful glances so I went and brewed more of that terrible liquid. I'd have made myself an egg but I once cracked one at home and there inside was an almost fully formed live chick. Now I wait for birds to do the cooking, or go without. After all, what are women for? They can't go about doing nothing all blinking day, not even in America.

The kitchen people were obsessional about their ovens, so I switched the electric ones on and lit the gas under the ones that looked as if they needed it. I heated some water, which I thought a really sensible move. We usually had quite a few people in for breakfast, who sat along the bar. I put the telly on, more unbelievable game shows with everybody clapping all the time.

"Yes, guv?"

Fredo was breathing hard, but sitting down now. The bobby was glaring. My heart sank. Morning of my fourth day in America, and it looked like I was for it.

"The money's right," Fredo accused. His words hurt him. I gazed blankly back. "I know. Della tilled up last night."

"Why's he talk like that?" the cop said.

"Who minded the store, Lovejoy?"

I thought that one out. Some idiom? Guarded the restaurant, probably. "Stayed here? Me. I couldn't work the alarm."

The cop looked troubled, but shrugged and left when Fredo gave him a series of long slow nods. That left us two, except Josephus trundled in like a sleepy troll and Lil, Della, and the rest arriving, hallooing that "Hi, there."

"In here, Lovejoy." Fredo walked with a limp as we made his office. He yelled for coffee through his hatch and got a chorus of cheery rejoinders. God, but morning heartiness is depressing stuff. I wasn't sure how much more I could take.

"Lovejoy. You stayed?"

Patiently I recounted my feat of having dozed on the bench during the night. He listened, staring.

"O'Leary was waiting for you to make a break for it."

"Break?" Run away? As from a robbery . . . ? My mind cleared. "You mean the constable expected me to steal our money?"

Fredo corrected, "*My* money, Lovejoy. You barricaded yourself in. O'Leary heard. He covered the rear exit."

I shrugged. So the police waste their time here as well. "Big deal," I brought out my Americanism proudly.

"Lovejoy. You stay downtown, right?" I still don't know what Americans mean by downtown. Ask what they mean, they'll define it a zillion different ways. They know where *theirs* is, though, which I suppose is what matters. "And you're new off the boat, right? The money's right." He pondered me.

"I know." This was mystifying. And the outer doors were clicking as New York poured in for nosh. "Look, guv. We've already said this twice round. Customers. If you want me to say it a third time, just call, eh?"

Apron, wash hands, and leap into a whirlpool of noisy greetings over the biggest breakfasts you ever could imagine.

Jonie, a lanky lad who shared Josephus's rotten taste in rotten music, told me Fredo had suffered an accident on Grand Central Parkway, been unconscious all night. Jonie, a merry soul who dressed like a jogger itching to go, laughed at his own joke: "Business worries got him hospitalized, Lovejoy—and business worries woke him right up!" Everybody thought that hilarious. I grinned, quipped that dough worried everybody, got a chorus of "Right, right!" and pressed on serving coffees, shouting orders, and making sure the right sauces, pickles, condiments were on hand for whatever customers lurked behind those mounds of steaming food we served and served. And served.

"LOVEJOY?"

"Evening, Rose." I was tired by eight. She was in, same stool, had her tunny fish salad and sliced eggs and coffee and a glass of white wine.

"Want me to buy you a drink?"

I thought I'd misheard at first. "Er, thanks, love. But I don't drink on duty." Then I contemplated the alternative, the terrible cinnamon tea of America, and relaxed my rule, but insisted on paying for it myself. She frowned slightly, heaven knows why. I got some American white wine.

"Why d'you lot import so much European stuff when yours is better?" I mused between customers, on the principle that compliments stop women frowning. "Like your American cut glass."

"Cut glass?"

"Late Victorian. It's miles better than . . . er, foreign antiques of that vintage." I'd caught myself in the nick of time, reminded myself that I was a Yank, not an illegal immigrant hopefully passing through.

"You and antiques. We take in that exhibition?"

"Give me half a chance, love."

"It's a date. Tomorrow afternoon?" She saw my hesitation, reminded me tomorrow was Sunday. I agreed with ecstasy. Antiques *and* time to think? "Then you can concentrate on legit antiques, Lovejoy."

She smiled, tilting her head toward the lovely woman in the corner who'd captured my attention an hour previously by her accessories. Her purse was a genuine Victorian Belgian gold-mesh chained handbag—I was practically certain it had a garnet clasp and a gold dance pencil on its chain. It may sound silly, but purses and handbags are still among the easier antiques to find. And they're still relatively cheap (though by the time this goes to press . . .). I must have stared rather. The woman, aloof from us rabble, actually used a cigarette case with the old Czarist tricolor enameled between gold mounts. Surely not Fabergé, here in New York?

"Lovejoy ma man, Fredo wants you."

I served one customer a gallon of bourbon (mounds of freezing ice, poor bloke) and left them to it. Josephus took over. He hated this. It stopped him singing because people along the bar talked and he had to answer. Fredo was in his office, ashen now.

"Lovejoy. You gotta do a job for me tonight, y'hear?"

"Tonight?" I was knackered. I'd never thought the prospect of snoring my head off in that grotty little hotel would seem like paradise. But Fredo looked worse than I felt. His eyes were bloodshot and he was slanted in his chair. He was on whiskey. "Shouldn't you be in hospital?"

"I been in the hospital, goddammit." He groaned at the effort, sweat pouring down his face. "A thousand dollars for nuthin', send you home worsen before, for chrissakes."

He was worrying me. "Look, Fredo. Close Manfredi's just for tonight, eh? Call your doctor—"

"Lovejoy." He spoke with drained patience. "You do my outside job tonight, right? Juss *do* it, ya hear?"

So I got this job, dead on nine. Wasn't there some old play once by that title, where somebody finishes up shot? It didn't turn out like that. Not immediately anyhow.

WHEN you're in some new country, city, anywhere, it's only natural to want to look, get the feel, be amazed at whatever's there to be amazed at. Tired as I was, I was impatient to see New York, walk and gawp. So far I hadn't had a chance. I'd been in two shops—I'd bought essentials, razor, street map, and that—plus Manfredi's Eatery, plus my microscopic drossy pit. So Fredo's command to get in a taxi and go to a written address pleased me: chance to see New York at last! I waved to Rose and explained to Josephus and Jonie and Della and Lil, left them arguing the toss about who was to do what, and left.

The taxi man was local. "I'm the only remaining New Yorker behind a wheel," he told me. "You're lucky you got me. Now, they're all African, Hispanos, Europe, you name it. Next month I quit, run my own service on Long Island with my dumb brother-in-law. He's a schmuck . . ."

I listened in bafflement as his family hatreds came out. I'd never heard anyone speak like this before. Was it the custom? To tell a stranger your native city stank from garbage? That you'd kill the mayor if you could? That your president shoulda done law 'cos he's stoopid? That your son was a bum? By the end of the journey I was stunned. I hadn't even looked out of the window.

"How much?" I asked, alighting in this enormous driveway. A large house loomed above up narrow stone steps, an ominous place in spite of the lights and music on the terrace.

He spoke with disgust, explained, "It's down to Fredo, my brother-in-law. You believe my luck?" And drove away into the glittering night leaving me standing there being watched by two silent goons.

One beckoned, examined my bag. I felt my nape hairs rise. Being looked at like that brings out the coward in me every single time. Life's always on the wobble, and men this tranquil exist solely to tip life out of control.

"My waiter's things," I said, nervous.

Silence, broken after a couple of centuries by a woman's irritated voice calling was he here at last and get him in here. I received my bag and was shoved to the rear entrance, where another bulky goon was standing, knowing I was coming and saying nothing. His hands hung down. He made no reply to my nervous "Hi there!"

"Where the hell have you been?" The same woman, by her voice, light hair and smart in dark blue and ruffles, comely but modern.

"I only knew a little while ago, ma'am. Mr. Manfredi sent me. He's had a road accident."

"In there. You're *on*. They're just going in."

The place was beautiful in a modern way, by which I mean clean and spacious and wretchedly dull. As I changed into the jacket—slightly too big, but it had to do—I could hear music and a faint kitchen clatter. The aromas were mouth-watering. I managed to get the shoes on, too tight but no time to argue, and tried combing my hair. It never works. Ready.

14

"For chrissakes! What've you been *doing*? This way!"

Shapely walk, white gleaming corridors of below-stairs, following into a lift—incredible. A lift! In somebody's house!—then a pit stop at some unnumbered floor.

"Manners above all. Y'hear? You done this before?" Her voice was a whispering bandsaw. This was a lady with whom I would never argue.

"Yes, ma'am."

The place was plush. Other flunkies were standing about the edges of the concourse. Pale lavender carpet, a grand staircase asking for gowned starlets to make riveting descents, chandeliers and antiques. Paintings on the walls that bonged into my chest and shut my mind off from common sense. A superb Chippendale library table that some lunatic had placed against the wall where its loveliness would be concealed. Sacrilege. Why not in the library, for God's sake? I found myself tutting in annoyance. The woman furiously told me to pay attention.

"The butler's Mr. Granger. I'm Jennie, catering. The captain's Orly, okay?"

"Mr. Granger, Jennie, Orly." The white-gloved old bloke was straight out of rep theater.

"Follow Orly's instructions. Don't speak if you can help it. Got it?"

"Thank you, ma'am."

She wasn't a catering manageress. She was a very very frightened catering manageress. Like I was a scared waiter. I wondered if we were all terrified. On the way into the lavishly appointed corridor—too much rococo wallwork for my liking—I realized some flunkies were more flunkies than others. Two waiters were nervous as I was; three others similarly attired were not nervous at all. These were stiller than the rest. They didn't look at the guests. They looked at me, the other waiters, the spaces between.

"Just in time. That's Orly. Take position by him."

Orly was an agitated smoothie positioned across the spacious entrance hall. Dark slicked hair, very mannered, slim, colorlessly delighted to be in charge. Only twenty guests, I counted, so nothing major.

Jennie glided away into the servants' regions. I took stock.

This was class. The ladies were glamorous, stylish from the certainty that all this richness would still be here in the morning. Looking young was their game. A couple were middle-aged but doing brave battle—we'd have trouble selling spuds tonight. The men were monosyllabic, except for a garrulous laugher with silvered waved hair. Politician? The remainder were too economical for my liking. Economy always chills me. They were economical with smiles, words, gestures, though they'd have passed for a first-night crowd anywhere on earth. Dinner jackets tailored, rings a little too flashily genuine. There was tension in the air, with everybody eager to pretend otherwise.

We got down to it at a gesture from Mr. Granger. The grub looked superb, but I was more interested in the antiques around the room. Twenty's no great number, is it, and I had time to fall in love with a vase on a pedestal—daft, really, sticking a Greek krater where us blundering servants might knock it off. These are worth a fortune. Think early Wedgwood if you've never seen one. It almost made me moan with lust. It stood glowing, its twenty-four centuries emitting radiance you can't buy. (Well, you can, but you know what I mean.) I kept trying to get near its inverted-bell shape to see if its two handles had ever been injured and re-stuck. The red-figure styles, like this, are the sort to go for. It was worth this whole house. . . .

Orly gestured so I leapt to it, serving vegetables. Italian seemed to be the grub theme, but well done. Somebody expert in the kitchens tonight, thank heavens. Veal done in some posh way, broccoli, some sweet-aroma pale things I'd never seen before, and boats of other veg, it looked good enough to eat (joke). They left almost everything, ungrateful swine. It broke my heart. I could have wolfed the lot.

"Certainly, ma'am."

The hostess was an elegant youngish blonde wearing an enormously long diamond neck chain from the shoulders. She'd indicated that a Spanish bloke wanted some grub, so I hurtled decorously trying to look, as waiters do, as if I'd just been about to get round to him any second. As I served—Royal Doulton, no less—I caught a momentary flash

16

of complicity between two glances. Well, my business was to see this guest got his fair share of mangetout peas, never mind if he had something going with the hostess.

"Lovejoy." Orly's quiet murmur took me out of the dining room in a lull.

"Yes?"

He rounded on me. "Pay *attention* in there! Can't you concentrate a single moment?"

"Eh? I am, I am!" I'd thought I was doing brilliantly.

"You're not!" He gave instructions. "No more staring at the walls. What *is* the matter? You'll have us cemented in the East River. Don't you know who these people *are*?"

Well, no. "Okay, okay." I returned to the trenches as Orly clapped his hands imperiously for the waitresses to clear the main course away. I'd met blokes of Orly's temperament before, of course. His sort gets worked up over nothing.

The pudding was some impossible concoction—hot outside pastry with a cold fruit middle—which I served smiling to prove I was all attention. I almost dribbled into their dishes, I was so hungry. I even earned a smile from a dark lady in deep blue velvet who wanted some more wine. Her neighbor was a showy bloke who was all teeth. I was sure I'd seen his teeth somewhere on television.

And that was it, really. The reason I'm going on about this dinner is that it nearly got me killed. As in death.

IT was afterward that my problems began. The guests drifted out to a loose chat, drinks and coffee in the larger of the two salons. My first real glimpse into American affluence. It convinced me that America was and is the mightiest nation that ever was. It has quirks, I knew, for wasn't that a Thomas Cole landscape painting placed beside a genuine Persian seventeenth-century tile wall panel—over a hideous modern lounge suite? Well, no explaining what money will get up to.

One small incident: The host, a neat compact man who could shut people up by simply drawing breath to speak, made an announcement when everybody was sprung from the nosh. Orly signaled me to freeze. Mr. Granger stood self-effacingly among the foliage. We serfs were not to be noticed.

"Ladies and gentlemen. A toast. I give you the game."

"The game! Win, Nicko!"

Nobody stood, though everybody seemed happily enthusiastic. Oddly, the blue velvet lady, Sophie Somebody, had to strain her grimace to its limit. Didn't like games? I caught her careful evasion of the Spanish gent's gaze, and his of hers, because I was standing nearby her at the time with a tray—silver, a genuine antique Boulton and lovely to clutch. I was dying to look for the hallmark. She wanted some more wine. I naturally stooped to pour, and found something worrying.

She was wearing some lovely jewelry—except it was modern crap. Diamonds really are precious, but phony diamonds aren't. Maybe wearing nondiamonds in the super circuit was the reason for her concealed anxiety? There's nothing really wrong with a bit of fakery. I mean, look at me.

Mr. Granger inclined his head. I zoomed for glasses, refills, after-supper chocolates. The glass wasn't quite Jacob Sang, but it was rich Edwardian so I was pleased. And Mrs. Sophie Velvet caused me another pang a second or two later because I saw she'd put her glass on the Sheraton Pembroke table and the glass foot *was wet*, silly cow. She was moving across to speak to Spanish, whose wife was laughing merrily with the politician, so there was no telling how long it had been there. I crossed quickly, blotted it dry, whispered to Orly that I'd attend to it later, and the party chattered on with nobody noticing we were into danger time.

THE guests left about one in the morning. I'd been helping to clear away. Then Jennie caught me examining the Sheraton piece, on my own. Its surface was marvelous, took my breath away.

"Lovejoy? What are you doing?"

"Eh?" I straightened up, worried by the stain. Satinwood can be a pig. "Oh, there's a mark on this wood, ma'am. I caught it in time, but—"

18

"Sure that's all?" She was looking about suspiciously. I was narked at her tone.

All right, so there was nobody else about and Orly and the rest were packing up to go, but a mark is death even on the best furniture.

"Knock it off, love. These library steps are worth a mint."

"Jennie?"

Light flooded down the lounge from a tall doorway. Nicko stood there, his wife Gina and the politician visible inside the room behind. It seemed to be a large study, loads of books lining the walls. Lovely. "It's this waiter, Nicko. I caught him going through the drawers."

I licked my lips in a panic. Jennie was looking at me in a mixture of apology and anger. "There *are* no drawers, guv."

We did the what's-this-guv-bit for a second or two. Nicko moved closer. I noticed two of the silent flunkies had silently reappeared.

The host positioned himself directly in front of me, but his eyes stared obliquely off at an angle. It gave me the creeps.

"What were you doing?"

"It's a set of library steps made to look like a table. Sheraton often did that. And Ince and Mayhew—"

"Jennie?"

For a bloke with a quiet voice his words could penetrate. Jennie drew breath.

"Sheraton's the antique maker, Nicko. A couple of centuries back."

Wrong dates, but I shut up in case Nicko disagreed. Might is right in these situations.

"What steps?"

Jennie hesitated. She didn't know. I carefully opened the Pembroke table to show them it was phony clever, as made by the immortal Sheraton. "See? This table's really steps. Sheraton often did that trick. Made them like leather-covered stools as well." Hadn't they ever looked, for heaven's sake?

Nicko glanced down. It might have been a plank, instead of the most beautiful furniture ever made by the hand of man. A cret, though a scary one.

"Has he excuse to be here?" he asked the air beside Jennie.

"Something about a mark on the surface, Nicko."

"You crept in here? To check a scratch?"

I showed him that too, him staring off into the middle distance. Jennie examined it.

"Shouldn't we rub it off?" she asked.

"No. Leave it. Rub it well when it's hard, never straight away. It might not need repolishing, with luck."

Nicko turned away, but like a fool I opened my mouth.

"Er, excuse me, sir. It was the lady with the zircons did it, not me."

Jennie's sharp intake of breath should have warned me, but I'm basically thick. So I went on to describe how she'd put the glass down and moved away to talk to the Spanish gentleman . . .

Nicko inclined his head and Jennie went with him as they talked. Me standing beside the Sheraton, worrying what I'd said wrong. I was barely ten feet from them and couldn't hear a word. She returned as Nicko went to the study, the door closing behind him. The two Suits evaporated.

She looked at me. "You're from Fredo, Lovejoy?"

"Yes, ma'am." I paused, not quite knowing what was going on. "You can check."

She paced a step or two, not quite wringing her hands. For a happy supper party there was a lot of anguish here. I was tired enough to fall down. And us serfs hadn't been offered a bite, not even with tons left over.

Then she said, "Zircons? Mrs. Brandau wore zircons?"

"Yes. The lady in the blue velvet dress, ma'am."

They paid me, got me a taxi back to Manhattan, making sure I had all my things.

Simple as that, and I'd earned a few dollars on the side. I was so pleased with myself. Like a milliard others, me and Americans were an instant success.

When I'm stupid I go all the way.

2

"NEW York's a collection of islands, then?"

Rose laughed, vivacious. The breeze along the boat kept blowing her hair. I'd have told her she was bonny, but she believed she was ordinary. They're full of daft ideas. We were just docking after a circular trip round Manhattan.

"The song, Lovejoy! To the New York Islands ..." She pointed across the Hudson River, singing about this land being her land or something.

"Oh, aye," I exclaimed quickly so she'd know I'd only forgotten for a sec. "That barge?"

"Every day, Lovejoy. Garbage goes out on barges, dropped into the ocean. The city's almost blocked with the stuff we New Yorkers throw out. Unbelievable."

"I'm struck by the buildings." And I was.

Everything in a new country's astonishing, I know, but New York is beyond belief. Until then I'd only seen New York in rain. My images had been formed from cinemas, that skyline they always show you—skyscrapers, tugboats, traffic on those bridges, the same old long shot of people crossing that long street between blocks.

I now saw New York was beautiful, kaleidoscopically and mesmerizingly lovely.

Many of Manhattan's buildings are no more than three or four stories, all different. And the ferryboat had steamed between forested hillsides and cliffs studded with lovely houses, chalets, countryside so colorful it could have been Tuscany. I was so taken aback I'd asked Rose, "Are we still in New York?" when I'd run out of landmarks. Several people standing along the boat's railings had turned and laughed, made jokey remarks.

"Not often New York gets such a good press, Lovejoy," Rose said as we watched the docking. "Especially from a Californian."

21

"Why not?"

She gazed at me. "East coast and west coast. Sibling rivalry."

"Oh, *that* old thing." I laughed, I thought convincingly.

The city seemed really . . . well, bright. Remade yet sound, not at all like the brash New World I'd expected. And such friendly people. Preconceptions are always wrong.

We got a taxi.

"Hey!" I'd spotted something. "There's a pattern. Avenues north to south? Streets east to west?"

Rose laughed at my excitement. "Sure. The rule here."

"And numbered!" I was more thrilled than Columbus. "In *sequence!*" How simple it all was.

"Except for Broadway," the taxi driver cut in. "And lower'n Fourteenth Street's real bad. Old-fashioned, y'know?"

He and Rose engaged in an incomprehensible dialogue about whether all even-numbered streets should have eastbound traffic. I looked out. The place was heaving, for all that it was Sunday. Rose had told him to go round the southern end of Manhattan to show me SoHo and Greenwich Village. I thought it all wonderful. And I was safe here, which was more than could be said for the place I'd left.

More parks and open spaces and different architectures than the parson preached about. I was exhilarated when we stopped on West Fifty-sixth Street to disembark. I had an ugly moment of terror about the tip. Rose explained.

"A tenth, fifteen percent if you're pleased."

We were standing in a quiet street outside an antiquarian bookshop of the name Hawkins. Hardly any traffic, and Rose looking distinctly flushed as she fumbled for a key. Why was she nervous? I'd not made any serious mistakes, not said the wrong thing.

"I work here, Lovejoy. I'd like you to see it."

If she said so. I followed her up the steps into a pleasant but confined shop. She seemed a little breathless, talking too much.

"My sister's business, really. She's the one with the knowledge. I'm just a hanger-on."

"Mmmh, mmmh," I went, saying the books were really quite good, the usual lies. There's a feel you get from reading old pages that you don't from new. I thought Blake a swine until I read his own printing.

"That glass case holds Moira's special sale stock."

I paused. Nothing special, save a tatty copy of *Martin Chuzzlewit*. It bonged me like the first edition, which is fine but common. "Great," I said heartily, trying to please.

"Of course, Moira dreams of the one really big find." Rose switching lights on so I could be impressed all the more.

"Don't we all, love," I said with feeling. "Same back home. Er, in California."

There was a desk at an angle between the cabinet and the door, with unanswered letters spread about.

"We have associates in England, France, Germany. Coffee?"

She had a silvery pot all ready, fresh milk in a carton, cups. Modern gunge.

"Please." I didn't like Rose's let's-pretend conversation. But that alone wasn't what was worrying me.

One of the addresses I could see on the letters was not far from where I live. Lived.

"Moira's on the trail of something now." Rose already had the pot making a noise. I watched her.

"Special?"

"Something drastic, fantastic."

Oh, dear. I almost switched off. Antiques are an open invitation for every extraterrestrial to orbit in from Planet Greed. We're all avaricious, wanting Tutankamen's gold bracelet for a song, dreaming of finding a Turner watercolor behind the wainscoting so we can ballock the boss and eagle off to Monte Carlo. And legends don't help, teaching us about King Arthur's lost crown, Shakespeare's autobiography, the fabled gold ship lost in the North Sea. Newspapers make us worse, always full of little lads digging up early Christian silver chalices, old aunties discovering that their plain gilt earrings are the ones Cleopatra lost in the Nile, all that. You think I'm against romance? Work a week in antiques. You'll get weary with reports of miraculous finds that turn out to be utter dross. It's always somebody else's exultant face under the banner headline, never mine.

Still, friends justify the means. And Rose was a sort of pal. So I smiled and went, "Mmmh."

"Moira was the same when she found that Book of Hours. Cream?"

"No, ta." What's wrong with milk? "Where, love?"

"The cabinet. Sixteenth century, French." She pointed.

"Eh? Oh, aye."

Pull the other one, I thought. It stood there among the parchment bindings. Phony now, phony always. I think it knew it, too. But next to it was a tattered relic volume that beamed out enough radiance to warm any dealer's vitals. It was labeled Burnet, probably that thesaurus that the crabby old doctor had published in Venice about 1700. (Tip: Nothing—repeat, zilch—has soared in price quite so much as the devotional Books of Hours did a few years ago. But be careful. Fakes are flooding onto the market, the better class ones priced about the same as your average Rolls.)

"I play a game, Lovejoy . . ."

I on the other hand was wondering about the elegant woman sitting in the back room. She'd been there when we arrived. Rose knew it. She'd maneuvered me round the wrong side of the desk so I wouldn't see her. Sister Moira? Only a glimpse, but I was sure she was the aloof lassie who sat and read in Fredo's. I'd caught her in the reflection of the glass door.

"What game?" Nicko had toasted some game.

"What I'd buy if I had the money."

"The Burnet," I said, in for a penny in for a pound.

"Not the Books of Hours?"

I mumbled something in reply. She heard me out. Then, "Lovejoy. How long will you stay?"

"I'm for California, as soon as I can. See the, er, folks."

"What d'you get at Manfredi's?"

A slow inhale. American confidences have three-league boots. But I was being my up-front Californian self, so I told her and she shook her head.

"That's peanuts, Lovejoy."

"I made some extra last night, waiting on at a private party." I cursed myself for sounding defensive. Why should I defend stingy old Fredo? "Fredo's okay."

We talked of money in the book trade. Actually, book dealers are my least favorite antiquarians. They're demon elbowers at book fairs, chiselers with each other and worse with customers. Go to any provincial book fair in England. Booksellers' commonest moan is, "There's no books to *buy!*" Meaning there's a shortage of cheap rarities they—booksellers—can salt away for themselves. The elegant woman didn't emerge.

We finished the coffee, both pretending, and went to the antiques show she'd promised me. On the way I heard a girl yell abuse at a taxi. I heard a man tell another, "Get outa here, ya bum." We saw buskers playing wonderful street music. I nearly had my toes whisked off by every passing car. Noticed that the street corners are curbed in iron! Asked why the manhole covers steamed so, got no answer. Learned the murder rate in New York topped anybody else's, though Washington was a contender.

But beautiful it is. Despite what happened it'll stay that way in my memory for ever and ever.

WE WALKED alongside Central Park to the New-York Historical Society's place.

"Note that hyphen, Lovejoy," Rose warned. "They're compulsives!"

"Show me a museum curator who isn't."

The elegant woman was there ahead of us, standing on the corner of West Seventy-seventh, ostensibly admiring the Natural History place next road along. I didn't wave, but wondered uneasily about Rose's pale indentation on her ring finger. I knew from ancient Doris Day films that marriage holds a special place in American lawyers' hearts. Was I a prospect, Moira along to suss me? She followed us in.

The exhibition gobsmacked me. I'm not ashamed to admit it. Here was quite a small building, not many people about, getting little attention. And inside they'd pulled together a staggering display of Regency furniture. I've seen most of the stuff that matters. I simply stood there, gaping.

Remember preconceptions? Even though I'd landed hoping simply to somehow scrape the transatlantic fare home, I'd been an arrogant swine, imbued with that Old World toffee-nosed attitude: The United States of America's got no culture, not deep down.

The first glory I saw was a Hepplewhite piece, then a blinding Ince cabinet, two—that's *two*—Sheratons, then a Chippendale . . . I filled up, had to pretend I had a sudden cough. It was like suddenly meeting a houseful of friends and lovers.

There's only one way to greet people you love, including antiques. And that's to drift. I kept losing Rose in the process. Finally I chucked in the sponge of pretense as the hours flew away. Until then I'd been trying my best to be the returned expatriate. Now I thought, what the hell, I'll probably never even see Rose again. I started answering naturally when she asked about things.

"No, Rose," I remember grinning like a fool. "They loved brass. See that brass inlay, all round the sofa table? They couldn't resist it. Good old George the Fourth. He has more influence on everyday life through furniture and household decoration than we care to remember. Of course, he was a bit of a ram, women all over the kingdom . . ." I saw people looking. "Er, he was a libertine."

"Why did you pull a face at that one?"

"It's a fraud, love. See the woods? Coromandel's a devil to use, hard as iron, difficult to plane just like the Regency makers did. In fact, it's as if they filed rather than planed. We use fierce electric sanders and routing planes. If you were to look with a McArthur microscope at the surface, you'd see microscopic . . ."

More folk listening, one gentleman stern, two others casual. And the elegant beauty. In an odd moment she'd crossed glances with Rose, though neither had shown recognition. I moved Rose on underneath a silver chandelier.

"There's only a dozen known, replicas excepted. Find one and you've pulled off the biggie." That was a thought, because in the USA possession of a silversmith's die—with which each made his hallmark—isn't illegal, whereas back in dozy old East Anglia . . . So anybody could make a *new* silver chandelier, get an original Regency silversmith's die, and in a trice be the proud owner of a "genuine" Regency silver chandelier, one of the world's greatest rarities. I wasn't really serious. Only daydreaming, as I told Rose when she called me to earth.

The clocks were disappointing. Some goon nearby started expounding about the 1820s being the peak of London's longcase clockmakers—the nerk called them "grandfather" clocks. He would. This sort of thing's often quoted from the slithery catalogue spiel of auctioneers. You have to arm yourself with truth to counteract it. London clockmakers let longcase clocks alone after about 1804 or so, when the provinces took over. There was a bonny archtop bracket clock in mahogany I would have found room for under my jacket if I'd been the only visitor (only kidding) and a pearlware Wedgwood jug with that priceless yellowish tinge they couldn't get rid of until they discovered that a little touch of cobalt made all the difference.

"For myself," I was saying as we left—it shut at teatime— "I'd rather have the lemonish tint."

I ignored the glimpse of the elegant woman to one side of the entrance, because what did it matter? Her sister was overprotective. So what?

We shared a gentle meal in a self-service place and said so long. Rose suggested we meet some time. I agreed because it's my only response with women. I waved her off near Columbus Circle, started walking.

I'd gone a hundred yards when I was taken in custody by a couple of plainclothesmen who flashed badges at me just like in the pictures and bundled me inside a motor the length of a cathedral. I was made to believe that any attempt at discussion would be ill-received.

4

IT WASN'T a police car, not like I'd seen. Some special division, arresting me for being an illegal alien? From jail I'd write to Rose, c/o Fredo's nosh bar, or her bookshop. We'd driven into an enormous tunnel.

"Excuse me, please. Where are we going?"

Neither answered. My mouth was already dry, but it dehydrated some more. My anxiety gelled into fright. This was no arrest. At times like this I'm even more pathetic than usual, lost, helpless, every neuron on hold.

Emerging, daylight showed me signposts. New Jersey? Wasn't that vaguely in Los Angeles? Or not? TV latenighters, hitherto my sources on America, are never precise on geography. Here was New Jersey, stuck right onto New York, as pretty as the rest of the place. Why I should be so astonished by trees, colorful gardens, chalets and imposing dwellings, handsome architecture, I don't know. I mean, I've never been to France or Tibet, yet I've read quite a bit about them. But here I was in the United States and ignorant as sin. Maybe it's that we *suppose* we know, when really we don't. Guilty, of willful ignorance.

The grand house we stopped at was familiar even in daylight. And the frantic girl who came to wring her hands on the steps. She was pale as death, though bonny in her taupe sheath dress. I had the feeling that somehow Jennie wasn't quite the same status by daylight. She'd been the catering manageress; now she was no more than a gofer. Terror still showed. I hoped mine didn't.

MR. GRANGER conducted me and Jennie across acres of carpet, modern crud attractive as an oil slick. For the same price they could have had a lovely Edwardian or Mesopotamian. It's the same with people who buy new dinner services or with household lace, late decorative glassware. Folk never listen.

Nicko was seated between two people. One was his wife. The other was Orly, erstwhile my off-table boss, only now much less camp and very solemn. Daylight altered status all round. I prayed it didn't change mine too much. Mrs. Nicko sat in an apple green afternoon dress, emeralds picking light from everywhere. Lovely. Nice to see a woman choosing the right colors for once. I honestly do believe they make more mistakes in colors than in hair styles, dress, fashion, textures of materials, food menus . . .

"What's with him?" somebody was asking.

"Lovejoy. Tell Mr. Aquilina what you said last night."

I dragged my eyes from Mrs. Nicko, licked my dry lips. My voice came out a croak. "Er, well, Sheraton—" Nicko gazed obliquely past me, still as a stoat.

"No. The lady, Lovejoy. Mrs. Sophie Brandau."

"Blue velvet? Yes. I saw her do it." Suddenly I really honestly didn't want to be guilty of marking their frigging table. I wanted to prove my innocence to the hilt. "Orly saw her. You served her the glass, Orly."

I swear my knees were quivering. Sometimes I disgust me.

"He said zircons, Gina," Nicko told the wall.

Mrs. Nicko did a woman's meticulous nonsmile that speaks volumes. I didn't want to get on the wrong side of her, either. She said, "Truly, Lovejoy?"

Odd that bosses have first names in America. Was it the custom? Chat and fright are immiscible, the way chat and love are not.

"Well, the setting was a bit too much for the style," I began helpfully. "The ring stone was about J/K color, Edwardian cut, put into platinum." Faces blank in my pause for breath. Was Nicko going to go spare if I said I didn't like the setting? "Er, I thought the mount crap—sorry, not well designed. There's a limit to what a slender Edwardian mount can get away with . . ."

Nicko's attitude had changed. Jennie jumped in. Fright makes a woman ugly, as if it scars her soul. Odd, because excitement makes them more attractive. I wonder why.

"Zircons, Lovejoy? Not diamonds?"

I eased. Was that all? Had I been brought all this way and scared witless just for society gossip?

"You mean am I sure? Zircon shows a double edge. Diamond doesn't. You need a hand lens to make certain, so I—" I glanced worriedly at Orly—"filled her water glass, handed it to her." Into their silence I explained that parts of a filled glass can magnify.

"This zircon," Nicko asked infinity.

"They're old-fashioned now, really," I said, cheering by the second. Home ground. "They were the favorite diamond lookalike once. Now there are superb cheaper manmakes."

"How cheap?"

"Peanuts." I spoke my Americanism proudly. "Some cubic zirconias and whatnot you can buy for virtually the cost of cutting them. Even amateur jewelers turn them out."

"So?"

I wished he'd raise his voice, give it some inflection now and then. Maybe it wouldn't put the mockers on me quite so badly. I shrugged.

"She should have had a synthetic." This was none of my business. "Some manmakes are red hot. I mean, cubic zirconias usually won't chip, which natural zircon sometimes does—not as hard, you see, though nothing's quite up to diamond. And finding a big natural zircon can be a pig because they're usually pretty small."

More silence, everybody looking. I cleared my throat, running out of facts.

"Ceylon exports them. People used to call colorless zircons Matara diamonds, after a town there." Pause. That was my lot, unless they got me a good library. "I like natural zircon. Mrs. Brandau's were terrific, though not worth much. Zircon," I bleated on desperately, "gets a bad press. Like colorless sapphires. You can't give them away nowadays, yet they're beautiful stones."

No response. I began to sweat, casting about in my mind for more bits gleaned from my sordid past. Mrs. Aquilina crossed her legs, driving me mad just when I wanted to concentrate. Jennie and Orly were intent, Nicko gazing off somewhere. His wife was nearly smiling, hard eyes on me.

"The woman," she said softly. I swallowed.

"The only reason women wear natural zircons nowadays is if it's their zodiac thing. Or if the setting's complicated and old and it'd take too long to have replicas made." I gave a stiff grin. End with a joke. "There's a lot of thieves about. So I'd use the antique phonies because the setting'd convince even if the gemstones wouldn't . . ."

And I wished I hadn't, because suddenly it was no joke. I learned that when Nicko moved. His head swiveled, but so slowly it was like waiting for a salvo. His eyes stilled me. Black as coal. I felt my feeble smile fade.

"Try him out," he said.

THEY took me to a small room a mile down some corridor. God, but white corridors daunt your spirits, don't they. What's wrong with a bit of color, for God's sake?

For an hour Orly and Jennie showed me stones of varying sorts, including zircons in various cuts, spinels, and colorless stones, mounted and unmounted. I was worn out, but becoming less scared as I worked through the gems in their plastic envelopes. Mrs. Aquilina came in to watch from time to time, smoking her head off but graceful with her cigarette and giving submerged looks. An elderly man called Sokolowsky had brought the gems. He sat by, saying nothing. Presumably the jeweler. He'd brought the instruments every antique dealer knows and hates—they tell whether a dealer's speaking the truth. You can put the fear of God in a jeweler by simply asking for a hand lens, a microscope, a refraction gadget. (Don't let him tell you he hasn't got these essentials handy—notice that all jewelers have a little dark alcove behind the counter?) I was nearly thrown with a synthetic turquoise; the sod had treated it with paraffin, as if it were a natural stone, so I had a bad minute with the microscope. The most valuable instrument is an old pair of Polaroid sunglasses, but I shelved that dealer's trick and did it all properly, for show.

All the while I was thinking, a brilliant-cut diamond of six carats isn't much less than half an inch across, if the proportions are about right. Sophie Brandau's zircons had been way above that diameter, from what I could remember. So her real ones must have been worth a king's ransom. Yet what did it matter if she'd decided to wear el cheapo copies? Women often do that for security, leaving their priceless

31

tom in the bank. Sweating less, I handed Jennie the list of the forty gems they'd given me, and waited while the old bloke ticked them off, nodded, packed his stuff, and departed with a wheeze.

Orly sat with me, talked animatedly and with open friendliness about last night's party, being witty about the guests, making me relax. Then I was sent for by Nicko, who told the middle distance, "He's hired."

"Hired?" I glanced from Nicko to Jennie, to Orly, to Gina, who by now had worked up into a genuinely frank actual smile, and very lovely it was.

"Well, thanks, er Nicko, I've already got a job. I honestly think I'd better stick with it."

The world iced.

"Is he real?" Nicko asked, passing a hand in front of his forehead.

Jennie wasn't so pale now. She gave a hand flap. Two suited blokes lifted me off my feet and flung me out, along, down, into a limo. All the way I was thinking, Hired? Hired for what? I mean, what good was I to a man like Nicko? To Jennie, Orly? To New Jersey, even, now I'd got it pinpointed on the world map?

I had a headache, my freedom, two jobs, and a growing terrible notion that I suddenly knew far too many people in America.

Thank goodness I hadn't told Nicko's lot quite everything about the blue velvet lady. Like an idiot, I actually thought I'd got away with something.

5

THAT Monday started so odd that I began to wonder what I was doing wrong. Or right. I had a visitor, discovered a familiar face, and got yet another job.

The minute I arrived at Manfredi's I got an envelope. The place was hardly open when in came a Suit. It was the huge truncated man who'd sat beside the limo driver the previous night. He gave me a thick manila, asked for coffee.

"I'm Tye Dee, Lovejoy," he said without blinking. He sat on a stool like a cartoon elephant, overflowing all round. "I bring the word. Capeesh?"

"Sure, sure." The word?

He watched me pour coffee, then left without touching it. Lil was close by and gave a phew.

"Ya got him for a friend, Lovejoy, ya gotta friend."

Well, hardly a friend. I opened the envelope, found it stocked with money. Hastily I hid it and hoped nobody had seen. Josephus and Jonie were busy, and Della was in Fredo's office signing on a new waitress. Maybe this was my pay for my extra unknowable job. The speed of America was bewildering. Should I tell Fredo? Was there a message in with the gelt? I was scared to look, with Manfredi's starting to fill with breakfast customers. I gave Fredo the envelope to stick in his office safe.

That day, I started taking an interest in the bar's television. We always kept it on. As the hours slid by in a cacophony of talk I kept watch, throwing in the occasional comment about politicians, bankers, show biz personalities as they appeared on screen. I wasn't being nosy, you understand. Just human. Fredo had been blunt: I should say nothing about the special job he'd sent me on. I understood that. Us illegal immigrant workers love anonymity. But there's nothing wrong with learning about a city, is there?

33

By evening I started activating the customers. I'd got nowhere with the telly.

"Hey, man," I responded to one enthusiast who'd challenged my supreme ignorance about New York. "I'm from the West Coast. What do I know?"

He was a regular, a cheery early-nighter from Brooklyn. I got him onto local politicians, easy with so many news bulletins on the million TV channels they have.

"See, N'York's a kinda special case," he told me, well into his third manhattan. "This city's the world's business leader. The federal government should help, 'stead of trying to tax us out of existence."

A lively debate struck up. Everybody seemed to be from somewhere else, but with know-all opinions about running New York.

The elegant lady—she of the Belgian gold handbag—was in the far corner soon after six, silently reading, but listening.

"Look at the way Washington treats N'York . . ."

"Mmmmh," I went, polishing glasses, serving. "Sure does."

Background was my role in life. Get enough money for the fare homeward. Until then, be silent as wallpaper, your friendly barman.

"Hi, Lovejoy. Remember me?"

"Hi, Rose." It was a careful greeting. She'd cautioned me yesterday about saying "Howdy." I was narked, but she'd said it's cowboy. "What can I get you?"

"You have to ask, Lovejoy?"

Tunny fish salad, sliced eggs, coffee, glass of white wine. And her usual end stool. I served as Brooklyn's argument heated up. Lil chipped in. It was all so friendly. Lovely, innocent, and so American.

Still no recognizable faces on the news. Good newscasters, a hundred times better than ours back home. One up for U.S.A.

Maybe it was preying on my mind, but by now I was almost certain I'd seen *two* of the faces before. I could only have seen them on the news. I'm hopeless with names, but I love faces. The trouble is we disguise ourselves with posh speech, fine clothes. We go about hoping everybody thinks we went to a better school than we actually did. Or that we're richer. Anything but truth. Faces are often the only way in to the real person beneath. I wish I'd remembered that. It might have saved a life.

Rose spun out her meal for well over two hours. By then Manfredi's was quiet, the cheerful arguers reduced to sports grumblers. She put it to me as I passed her the chit.

"Lovejoy. Moira wants to know if you'll call. Maybe come round for coffee after work?" She smiled at my hesitation. "She'll pay the taxi to your hotel."

"I'm not good with relatives, love."

"A paying job, Lovejoy. Antique stuff."

She was speaking confidentially. Nobody else within earshot.

"Fine."

She slid off the stool. "You remember the address?"

"It's the only one I know in New York." She left a tip, to my embarrassment, but Della barked at me when I demurred.

"We're taxed eight per cent of our salary, Lovejoy. Refuse a tip, you're subsidising Uncle Sam."

"Thank you, miss," I called after Rose. A minute later, the elegant woman in the corner also left. No coincidence, not any more. She was Moira all right. But why the secrecy?

What harm could a third job do? I'd already got two. I joked my way toward closing time. Fredo quietly told me he was pleased I'd done well at Mr. Aquilina's, and to leave an hour earlier that night. He looked rough and tired, so I said I'd stay. He insisted. I obeyed.

NINEISH on a wet New York evening isn't beautiful. I walked carefully, keeping to the well-lit areas as Rose had told me. I saw some old geezer preaching God Is Love and was coming to exterminate us. Two blokes were brawling on the pavement with drunken sluggishness. People in doorways start soliciting an hour after dark, demanding change and offering packets of God-knows-what. Taxis always seem to be heading the opposite way.

Odd, but the dozy old man on the hotel counter gave me a greeting, his first ever. Really unnerved, I climbed up to my grotty pad, and found Jennie there. Now, I always keep the room key whenever I'm in a hotel, so she was a surprise.

She didn't move, just pointed to the chair opposite. No smile. I exhaled, having had some ludicrous notion of asking what the hell but deciding better of it. Where Nicko's catering manageress was, various goons wouldn't be far behind.

"Zircons, Lovejoy."

I was beginning to wish I'd never mentioned the bloody things. "Did I get some wrong, then?" I meant the jewel tests they'd made me do.

"No." She was eyeing me like I was a curiosity. For women this is nothing new, but I'd thought America would be different. "Hundred percent. Even the mounted gems."

Oh-oh. I knew what was coming. There'd been a piece of beautiful amber in a Balkan wooden carved mount. I'd loved it. These votive pieces are religious objects, nothing truly valuable in themselves but exquisite antiques. (Take care. There's a zillion forgeries about, usually copal resin with carved walnut wood, mostly made in Italy.) It had chimed warmly at me. It was authentic all right. At the time, I'd vaguely wondered about the coincidence. Rose's amber, now this.

"One of which you didn't even touch, Lovejoy."

"Miss one, did I?" I said brightly. "Well, get the old soak to drop it by and I'll—"

"Sokolowsky says you didn't. A wooden-cased amber pendant. Yet you scored it genuine."

"He'd nodded off, Jennie," I lied quickly.

"We video everything at Brookmount." She stood, walked the one pace and twitched the curtain. It shed dust over her. "You're some sort of divvy, Sokolowsky tells us."

Good old Mr. Sokolowsky, not as sleepy as he'd seemed. And who was this *us*?

"Guesswork."

"Could you repeat the test, Lovejoy? On other items of our choosing?"

She spoke with authority greater than that of the usual serf. Jennie was big medicine. In fact, I bet that she and Nicko . . . I tried a disingenuous smile, little boy found out.

I said offhand, "Sometimes guesses work."

"Life or death on it, Lovejoy?"

I swallowed. "Er, look Jennie, I, er . . ."

"Just tell me the truth." She was simply asking, perhaps even a little sad. "If you aren't a divvy, that's fine. Nicko wouldn't blame you for a skill you haven't got. If you are, that's fine too. Just don't lie."

Her voice had gone hard. I nodded a yes.

"Only for antiques, Jennie."

That made her think. She started to speak, cut out, reached inner agreement.

"Very well. Be here two o'clock tomorrow. Nicko has an idea."

"I'm sorry, but I . . ." Her expression changed to a light sleet. I smiled my most ingratiating smile. "Right, right."

She paused on her way to the door. "Good luck, Lovejoy. Mrs. Aquilina is very . . . strict with all employees."

"Meaning what?" I asked, but the door wafted her away into New York, leaving me alone.

Lovely lass, worried sick and living on her nerves. Nicko her lover, yet she warns me about Nicko's wife's fearsome nature. I could do without all those implied threats. But that tip about Mrs. Aquilina unsettled me.

I put the telly news on to get the time, and coming back from the washroom with my one towel I caught sight of a face I recognized. It was Brandau, his wife Sophie beside him. That was why I couldn't decide why it was one face or two. I switched off and went out to get a taxi, smiling at the irony. Maybe they'd be in some newspaper tomorrow—if newspapers in America did what newspapers do all the time back home, simply filch their scoops off the nine o'clock news and pretend.

"SORRY I'm late."

Rose let me in, more flustery than usual. I'd have said edgily excited, had I known her better.

"I'm pleased you came, Lovejoy." She smiled me into a chair, sat with an intent frown.

"Do you know anything about Sherlock Holmes, Lovejoy? Conan Doyle?"

"Nothing. I remember the Basil Rathbone films, though."

She winced. I sighed inwardly. Was she one of those truly boring fans who dress up?

"Not quite the same thing as Dr. Watson's accounts, Lovejoy."

She made it a reprimand. I mmmmhed to show I thought the same, though quite honestly these nerks who forever delve into fictional characters as if they were real people annoy me. She spoke as if Dr. Watson were real, which tipped me the wink that she was one of those loons who'd come to believe the writer's fantasy. It's a danger we all skate near.

"Dr. Watson didn't write the stories, love," I said clearly, nipping delusions in the bud. "He was fictitious. The real-life physician was Conan Doyle."

"Lovejoy. My sister has made a lifelong study of the Holmes literature."

"Good." I waited. Rose was acting on Moira's instructions.

"I've a proposition, Lovejoy. Your antiques expertise convinces me you are the right person."

My newest new job loomed. I donned a pleasant you-can't-mean-me smile. "I doubt it, Rose. You need an antiquarian if you're making a collection of Sherlockiana."

"Let me tell you a story, Lovejoy." Rose was hovering, tidying piles of papers, quietly placing books. "It's the most valuable of all modern manuscripts."

"Not that old joke about some beautiful?"

It was honestly meant as a quip, but I saw her face set in anger, suddenly suppressed. She knew instantly what I meant. A "beautiful" in the antiques trade is a long-lost treasure. Captain Kidd's chests of gold, Chippendale's secret warehouse in Wapping, that ton of priceless pearls hidden under Birmingham, the whole dustbin of burdensome fable that troubles us antique dealers night, day, and dawn. I'm not being unromantic. It's just that the public ought to grow up. George Washington's secret treaties with the Emperor of China, King George, or Napoleon are so secret they never existed at all. See what I mean? Getting close to myths is dangerous. You start believing.

She calmed, with effort. "Lovejoy. I expected better from you. It's a matter of simple record that Dr. Conan Doyle wrote *The Narrative of John Smith* about the time he married Louise Hawkins. His first novel! The manuscript was lost in the mail."

Well, what's in a name? Though I should talk, with a name like Lovejoy. I tried to remember. Conan Doyle? It's one of those names that slip in and out of consciousness like sparrows through your headlights, gone unremarked. I'd better own up.

"I know nowt about him, love."

"My father's people came from Southsea. Where Dr. Conan Doyle practiced. Where, in fact, he wrote it."

"This being the Sherlock beautiful? The *John Smith* novel?"

"Of course."

Pity. I decided that the U.S.A. was now a terrible disappointment. America should have done better. What about all those ancient land deals with the Red Indians? The lost deeds to whole silver mountains? Columbus's long-lost maps, Captain Henry Morgan's treasure from sacking Panama? If I started starving here I'd have to fake a few Eric the Red mementos.

"Thanks for the offer, Rose. I'd best be getting back. Big working day tomorrow."

Rose watched me rise. I hesitated, but what claim did she have on me? I mean, okay, Rose had befriended me. And I'd welcomed it. But that didn't mean I had to listen to her barmy ramblings.

"See you," I said cheerfully.

I was making my way to the door when Rose spoke. "Moira?"

The elegant woman stepped into the room. I'd assumed the little door led to a closet, toilet, some nook. Careless old Lovejoy.

"My sister, Lovejoy," she explained apologetically.

"You'll help us, Lovejoy." Her voice was as melodious as she looked, but with added threat.

"Not me, love."

"Lovejoy," Moira said, perching on the desk with such style that like a fool I stopped to gape. "Late of Hong Kong. Before that, East Anglia." She even gave the address of my cottage. "Divvy, wanted by your own police. By antique dealer syndicates. In debt to seventeen antique dealers, two finance houses, three mortgage companies. All that plus six lawsuits, Lovejoy—as soon as I have you deported as an illegal alien."

Rose was pale as her sister spoke. I dithered, returned, cleared my throat, looked at the time. Nigh midnight, and me being blackmailed into balderdash.

"You've got the wrong bloke, Moira," I tried for the record.

"Rose?"

"Yes, Moira." Rose passed me a sheaf of typewritten notes. Taking them, my mind went: My career was documented pretty well, but with that bizarre slant with which libel uses truth. "We are associated with antiquarians in England, Lovejoy. It took only an evening's phoning. People didn't even have to look you up. They already knew you."

See how falsehoods spread? I was indignant with the sly bitch, but swallowed my ire. Why was deportation such a threat? Maybe America deports illegals to wherever they want to go! I could try for Australia, if they'd let me. Yes. That was clearly the way. Resist this attempt to blackmail me into helping the loony women. Bluff and double bluff. Be strong, show defiance. The American Way!

"All right," I said weakly. "What do I have to do?"

BEING in the greatest of all lands is all very well, but antiques are antiques. And money rules. I was fast learning that America knew money. It is very, very dear to the U.S. of A.'s big beating heart.

In my time as a dealer I've seen all sorts of legend about priceless antiques. Every dealer has. Crazy, daft, loony—but they've generated fortunes, liaisons, and affairs that have led to multiple murders, robberies galore. I've seen a million ancient charts to lost cities, King Solomon's mines, Merlin's magic wands, Beethoven's missing symphonies, and extinct species of plants living on under the Cotswold hills. All pure imagination, maybe nothing more than wishes formed of faded sorrows. But—remember this—*all* confidence tricks have a basis in greed. And cons make money, right?

So I did a little diligent spadework using New York's phones. And after a fortune in coins so minute I kept dropping the damned things, I got through to Thurlough in Buxton, Derbyshire. It felt really strange talking with somebody on the other side of the Atlantic but who sounded within reach. I had to shout over the night traffic.

"Thurly? Lovejoy. I haven't got long."

"Lovejoy? Do you know what frigging time it is?"

"Sod the time, Thurly. Look. A Sherlock Holmes bookseller . . .?"

"The best?" He took time off to complain to his missus that Lovejoy was ringing at this hour. They sounded in bed. "That'll be Brian Cheeryble."

Cheeryble, opposite the British Museum, up those rickety stairs. I got Thurly to find me the number, and when he tried to suss me out told him I had a chance of an earthenware bust of Conan Doyle, probably a modern fake. He rang off still grumbling, old misery. Brian Cheeryble. He'd know about any Conan Doyle grailer, if anyone would. I'd not contact him until I'd learned what I was really contacting him about.

6

THE commonest question is, how can you stay poor yet recognize antiques a mile off, by vibe? The answer's pretty grim: Imagine having responsibilities to every antique you ever met. A divvy has exactly that. It comes with the gift. Like being dad to all the children on earth, you never know where you are, what to do. Even the Old Woman Who Lived in a Shoe only had forty kids. She had it made. She should have been a divvy, and learned the hard way.

Plus this thing called crime. Tell anyone that you're a divvy, and you can see evil thoughts flit through their minds. And they aren't innocent good-heavens-how-interesting thoughts. They're greedy how-can-we-use-this-nerk-for-sordid-gain thoughts. I've seen it a hundred times. And don't pretend you'd be any different. You wouldn't be. Why am I so certain? Because avarice rules, that's why.

Antiques equal treasure, yes indeed. But some are more equal than others.

Look at your average newspaper. In one week the Greeks re-excavate a temple to the God Poseidon in Corinth, and Boston University architects date it a sensational 665 B.C.; the Chinese find their earliest known celestial map, painted on a tomb's vaulted roofing over twenty-one centuries ago; and two new living species of fly are discovered in Wales. I'm thrilled by the first two, because they're antiques. But the flies are a yawn. Don't misunderstand me—I'm all for conservation. Flies have to manage as best they can, and have wings and whatnot to do it with. But antiques can't. They have nothing except soul. And they can only become fewer and shoddier, as we batter and revarnish and "mend" them whenever we think we'll have a hamfisted go . . . See? Somebody has to be on their side. So far, I've only found me.

♦ ♦ ♦

Two o'clock I went to my crummy hotel, and found Zole in the lobby trying to lever open something under the desk.

"Hi, ma man. Watch yo back, Lovejoy. Tye's waitin' n' baitin'."

The greetings alone are enough to wear you out. "Hello, Zole." I warned him in passing that the desk dozer was coming back down the corridor, and saw him ease silently out into the street. A mini-gangster, that one. What had he said? Watch my back? Tye Dee was waiting in my room, talking with Magda. He turned from her the instant he saw me, cutting her dead. It seemed odd at the time, but not later. I gave her a wave, got one in return.

Quarter past, we were in a skyscraper's lift rising in grand style. We shared the lift with a suave bloke wearing an antique stock pin in his tie, the cret. Can you imagine? It had the true zigzag stem—I could actually see its shape—projecting slightly from his idiot modern tie. Well, I'm used to these Flash Harrys back home so I just glared a bit when he got out on the eighteenth floor in a waft of expensive aftershave.

On the nineteenth floor Mrs. Aquilina was waiting. Not Nicko, not Jennie.

Sumptuous was the only word. I stood in the doorway being searched for concealed ironmongery by Tye while she strolled and blew cigarette smoke toward the vast expanse of windows. She wore a confining black dress, scallop neck, and looked half as young as before.

"Clean," Tye announced in his gravelly bark, and closed the doors as he left.

"I don't doubt it." Mrs. Aquilina avoided smiling, gestured me to sit opposite, a callous trick to play on someone undergoing enforced celibacy. A log fire seemed genuine. The air hummed coolth. The vast flat was dull as ditchwater, everything modern and expensive and thoroughly objectionable. Tastefully decorated, but who cared?

"Today I'm going shopping, Lovejoy." She had aloofness, but not her husband's terrifying knack of speaking to distant planets.

"Yes?"

43

A pause. She didn't drum her fingers, but was impatient. She returned my gaze, squared. "You're going to buy me some jewelry."

"Sorry, missus," I said apologetically. "I'm not well up in modern stuff. You've got some good tom shops in New York—"

"You proved your worth with gems, Lovejoy."

"Spotting Mrs. Brandau's jewelry was accidental, Mrs. Aquilina."

"Sokolowsky gave you full marks. Yes, Blanche. Martini." A bonny maid appeared and vanished. I wasn't offered any revelry. "One hour, Lovejoy. Go and dress. Be in the foyer. Dee will show you."

Dress? I was already clothed. I rose and like an idiot thanked her. For what?

"One thing, Lovejoy." She ground out her cigarette. "I will not tolerate any more insolence. Last warning."

"Right. Thank you, Mrs. Aquilina." I almost nutted the carpet making an exit bow. Blanche's glance avoided me as I left, but it felt sympathetic.

EXACTLY an hour later I was in the foyer, standing like a lemon with Tye Dee. I kept wondering how I'd been insolent. I'd done my maximum grovel, agreed with everything she said, not complained when she'd not offered me any victuals. I'd been for a shower, shaved again in case I'd missed a chin patch. I was hungry as hell, not having had time to snatch a bite while hurrying down the New York canyons.

Tye Dee had inspected me doubtfully when I arrived. "You okay like that?"

"Fine, thank you."

Kind of him, I thought in my innocence. He looked monolithic, even bigger in daylight. I felt as if I were standing beside a gasworks. I watched people come and go through the foyer.

"Lookin' at people?" he said after a while, suspicious rather than interested.

"Eh? Oh. I try to guess what they do."

The foyer was marble and brass. A modern desk was set out for the receptionist, flowers and notepads and console, a couple of couches for waiting serfs. Except Tye had told me to stand beside him at the windows. A doorman in comic opera regimentals strode about marshaling taxis and leaping to serve. Mostly ladies, one or two with the tiniest dogs you ever did see. Fantastic. One was no bigger than a mouse, and wore a collar worth me twice.

"Rum world, eh?" I said conversationally.

"Uh?"

"Rum world, Tye." I nodded to indicate the diminutive hound being passed to a liveried chauffeur. "Bet that dog's got more servants than—"

He did an odd thing. He spun me round to face him. It took hardly any effort on his part, but I was held in a vise, completely immobile. I'd never seen anybody move so fast. His face lowered and he spoke softly.

"You say nuthin', Lovejoy, less'n you're spoke to. Got that?"

"If you say so, Tye," I got out, throttled.

"No names. We're not here, see? Gina's our total responsibility."

He lowered me to the ground and let go. I straightened and recovered my breath. Don't speak. Don't mention names. Protect Mrs. Aquilina. Do as you're expected to do, which meant be invisible and anonymous. Take the money and do the job, in whatever order either comes. I sighed inwardly as the lift went and sundry serfs leapt to fawn on Mrs. Aquilina as she emerged. Okay America, I thought, you're the boss. I too advanced, smiling the anxious smile of the abject ingrate.

She swept by me without a word, doors parting and kulaks bowing and scraping. I trotted after, a humble ninth in the entourage. Except there was something wrong. And it wasn't that Mrs. Aquilina also seemed mad at me. It was that a bloke stepping forward in the morning coat of a hotel manager had a luscious eighteenth-century stock pin, ruby head and zigzag stem, in his lapel. Lovely stone, glamorous design, gold mount all just the same as earlier. I've only seen about six in my life. Now two on the same day, in one building? Were there scores in New York? And he'd grown a moustache—in an hour?

"Excuse me," I said, plucking Tye's sleeve as our lady stopped and we all collided up against each other.

"Shtum." It was more than a hiss, not proper speech. I only wanted to explain about the bloke with the tiepin, ask why a stylish gent in sunglasses and suave gear would want to change into serf's uniform. Was he too one of us hirelings, on perpetual guard against New York's unknowable mayhem? If so, it was overdoing things a bit. This Nicko lot seemed to live on its nerves. . . . Then I saw Tiepin look at a dark blue motor down the street, surreptitiously raise his hand. Two men. Tye was facing the other way, though he scanned the traffic closely as we left the foyer for the pavement.

Mrs. Aquilina got into her limo. I recognized the driver. Tye said, "Hi, Tony," so that was all right. I made to follow her into the motor. She rounded on me from the interior.

"Out!" she snapped. I'd never seen anybody so furious. "You look like a hobo! *Out!*"

Tye hauled me back onto the pavement, saying desperately, "Wait, Gina—"

"*Andiamo!*"

Tiepin disappeared into the building, moving faster than a major domo should. They stroll, august and serene. This one was . . . escaping? Definitely at a fast trot. Wrong. Our limo containing Mrs. Aquilina moved off, I thought a little slower than normal. And Tony's gloved hand reached out of his window and slickly tapped the limo's roof. Why?

The big dark motor down the street started up, rolled after her no more than sixty feet.

Tye was signaling to a taxi—so the strange motor with the two men couldn't be ours. Therefore they were . . .

I barged the commissionaire aside, grabbed his posh metal stand, and heaved the damned thing into the road, catching the blue motor. Two other cars swerved. The blue limo tried hard, but dived into a skidding yellow taxi. Tires squealed, glass fractured, and horns parped.

A passing scruff delightedly went, "Wow-eeee, man!"

Drivers began bawling with that immediacy New Yorkers manage so easily. I'd never seen so many gestures. Even pedestrians joined in, exclaiming and gesticulating and thronging about. Tye had vanished. Some friend, I thought bitterly. Just when I wanted him.

The commissionaire had me in some deathlock. It had taken ten seconds. I was alone, the center of attention. In one minute flat I was arrested. The druggie bent to peer in at me as I was clouted into the police car. "Wow-eeee!" he cried after us. I wore handcuffs, heavier and more service-able than ours. The policemen were about two stone over-weight, and brutal masters of invective. Genuine police, at last. I'd made it back to normal.

7

WELL, all right America, I still love you. I just have my doubts about your constabulary.

NEW York's joke is, "You can't beat our cops." True, true. (They do the beating, get it?) I was black and blue when I came to rest among other miscreants, but nowhere did it show. Clever. My face and hands were untouched, yet I could hardly stand. They slung me into some pit amid sounds like a clanging echo chamber. Nine of us, mostly wearing jeans, tattered denim, and truculent sneers. I avoided eye contact, slid down the wall bone tired. I realized that irritating groaning was me. I stopped, hoping to avoid attention.

"What yo fo, bo?" somebody asked me, a treble bass voice.

"Attempted murder," I said to the single bulb a mile out of reach through a grid that covered our domain. It was hardly a glim, but hurt. I closed my eyes.

"Who'd ya trah?"

"International art dealer." I'd worked it out. By the time this lot learned the truth, I'd be deported, shipped home for my long-awaited trial elsewhere.

This time I got "Whafo?" and "How?" I was among sociologists. A doze was called for, out of all this. If they'd let me. Jails and violence are synergistic, not mutual exclusives.

Somebody was picking my pocket. Talk about inexpert. Where I come from he'd starve. I roused to answer when somebody shook me, asking.

"Eh? Oh. I'd done him a load of antiques. He didn't . . ." Americanisms might save me from being butchered as an Olde Worlde guest on these shores. "He didn't make wit de bread, man. I threw a hotel stand at his motor, uh, automobile."

As improvisation it wasn't bad.

"Shoulda trahd yo gun, man," the resonant voice said. I'd never heard such a bass, quiet as that.

"Boss says no guns. He'll be—" what was Americanese for infuriated?—"real sore at me for this."

A desultory talk began while I tried to rest. They discussed ways of inflicting death and/or destruction without guns. They thought my effort with the stand feeble.

The clamor from the clink intensified. Like living in a foundry. A couple of people came and went, subjected to the same interrogation I'd undergone. My few dollars went from my back pocket. I dozed fitfully, was hauled out for interrogation twice—reason for blamming a vehicle, causing mayhem in Manhattan—was thumped back to the cell. We'd shrunk to eight, one clearly stoned out of his mind on spiritual substances. He was clobbered to the floor by the treble bass voice. I did my weary slide, now blacker and bluer.

"Hey, man. Bettune?"

"Eh?"

The bloke who'd slammed the druggie was crouching by me. He was a giant, even bigger than Josephus.

"Yo dealer man. Bettune? East Seventy-fourth?"

What the hell was he on about? I squinted up at him. "Boss says no names, man."

"Rahd own." Right on. The great head nodded slowly, big as a bison's and biblical with it. He waited a moment, staring at me with vast bloodshot eyes, then snapped his fingers and without having to look caught a clutch of dollars somebody instantly passed him. "Yo cash, man."

"Thank you."

I remember very little else for seven or eight hours after that. Somebody playing a mouth organ, everybody having awkward pees with everybody else grumbling, the druggie waking to the shakes in a screaming fit, that persistent clanging, occasional shouts, vehicles wahwahing outside.

They called me about six in the morning. Except it was the brightest-suited lawyer I'd ever seen, all smiles and brilliant teeth. A holiday camp of a lawyer if ever I'd seen one. He knew everybody, slapped backs, had a million jokes, a cheroot, expensive tan, and a briefcase chained to his wrist.

49

It held one sheet of paper, which he produced with a magician's flourish. I never did learn what was on it, but it sprung me.

"See yaz, Lovejowa," boomed the bass after me.

"Oh, yes. Bye. And thanks, er . . ." How did he know me?

"Busman. West Forty-second station, yo in town." The bass varoomed a laugh octaves down.

"Cheers, Busman."

"Name of Gordino," the lawyer told me, shaking my hand. I blinked at the light while he signed at a desk. I'd never seen so many police in such a hurry. Like a commuter rush, barging past and yelling things like, "Yo!" They had more hardware on their belts than most tinkers' carts. "This way, Lovejoy."

"Er, thank you, Mr. Gordino. It's most kind of you to—"

"That's all, Lovejoy." He muttered the instruction from the side of his mouth, impressing me. I knew I'd be trying to do it in front of the mirror as soon as I made it back to the hotel.

As we left the cop shop he made a regal progress, acknowledging everybody, any rank and role. "Hey, Al! How ya doin'?" and "Tom? Okay Thursday, get beaten by a slicker handicap?" Our departure was a crazy crosstalk act, him the cheerleader, pally police an amiable gauntlet.

We made the car park and he changed into a bitter unsmiling man.

"You bastard," he said, lips tight, sinking into a saloon. Tye Dee was sitting beside the driver. It was Tony the roof-tapper. He said nothing, so neither did I. Gordino cursed me. "You double mother of a bastard. Never try that on me again, ya hear?"

"Right, sir," I said anxiously.

"Why the frigging fuck you not lay out the wire?" he said through his slit. If he loved the police, he hated me for not laying out his wire. I nodded blankly. "It took me nine—repeat nine—long hours to find you."

"I'm sorry. I promise." But promise what? So far, nobody in America had understood me. And I was lagging in the comprehension stakes by a mile.

Gordino mopped his face with a crimson handkerchief.

He was trembling, here in broad daylight. I looked out, trying to see where we were going, but Tye's eyes caught me in the rear mirror and I sank down so as not to see.

"Double bastard," the lawyer muttered a couple of times.

We drove out of Manhattan, some tunnel to somewhere. Wherever it was was sure to be beautiful, leafy, affluent, and baffling as the rest of America. I started scratching, having caught lice from the jail. I wondered about Busman, Bettune, Seventy-fourth Street, having my money returned by robbers for nothing. And, of course, why I was a swine to Gordino on account of some wire. And why Tye Dee looked scared for his skin. I was scared for mine, of course, but that was normal.

It was about eight o'clock, the morning rush hour. I drew breath to suggest that I'd best be making tracks for Fredo's bar, but stayed silent.

IT WAS more than a yacht. It was a cruiser, white as a goose. Twin masts and striped awnings. They didn't have vessels like this in the Blackwater at home. This was a cocktails-and-caviar boat, not a coastal slogger ready for gales such as I was used to. It was the only vessel at the small pier.

The crew weren't uniformed so much as standardized, which was much less reassuring. Only half a dozen of them, but fit and wary. One just stood there in the stern, scanning the distant wooded riverbank and talking quietly into his chest whenever another boat glided by.

I went up the gangplank after Gordino. He was into his windmill mode, a big hello and cheroot, pretending to throw up over the side when the boat rocked slightly in a wash.

"Follow me," Tye Dee said. He was uncomfortably close behind me.

It was a lovely morning, the sun already up and a few boats plying the water. Cars winked windscreens on tiny roads parallel to shore. A few gulls planed over. Several other yachts were moored further downriver. It felt good to be alive. God, but yes it did. I warmed again to America, not solely because there was Gina Aquilina in a white toweling dressing gown observing our arrival from under an awning on the top deck.

Nicko cooled my pleasure at this nautical scene. His stare was somewhere to the northwest, his voice sibilant. Jennie wasn't there. Orly was, seething at me as usual.

"Lovejoy's done well," Nicko said. "He gets bonused."

Bonus a verb too? I grinned, but my face wouldn't play, stood there like a lemon.

"Tye, man." Nicko heaved a moderate sigh. "About you."

"Let Lovejoy tell it, Nicko," Mrs. Aquilina begged. Funny sort of begging, though. Quiet, yet the words piercing everybody's reluctance. I spoke up, worried about the outcome but avoiding scratching at the lice. Fleas get poems written in their honor. Lice are just misery.

"Why didn't you warn Tye, Lovejoy?" she asked.

"About the men in the motor? I . . . I didn't know if I was wrong." I'd explained about the tiepin man, his sudden moustache and quick change, his running exit, the signal to the two men. Except I'd tried, and Tye had almost flattened me. I left that bit out.

"Why didn't you warn Gina?" Nicko asked.

This one was more difficult. A simple lie to save Tye's bacon was fair, but dare I try the same for Mrs. Aquilina? The space between husbands and wives is a minefield.

"I . . . I was too slow getting into the motor car, Nicko."

"He looked like a hobo, Nicko," his wife said.

"I'd no other clothes, you stupid cow!" I yelled, narked. Then swallowed myself into docility again. "Sorry, missus."

"Good." Nicko nodded to the distant shore. "I like that. He lies good." He thought, glanced at the shore where Tony waited by the limo having a smoke. He wasn't relaxed, kept looking up at the yacht. "Berto?"

Gordino said, "Lovejoy told nothing down the precinct. But he shoulda got on the wire, saved me a ton a trouble."

"That's okay," Nicko forgave. "I like that. He telled nothing." He stared at Orly. "He's filthy. Clean him up, bring him for prima collazione."

Breakfast! Grub on the way! And bonused! I was in some sort of favor, an experience so rare I'd been slow to realize it.

"Who's the broad?" he asked the river.

"Rose Hawkins, Nicko," Tye replied for me. "Bookseller. She's hot for Lovejoy. Has some book job for him is all."

"Excuse me, er, Nicko." I ducked slightly as his head rotated. It turned like a gun's swivel mount in a turret, stopped short of my face, thank God.

Silence, except for sea gull sounds by the gallery portholes.

"Er, can I ask Mr. Gordino to do something? I'd pay—well, owe him, if it's okay by you." Mrs. Aquilina had a sudden alert interest, a stoat about to start its rabbit-transfixing dance. "There's a bloke—guy—in the police station. Can you try to help him? Busman. He was kindly."

Nicko thought, said okay. Gordino asked, "Chico? Spic? Nigruh? Wasp?"

"I don't know his surname. He's just called Busman."

Mrs. Aquilina stifled a giggle. Nicko's gaze reached me this time, like a puzzled Last Judgment. He decided I was thick. "Orly. See about Tony."

Orly nodded, left us for a moment. We all waited. The rest seemed content. I kept clearing my throat, shuffling, whistled a bit until I realized it made me feel more ridiculous.

Two crewmen went down to Tony. He stood on his fag end, almost came to attention as they approached.

"Nicko," he called, in his voice an ugly quavering. "Can I speak with you?"

Nobody moved or answered.

"Er, I think Tony's calling, Nicko . . ." I petered out.

The crewmen shoved Tony inside the motor. One sat behind him as the other drove the car up the slope and away. Sacked? Perhaps for lacking vigilance? On the boat life instantly resumed.

"Right," Nicko said. "Let's go."

"To help Busman? There's no need for us all," I thanked him. "Just Mr. Gordino, if he could . . ."

Nicko departed, shaking his head. The lawyer sprinted ashore after darting me a malevolent glance. The crew sprang into action. Orly left at a peremptory signal from Gina. There are some people who, whatever they do, look

53

as if they're always sweeping up after the boss. Orly was one. Mind you, Gina would be lovely to associate with in any circumstances—or so I thought, then.

"Don't go, Lovejoy."

"Yes, Mrs. Aquilina?"

Tye Dee beckoned a crewman, who eyed my measures doubtfully. They went below through heavily varnished doors.

Gina was so desirable my throat had practically closed. I stood, mesmerized and in difficulties.

"I'm grateful. You saved my life. You know you could have gotten yourself shot?"

"Well." I struggled with my airway.

She gazed out at the river. Sunlight consorts with a woman, doesn't it. I looked. She turned to gaze at me.

"There's only one thing makes a man take a stupid risk like that, Lovejoy. I just want you to know I understand. But it's out of the question. However, you deserve some sort of reward. You can have your pick of the staff. As long as you are discreet about it, and the girl goes along."

I pondered. What the hell was she saying? That I was lovelorn? That I'd acted from adoration, or what? I got breath and was about to explain that she'd got it wrong. I mean, don't misunderstand me. She was blindingly beautiful, and knew it. And I'd have given anything just to, well. But when a living creature's in mortal danger, I mean any bloke in his right mind would do the same thing without weighing the pros and cons, right? I've rushed across motorway traffic to save a bewildered hedgehog before now. It's what people do. Instinct or something.

"Well, Gina . . ." Then I thought. My one brain cell shrieked to beware.

It's this business of women and love. It lies at the root of all of life. Everybody loves a lover, true. But does every woman love a lover equally? Not on your life she doesn't. Oh, they adore Abelard, crazy for Heloise. They revere Romeo's lust for Juliet, John Whatsisname for Lorna Doone. And here was the lady who had everything—power, wealth, beauty, youth—saying openly that she approved of me, your one-off destitute scruff, solely because she believed that I'd fallen for her. Of course, she was right. But it was true of her maid Blanche, of Rose Hawkins, her imperious sister Moira. For Della, Lil at Fredo's bar, for . . . No. The great mistake loomed. Hell hath no fury like a woman substituted.

"No, thank you."

"What?" She leaned on the ship's rail, taking stock.

"No, thank you." I tried to look abashed, embarrassed, brave but melancholic. A bidden blush never comes, does it. It's only when I try to seem supercool that I go red. "I know you're out of my reach, Gina. I'll not settle for less."

"Of all the . . ." Her anger faded. She turned away. "Get below and clean up. You look like a derelict."

I went inside to find Tye, more cheerful than I'd been. I'd risen in Gina's esteem. And my determination to stay pure needn't last more than a few minutes. There were several maids laying for a party on the upper deck arena. As long as Gina didn't find out. She'd not want me to lower my standards.

The engines started and nautical sequences began. We were going on a voyage.

"CHICO, Spic, Nigruh, mean color, Lovejoy." Tye Dee was swilling a whisky while I showered. (Dear U.S.A.: Need your showers be so forceful they slam you against the tiles?)

Color? How could Busman's color help? There couldn't be more than one with that nickname. I soaped industriously with a loofah. Lice are simple to shed. Damage the fragile little things and they've had it.

"Another thing, Lovejoy. Orly and Mrs. Aquilina are . . . friends. So's Jennie and Nicko. Okay?"

That halted my scrubbing for a second. I resumed, slower. "Thanks, Tye."

"And ya get took, ya phone Gordino. Okay?"

God, but whisky stinks foul in the early morning. Its aroma almost made me gag. I'd bagged my clothes in plastic, and tied the neck. A crewman's gear was laid out on the bunk. My second job, at last? Dressed, I went and lost my way a dozen times.

Breakfast was gigantic even by American standards. Gina finally came, had an ounce of orange juice and three grapes.

55

Orly had a couple of pancakes. Nicko had a croissant and coffee. I had hash browns—think fried mash—and everything within reach. Three times I narrowly escaped having syrup poured over it all.

During the gargantuan nosh I tried asking where we were going. The Hudson? No, for we were amid several islands. The Statue of Liberty, and us turning away northward, bridges ahead and a crowded mass of habitations to the right.

Gina was being amused. "How marvelous to see you eat, Lovejoy! The galley will be delighted."

Well, there was no telling where my next meal would come from. And you can't muck hunger about, or any other appetite for that matter.

"I'm worried about Mr. Manfredi, er, Gina. He'll be in the middle of his morning rush."

"That's taken care of, Lovejoy." Then, just as I was settling down to the new batch of grub, "You seemed to take a particular interest in Sophie, Lovejoy. Why?" I rescued myself from a choke. "Sophie Brandau, Lovejoy. The lady in blue velvet."

"I saw her bloke on television. I looked their name up."

There's not a problem in human affairs that crime can't solve. So crime had to be my explanation.

"He's a politician, Gina. I was scared, because I'm in political trouble."

She was enjoying my discomfiture, chin on her linked hands, very fetching 1920s while Orly glowered. Nicko and Tye were listening.

"I'm not American," I confessed. "I'm from East Anglia. Illegal immigrant, trying to work my way home. I'm wanted by the police there."

"We know, Lovejoy. You're not exactly our streetwise New York spoiler."

Sandpaper grated nearby. We all looked. It was Nicko, laughing, shaking up and down in his deck chair.

"Lovejoy. You think you'll put the bite on Denzie Brandau?"

Nicko fell about. It really narked me. I'd been so American I'd convinced myself completely. Gina was nodding.

"Through Sophie, perhaps," she murmured. "Except generosity's never been her strong point."

She and Nicko exchanged glances. Tye Dee was with me still, noshing but keeping out of it. Orly put his oar in.

"Lovejoy'll be able to try his hand at exploitation—when the Brandaus come aboard this afternoon."

We were turning toward the east, leaving Manhattan behind. I felt entitled to ask, myself again.

"Is this still New York?"

"Both sides. We're headed for Long Island Sound." Gina extended a hand. Orly leapt to take it, haul her up.

Nicko showed no emotion as Gina and Orly paired away. He was reading from a folder. I avoided asking the obvious. Their business.

"Excuse me, Nicko. What am I here for, exactly?"

He didn't look up. "To help decide fraud, Lovejoy. And play a game."

It didn't sound my thing. I lowered my knife and fork.

"I'm sorry, Nicko, but I want out . . ."

Tye suddenly shoved a plate of scrambled eggs and waffles across the table, warning. Nicko hadn't interrupted his reading.

"Great, great," I said quickly. "Look forward to it, Nicko. Fraud's my thing." Thereby being responsible for the deaths of two people. One was a foe, one a sort of friend. And one was nearly me.

FOR an hour I stood on the after deck watching New York glide by. Tye described where we were. The names were oddly familiar, the places resonant of some primeval dream time: Brooklyn, Queens, the Bronx, New Rochelle. The old jeweler Mr. Sokolowsky astonished me by coming out to stand and reminisce. He was amusing, got me laughing about local quirks in buying silver, pricing jewels, a goldsmith's slender finances ha ha ha. A witty old bloke with shrugged-off humor. Orly passed by once, to say I was to "get something decent on by the time we hit the Sound."

"Long Island Sound," Tye translated. "That's where it happens."

"Oy vey," Mr. Sokolowsky lamented, shrugging. "Happenings should wait a liddle now and then."

Gina sent her Blanche with a message that she wanted me. It was to do with clothes. She'd had the vessel combed for clobber. It was highly fashionable, which I am not. I settled for some loose gray trousers and a white shirt. She pulled a face when finally I showed myself. I grimaced back, grinning to set her laughing. It was the last laugh for some time.

I wanted to know what happened to Tony, if Berto Gordino had managed to spring Busman, what Della and Lil were telling Rose when she came by Fredo's and asked where I'd got to. But by then the boat was thrusting through some narrows into Long Island Sound, breathtaking in its expanse and shores, and my duties began.

THEY started coming aboard about mid-afternoon. I watched them from the rail, a mere bystander like the crew.

Glamor isn't simply something in the eye of the beholder. It's a kind of heat emanating from the glamorous. But it's cold, heat that doesn't warm. Which I suppose is one way of saying it's radiation, the stuff that eventually kills. This thought struck me when I recognized a familiar elegant lady ascending our gangway from a small power boat. Good old Moira Hawkins was accompanied by Sophie Brandau and her politician husband. My head didn't quite spin off, but my breathing went funny. Was I the link? I hated this notion, because chains have a tough time. A score or more arrived, laughing and full of that strange chilled charm only the rich exude.

Long Island is, well, sort of a long island, if you follow. Everything tends to astonish me, so America had it made. But why should I be dumbfounded by the Atlantic's proximity? And by Long Island's enormity, its beauty? Glamor is America's par, wealth an incidental. Everything's so vast that your eyes run out of vision. Tye Dee was supervising the welcomes—which probably meant seeing they all arrived unarmed—so I'd nobody to ask. Old Sokolowsky had vanished. How strange that he was along, on a fantastic cruise like this. Mind you, the same went for me. Except the old jeweler and me were two of a kind; different bookends, same purpose. Sokolowsky was the experienced gelt merchant, techniques to his fingertips. I was the . . . the what? Neither Gina nor Nicko had mentioned antiques, which is basically what I'm for. Sole purpose in life. Tye Dee was simply a trusted bouncer, with his thick holster bulging his chest lopsidedly. Orly was Mrs. Aquilina's "friend" again today.

It was a pleasantly open day, light breeze, rich thick American sunshine. Innocent, fresh.

The little boats shuttled between the shore and us. A small township, its streets open and the traffic casually undeterred by the growing aggregate of Rolls Royces and lengthy American cars I couldn't name. How pleasant to live in such a place, I was thinking, when I saw Jennie alighting from a limo with a fat man. They made quite a pair, him flashy and corpulent and Nicko's lassie slender and pert. Wasn't I thinking a lot about gelt? Something in the climate.

Fatty and Jennie were the last, the occasion for much jibing from the party on the afterdeck.

"Hey, Jim!" one voice yelled through the growing music. "Antiques doin' okay, keeping you late."

"Don't hold your breath, Denzie!" the fat man bawled as his boat slowed. "You politicians ride on my back, man!"

Desperate needling, it seemed to me, but it earned a roar of laughter. You can say anything in America, as long as you grin. Orly's shoulder tap made me turn. I wished he'd stop doing that. Worse, he prodded my chest.

"Lovejoy, go help Bill in the bar. You know how?"

"Yes."

"Tell Tye to close the rail. Mr. Bethune's always last."

Antiques, Jim Bethune. Busman had asked about some art dealer, Bettune ... Orly shoved me so I almost stumbled.

"Move your ass, Lovejoy."

"I'm hurrying, I'm hurrying."

Correction: *Almost* everybody in the U.S.A. is charming. If Orly prodded me once more I'd break his digit, in a charming sort of way of course. I sprinted to obey, fuming but silent.

THE pace of the Aquilinas' party was sedate, compared to Fredo's in full spate. It was noisier, and the grub went almost untouched. I was astonished at the transformations the guests had undergone. They'd changed, instant butterflies, even Jennie emerging gorgeous from the cabins.

Bill the barman was twice as fast as I'd ever be. He was tall, lean, tanned, wavy-haired, the sort I always think must be every woman's heartthrob, straight off a surfboard. Blokes like him evoke archaic slang.

"Handle the ladies when two come together, Lovejoy," he ordered. He didn't tap or prod. I warmed to him.

The women? I went red. Barmen the world over hate women customers. Men are more decided, can be served fast. Women take their time, change minds, negotiate. That's why sluggardly barkeeps get the slowest jobs. And me a veteran of Fredo's famed happy hour! I swallowed the insult.

In spite of being narked I slotted in, doing my stuff, trying to remember to maintain that wide American smile. The crowd swelled to thirty, as guests already on board before the influx made their colorful entrances amid hullabaloo. Quite frankly, I admire people who put on a show of style. I mean, it's something I could never do in a million years. The women were bonny, slim, slick. I'd never seen what I call evening dresses worn during the afternoon before. Jewelry gleamed genuine gleams and antique settings bonged into my chest, but I kept my mind on my job, trying to please. It was a pretty scene. I avoided Mrs. Brandau's eye, didn't look at Jennie, tried my damnedest not to lust too obviously after Gina when she queened into the deck arena amid a storm of applause. The men were not my concern.

Denzie Brandau was smooth, suave, your friendly politician. He was perfectly attired, cuffs mathematical and suit impeccable, his manner subtly saying that he was slumming but was too polite to say so. Power anywhere is a threat, very like glamor.

"Hey, Bill," I said in sudden thought as the bar slackened. Other serfs started circulating with trays of food to encourage the starving. "Am I replacing Tony?"

"Sure are, Lovejoy." He was shaking a cocktail. I watched enviously.

"I can't drive." A lie at home, but true in America.

"Drivers we got. Only here in the bar."

"That Tony owes me ten dollars," I invented.

Bill dazzled the ocean with a brilliant grin. "Then you are strictly minus ten, Lovejoy. Like forevuh."

We chuckled, me shaking my head at the vagaries of fortune. I tapped my foot along with the music, smiling with the peasant's pride as Fatty Bethune staved off his anorexia by wolfing all the grub within reach. Oh, I was so merry.

And my soul cold as charity. Tony was extinct. My fault? I leaped to serve as Sophie Brandau and Gina drifted to the bar asking for Bloody Marys. But a lone neuron shrieked outrage. What the frigging hell did it matter whose fault it was? I get narked with myself. I don't run the frigging universe. I only live here.

"Lovejoy tends to ignore the ice," Gina said mischievously. "Something in his background, I suspect."

"Is he new?" Mrs. Brandau was distantly bored by serfs.

"Practically." The hostess took her drink. "On probation, you might say."

"I aim to please, madam." Groveling's pathetic, but my job.

The ladies drifted. I turned. Bill was watching me. He wore his professional smile, and spoke softly.

"Lovejoy. Don't look murder. It shows."

"Ta, Bill. It's er, all that grub."

"Hungry? We get ours during the game."

"Will it be long?" I noticed Blanche undulating past, mingling merrily with a tray of edibles. I love seafood, as long as the poor creature's unrecognizable. I mean, shrimps that need beheading and lobsters looking like they've just clawed over the gunwale make me run a mile. To eat, something has to die even if it's only a plate of chips.

"An hour or two."

God, would I survive? I served Mr. Brandau while he talked with the dark Simon Bolivar lookalike who'd exchanged secret glances with Sophie at Nicko's. They talked of percentages, cut-ins and shutouts. Was this the yacht's secret, a clandestine investment company? Or was there simply no secret, except a bit of body-rodding? La dolce vita was hardly tomorrow's news.

"Who needs cut-ins, Charlie?" Brandau was saying. "I can be bored in the Senate!"

The swarthy Charlie laughed, joked his way out of some dilemma. Sophie Brandau's face tightened and she floated over, lovely as a dream.

"Mr. Sarpi shouldn't think that politics bores you, Denzie. Think of the effect on the electorate!"

I caught Bill's glance warning me not to listen. I whistled, being busy.

"Hell, Sophie," her husband joshed. "I'm gonna *buy* the electorate!"

Moira Hawkins was being introduced to Jim Bethune. The podgy man would have fondled, except Jennie did a neat interception. I noticed Gina Aquilina watching me. I raised my eyebrows in mute appeal, and asked Bill if I could cadge some of the buffet food on account.

"No, Lovejoy." He had a marvelous delivery, not a decibel misdirected. He should have been a spy.

"Okay, okay." I carried on serving, smiling, giving out pleasantries.

Charlie Sarpi and Denzie Brandau drifted away, mingling with Nicko's group. Sophie Brandau hesitated by the bar, then did a simulated start of surprise to notice a restless young blonde who was definitely on the toxic twitch. She had the look of a luscious plumpster who'd slid the snake to become skeletal in a matter of months.

"Why, Kelly Palumba! I didn't even see—!"

"Hey, Sophie—!"

The party was so glad the jittery lass and Sophie were glad that even I felt glad, and served Miss Palumba her brandy sour with a beaming heart. Gladness is contagious, I find, even where something murderous is beginning to scratch your spine.

"Beg your pardon, miss." I was baffled. The blonde had leaned close and asked for something. "Bill?"

He was cool. "Sorry, Miss Palumba. We're right out."

"Sheet," she said distinctly, swigging her drink and replacing the glass with a commanding tap. I poured. And encore. And twice more, to the brim.

She had said to lift her drink. Lift where? To her lips? Or was it Americanese for strengthen? But with what? It was already as potent as distillers could make it. I shrugged as Sophie Brandau edged the girl away into the socialite press with the "How's the family, Kelly?" kind of prattle. I tried not to look at the blonde, but when you see somebody screaming so silently it's difficult.

Tap on my shoulder. I turned. Prod. "Hi, Orly."

"Mrs. Aquilina wants you, Lovejoy. Main cabin."

I heard Bill's warning, nodded, wiped my hands and went.

THEY were setting out a long table. I would have called it lovely but for its newness. Gina was supervising flowers and suchlike. Blanche was scurrying, two other serfs placing chairs. Somebody was changing a picture, a Philip Steer painted in a milliard divisionistic dots, two girls running on a waterside pier. I smiled, then frowned to show Orly and Mrs. Aquilina I was all attention.

"Blanche. A tray of hors d'oeuvre in the anteroom. This way, Lovejoy."

An archway led through half-drawn curtains to a slender cabin, more of an alcove. She reclined on a chaise longue and gestured me to sit opposite.

"That's all, Orly. Go check the arena."

He gave me a lethal glance and left me to be dissected by this smiling lady. She said nothing. My feet shuffled as usual under this treatment. I found myself reddening slowly. I cleared my throat, tried to look offhandedly through to see how the other kulaks were managing. Surely not laying for another nosh? But the table was bare, almost. Just small boxes of playing cards. And a couple of computer screens coming to life with that irritating come-hither bleep they make. Like a boardroom. Who cared?

"Thank you, Blanche."

A silver tray of food. My mouth watered. Blanche returned to her task. I dragged my eyes from her receding form, tried not to ogle the grub, failed on both counts.

"I'm not usually taken in, Lovejoy," Mrs. Aquilina said.

Now what? I was suddenly so homesick. In a new country I find I return home a lot more than I arrive, if you follow.

"I'm sure you're not, missus."

"Gina, please. Do have something . . ."

I fell on the tiny things. There's not much in one, so I had to take a few at a time. You get famished in sea air. "Sorry, er, Gina. But it's been hours since breakfast."

"Of course it has," she said. She was carefully not laughing, the way they do, but really rolling in the aisles.

"Want some?" I can be charming, too.

She tasted one small biscuit with a fractionated sardine balanced on its rim. It really beats me how women survive half the time. Some biochemistry we haven't got, I suppose. I didn't like that "taken in" bit, but it's a wise prophet who knows where his next meal will come from.

"Lovejoy. You seem to be troubled. All eyes and ears." She smiled. "Then I saw where your attentions really lay." She indicated the shrinking victuals and shot an appraising look to the preparations in the long cabin.

"Look, Gina. I can't help being hungry. I can't stop women from walking past, either."

"Of course not." She gave a sign and Blanche's mob withdrew. "Tell me about Bill, Lovejoy."

"Bill?" She was full of surprises, this one. Did she fancy him, or what? "Nice bloke, good barman. But something's wrong."

She stilled with a woman's scary tranquillity. "Explain."

"Well, I think he's a thick. I tried asking him about antiques. He wasn't interested. Hadn't even heard of your 1760 Goddard-Townsend cabinetmakers from Rhode Island—when a single one of their mahogany secretary desks goes for zillions." She stared back at me. Obviously she was thick too. Annoyed, I gave it her in detail. "Furniture that exquisite'll never come again, never on this planet. It's all made of mahogany we call *grand*, natural unforced trees, not this spongiform crap—sorry, love—that they force-grow nowadays."

She was still blank. I found myself up, walking about. "For Christ's sake, love," I cried, exasperated. "Can't you see? That's why the values increase faster than the national debt! It's like a Gainsborough, irreplaceable."

"You're telling me Bill's odd because he isn't interested in antiques?"

Give me strength. I'd thought all Yanks were fascinated by antiques, but here I was having a hard time telling them about the treasures on their own doorstep.

"Look, love. You know that Manhattan building somebody sold for, what was it, zillions? On the news two days agone. Remember it? Well, the secretary desk I mentioned could buy two such buildings, and leave change. You follow?" She nodded slowly. God, she was beautiful, yet gorgeous women drive me at least as mad as the lesser lights.

"I see."

"And a *small* Philadelphia pier table—" I held my hand less than a yard above her carpet—"could buy the very next hotel." I was yelling down at the numskull. "You can't criticize Bill for not being interested when you're stupid as him—"

"Sit down, Lovejoy."

Her tone chilled me. I sat, suddenly less narked. Her brain was clicking, her gaze distant and venomous. I wished I was back at the bar. We sat for a full minute. She stirred.

"Lovejoy. Sophie Brandau. Her jewelry today."

"Looked genuine, Gina." Safe ground?

"Was everybody's?"

"What do you think I am?" I said indignantly. "I was behind the bar. All the tom—er, jewelry—I saw was genuine, far as I could tell. I liked that eighteenth-century Milanese brooch Miss Palumba was wearing, though some nerk had tried to restore it with platinum." Silence. "You see—"

"Lovejoy." She meant shut up. Then why had the stupid cow asked me to speak? I tried not to sulk while she did more of her long-range venom. When she spoke it was muted, sibilant.

"Make up to Sophie, Lovejoy."

We'd not had a row. "Beg pardon?"

The curtain glided open, some electronic trick. Nicko was sitting alone at the long board table, reading his endless printouts.

"Become special to her."

I checked my hearing against memory, decided I wasn't hallucinating. "Er, exactly what is it you're—"

"*Do it!*" she spat. I shot to my feet, edged away.

"Do you mean . . . ?"

"Into Sophie Brandau. And report her pillow talk."

"Look, Gina." I retreated, babbling. "That's something I can't—"

"Nicko?"

Her husband spoke, still flicking along those lists. "You opened a packet of money, Lovejoy?"

"From Tye Dee?" Maybe they wanted it back.

"Your prints are on it. The money's traceable. It was stolen from a Pittsburgh bank. A guard was killed. The bullet matches the gun in your hotel room."

My voice went faint. "Pittsburgh? I've only just arrived in the U.S. It's marked on my passport."

"Illegal migrant worker? Criminal history? Now a lethal bank robber?" Nicko brought out my passport. "No record of any date stamp in this, Lovejoy."

I'd seen the immigration man stamp it at the airport. I sat. Gina was suddenly impatient.

"You've your orders, Lovejoy. And keep me informed of the Hawkins project."

The what? Why didn't she just ask Moira Hawkins? She was only yards away, swanning around the deck arena with Fat Jim Bethune. And why did this megabuck outfit worry about a cheap dream in a cheap bookshop?

"It's just some loony scheme about a missing manuscript."

"Realistic? A practical proposition?"

"Well . . ." I felt it was time to splash over the side, somehow jump ship and make a run for it. Less than a few hours ago my only worry was being late at Fredo's diner. "Her sister's the grailer. That's a nickname for crets who waste their lives chasing a rainbow. The Holy Grail, see? The Hawkins daftness is only a Sherlock Holmes novel. It went missing in the Victorian postal system. Every nation has its loonies," I said apologetically, in case Gina or Nicko took umbrage. "We have folk who're chasing two of the Virgin Mary's milk teeth, supposedly in a pot in Syria. Fakes are life's real trouble."

Gina said softly. "That's so, so right. Go now."

I decided to play along as ordered but to cut out first chance I got. So whatever I promised now would be superfluous, since I wouldn't be here to be checked on. I'd smile my very best at Sophie Brandau, tell Gina the gossip, then exit pursued by bear.

"How often do I report?"

"Nightly," she said, making my mouth gape by adding, "You come to my cabin."

And Nicko sitting there, deep in his numbers, while his

wife tells a stranger to come tiptoeing into her boudoir in the candle hours? "Er, wouldn't it be best if I—?"

"*Out!*"

I crept away like a night-stealer. Just in time to get pinned against the nearest bulkhead by Orly. He was ten times tougher than he looked.

"Lovejoy. You keep away, capeesh? Gina's not switching, hear? Not to you, not anyone."

"Okay, okay!"

It was Tye who prised Orly off. I recovered my wind while Tye shook his head and lowered Orly to the deck. He'd lifted him one-handed with barely a grunt of effort. At least I'd one ally. That's what I thought then.

"Leave Lovejoy, Orly," Tye said. "He's taking orders, same as the rest of us. You want changes, you ask Jennie, okay?"

Ask Jennie? Not Nicko, Gina? I watched Orly hate me out of sight, and followed Tye toward the sound of the music and glam shambles. I'd be sorry to land Tye in it when I ran for it and shook the dust of New York off my shoes.

Tye paused at the foot of the gangway. "A tip, Lovejoy. This is big. Nobody gets outa here less'n he's allowed. 'Kay?"

"I'll ask first, Tye. That's a promise."

He gave me the bent eye for a moment.

"I can't tell if you're stoopid or clever. Know that?" He sighed and started to climb to the upper deck. "Trouble is, it's the same thing."

With ignorance born of idiocy, I ignored that warning too.

As I rejoined Bill behind the bar the tannoy was announcing that the opening game would commence in one hour. O'Cody, portly gray-hair in the magenta silk waistcoat of a monsignor, chuckled when Jennie joked there was still time for a quick prayer. Others laughed along. Puzzling, because I hadn't seen a cleric come aboard, though somebody very like him had. I shelved the oddity, smiled, located Sophie Brandau in the glittering throng, whispered to Tye to have somebody spill a little vino rosso on the lovely Sophie's dress, caught up a silver tray—gadrooned, my favorite style—and briskly went to start my compulsory courting.

9

ASPILLAGE on a woman's dress is an indictable offense. Funny, that, when it's supposed to be lucky. The old Queen Mum used to say ta to nervous waiters when they plopped a drop on her lap, for luck given. Sophie Brandau didn't quite go spare, but Blanche zoomed to the rescue when Tye—too clever to commit the crime himself—sent a waiter to accidentally tilt a carafe in passing. Kelly Palumba and a thin straw-haired wastrel called Epsilon were especially concerned. Denzie Brandau gave a bored half-glance, made some remark to Moira Hawkins, causing people to fall about. I diagnosed a husband making capital from his wife's clumsiness. I was beginning to dislike the politician. I took over from Kelly Palumba, who cracked to her pal, "Better than your TV productions, Epsilon!" I didn't care much for her, either.

"Mind, Mrs. Brandau," I said. "Don't stretch the material." People don't think. Her dress was a rich brocade, royal blue with sky sleeves. I commandeered a water decanter from a waiter and drenched a serviette. "Macon wine leaves a stain otherwise."

I drew her to one side as the chatter reasserted itself. We were by the rail, landward side. "A few more linens, Blanche, please," whittled the gathering down.

That left Sophie Brandau and myself. Fussing like I imagined a meticulous waiter would, I blotted the brocade. It was near the hem, and took a few minutes. During it, I passed comments on the surroundings. Which made me notice the man in the motor opposite the pier. He didn't look much like a photographer, but the motionless Wildlife Internations van nearby with its odd black-sheening windows could be full of them. He was talking into a car phone. So?

On board, however, Mrs. Brandau and me were no longer the center of attention. I placed everything on the tray, and happened to notice her face with a start of astonishment. Overacting, of course.

"Good heavens!" I said. "I remember you now! That beautiful sautoir, wasn't it?"

The diamond chain was there, worn as it should be from both shoulders. (I hate the one-shoulder *sur l'epaule* style so popular in nineteenth-century France, because what the hell's the pendant to do?) The pendant was there, tassel shape, four compound strands. Diamonds genuine as genuine is, and antique old. The central diamond was huge, bigger than the poor lumbering zircon she'd substituted for it. Seventeen carats? Nearer twenty, and brilliant-cut, which was good going for that kind of date.

"You noticed," she said, quiet and pale.

"Did I stare? I apologize, Mrs. Brandau."

You have to feel sorry for any woman caught out in deception. It's routine for a man. Okay, when some bird rumbles you it's uncomfortable for a few weeks—well, ten minutes—but then you get over it and life's rich pageant rolls on. "I said nothing, about the pendant."

"I guessed from the way you looked at it," she said. "You're Lovejoy? The one Nicko had the trouble with over the furniture?"

That sounded nasty. "I'm the one who advised Nicko how not to ruin his antique," I corrected stiffly.

"You've become quite a joke," she said, not even near laughing. "Facing Nicko down over a wine stain."

I said, narked, "We don't deserve the antiques we've got. The moron you got to dock your sautoir pendant and substitute with zircons wants locking up."

"You're good at antiques?" Her eyes were so sad, but still wearing that calculating quality women find hard to forgive themselves for. "Can you do valuations?"

"Accurately. But . . ." I hesitated. Her eyes were lovely, brown, deep and broad in a slender face. She looked out of place among this lot. "But sometimes people don't like the truth. Antiques deserve it." Well, hang veracity. I'd got orders.

"And restorations? Antiques firms give such conflicting

opinions." She said it like lines in a rehearsal. She'd been as glad of the spillage excuse as I. Maybe she had orders, too.

"They would," I said with feeling. "Valuation companies are on the fiddle. I do everything free—for genuine antiques, that is." I don't, of course. Never have. But my life might be at stake.

She thought a second. A gust of laughter rose from the party over something political.

"Tell one of the waitresses to get me a bitter soda, Lovejoy," she said quickly. "The game starts soon. When it's quiet, bring a drink to my cabin. It's zero two zero."

American for twenty. "Right. What drink, exactly?"

She stared at me, shook her head as if having difficulty. "Anything convincing, Lovejoy."

What drink was convincing, in Long Island Sound?

"Will there be a stain?" she was asking pointedly as people started drifting from the canopied arena. I recognized feminine obfuscation at work, and loudly played along.

"Certainly not, Mrs. Brandau." I felt like telling her it hadn't been wine, only water, another of my deceits, but I needed all my honesty in reserve. One of the guests was now in a military uniform, I saw as I made my way back to Bill. I hadn't noticed any general arriving. What was it, fancy dress? But ranks above corporal are where the mysterious Orient begins, as far as I'm concerned.

"Here, Bill. What's three stars mean?"

"They mean you saw nuttin', Lovejoy." Bill was flipping a last-minute cocktail for Kelly Palumba, who was now sloshed. She giggled.

"Hey, Lovejoy! Tell this hunk I'm gonna get some work outa him real soon . . ."

Epsilon was pouting. "I have to go, Kelly. See you here in an hour." What card game lasts exactly an hour?

"That's time enough," Kelly told Bill. A woman leering is not a pretty sight. I was glad when she started to slide.

I caught her as her knees buckled. Blanche and two waitresses flew up, hustling her out of sight with that concealed anger they reserve for a transgressing sister.

The party was thinning. Seeing nuttin', I didn't notice

Denzie Brandau smoothing Moira Hawkins's bottom as they strolled off together. Nor did I notice the covert sign the monsignor made to the general, fingers tapping palms in the universal let's-cut-percentages plot. Nor the unconcerned way Nicko indicated his watch when Jennie started rounding up the strays like an eager sheepdog.

But I did notice the way Bill rearranged my clean glasses that I'd placed on the counter. And the glint of the low sun showing the people on shore. You don't hide a watcher among trees, nor conceal him behind a window sill. You put him in a motor, where shoppers park their cars. Like the man Bill had continually checked on with a casual glance now and then ever since the party had started. Still, all was normal.

Except it all wasn't. We were under surveillance. Bill was in on it, with his signaling glasses and his flashy tricks with cocktail shakers. I was anxious to warn him about Gina's questioning, but got interrupted by a last-minute matron, one who'd had more face-lifts than Tower Bridge. She was a born gusher, had fawned continuously on the monsignor, and now swigged her sixth martini like medicine, grimacing as it took effect.

"Wish me luck, honey," she said, pondering whether to go for another. I decided to get shut of her.

"Luck? Here. Take this." I took out a cent. "It was my first ever American coin. You know the old saying, your first penny buys an hour's luck."

"I never heard that one."

She couldn't have. I'd just made it up. Women who doubt really nark me. "It's true. Here." I passed it over with a discreet smile, which mercifully got rid of her.

"Is that proverb straight, Lovejoy?"

"Certainly!" Now even Bill was skeptical. I hate mistrust in other people. We started to clear up.

"Do a deal, Bill?" The deck arena was clear of guests. Gina Aquilina drifted through—changed again, exquisitely sheathed in a risky purple, silver chain accessories—with Orly prattling amusing prattle. He'd changed too, a smoothie's white tuxedo. I waited until they'd strolled inside.

"Could I afford it?"

Witticisms gall me, when they're at my expense. "Watch your back, that's all." Zole's words.

"My back?" He laughed, but eyes alert and wary.

"Gina asked about you. I said you were a great barman." I glanced over his shoulder at the shore, made sure he knew where I was looking. "I could have dropped you in the clag, Bill. That means you owe me."

"How much, Lovejoy?"

"The ten dollars Tony owed. I could have said you were hopeless, got you the sack."

"I didn't figure you for a mercenary, Lovejoy." He brought out a ten-dollar bill, placed it on the serving basin. He was puzzled now, and even warier.

"I'm working my passage up, up, and away. I need every groat I can get. Thanks." I slid the ten dollars back to him, finished wiping the glasses. The bar might be wired for sound, vision, heaven knows what. Just like the party area, or the rails where I'd attended to Sophie Brandau.

Bill looked at the money. He finally recovered it, said nothing more, except gave a curt nod of recognition. We wound up the bar.

"Reckon Kelly Palumba's recovered?"

"No names, Lovejoy. House rules."

"Right. Only, it's been about an hour since she went moribund." I drew breath. Come darkness, I'd be over the side and swimming for it, or being smuggled away in some kind lady's purse. Sophie Brandau was that lady. "Bill. What would you call a really convincing drink, for a lady?"

CABIN 020 was midships, port side. That meant its portholes faced the open sound. Light was dwindling now, sailing boats and small craft setting sailing lights shimmering the darkening waters. The *Gina* was starting to sway almost imperceptibly. I knocked, licked my hand to smooth my uncontrollable thatch, and donned a bright waiter's beam.

Mrs. Brandau's welcome wasn't much. "Come in, Lovejoy. Sit."

Hell, like a dog. Reluctantly I deposited the tray, an old Burmese original lacquer. Criminal to use it. I'd only chosen it to prevent Bill from scouring it to extinction. It was 150 years old, living on borrowed time in this company of millionaire scatterbrains.

The cabin was a shipboard compact, folding tables and furniture screwed down and all that. It was highly feminine, three mirrors, of which one was a true Regency that caught my eye. I sat on a low settee, modern crud, and tried to think polite thoughts about the lovely woman opposite.

Worry shreds a woman's confidence, doesn't it. It takes the steam out of the face somehow, shows in the eyes. This lady was never going to bat for America, not the way she'd crumpled inwardly.

"Something I said, love?" I asked.

"You were kind, Lovejoy. I need somebody kind."

This sort of talk dismays me. We're vulnerable enough without trust raising its fearful head.

"Look, lady. I'm knee-deep in muck and bullets. I've hardly a bean. All I really know, between ourselves, is antiques and nothing but antiques. I'm also . . ." How to phrase it so I sounded superb? "Don't trust me, is all I'm saying."

"Sophie," she said listlessly. Women take no notice. You might as well talk to the wall. "It's my husband, Lovejoy."

Oh, hell. I half-rose. She gestured me down.

"How can I stop him?" She noticed my face, which must have de-beamed somewhere along the line. "You're the one doing the Sherlock with Moira Hawkins. Denzie's crazy. It's not the first time he's been stupid. She's dragging him in. We're in over our heads. She's persuaded him it'll bring fame, a fortune. The biggest PR fillip ever. Even push him to the presidency. He's like a man demented. And she's playing on it."

That was it. Expectancy lifted her eyebrows. "Well, Lovejoy?"

Clearly this was no seduction scene between randy serf and lusting contessa. Disappointed, I revealed how I'd encountered the Hawkins. "All I know is that Moira's sister Rose frequents the bar where I work . . ."

Sophie heard me out. She lit a cigarette, clicking the lighter a few times. "I'd hoped you would be more cooperative. If it's a deal you want . . ."

I'd nothing to deal with. Yet here was a millionaire's wife

offering ... suddenly I wanted to know more, more about Moira Hawkins's project, why Sophie was so concerned. I mean, I'd seen the Hawkins place. It was mundane, cheap even. This lady's emerald solitaire could buy Rose, Moira, bookshop and all. I'd been ordered to play along with this delectable bird, so I'd be in the clear with Gina even if I said, "Okay, love. I'll do what you want."

Her face lit, losing that waxy cast and hueing into animation. "You will? Truly, Lovejoy?"

She came to fold herself beside me. "You know the risks?"

"You're worth it," I lied, hoping Gina's recorded tapes of this conversation would exonerate me one hundred percent.

Her eyes fluttered, lowered. "Don't be under any illusion, Lovejoy. There's a limit to what I can do."

"That's always the danger." I felt noble, a knight on a white charger. "You want me to have a word with Moira?"

She gave a harsh laugh. "No, Lovejoy. You'll have to end it. The Sherlock enterprise. It's the one thing that'll make him drop that Hawkins bitch."

End? That all? I cheered up. Moira's plot hinged on a grailer scam, and they're always failures. Dreams are dud, which is why they stay dreams and never become reality.

"Easy, Sophie," I said. "Leave it to me."

"You will? Oh, you darling man! Thank you!"

For one second I knew I could have joined her in communal happiness, so to speak, but I heard someone coming down the corridor. My hand never even reached her breast.

"Invite me to your place," I said, thinking quickly. "To, what, restore your antiques."

She slipped me a card from her handbag.

"I'll okay it with Jennie," she said. "I've a collection; Jim Bethune supplied most. You want me to damage one or two, make it look convincing?"

I went cold, nearly throttled her but kept control. Her hand cupped, grasped mine. She kissed my palm, eyes filling. I'd never seen so much gratitude at one go.

"Don't ever damage an antique, Sophie. Promise?"

"I'll do anything in my power for you. I swear."

I left then, her gratitude flowing out into the corridor

after me like a cloying perfume. Mr. Sokolowsky was approaching. He said a cheery hello, asked how I was liking life on board ship. I was making some sort of inane reply when he leant close confidentially.

"Help her, Lovejoy," he whispered, and went on his way, the sentimental old fool. I presumed he meant Sophie. I shrugged it off, only one more bemusement among many.

When I returned, Bill had gone. The deck arena looked uninviting. Nothing so forlorn as drooping bunting. All was left for sea gulls and the evening breeze.

Onshore the Wildlife van remained. I looked down at the water. Still enough daylight to make a swim for it. A small white motor launch was purring across the bay, heading parallel to the shore. One crewman, and Bill. The *Gina*'s inshore boat. I yelled, "Hey, Bill!" but he didn't turn. All right, I thought, narked. Not even the manners to say so long.

I decided I'd better report to Gina as soon as darkness covered the day, and went to find the galley for some nosh to keep the wolf from the door. It was on the way that I got the key to most, if not all.

The cruiser was almost silent, rocking somnolently with its lines tapping as the breeze flicked them. The companionway led down a deck. You double back toward the stern, for the crews' quarters. I'd been told our scoff was there and nowhere else. Tye Dee must already be there, I'd decided. Like an obedient hound I would report to Gina on the dot, allaying all her suspicions.

"Lovejoy?"

I almost fainted with fright when she grabbed my arm, coming out of nowhere.

"You silly mare! You scared me to death!"

Normally Kelly Palumba would have giggled, having put one over on the universe. She was in no state for levity. She was shaking, teeth chattering and limbs a-twitch. A fleck of vomit touched the corner of her mouth. God, she was a mess.

"Lovejoy. Where the fuck's Bill?"

"How the hell should I know?" She clung and trailed,

clawing. She babbled inanely. I pushed her back into her cabin and stepped after. "Look. Wait here. I'll call Blanche."

"Wait?" she shrilled. "What the fuck's with *wait?*" She wept, shivering. Her dress was soiled. I looked away, stuck to my fair-minded task of getting the hell out and leaving her to stew in her own pot. "Get for me, Lovejoy. I'm dyin'."

Some sort of drugs. "I'm sorry. I haven't got any." I pressed the button frantically. This nightmare wasn't the prelude I wanted to my clandestine escape. "Who's your stewardess?"

"Fuck the stewardess!" She slumped against the door, sobbing, muscles in spasm, retching. "Where's Bill?" It was a cry from the heart. I tried dragging her away so I could get out. Where the hell was Blanche and her team? "Bill sees me right every time. You're all against me . . ."

Bill the drug supplier, to this ruin? I almost joined in her wailing from self-pity.

"Let me out. I'll get Bill. He'll bring you your, er, tablets. Honest, love."

She flailed against the cabin door in some sort of epilepsy. Why had I let her lean against the damned door, trapping me like this? I reached for a towel by the bedside, scattering syringes, silver foil, and rolled it under her head. I vaguely knew there was something about an epileptic's tongue, but what?

Gradually she quietened. I was drenched in sweat, breathing hard.

"They won't even let me play the game," she whimpered. "Just because I've a small habit. Who hasn't, Lovejoy?"

"Mmmh," I said. "Rotten sods."

She sobbed uncontrollably. "Now I'll be out of the California game. It happened before." Her voice crescendoed. "They won't let me go to L.A."

I tried to step over her toward the door but she clutched my leg. "They wouldn't do a thing like that. I'll ask them—"

"Fix me, Lovejoy." She tried a smile. A pathetic eager grin for a horror film. "I'll be nice for you. Ask Bill. I'll do anything if you make me sing."

I was worn out. The cabin was insufferably hot. There must be something stupendous in drugs to reduce a complete human to this. She'd been nearly exquisite two hours since.

"Right!" I said brightly. "I'll get the, er, tablets for you. I have nine, maybe a dozen. Just let me pass . . ." All the time I was pushing the bloody button and not one of the idle bitches was coming. I'd belt the lazy cows.

She started her retching, holding on. I got a hand on the door latch, but made it no further, frantically started knocking on the panel calling out Blanche's name, bawling for Tye Dee, anybody for God's sake. She hung on, weeping and stinking, babbling not to leave her like this, promising anything.

"I'll get you a place in the game, Lovejoy," she wheedled, her ravaged face staring up at me. "I'll fund you!"

"Help!" I bawled, sick and shaking almost as bad as she was. "Blanche, for Christ's *sake*—"

The door handle turned, and Blanche came whizzing in, forcing the girl bodily up from the floor in an amazing display of strength. Tye crowded in after. I reeled out.

"Where the hell have you been?" I yelled. "I've been pressing that frigging button and knocking the bloody door for six hours, while you idle gets sat on your fat arses and—"

Tye clamped a hand over my mouth and hauled me along to the next cabin. He slammed me in and shut the door.

"You call yourself a friend?" I was yelling. "Leaving me—"

"Shtum, Lovejoy." He listened. The faint thumping from the adjacent room quietened, stilled. He relaxed, sat on the bunk.

I went to the bathroom, washed my hands and face, sniffing at my clothes for traces of Kelly . . . and noticed that Tye wore only trousers and a gaping shirt. He was barefoot. My hands in the basin's warm water, I stared at my reflection. Come to think of it, Blanche had hardly been what you might call eminently presentable, either. She'd looked just rising from a good night's, ah, rest.

Tye was pulling on socks, fumbling for shoes beneath the

bed. Silk stockings were draped on a chair. The bed linen was disordered. A hard day's night had been had by all. I straightened, found a towel.

"No wonder you were slow coming," I said evenly.

He cocked an ear, nodded as a buzzer sounded three faint zeds. "We have to talk."

Blanche entered. She was pale under her dark skin, almost purple round the eyes. Lovely, but scared and looking at Tye for direction. She carried a small tray holding a syringe, needles, ampoules. They made me feel queasy.

"I've fixed her good, Tye," she said in a wobbly voice. She looked in a worse state than me. Partners in paradise, while I'd been in hell next door.

"You'd better know something, Lovejoy," Tye said. "All that went on in Kelly Palumba's cabin'll be taped, sound and video."

"Thank God for that!" I said vehemently. "It'll prove she dragged me in. When Nicko and Gina see the tape they'll see I was bawling my head off for you two . . ."

Aha. I paused, looked from Blanche to Tye.

"You see the problem, Lovejoy."

Blanche was finishing dressing. I tried not to see her lovely legs sheathing into her silks. Tye stood, buttoning his collar.

"Aye." And I did. The camera record would show me all innocent, trying to cope with the sick lass—and it would reveal that Tye and Blanche were in dereliction of duty. "You two'll get your wrists slapped?"

"Sort of, Lovejoy."

"But this . . ." Like a fool I glanced about the cabin, as if bugging devices would be in view and clearly labeled.

Blanche answered, doing her hair at the mirror. "I have an arrangement with the recordist, Lovejoy. To default the circuits."

She evaded my eyes in the mirror. Well, she had powers of persuasion any electrician would accede to.

Tye spoke, fastening his holster. I watched, amazed. It was the first real holster I'd ever seen. I'd no idea they were so bulky. How ever did undercover agents manage?

"We can erase Kelly Palumba's, Lovejoy."

Into the ensuing silence Blanche spoke softly. "If you stay quiet, Lovejoy."

Now her eyes met mine. It wasn't a simple threat. It was more like, well, a country woman's promise of coming weather, certain it would come but hoping for maximum clemency. A rainstorm, we'd all get soaked.

"What's the risk to me?" I was conscious I was missing some sort of opportunity, but was too feeble-minded to think it through. "I've promised loyalty to Gina all sorts of ways."

"Haven't we all, Lovejoy?" Tye donned his jacket. He looked surprisingly neat, if a trifle bulky. So those holsters were tailored! The things you learn.

"There'll be no comeback from Gina," Blanche said. "Where's the harm in a little fun?" She did that erotic magic with lipstick that always makes me swallow and think hard unyielding thoughts. She smiled to herself. And Tye smiled too.

"Everybody needs a little fun now and then. Right?"

I swallowed. "Right, right."

That was where we left it, we of the good ship *Gina*, me going to change into clean gear, then totter along to the galley for a nosh, Tye strolling to resume his patrol, Blanche staring at her reflection slowly sucking her lips in to even her lipstick. And the drugged girl somewhere in that chemical paradise from which few travelers ever really return.

10

IT WAS Chanel who came to tell me I was wanted. I liked Chanel. She was personal maid to Mrs. Van Cordlant, my one-cent lucky lady. I'd have stayed in the galley to explain that eating was a good means of preventing starvation, but it'd have been no good.

I climbed to the next deck. Think of what that poor Kelly had told me. What was it? They wouldn't even let her go to L.A., for the California game. She tried bribing me with her poor ravaged body, just like she'd paid Mr. Squeaky Clean Bill for providing her drugs.

Weird words.

The poor lass was just demented—or else she was also addicted to gambling. I knocked at the door Chanel had told me: the long conference cabin. I was glad I'd donned clean and was scented like a rose garden. Maybe this was my reward, Gina wreaking her unsated lust on my poor defenseless frame?

The long boardroom was empty. A few papers were strewn here and there, crumples being fed into a portable shredder by Blanche and two stewardesses. Gina reclined, good enough to eat.

"Yes, Gina?" I said, all confidence and intimacy.

She hardly glanced up.

"Oh, Lovejoy." I was suddenly new and insignificant. "To Manfredi's. Soonest." She looked past me. "Blanche? Get me that Harvard architect. Two minutes."

"Yes, Miz Gina."

"Er . . . ?" I said, still oozing charm.

She noticed me with irritation. "Manfredi's, Lovejoy. Go."

I cleared my throat. "Er, I don't think I quite understand—"

Hands grabbed me, mostly Tye's but with assistance from

two other hulks. I was flung into my old gear, mercifully cleaned, hustled into the shore boat, and rushed breathless and bewildered to a waiting motor on shore.

Well, I'd prayed for an end to my servitude, but I was narked now it had come.

I didn't know it, but next dawn was the day I'd start killing people.

ONCE, I knew this bloke Ted who wrote what he called copy. Ted was a university academic, and like the rest he moonlighted on his Eng Lit job by scribing for newspapers. A sad bloke, he was simply one of these geezers who'd never done anything except teach—never known an honest day's labor. He was made redundant in the Great Cutbacks. Suddenly he found himself facing the stark truth that he was unemployable. Now he trundles a handcart about Surrey villages scouring for tat, old rubbish that he tries to sell. He does it badly, needless to say. If he'd ever worked, with hands, he'd have been okay. As it is, he's had to invent a conspiracy among his university alumni to justify his bitterness. Tells everybody they were all jealous.

We all do it. I did it, that morning when Fredo arrived and found me disgruntled on the pavement. He said very little, just to get the garbage out in the alleyway because Josephus was having woman trouble.

"I asked Nicko for a few days off," I lied brightly.

"Sure." New York's elastic word speaks volumes.

Della was thrilled I was with them again. Jonie came and told me I'd missed a brawl in the bar between two guys berserk over the Super Bowl. Lil told me she'd known all along I was crazy over her. Two new waitresses, and a new shabby shuffler to help Fredo in the kitchen, and we were ready to cope with Manhattan. I was angry, dejected in the best Ted manner, fuming to myself as I started smiling, giving out my cheery "Hi, there!" to all and sundry.

I'm not really posh-minded. No, honestly I'm not. But I really had thought that on the *Gina*, first names with Nicko and all that, I was plugged in to something special. As New Yorkers bowled in for breakfast and my routine banter, I found myself thinking over oddities. Bill—who was he?

Nicko owned the world, sure. And Gina ran much of it, sure. But whenever anybody spoke of reporting or checking or approving, it was always Jennie's name that cropped up. And Orly was her oppo.

"I reckon the Dallas Cowboys aren't in it this year," I told a driver I recognized. I didn't understand who the Cowboys were, but remembered he was for. His trigger phrase reflexed him into a soliloquoy that gave me time to think.

The California game? I'd been given orders to report nightly to Gina. Any progress on Moira Hawkins and her loony Sherlock plan. Yet here I was washing and serving at Fredo's joint when Gina and the *Gina* were a-bobbing on the briny of Long Island Sound.

"They're too erratic, for one thing," I challenged my customer, into his third mound of pancakes. (You won't believe this, but he poured syrup over them, next to four rashers of bacon. Warning: American grub's lovely; its arrangement takes some beating.)

"Tell me who's more consistent!"

"Look at the league tables," I said, doing that American shrug—a simultaneous grin and nodded headwag that encourages instant denials.

Did Gina *now* expect me to phone every evening with my progress report? There couldn't of course *be* any progress. There never is on a grailer. There can't be, for they're all myths, dreamed up by mystics and purveyors of illicit scams. You can invent some yourself. Do it today: precious diamonds from South Africa bigger than any on earth; limitless gold from the ocean floor; rare antiques in attics the world over. You only have to dream it up, and antique dealers will rush to market it for you. The fact that it doesn't exist won't matter. That's what a grailer is, rainbow gold. I'm not being unromantic. I'm only trying to warn you your friend's scheme of importing rare tapestries from the Punjab, ten cents a time and unlimited profit, is crud.

"Dallas, schmallas." I replenished my customer's coffee while he went wild and started calling along the counter for allies to set this jerk straight.

I mean, I know an actor who's fourteenth in line to the throne. (Incidentally so does everybody else in the U.K.,

83

but we're all too polite to mention it, him being the wrong side of the blanket and everything, and anyway we all like his TV series, evening Thursdays unless they've changed it). Well, this right royal bloke could reap the world, if you think of it. He's a born grailer. Why? Because he could sell his story, his opinions, even his name for vasto gelto, and live plushly ever after. And does he? Not on your life. He simply ploughs the theaters, does auditions, is downcast when he doesn't get them, rejoices when he does, the whole acting gig.

Why doesn't he? Because he's not thick, that's why. I once met him at an antiques auction. He was bidding for a miniature portrait. I tipped him off that it was on ivory and badly warped. He said ta, slipped me a fiver, and we had a bit of a chat. I waxed indignant that the auctioneer—it wasn't a thousand miles from Sotheby's, Bond Street—hadn't sent somebody over to point the defect out, him being the czar or whatever. "Maybe he doesn't know," he said, smiling. "You could have told him," I said. "Mmmmh," he concurred, "*but then what?*" And I saw the problem. His life would be an instant media circus. Reporters would rifle his dustbins. Every female he raised his hat to would be hounded to suicide. He would be dissected in public with that well-known frenzy the media reserve for ante-mortems.

"No what?" the Dallas supporter was asking.

God, I must have spoken out loud. "No way," I said. "They ain't got the pitchers."

"Pitchers is baseball, jerko."

Hell fire. "Shows how much them Cowboys know," I improvised quickly. "They're advertising for pitchers in the *Herald Tribune*."

That got a chorus of shouts and laughs. In the middle of it an old and valued customer arrived.

"Hello, Lovejoy." She was hugging herself.

"Too early for wine, Rose."

"Coffee, two eggs, toast."

"Coming right up." I shot the order through, eyed her. "I had to go on a visit, love. Sorry."

"Back just in time, Lovejoy. We've located a precious heap of paper for you."

I stared. "You have?" I'd never heard of a grailer actually becoming reality. Fakes do, of course. Trillion to one, I gave mental odds. News indeed for Gina; she was so endearing it'd be a shame to disappoint her.

"Hand it over, then. Let's have a look."

"I said located, not obtained."

Surprise, surprise. I tried to look enthralled, but probably failed, being distracted by Bill, who blew my theory about then by suddenly not being dead after all. He went straight across to the nooks, sat and read his paper. I made demented smalltalk with Rose, the Cowboy fan, a state-of-the-city grouse. Bill left after a quick serving, paid Della on the till. No sign from him. Meantime, Rose had been telling me some cock-and-bull tale about letters received, transatlantic phone calls . . .

If Bill wasn't dead, was Tony? I felt a bit let down, decided the entire episode was my spooky imagination. All over. I felt relieved. I smiled at Rose's charming features. A bird in the hand is worth two in the bush, as the wicked old treble entendre has it.

". . . to England," she was saying.

"Really?" How convenient for me, if Moira wanted somebody to cross the pond and bring it over! "How interesting, Rose." I looked into her eyes, sincerely as I could while serving a bloke with a breakfast I could hardly lift.

"Hey, I was in England once!" the customer put in, just when I wanted to tell Rose how deeply I'd missed her.

Conversation struck up from all around. No time for chat with desirable ladies. I resumed my loud comments on the telly newscasts, the plight of City Hall, the nation's finances. And promised Rose when finally she left that yes, I'd be along to the bookshop the minute Fredo's closed, to discuss plans.

Two letters came for me that morning. One was by special messenger, a bicycle dervish with his head clamped into trannie muffs. The other was handed in by a uniformed chauffeur. I saw Della looking, grinned, and told her it was the circles I moved in. I stuffed them into my pocket. More marked money from Nicko's Pittsburgh robbery? It could do without my fingerprints.

I worked on, surprised to find myself thinking less now of escape to Somewhere Else, U.S.A. Magic California? I didn't realize it then, being thick, but America's favorite risk was already setting in. I was being amused by the good cheer, the bustle, the aggressive glee all around. And the noise, the sheer willing ease of encounter. That American risk called seduction.

My grotty walk to the grotty Benidormo was interrupted. A few seconds after I'd called goodnights to Fredo and Della, envying as I did Della's special friendliness towards Fredo this particular evening, I caught sight of a reflection in a shop window. He was behind me, closing casually but fast. One flash of a passing police car's blue was all it took. I paused to let him catch up, not looking.

"Wotcher, Bill. Not dead, then?" Now I wish I'd not said it.

"Good eyes, Lovejoy." He was amused, cool, in charge. As a luxury yacht barman, I hadn't been certain. One look on this street and I had him sussed.

"All the better for seeing you, officer."

He paused to let some theatergoers pass, chasing taxis. "You have two ways, Lovejoy. Out, or in. Either way, you're recruited."

Another job? Three, or was it four? Maybe the letters in my pocket were offers from Paramount. I suddenly wanted to be in that museum Rose had taken me to, safe among antiques where life was simple and any other *Homo sapiens* was a foe.

"Who're we against?"

"Everybody, Lovejoy. Far as we know."

A three-star general, a monsignor, antiques magnate, bullion heiress, bankers, drug handlers, property baronesses, television moguls . . . they'd all been there. Plus politicians, and somebody the guests had called commissioner. As in police?

"I'd come like a shot, Bill. But I'm on my way to a job."

He was amused. "That Sherlock gig? We know all about that, Lovejoy. What we don't know is what it's *for*. Suppose you find out from Miss Hawkins and tell us, huh? Your first assignment."

"Sure," I promised. One more tyranny's nothing to a serf. "How'll I contact you?" As if I ever would.

"You agreed too fast, Lovejoy."

I was so tired. "Look, Bill, if that's your real name. I'm in a cleft stick. You're in the law. You've given me orders. I'll comply. Now leave me alone. I've a chance of seeing a bird for a few minutes' quiet nooky."

"Phone number in your pocket, Lovejoy." He moved off, blending expertly among pedestrians. I thought I saw him fade through a doorway, but couldn't be sure. It was a card with a typed phone number. I walked on, head down and thinking.

Tyrants. It's all very well for them. Even among other tyrants they can make a living. It's us that catch it. I paused, hurried on, and found a phone. I caught Fredo at the bar. He sounded a little breathless, relieved it was only me.

"Fredo? I need Gina's phone number."

"Christ, Lovejoy!" He spoke off phone to somebody. I heard a woman's offended expletive, a door slam. "I can't, Lovejoy. Even a dickhead like you should know the score by now."

"Listen. Gina said I was to report in. What must I do, send a carrier pigeon? Tell me Nicko's, then. Or Jennie's. It's urgent." I hesitated for only a second, opted for betrayal. "That barman, Bill. He's police. Asked about Moira Hawkins."

"Wait, wait." He came on in another second, asked where I was ringing from, and finally gave me a number.

While the traffic rushed past and people tried to hustle me, I got it picked up first ring.

"Hello? This is Lovejoy. I need to speak to Gina, please."

"Jennie, Lovejoy. Why are you ringing this number?"

I explained I'd got it from Fredo. "I was ordered to report to Gina."

"What is it?"

"Bill. The barman on the *Gina*, remember him? He's a bobby. He's just asked me to spy on the Hawkins family."

"Bobby? You mean police?" She made me repeat his every word. I did, almost with impeccable accuracy.

"Look, Jennie. I don't know what I'm supposed to do any more."

"You did right, Lovejoy. Just behave normally. Leave things to me."

"Look," I started to tell the phone, but it was dead and the queue was threatening my life. I escaped.

SOME things go wrong, don't they. Had I caused them to, telling Jennie about Bill? Fredo didn't matter. Anyhow, he was only interested in making smiles with Della.

Zole was in my room. I looked at the key in my hand. I'd had to unlock the door. He was eating a hamburger and watching a small color television from the bed.

"Hey, Lovejoy ma man. This gasket's gonna blow."

A cop chase, to gunfire. "The hotel management upping its image?" I got my soap and towel, still damp from morning.

"You talk sheet, Lovejoy. It's yo' present, y'know?"

He still didn't think much of me. I went the length of the corridor, washed, did a weary shave, and returned as Magda saw a client off the premises.

She came with me. "You're great with Zole, Lovejoy. He's talked about nothing all day, except how pleased you'd be with the set."

"Look, Magda." I hated to say it. "How did Zole come by it? Might it have been, well, stolen?"

She stared at me so long I thought she was controlling outrage at the scandalous suggestion.

"Of course it's stolen, Lovejoy! Jeech! You know how much they *cost*? Zole works the stores with three other kids."

She took my arm and walked me. Zole was yelling obscenities, exhorting the gunmen to even greater mayhem. "Tell him you like it, Lovejoy," she whispered. "He'll be thrilled."

I cleared my throat, put my soap and towel away. "Zole. That set's the very best I ever saw. It's splendid. Thank you."

"Ain't nuthin', rube," he said, engrossed.

That was it. Zole, aged seven, was also a gang leader. I said so long, started downstairs with Magda along.

"Look, love," I said. "This is a bit awkward to say. But if

the police catch me with a stolen television I'll be in real trouble. Can you tell Zole no more presents, please?"

She laughed. We came into the hallway. The desk man was watching a quiz show, impatiently muttering answers to himself.

"Lovejoy. Watch out for yourself, okay? There's people watching you. I just want you to know."

"Me? You sure, Magda?"

She made to move off. I caught her. "Look, love. What about Zole? Who's looking after him while you're, er, working?"

All she did was laugh at me. "Murder, man," she said.

I must have recoiled because she stopped scanning cruising cars and looked at me directly. She didn't often do that. "Hey." Yanks are brilliant at inflection. She squeezed more compassion into that one syllable than Molière averaged in a Paris rep. "I mean you're weird, okay?"

"Sorry, Magda. Just spooked, is all." It was a phrase picked up from a dozing bar bum. "I just wish I could help. You have a difficult time, the pair of you."

She smiled. "Most guys are shovers or pullers, Lovejoy. You're weird because you're neither. You off to see that skinny bitch?"

I said nothing.

"She won't fly you far, hon. Fly Magda Airlines some time."

If it hadn't been for the prickly feeling of unease I'd have talked longer. Anyhow, a crumpled motor crawled by and she trotted off to answer the whistled summons. I sighed and walked off. People do what they're good at, I always think.

As I started off, I tried working out this land of opportunity's determinants. Like, how come Kelly Palumba was rich beyond the dreams of whatnot, while same-age Magda was a street prostitute? It couldn't simply be silver-spoon-at-birth, could it? Kelly had offered me more money for a pinch of drugs than Magda saw in a month. Maybe our olden day system was simply continued here in the U.S.A.? Except in America the bosses didn't wear emblazoned coats-of-arms.

Then I heard sirens, denoting carnage somewhere close. It wasn't far, maybe three hundred yards, to where the cars congregated around the man lying near the pavement.

Taxi drivers were yelling and horns blared accompaniment. I didn't bother listening to the explanations and shouts of whose fault it all was, how some car had suddenly accelerated and the man suddenly fell off the curb . . . I went on past the crowd, sick to my soul. No question of what had happened to Tony, not now I'd seen Bill lying there. The taxi drivers were wrong. It was my fault. I'd assumed the police were invulnerable, that nobody could possibly harm a special agent, or whatever Bill was. Had been. I'd rung the Aquilina number to ingratiate myself. I knew that. Well, I'd made myself secure now. Bill had paid up, for me.

Against all habit I went into a late-night bar up from Times Square. I had some Californian wine, pale and faintly opalescent. I vowed no revenge. How could I? I was just badly shaken, even leaping like a scalded cat when the bar door banged in the night wind. I was frightened. I didn't know what I was into. Stupidly, I'd assumed I was free of obligations to Nicko's crowd once Gina had sent me back to pasture in Manhattan.

In Apple Zee's nutritious joint I pulled out the letters. I memorized Bill's phone number, but kept the card to give to Nicko. It wouldn't matter to Bill, not now. All betrayal is a one-off, complete and entire of itself. The card would add nothing, but be proof of my good faith. The second was a note from Sophie Brandau's secretary, on scented notepaper that must have cost a bomb. It said to call on Mrs. Brandau at my earliest convenience, Park Avenue. The third was a scrawled note from a Mrs. Van Cordlant's secretary's assistant, saying to call, on Madison Avenue.

Not much. So? The only way was to feel my way out of New York, along any thread. Rose was my least likely thread. The others? Well, Sophie might reveal most. Except this Mrs. Van Cordlant coming out of the blue. . . . When in doubt, grab for antiques. Therefore Sophie, Park Avenue.

I was about to go when Zole slipped in beside me.

"Two more burgers, ma man," Zole sang. He had his star-spangled yo-yo.

"Not for me, ta. And put that yo-yo away."

"You ain't gettin', rube."

I watched him in the bar mirror, grabbing the food. A lad after my own heart. "Eat well, Zole."

"Your pal was dead before he got hit," Zole said conversationally. "He got *throwed*, man."

"I guessed." Bill was no accident-prone stumbler. He was a capable bloke.

"Hey, Lovejoy! You ain't such a rube."

"He was the one watching the hotel?"

"Him, a bad news pig, and two brothers."

Whatever that meant. "Brothers? He had brothers?"

Zole guffawed, a gaping mouth filled with a mash of ketchup-soaked hamburger, and mocked, "Ah mean *black*, Lovejoy. Ya know *colored*? Jeech!"

Leaving, I made him replace the cutlery and two saucers that had somehow fallen under his T-shirt. We parted, me to get an armful of newspapers from an all-nighter, him to hustle a john for Magda, he said. I nearly didn't believe him, but worried in case it was true.

The Benidormo was jumping, forgive the pun. Magda's room thumped to an ancient rhythm. The other side was a pandemonium of a man and bird having a brawl, best of six pinfalls and threats of murder with free abuse.

Before I could settle down to tranquillity, the bad news pig shouldered in and stood there apologetically.

"Sorry, Lovejoy. I gotta do this."

My heart sank. Between the orgiastic moans from Magda's and the howls from screamsville, my own pad had somehow earned a bludgeoning.

"What's up, Tye?"

"Gina says you aren't following orders, okay?"

He said the same okay four times, each time hauling me erect and clouting me in the belly so I whoomfed double. I tried asking what orders for chrissakes but he didn't answer. He was really sorrowful, though, and expressed sincere regret as I crouched and retched onto the bare linoleum.

"It's not me, understand," he said with compassion. "It's Gina, okay? You didn't report in."

I gagged. My sweat dripped onto my hands, into the puddled sick between them. God, I felt like death. "Okay. Sure." What else meant concurrence?

An hour after Tye'd left I finished mopping the floor and went down the corridor to wash my towel. Magda came to stand in the doorway behind me. She looked sympathetic. My heart sank further. I definitely needed no more help.

"No compassion, Magda. I've had enough to be going on with, ta."

"Lovejoy, honey," she said softly, "leave N'York. Soon."

"Am I allowed one phone call first?"

She sighed. "Dumb," she said.

For the next hour, until midnight, sprawled on the mattress between two shaking walls, I ogled my gift TV and read the newspapers, under a snowfall of flaking plaster. I'd at last set to, learning New York's news. Then at the witching hour I phoned the number Fredo had given me, and told a recording machine a negative report, but that I was invited to see the lady in question next day when I'd report in full.

And slept, fitfully dreaming of Bill's body being lobbed under an approaching car. I didn't go to see Rose that night.

11

AMERICA'S not perfect, mind. Disillusion's the bus station, West Forty-second Street.

Sheer size is agorophobia's ally. I'd learnt the word panhandler from Zole the day before. The world center of hustling, panhandling, drug pushing, aggressive dereliction is surely here. I'd never seen so many buses in my life, commuter roarers and long-distance racers all the colors of the rainbow. It seems they're all private companies. Passengers too are all shades and sizes. Tip: Don't go for a pee—bottle it until you reach home.

A whole hour it took me, finding the times and places of the California runs, for my escape. The drifters with their aggressive sales pitches frightened me to death. One shabby bloke wide as a barn stopped me in the open crowd by simply shoving a flat hand on my chest.

"Hey. Whachoo want, man?" he threatened.

"Er . . ." I tried to edge away among some passengers.

"You gotta want somethin', man." He dragged at me.

"I've no money," I said feebly.

"Sheet." He let go so I fell, got up, and scarpered to palpitating safety among a horde of people queueing for hamburgers.

The trick is to stay ungrabbable, which means beyond arm's reach of passersby. This means deep in a queue of ordinary folk, or ensconced in a nosh bar where the proprietor is protection for as long as you're buying. Remember that. Solitude prevails in any loo, except here it's a mangler's mart, with blokes of all ages soliciting, injecting, selling syringes, even fighting over vulnerable travelers with knives. Police are on hand, sometimes. But bloodstained tiles do nothing for confidence.

Japanese tourists are useful, going in clusters like they do. I found them a practical aid, and hopped from group to camera-loaded group like a child crossing a turbulent stream on stepping stones.

And got taken forcibly just when I'd discovered the bus numbers, price, and worked out a policy to avoid the perils of passengerhood. Perhaps midday departure to San Francisco would be the best? Being trapped on a charabanc with a load of streetwise hustlers scared me. Or maybe these weapon-toting clutchers never actually went on the buses at all?

"This way, man."

Three blokes grabbed me. I tried squawking for help, struggling, shouting for police, anything. I was yanked down some stairs, God knows where. Two prostitutes were having a wrangle on a landing while a bemused city dresser looked on. Four or five blokes were trading money for screws of paper, slick as light. The staircases were concrete. I got bruised against the handrails in the rush downward. A couple were fornicating in a doorway, the woman against the wall, nonchalantly smoking, gazing into space. The tunnels and staircases reverberated to the echoes of shouts, quite casual, distant thunder of traffic, people talking, cars starting up. My mind reeled backward. Incongruity's supposed to be the essence of humor, not chaos. Down here all rules vanished. We reached some level that stank of urine. My three captors were talking quite offhandedly among themselves, as if they weren't hauling a struggling captive along dank concrete terraces. We seemed to be near an umpteen-tiered car park. The sweet smell of excess mingled aromatically with petrol's thick scent. A man whooped as if in some echo chamber. I glimpsed some geezers around a trestle table under a naked bulb. "After you wit' heem," a bird called laconically, squeezing past going the other way and tutting in annoyance when they shoved her aside.

"Hey, Lovejoy ma man!"

We'd stopped in a concrete bunker of some style, the door not hanging off and a score of television monitors on the go round the walls.

I was plonked in front of a desk—desk, if you please, in this warren. Numerous people sat about, several birds. They were talking, watching the consoles, professionals of a sort.

I tried to get breath, but got giddier the more I inhaled. The fumes were literally intoxicating, sending my mind on a strange unplanned trip. A control room?

"What you doin' here, Lovejoy?" He pronounced it love-jo-a. "Why'ncha come ta me, man?"

A little unused air happened into my lungs and I found voice. "For chrissakes, Busman!" I yelled. "What the hell you do that for? You scared the hell out of me, you stupid burke!"

The place stunned into silence. Busman rotated his chair, smiling hugely at his people.

"Ain't he somethin'?" he demanded. "He ain't crazy, jess sorta weird. Squat it, Lovejoy."

A chair rolled under me. I fell into it, sucking where my knuckles had scraped along the walls.

"Silly sod." I was really narked, mostly from having been terrified.

He boomed a laugh from forty fathoms. I swear the ground vibrated. "Lovejoy's the bad who got me shucked, people. Believe it."

They resumed talking, glancing between their consoles and me. The screens showed the concourses, departure points, ticket agencies, the nosh concessions. Even the stairwells were there, hustlers and activities in all their glory.

"Is this where you work, Busman?"

His amusement thundered out. He shook, his desk throbbed, his teams fell about. Typical. I was getting narked and said so. I'd thought I was being polite.

"Love-jo-a," he said, wiping his eyes on his sleeve. "You *is* weird, an' thassa fact. I don't work here, man. I *works*."

More rolling in the aisles from all and sundry. I sat, nodding with a feeble show of interest. Whatever turns this lot on, I thought, then let me get out of here and I'll go by train, canal, hire a yak. Anywhere'd do.

"I *controls*, Lovejoy. You know control?"

Who pays them to watch the concourse so fervently, I wondered idly. I didn't really care. If I asked the question they'd only roar and shake their heads. Even the birds were eyeing me, tittering.

"Lovejoy." Busman came in to land, leaning forward. God, he was big. He'd make ten of me and have leftovers. "You sprung me. Why?"

I brightened. A sentence I could recognize, at last. Berto Gordino must have got him out.

"It wasn't me, Busman. I just asked a lawyer to try."

He closed his eyes, shook his head, roused as if coming round from an anesthetic.

"You don't work fo' no Bethune, Lovejoy." It was an accusation. I swallowed, nodded.

"I lied, Busman. I was scared. I'm only a bar help at Manfredi's. I did extra waiting for some society folk. It was Mrs. Aquilina in the car. Her lawyer—"

"I got it, Lovejoy." He beckoned a confrere, sounding mystified. "See what I mean, Trazz? Anybody else'd claim *serious*. Lovejoy just says it like is."

"It was my idea, though," I put in quickly, not wanting to be left out of any free praise.

Trazz was a tiny man of skeletal thinness, warped by some deformity so he stood at an angle from his waist up. He had a cigarette between his lips, eyes crinkled against ascending smoke.

"He's not so dumb," Trazz said. It was a hoarse whisper so slight you had to strain to listen. "Not like today's mob. See the screen, Busman? They've hacked the delivery. Makes two times, Busman. We godda *move*."

"They stupid they have, Trazz." Busman rolled his chair across the floor, staring intently from screen to screen as buses disgorged passengers and bags. "Who's the shipper?"

"They's Sarpi's. Got hisself Miamis, Haitians, Jamaican." Trazz crinkled, went tsss-tsss. I watched a second, scored it as wry laughter. "He knowed best, Busman, tsss-tsss."

"Hit his smurfs, Trazz. How many he got?"

"Today? Sixty-eight, not counting Mexican."

People all about laughed at this sally. I tried to grin along but my face had gone tight. Hit?

"Forty too much?"

Trazz went tsss-tsss some more, said, "Forty twenny-eight short, Busman " More hearty laughs. A jocular company.

Trazz swayed away, pivoting on his right hip. Quiet and speed together, for all his deformity.

"See, Lovejoy? N'York's way." Busman rose from his chair, darkening the known world, nodded me along with him. We walked the screen-studded walls. "We see the goods come, charge a percennage. Only small, nuthin' spectacular."

"What's a smurf, Busman?" I had to look upward almost at right angles.

Folk nearby chuckled. A girl snorted in disbelief, hurriedly composed herself when Busman idly looked round.

"Smurf is a mule, Lovejoy. Carries the bag, see? Drugs, money fo' washing in these clean white streets of ours, guns, anythin' the man wants, see? Six cents on the dollar."

"Who's this man, then?"

He laughed so much he almost fell down, literally sagging helplessly. I had to try and prop the bloody nerk up. Nobody came to help, even though I cried out when my spine buckled, because they were all rolling in the aisles too. I got him to a chair at a screen showing the panel of long-distance arrivals and lent him my hankie so he could snort and wipe his eyes. What the hell had I said?

"The man's who-evuh, Lovejoy," he said. "Poh-lice hack businessess, right? Then they *the man*, see? Canada goods hack mebbe four cents on the dollar by transport's bossman. Broker man's boys spread rumors some bank's foreclosin' so he makes a little zill, *he's* the man, see? Who-evuh."

"Not just one person?"

"You catchin' own, man!"

He strolled up deeper into the room. It was extensive. At the inner end a row of American pool tables. Trazz was there, allocating jobs to a small crowd of men, all sizes and shapes. We went through a doorway, along a corridor, and into a comfortable living room. A woman about Trazz's size came up smiling, got introduced.

"How d'you do, Lorrie?" I greeted. "Pleased to make your acquaintance."

Busman loved that. "We gotta gentleman here, no mistake. He sprunged me last week, that big society mouthpiece. Give him a drink."

We rested in deep leather armchairs. I was given some hooch that made my eyes water. Lorrie was thrilled, seeing my gasp as evidence of sensitivity.

Busman enjoyed himself telling her how I'd got myself almost dissected by the maelstrom in the concourse. I worked out that we were somewhere deep below West Forty-second Street, the bus station heaving and churning away way above our heads. I didn't like the sensation. I looked round. No antiques, which was a disappointment.

"Is this all a part of . . . ?"

"Sure is," Busman said. "They don't call for the rent, is all." He laughed. Lorrie laughed.

"Do they know this goes on?"

"Sure do, Lovejoy." He explained to Lorrie, "He don't know from nuthin' Lorrie. Like a chile, so say everythin' two times but start over part way in, see? Tell him it. I gotta check Trazz not too vicious this time." He went into an inner room that had more screens projecting from its walls.

She was fascinated, started to explain, repeating it slower as if I was gormless.

"You really don't understand," she marveled. "I think it's kinda sweet, y'know? Like . . ." She dug for a word. "Like innocent, y'know?"

Narked, I said I was following all right. She said hey sure, and went on telling me how Busman's world worked. Cash defaulters had to be punished. Sarpi's drug carriers arriving from the south today would be attacked, their merchandise seized. It was an illegal Customs and Excise.

"Why don't the police stop it?" I said at one point, which called for more repetition, slower still, Lorrie painstakingly mouthing the words as if I'd gone deaf.

"Police got their own hack, see? Smurfers take care of them, like airlines, like property developers, building trades. Like merger capital, see? Like bullion markups that happen of a sudden for no reason. Like movies that bomb, like million-dollar shows go turkey, a politician gets himself elected—"

"Elected?" I'd heard Yanks had universal suffrage.

"Sure. One's elected, the others not paid enough, see?"

"The man?" I guessed shrewdly.

She was delighted. "You got it, Lovejoy! It's *always* the man, see?"

I said. "Lorrie, I can't thank you enough for your kindness and patience. I'm grateful."

"Think nothing of it, Lovejoy," she said shyly. "It's our pleasure."

We talked of homes for a while, me saying about my cottage in England and trying hard to remember the price of groceries and all that so she could be outraged at differences higher or lower. Busman returned, downing a couple of whiskies more and saying that Trazz was putting too savage and that he'd have to go. He was proud that Lorrie had finally explained the way life worked. "She bright," he said. I concurred. She was ten times brighter than me.

"Honey, Lovejoy in that shitty Benidormo," she complained elegantly. "You not do something?"

"Thank you, love, but I'd rather stay there for a couple more nights, if that's all right. I do appreciate your generosity."

"You wants, you asks," Busman rumbled benevolently. We went and I got an usher from Trazz to the upper world of life and pleasant New York skies. It was still a dream, but now tinged with dark-rimmed clouds.

12

FREDO was mightily soured by the news that I had messages to carry for Nicko and couldn't work today. He complained, whined, appealed to the skies as he opened the bar.

"I'll stay, then. Can I phone Nicko?"

"No!" he screeched, going pasty white. "Ya wanna get me . . . ?"

Killed? I went my way.

New York's bus system's so orderly it's incomprehensible. You simply buy a ride, and get a permit from the driver entitling you to another ride on any bus whose route crosses yours. Get it? It all stems from this methodical crisscross system of numbering streets. I was baffled by its predictability, finally got a taxi.

"Th'ain't got this in England 'cos they dumb, man," the driver sang, laughing. "Like, you live say five hundred Fifth Avenue. Eerase that last zero, divide by two, okay? Add eighteen gives forty-three. You drops the fare Forty-third Street and you's home, man."

"How marvelous," I said through a headache.

"Sep you add thirty-four for Park Avenue."

Fantastically enough he dropped me right at the door. Where the commissionaire only reluctantly put a message through to the Brandau residence. I was told ten o'clock.

That left me walking through lovely New York's morning sunshine. I'd my Manhattan map, which showed these amazing streets. The shops were so varied, the traffic instant mayhem. I stopped just to look. The taller buildings caught sun against the blue. Even the deepest chasms were relieved by a distant sheet of sky, sometimes with an exhilarating stretch of waterway. A couple of times cars nearly ran me down— wrong side of the road, I remembered eventually. Manhattan was so wonderful it was a full hour before I caught myself wandering rather than aiming, called to mind Tye Dee's chastisement, and set about finding Mrs. Van Cordlant's address on Madison Avenue. The names thrilled me, from songs and films. I felt quite proud when I managed to say Madison without adding avenue. A real New Yorker.

My letter got me into the lift. It flung upward like a shuttle, casting me out at altitude into a plush ballroom that seemed to function as a corridor. You could have held a concert in it.

I was frightened by an instant screech as a lady I half recognized wafted to greet me.

"It's my lucky Libran!" She enveloped me. Perfume cut off my air supply. Something licked my face. I realized there were three of us in there, one a minute dog. "I'm so glad you could come, my dear. Chanel? Bring this gentleman his favorite drink this instant!"

"Yes, Mrs. Van Cordlant!"

A maid in full fig—I didn't say hello to Chanel—slicked the doors to and wheeled a tray of drink after us. The flat spread into the distance. Windows showed Central Park, a lake, the scaggy tops of edifices and expanses of lovely sky.

Mrs. Van Cordlant dragged me to a settee and shoved me down. She'd not been this decisive when I'd given her a cent to get rid of her on board the *Gina*. Then, she'd seemed driven to distraction. Now she was practically on top of me. Enveloping breasts seemed everywhere. I struggled to breathe.

"Just tea, please."

Chanel almost staggered with shock, but was a game girl and left us to it.

Mrs. Van Cordlant eyed me eagerly. "How long have you been clairvoyant, my dear? Was it from birth?"

"Er, well—"

"I *agree*, Lovejoy! My astro-psychic—been with her *years*—had *no notion!*—until she was struck by lightning in South Carolina. Can you imagine?"

"Good heavens," I said gravely, thinking she was a right nut. The bloody dog, a King Charles the size of a shrew, was trying to hump my foot. I tried to disengage without booting it into the Guggenheim.

She was eyeing me admiringly. I felt odd. Admiration hadn't happened since I'd landed.

"Do you want repaying now, Lovejoy, or shall we take care of the business in hand first?"

"Repaying?" I brightened. Then I remembered I'd only given her a single cent. Repayment on that scale was out.

I rose, frostier than her commissionaire, and toe-flicked her hound aside.

"Mrs. Van Cordlant," I intoned. "If you imply that I would demean myself by accepting repayment for the small service I did you, I'm afraid I must decline."

"But I—" Her features were quite appalled.

I went all stern. "No, Mrs. Van Cordlant. Thank you. But I gave you that coin in all good faith, knowing it would assist. *Any* compensation to me would instantly devalue your luck. I can't accept money. The . . ." what were they? Star signs? "The forces of fortune are *life*, Mrs. Van Cordlant. They can't be bartered, like commodities."

"Oh, I'm so sorry, Lovejoy. I'd no idea!"

"Please may I take my leave, Mrs. Van Cordlant?"

"Oh, please. I—"

Melodie quickly mollified me enough to have me sitting down. We were frosty friends at opposite ends of the settee, a mere mile apart, while Melodie apologized repeatedly. I was aloof.

"You hear that, Chanel?" she told the maid with brimming eyes while I looked soulful. "Lovejoy here—a true clairvoyant, though he's Libran—refused twenty thousand, so's not to spoil the luck he *gave* me! Isn't that just beautiful?"

Melodie choked, Chanel looked astonished. I almost fainted, and did a bit of choking on my own. I came to with my ears ringing disbelief.

"Lovejoy," the silly old bat said, emotion brimming from her eyes. "You are the most sincere person I have ever met. Do you know what it's like to be rich in New York?"

"No, Melodie," I said with honesty. Or anywhere else.

Her voice sank to a whisper. Chanel left, looking back in disbelief. "It's punishment, Lovejoy. Purgatory."

"It is?" I tried more soulful, this time didn't make it.

"It's people, Lovejoy. Mercenary, grasping."

Women are odd. I really mean that. A woman doesn't know the effect she has on a man. Any woman affects every man with instant global tonnage every single time. But women all go about teaching each other it isn't true, God knows why. They reach for doubt, where we blokes go for hope. This accounts for much of their behavior. Here was Melodie, for instance, wanting some excuse to justify our evident valency, and finding approval for her desires in this mystic claptrap. I was glad, wanting desperately to get back to where that fortune had so briefly winked its golden eye.

Chanel safely out of the way, I took her hand forgivingly. "Don't, Melodie. You're distressing yourself. Distress isn't the way of, er, those psychic influences. We can keep ourselves mindful of truth, and love."

All that frigging gelt, my baser elements were sobbing. I could have been winging my way out on my own personal frigging jet.

She was filling up again. We were both awash. She raised my hand to her lips, gave it a sucking kiss. "Oh, Lovejoy. I knew we'd bond. No wonder Gina values you."

"Please, Melodie." I moved away, thinking what to say. In the grief of losing all that gelt, I'd forgotten this bird was a pal of the Nicko mob. "There's something I have to say."

"Yes, dear?" She came to stand with me, looking over the city. I put my arm round her waist.

"I have a psychic obligation to you, Melodie. It came to me right—" how the hell did psychic obligations come?— "out of the ether." I grasped her hands. They were a mass of rings I could hardly get my fingers round. "I had to guide your actions, transfer my luck to you."

"You did?" she breathed.

"Had to, love. But there's a psychic condition."

"What condition, Lovejoy?" She withdrew slightly, eyes narrowing. I recognized suspicion.

I gazed into her eyes, deeply sincere. "I want a promise, Melodie. Just your word that you'll not breathe a word of our friendship. This psychic, er, thing is solely between us. Is that understood?"

Her expression cleared. "Oh, yes, Lovejoy!"

"Can Chanel be trusted?"

"Perfectly. Her family's served mine for two generations."

Two generations? That was only her and her dad. Didn't she mean ten, twelve? I shelved the problem, bussed her, disengaged when she clung.

"Oh, Lovejoy." She broke down, weeping. "I have a terrible confession. A moment ago, when you said you wanted something . . ."

"I know, love," I soothed. "Don't forget I *am* psychic. Mercenary considerations crossed your mind, didn't they?"

She nodded, sniffing. The miniature hound started whimpering in a corner.

"*Never* think of money between us." I swallowed, almost blubbering myself at our profound emotional depths. Thoughts of all that money helped my sorrow along.

"Thank you, my dear," she said.

"Then all's forgiven." I led her gently to the settee. "And you can tell me—" brainwave!—"about how you carried it off, on the *Gina*."

We held hands. I stayed her from ringing for Chanel to pour, bravely said I'd manage. It was a modern scrolled silver, rubbish but worth its weight in, well, silver. The porcelain was crappy modern stuff. Unbelievable.

"Oh, Lovejoy. It was marvelous!" Her eyes were shining now. There's nothing so voluble as a woman telling a triumph. "I'd never felt so confident! It was your penny!"

Smiling, I corrected her gently. "Not the penny, love. The forces act *through* it."

"That's it!" she cried. "I felt the forces act *through*! I slipped it under my third ring—you'll know we're all searched. I took quite a risk, Lovejoy."

Her face was solemn now, serious.

"Risk?" I frowned. "Not with the force?"

"Oh, no! But I suddenly *knew* I should stake bullion profits. Out of the blue!" She was so thrilled. We were so close. "You know what I staked?" She tutted at herself. "Cool as you please! Two percent! Can you believe it?" She gave a naughty-girl giggle.

I chuckled, shaking my head. "I'd have loved to've seen you, Melodie. You have such natural grace."

"Oh, d'you think so?" She fluffed her hair the way they do. "Their faces! Especially Charlie Sarpi's. After the failure of the Japanese gold commemorative fakes from Europe, he thought his cartel was in the driver's seat."

"I was only sorry Kelly Palumba was unwell."

"Such a shame, poor dear. Epsilon tried, but I swear that young man's sometimes quite deranged. Really made a hash of poor Kelly's stake. He simply knows nothing of property values. She'll be so mad. He got in. Did all right with his silly TV stations, though."

"Well, his home ground." I spoke as if I knew what we were talking about.

"Sarpi didn't even come close, darling," she told me mistily. "Only the commissioner. Of course Jim Bethune's always in at the finish these days. Antiques is a crazy world."

She was telling *me* that? I hesitated. "You know, love, I feel as if I've known you in at least two previous incarnations."

"Lovejoy, I feel it too. Deeply. We've known each other a lifetime. Is that silly?" She went shy.

"Of course it is." You have to deny a woman's suspicions to confirm they're true, but gently. "If we'd been, well, lovers in a former incarnation, surely we'd probably . . . ?"

Confusion set in, especially when she agreed with me. I wasn't too sure I wanted to associate with her, not without a single antique in the whole rotten dump. Sophie Brandau on the other hand said she'd got several.

"Will it last, Lovejoy?" We'd migrated to the middle of the vast settee. "For the game itself, I mean."

"No, Melodie. I'll have to divine for you, explore the, er, ether. That way I'll reinforce fortune."

"You will?"

Gold rings clamped on my hands. "Melodie, Melodie," I chided softly. "You think I'd desert you, now we've found each other after all this time?" For a moment I floundered. How long did reincarnation take? Was it like a frog shedding its skin, ten minutes flat? Or was it something to do with the Egyptians?

"I know it! Look what happened last time, darling! That horrible Monsignor O'Cody *cleaned up.* Seven massive church debts rescinded. You know what that is in dollars, darling?"

"Yes," I lied with gravity, sighing. "Amazing."

She snorted angrily. "I don't want to seem a sore loser, Lovejoy. It cost me, like it did the others. Costs hurt." She gave a thrilled moan. I recognized the woe-filled ecstasy of the gambler. You see it every day in auction houses the world over. "But I think O'Cody's a nerve. His line bid one point nine percent of total funds last fall, and lost. Know what? He tried all sorts of persuasion. Indulgences, the Faith, every whining excuse you can imagine—"

"I wasn't here then, Melodie."

"You should have been, Lovejoy! You know what he tried to do? Reschedule diocese loan flotations. Jim Bethune appealed to Nicko, got that stopped. I ask you!"

"Good heavens! Did things go that far?" I was completely lost now.

"They did! How could anybody look the De Beer hackers in the eye after that? Jim'd staked his usual three percent auction levy. Kelly had some new theme park in the pot. And, I mean, diamonds are *diamonds,* Lovejoy!"

"True, Melodie. Long faces everywhere, I'll bet!"

"And the rest! Of course, this time there'll be none of that. Nicko's had to get quite firm. That's why I think Gina's so worried about this manuscript business. Fell like a lead balloon when Denzie staked it. I mean, he talked it up—the Second Coming! Worth quite a bit, I suppose, but nothing compared to, say, the commissioner's police hack."

I sighed. "But you try telling them!"

"One default, that's all it needs, darling. One default, and the whole house of cards falls apart." She had her arm around me. Her eyes filled my view.

"And antiques, Melodie, er, love."

"Of course! Jim Bethune could see his whole hack *vanishing.*" She was stroking my face. "You know, darling, I could easily—"

A distant buzzer sounded. The hound yelped, flew under the settee. Melodie moved away quickly, smoothing her hair. "Look at the time!" she said brightly.

I recognized all the signs of a returning husband. Time to go.

I raised Melodie's hand to my lips with maximum sincerity, hoping I was doing it right. "Until the next time, love."

She hurried me to the door. "When, darling? Quickly!"

"Tomorrow? Same time?"

"Yes! I've no visitors tomorrow. Take the stairs until the elevator's gone."

The lift whirred, on its way. As Melodie's door closed, I ignored the stairs and scooted along the corridor, guessing doors. A faint clatter guided me. I can always sense the servants' entrance, my natural habitat. Chanel was doing the coffee mystique as I ghosted in.

"Lovejoy!" Instantly down to whispers, with her woman's instinct for subterfuge. "What the—?"

"Shhh!" I made myself more frantic than I felt. "It's her husband!"

She laughed silently. "Dumb, Lovejoy. She ain't got a husband, just four exes!"

Four divorces? Melodie wasn't young, but her turnover rate seemed excessive. "Chanel. I had to see you."

The kitchen had two closed-circuit monitors mounted above the inner door, and a small wall panel. One showed the downstairs foyer, the other the penthouse corridor.

"Me?" Her surprise melted slowly into a smile. "You outa your skull, Lovejoy? You passed up a fortune there."

"When can I see you, love? I wanted to, er, date you on the *Gina*." A faint buzzer sounded. She pressed an I'm-coming button. "She wants me back tomorrow."

"Horny bitch," she scolded angrily. "You watch her, Lovejoy. Come an hour earlier. My room's down the hall."

The console showed the left gate opening. Two men strolled into view, one lighting a cigarette. The doorbell buzzed, its proximity making me jump. Chanel gestured me to stay and quickly left to answer, smoothing her dress. I waited until the screen showed Denzie Brandau and Jim Bethune admitted, then slid out into the corridor. I fled, the one thing I used to be good at.

Outside, New York'd never have known I'd been up to

no good with Mrs. Van Cordlant. Everything seemed so normal. Traffic poured about. People tried to jump the red. Pedestrians survived by the skin of their teeth. Shops traded. A siren wailed the American song.

Hack? What stakes, exactly? Kelly had mentioned a game. What game was played by a church? Police commissioner? Silver bullion heiress? Property magnate? And on down the queue of wealth. Right down to the Brandaus with their miserable little stake of a supposed manuscript, allegedly now appearing after a century or so, in a manner as yet unidentified.

Thinking, shallow as ever, I posted off Bill's card to Gina with a note saying it was the phone number I'd reported the night before.

13

AMERICA'S phones are bliss. Their habit of actually working is very disconcerting: Put in a coin, dial, and speak to whoever answers. I truly hope it catches on everywhere. In little over half an hour, I made ten transatlantic calls to East Anglia and London. Cost me an arm and a leg, but I was over the moon. In East Anglia, a public phone is a dangling flex.

"Get through, Lovejoy?"

"Eh?" I wished Zole wouldn't keep doing that, suddenly being there with his bloody yo-yo. Hearing my name in this exotic paradise was queer enough. "Oh, aye." I'd told Boyson's pal I'd ring in an hour. If he wasn't home and waiting I'd . . .

"Stay cool, Lovejoy." Zole was whizzing his damned yoyo past my ear. It sounded like a mosquito, the sort that wakes you up slapping at air. "Cool's no fool."

"Why do you Yanks talk so?" I asked, starting across the traffic with the sudden rush of pedestrians as the green light showed. I didn't particularly need to cross, but in New York you seize any opportunity. "Gossip's a trash flash, honesty's a sleaze freeze." I'd noticed this as soon as I arrived. A dim actor of notable physique was a punk hunk, a crosstown journey a side ride. All catchphrases.

"You mad 'cos you cain't talk, Lovejoy." Whizz, whizz.

"Maybe true, Zole. Coffee?"

We went into a shop I'd never seen closed, perched on stools overlooking the tormented traffic. Zole ordered numerous hamburgers. How had he survived until he'd acquired teeth?

"Lovejoy, you stupid."

I grabbed him by his T-shirt. "Listen, you arrogant little sod. Call me stupid again and I'll—"

"I'm doin' you favors here, man!" He dusted himself

down with dignity. "This is N'York, Lovejoy. You gotta do like N'York, see? Or you don't make it."

"Make what?"

He sighed, wading into his grub. Seeing him eat made me hungry so I went and bought two of the nearest things they had to a pasty.

"Like, I say you cain't talk, you don't agree, man. That's the stupid. I say you cain't talk, you gotta say the same back, but real mean."

"I have?" I was curious.

"And don't pay the fuckin' phone. You *works* it. Then you gets the call free, unnerstand? You think Magda pays when she calls Tye ever' night?"

Magda, phoning Tye? "It's illegal," I said, to keep him going. I was learning.

"Legal's stupid, Lovejoy. Legal's jess N'York puttin' you down. I'll show you." He looked about for a second, then appalled me by yelling, "Hey, lady! Where's the ketchup?"

I went red. "Shhhh, you little—"

"Comin' ride up," somebody called, quite unconcerned. I smiled apologetically as it arrived. Zole noshed on, mollified.

"See?" he said eventually. "I hollers no ketchup, you says you're sorry. They thinks you stupid. They *knows* I'm not. Like that book you buying."

I stilled. How much of my phoning had the little sod overheard? "Book?"

"Don't send dollars less'n you get it first, see? Stupid."

I smiled at the obnoxious little nerk. "Ah. That's just some money I owed him."

"He don't squeeze, you don't pay, Lovejoy. That's smart."

"It is?" I wondered if he had any leanings toward being an antique dealer. With his instinct for fraud, he'd do a bundle. "Get the whole book, Lovejoy. One page is stupid."

He'd heard everything. "But what if—"

He glared at me in fury, yelled, "Who's doin' the buying, man? You or him? You? Then don't pay's smart. Lemme talk to him."

We discussed this proposition until we'd finished. I said I'd follow his advice, meaning I'd make sure nobody was listening next time, meaning Zole. I just hoped he wouldn't say anything to Magda. With her circle of clients I'd be done for in a day.

BRIAN Tarnley can't be trusted either, but that's because he's an antiquarian bookseller. The important thing about him is he owns a dingy upstairs room near Floral Street, Covent Garden. There, Easy Boyson works rent-free.

It's a strange partnership, founded on two things. First is that Easy Boyson's daughter is Brian's wife. Second is that Boyson's on the run, has been these five years. He was unbelievably a major, as in rank. His august old regiment was understandably vexed when the regimental silver vaporized. The peelers failed to find Boyson, or the tom. Which was lucky for Brian, who'd married Easy's daughter and could provide the scarpering major with a safe nook. Investigations revealed gaping holes where the military's bulging bank accounts should have been.

Neighbors occasionally query the two Tarnley children's tales about a grandfather who lives in their attic and isn't allowed to come out and play. Brian tells everybody that Alice's dad's poorly.

Which is great for Brian, because Easy Boyson's a forger. And the police are still unraveling the handwriting on withdrawal forms in Glyn Mills, bankers of Pall Mall.

Zole followed me to the phone, eager to show me how to defraud the phone company. I declined, and told him I was phoning a lady and my talk was not for little boys. He went off disgusted.

"Easy Boyson? Wotcher. It's Lovejoy."

"Where the hell are you, Lovejoy? A tank exercise?"

Brisk, military. I warmed to him. He still rises at six, spick and span by seven, ready for action.

"Conan Doyle, Easy. Do me a Sherlock Holmes page. You'll find examples of his handwriting in —"

"Leave recce to me, Lovejoy. Degree of authenticity?"

"Complete," I said. Another fortune down the nick.

"Excellent!" Forgers love perfection. "Continuation?" He meant was there a chance the buyers would want the whole thing later on.

"Possibly."

"Right." He pondered a moment, named a price that staggered.

"Fair enough," I told him. "I'll have it collected."

"Good luck, Lovejoy. Regards to New York."

And rang off. I supposed it was the traffic or something gave my location away. But Easy Boyson was an officer and a gentleman. Word his bond. Thank goodness for standards.

Then I used my last dollars to do something truly momentous. I scribbled a note to Mrs. Gina Aquilina, saying I didn't quite know where I stood, but had faithfully followed her instructions, and had striven to identify the source of the Hawkins grailer. A sample page would soon be on hand, when I would send it. I signed it, put it in an envelope, and got a cycle courier to come to the coffee shop. He arrived in an unbelievable space-age time of two minutes, and hurtled off on payment of my last groat.

Nothing for it. I walked all the way back to Fredo's, signed in for the remainder of the day, and started my cheery greetings to all comers. Until the fire touched the fuse.

Middle of the midday rushed it happened, one o'clock and every seat in the place occupied, people arguing sports and politics and prices and traffic in the way I was growing to love, all peace and racket.

"Lovejoy? Take a break."

"Wotcher, Tye."

"Hey, what about my order?" a customer called angrily from along the counter as I doffed my apron. I shrugged. Zole had taught me how to yell, but not what to reply. Fredo tore out of his office in a state.

"Glad to catch your visit, Lovejoy," he groused.

"Not be long, boss."

Tye gave me a look that sank my spirits, conducting me to his car. It was illegally parked, but without a parking ticket.

"I don't know what it is about you, Lovejoy," he sighed, opening his passenger door. "But you're sure attracting Gina's attention lately."

When you need a light quip, none comes. Ever notice that?

THE road north from New York splits into a frond of motorways. We bent right, and distantly I recognized a stretch of water. "Hey, Tye!" I went, excited. "That's where we sailed!"

"Lovejoy. You wiseass or dumb?"

He'd obviously got out of bed the wrong side. I ogled the scenery. Small towns came and went. Connecticut's pronounced with a load of Ds it hasn't got. The sun lit hills. Trees shone a strange and lovely russet I'd never quite seen before, quite like Chinese amber. We drove less than two hours, to a mansion with porticos and white pillars, lawns that people hate you to call manicured. No gates, but a goon in seeming somnolence that fooled nobody. He bent, peered at Tye, me, the limo's interior, shrugged us through.

"Reckon there's Civil War antiques here, Tye?"

He sighed, made no reply. We alighted and Blanche, lovely as ever but even more distant, ushered me in to a drawing room whose very length tired the ankles. Gina was sitting writing letters at a pathetic rubbishy desk, fetchingly decorating a window alcove against sunlight and olivine curtains.

"Lovejoy." No sit down either. "You found *what?*"

"The grailer, Gina. I think."

She slowly ran her gaze from my scuffy shoes to my unruly thatch. I felt specimened, candidate for a museum jar.

Her slender hands held the card I'd posted, and my scribble. She didn't ask where, how, what. Just examined me. A reaming, draining inspection. Her eyes were bleak as a winter sea.

"What did I order you to do, Lovejoy?"

"Er, well, missus." My voice quivers when I'm scared and my throat dries so it's hard to get a conversation going.

"*What?*"

I jumped, stammered, "To, er, make up to Sophie Brandau, report what I learned."

She beckoned me gently. I went close, stooped when she crooked her finger. Her hand lashed my face. The silly cow nearly ripped my eye from its socket, missing by a whisker. My head spun.

"And did you?"

"I've no money, except the marked stuff that'll get me arrested."

She considered that.

"Lovejoy. I'm no longer interested in whether you're as innocent as you seem, or double shrewd."

She could have expressed slightly more enthusiasm. I'd saved her from kidnap, or worse.

"Now I'm changing the rules. I give you orders day to day, understand? You start now." Why do agitated women clutch their elbows when they march about? I dithered, not knowing if I had to follow her. She returned, halted, gorgeous. "Tell me about the Hawkins thing."

I did, speaking with utmost sincerity into her eyes and only occasionally losing my place. Whistling bravely past the graveyard, I said only what I'd rehearsed.

"I spent every cent on phone calls to England. Dealers I know, who owe me, ones I could trust. And I kept it down to no-name stuff." I fluttered my eyes, the best I could do for shyness. "A . . . lady I know. She's married. We used to be, well, close friends. I got her to sift her husband's reserve records. He's a big antiquarian."

"So it's true? This . . . ?"

"Manuscript thing? It seems so. She's getting me a single sheet, day after tomorrow. I'll divvy it." I waited. "I thought it'd be what you'd want me to do." I was pleased with myself. She wasn't responding much, but I felt my tide turn. "See, Moira could tell me anything. In bed or out, I'd have only her account to go on. I know me, see? I'm hopeless with women. I believe them."

Gina paced, stood looking.

I took her raised brows as an invitation to speak on. "Moira Hawkins is a lady who wants much more than she has. Deep down, she's ambitious. Look at me, Gina. I'm a scruff. I'm not Fauntleroy. Would she be seen in a restaurant in my company?"

"There's Rose."

"Or the Brandaus?"

"You mention them together, Lovejoy. Why?"

"They're lovers, Gina. I'm not that thick."

Suspicions are meat and drink to women so I kept going. "Sophie Brandau doesn't want the scam to succeed. She knows it's untrue anyway. Sophie's frightened. It's all got out of hand. She wants him to chuck it."

"How do you know this?"

"It's plain as a pikestaff. I think Sophie hocked her jewelry so she could maybe buy Denzie out of Moira's scam."

"What did she use the money for?"

"Buy the grailer?" I suggested, trying the American shrug. I tried it again, gave up.

She stood at the window, fingers tapping her elbows. "How much is a grailer?"

"Depends on the amps." Her head shook minutely so I'd explain. "Amplifying factors. They work to tell you the price of an antique, anywhere."

I lifted a gilt silhouette sugar bowl from the low cornish. The poor phony thing was trying to be genuine Hausmaler work from Augsburg, about 1725. "This fake's from Berlin—see how they tried to get the proper silhouette of these flying birds? They went mad for Chinese fashion in the eighteenth century. This doesn't . . ." My words run out when I try to explain what happens. My chest should tighten and chime. I turned the lidded bowl over. Zilch.

"It's an 1880s fake. Price? Only two months' wages. If it was genuine, that counts one amp. If you'd got an original bill of sale from Augsburg, that's provenance and counts another amp. And authentic manufacture counts a third. Rarity, four. Is it of special material or mint? Five. Signature of the master, Johann Aufenwerth? Six. Then there's the grail factor, last of all. Like, say this was owned by Abraham Lincoln himself! Makes seven. Seven times two is fourteen. Hence the lowest price you can afford to sell it at is fourteen times the average monthly wage. See?" I replaced the chinoiserie carefully. She was listening, saying nothing.

"Some antiques have a base price—that's only the same, but compounded of amps to get the unit. Pearls, say. Get the quality first, expressed as currency units. Our unit is one pound sterling. Say you've a pearl, right? You phone a jeweler: What's this week's unit base average for pearls, ma man?" I was embarrassed, caught out doing my dud accent. "He tells you it's one. Before you do anything else, you *weigh* the pearl, in grains. It's nine, a whopper. The cost is exactly nine times nine, equals eighty-one quid *that day*. The price fluctuates. Like, next week's average unit base price might be two. Then your pearl's zoomed to eighty-one times two, see?"

I was suddenly conscious of a stirring behind me. Jennie and Nicko stood there. Malice was in the air.

With one woman I've always the feeling I've a chance. With two and a criminally minded lover of one who was also the husband of the first, I was in irons.

"You see what I mean, Nicko?" Gina asked, her job done. She went to her Victorian chaise longe, early repro but none the worse for that. She embellished it by just reclining. I envied it, quickly went back to being humble.

"He's a risk," Jennie said. I disliked Jennie. She always sounded so bloody cold. I'd reported to her, not Gina, about Bill. Then Bill was killed. Then Gina sends Tye to duff me up for not reporting. Aha.

"Maybe worth taking," Gina suggested.

"For what, though?" Nicko lit a cigarette. "I can't have any slip, this late stage."

"For the game."

Jennie's sharp intake of breath endeared her to me even less. Nicko stilled her worry with a shrug.

"Where's the gain?" he asked. He stared balefully past me with his black eyes.

"We know Moira Hawkins is fronting something with Denzie Brandau, Nicko. We don't know what. Lovejoy here knows values. You heard him. Okay, so he's stupid—"

"Just a minute, Gina." They talked on over me.

"—but that doesn't mean he can't be used."

I tried to look useful, effective, anything to prevent my being taken away pleading like Tony.

"Used how?" Nicko asked.

"Like I tried. A plant."

Jennie couldn't control herself. "You tried that, dear."

Gina's smile was cold. "I underestimated Lovejoy. He's weird, but oddly effective. He's latched onto the Sherlock thing."

"He says, dear."

Women can put malice into that innocent word. It splashed like malevolent oil.

"He said himself it might not be the right one. But it's a superb effort without any resources."

I liked Gina. She was brainy as well as beautiful.

"He'd have got close to Sophie if we'd funded him from the start." I wanted to give Nicko a reproachful glance to remind him of his marked money business, but bottled out. "We take him on staff, tell Denzie openly that Lovejoy rides with them as our informant."

"Have you thought of risks at all, dear?" from Jennie.

"Wait."

Nicko sat staring into space. My attention wandered between the exquisite Gina and a piece of original Chelsea porcelain ceiling ornament above me. It was misplaced, of course, stuck there without any other decoration to support it on the walls, but it was exuding a lovely warmth that any genuine antique gives . . .

People were talking.

"Answer, Lovejoy," Gina commanded. "What will you require?"

"A small sum to send for the sample page." I explained I was getting it on tick. "And to know enough to stop being scared I'm making mistakes."

That earned me a blast of lack-eyed laser from Nicko's eyes. To my disgust I found myself begging.

"Well, for Christ's sake. I'm on a tightrope every waking hour. I'm given orders I don't understand, not knowing if I'm going to get myself topped or not, beaten up—"

"The number he gave checked out," Jennie said.

"Right, Gina. Do it. Your can, okay?" Nicko rose and walked from the room. Jennie had to scurry to catch up before the door closed.

Gina was smiling-not-smiling. "Allies, Lovejoy. Welcome to the team."

"Do I get the chance of a bath? Paid?"

"Money, yes. But not the reward you're holding out for." She smiled genuinely now, sipped her drink, feline. "Plus one very very special benefit."

"What?"

"You're in the California game, Lovejoy."

"Thanks, love." Like hell I am, I thought. I'm off out.

14

SHOPPING is hell. God knows what women get out of it, but for me it's Doom City. Today, it was even worse, because I'd been sent out with Orly, who clearly hated me.

"For a start," I grumbled as we trekked from shop to shop, "everything's new. Different with antiques."

"Lovejoy." He stopped, right there in the middle of Fifth Avenue, arms full of parcels, and tried to stare me down. It didn't work, because I was in the California game too, whatever it was. "I don't trust you. You're a loose cannon. You'll roll around the deck and sink our ship. I know it. Okay. But don't try charming me. You're today's Fifth Column."

"Don't hold back, Orly. Spit it out."

He didn't smile.

"There'll be a comeuppance, Lovejoy. You'll die the death. After you're buried I'll laugh all I want."

"Orly," I said, riling him who was determined to be riled. "Did you think that silk tie was worth the money? Only—"

He dumped the parcels in our limo—it was following us—and marched imperiously into the next stores.

"Orly," I tried every so often. "How comes it that you and Gina, well, y'know? While Nicko and Jennie are . . . ?"

"Stupid," was all he said back.

I noticed Zole ogling us from across the street. He saw me in a brand new off-the-peg suit, trendy shoes, striped shirt. His yo-yo almost froze in mid-air. He didn't come across, though I waved. I wondered what they'd say in Fredo's.

I got into the car after Orly and tapped our driver on the shoulder. "Manfredi's Eatery, mate."

"Orly?" the driver asked.

"Bugger Orly," I said. "I told you Manfredi's."

We drove to Manfredi's. I endured a few minutes of leg-pulling from Della and Lil, was congratulated by Josephus in a melodiously outdated rap, envied by Jonie, and caused Fredo moans of outright grief by resigning. No sign of Rose. I made them drop me off at the corner by Hawkins's, and got a satisfactory ping from the little bell over the bookshop door. Seeing Orly's thunderous face as the limo rolled away was pleasant.

Rose was at the desk, invoicing.

"Lovejoy!" she cried, flushing red as fire. "I thought you'd left us in the lurch!"

I bussed her cheek, looked round smiling. "Won a few quid on a, er, betting game."

"You look splendid! Moira'll be thrilled!"

"How's Moira?"

Her expression clouded. "Busy. She's at a meeting."

As ever, I added for her. With Denzie Brandau. I did a stroll. No customers behind the stacks.

"Listen, Rose. This money I've got. It could take you and me to Southsea. We could bring over the Sherlock!"

"Uh-huh." Another New York enigmatic, meaning anything you cared to read in. "Well, that's great, Lovejoy!"

Meaning I was to serve, not lead. Okay, but it wouldn't do.

"I'll book our flights, okay?" I coursed over her indecision. "Tell Moira we'll be there and back within a week."

"Wait, Lovejoy," she tried desperately, but I'd already bussed her and was out of the door heading off down the street calling that I'd be back about four.

For a couple of blissful hours I delved into the public library, Fifth Avenue west side, looking up California and various people, with patchy success. Nice library, though the white marble and the smug lions by the steps cloy and its marble candelabra are a bit much. I loved it. No sign of Zole at the corner, so I used the public phone. Still amazed by the cheapness of the U.S.A. phone system—ours in U.K.'s three times dearer.

"Lovejoy. Locations, please. Moira Hawkins, Sophie Brandau."

"One moment." And, less than five seconds I swear, the girl gave me both.

"Ta, love. I'm going to the latter."

Moira at a hotel restaurant in which, surprise surprise, Denzie Brandau happened to be chairing a campaign fund-raiser. Sophie was at home, so I phoned her, asked her could I see her urgently in strictest confidence. I got a taxi to Park Avenue, where the doorman fawned. Flung to the penthouse by a lift that just managed to judder to a halt before crashing out into orbit, I rang the bell. Sophie herself came to the door.

THE Theory of Sexual Understanding is mine. I created it. It works between a man and a woman. It's this: Everything's up to her. I coined it years ago over a bird I fell for over some antique she said she owned. God, I slogged, broke my heart, agonized, plotted, just to get near her. Nearly four whole days. I finally gave it up as hopeless on a rainy Thursday at an antiques auction. She came in, offhandedly told me she'd brought along her Roman mosaic glass bowl, about A.D. 10. (These small objects, astonishingly difficult to fake, are still pretty common.) I shrugged and went with her to the auctioneer's yard.

In her car, she practically raped me, whimpering and ripping at my clothes. The car windows mercifully steamed up and the auction was under way so nobody saw us. I hope. Her preoccupied husband was at the same auction. See what I mean? I'd set out to win her affections, against all odds, and failed. Then she decides on frontal assault, and it's the hallelujah smile. Of course, the lying cow really hadn't got a Roman mosaic glass anything, so my love didn't stand the test of time and I ditched her for a vicar's widow whose collection of continental barometers came up for sale about then.

My TOSU worked the second Sophie opened the door. I myself am never quite sure when a woman takes the decision. But I am certain it's always up to her. We blokes just trot along obediently, hoping the whim's in the right direction. But I knew I was favored. Not that she did anything to suggest she was about to. I mean, her reception of me was almost exactly the same as Gina's, by which I mean an erg above glacial. She looked imperial, gowned as if for an evening do.

No maid, I realized, but that incidental's never more than half a clue, and open to misinterpretation.

"No, thanks." I declined the offer of a drink. "I didn't come because of your antiques, Sophie." I didn't need to mimic hesitation. I was worried enough. "It's that something's really wrong. But I want to help, any way I can."

"I know." She didn't mind her hand in mine.

"Look, love. I've been taken on the payroll by Gina, to advise on antiques. I've been told it's to do with the California game. I'm telling you this well, because."

"What are you saying, Lovejoy?"

Why ask me? I wasn't really sure. "Anything I can do for you, love, I will. I promise." Aghast, my brain shrieked caution, not to make frigging promises that might get it killed. I wallowed on just because of the way she was looking at me.

"I need help, Lovejoy." Tears welled in her eyes. She suppressed them, came to.

"I don't mean I'll help Denzie. I mean help you."

Drive a harder bargain, you pillock! shrieked my brain in a panic. What's she giving in return for lobbing us both in jeopardy?

"Please, Lovejoy. He's not a bad man. Honestly. I promise you. He's just . . . wayward, driven by ambition. He's a consummate politician, capable, kind. Everybody'll tell you. He's in line for the next presidential nomination. People don't know Denzie. I don't know which way to turn, not since Moira inveigled him into taking half a share in the Sherlock stake."

I let her talk through her exhortations, hopes, fears. I rose and went to stand, as if in deep tortured thought, before a decorative shelf of pewter tankards that pulled me like a magnet. I'd been dying to inspect them ever since I'd stepped into the flat. I was so excited by what I saw I almost shouted the joyous news to Sophie. In the nick of time I remembered I was in spiritual anguish, and just loved that dulled glowing metal. They were stupendous, the only set of Channel Isles tankards I'd ever seen. The giveaway is the measure, for obstinate old Jersey people still use the "pot," which is a cool 69.5 fluid ounces. All six stood there, each with cunning little double acorns on the thumb catches. I stood, warmed with love. How many ancients had drunk from them in their two centuries? You don't get love like that anymore.

"Lovejoy?"

Sophie was asking me something. She'd come to stand beside me. I turned away from the pewters, heartbreak coming easy.

"Shhhh." I put my finger to her lips. "I promise I'll help Denzie."

"You will?"

My brain resigned, stormed out of ken shrieking abuse and insults. But what could I do? She was closer, letting her hands touch my jacket and gradually raising her gaze from my chest toward my face and then opening her mouth ever so slightly and keeping her eyes fixed on my mouth as she gave the gentlest of tugs so we were closer than ever and what could I do when it's women decide every single time?

"DARLING?"

Sophie moved with a woman's awkwardness from sin into confession. I never have any problem shifting these gears. They do.

"Mmmmmh?"

Women's greatest—maybe only—mistake is to chatter straight after love's made. Beats me why. What's there to say? But they find something, anything. If ever I find a woman willing to stay mum during that transitory death after loving, I'd love her for nowt. I know I keep on about this.

"Darling. I didn't ... you know? Just to ... y'know, Lovejoy?"

"Mmmh?" (See? They don't even know themselves.)

"I don't want you to think, well, just because."

"Mmmh."

"You don't, do you?" Apprehension raised the ending, so a denial would suit best.

I gave up, carried the small death along, rolled over to find her propped on one elbow. The bedroom was semidark, curtains drawn. We were a million feet off the ground, but she'd had to ensure we were safe from the prying balloonists.

"Look, love." I couldn't stop looking at her breasts. She

covered them by gathering her nightdress with her spare hand. I hadn't remembered her donning a nightie, but orthodoxy rules. "If you think I'm that cynical, then—"

She shushed me. "I just want to hear you say you don't think that way."

"Do I need to, love?" I'm easily confused. Was she asking me to deny an affirmative based on a denial of a suspicion . . . or the opposite?

"Please."

"Very well." No chance of escaping with a light laugh. I cupped her lovely face. "Sophie Brandau, your anxieties are unfounded. I admire you. I fell for you instantly. I'm head over heels in love with you." I gave her a quiet smile, my sincerity revealed.

She sighed in relief. The answer she'd needed was in there somewhere.

"Thank you." She lay back, thinking. I waited. After confession, the penance. They go for both together. Sometimes I wonder if it's women whose instincts determine religious liturgy. You could make out quite a case.

"Lovejoy. Were you . . . shocked by, well, by it all?"

What the hell now? "You want the truth?" I asked with reluctance. "Yes, quite frankly. It was something . . ." Words are such sods. I never know which ones women want.

"I knew it, darling. I could tell. But you must realize. America's a harsh country. Below the surface we don't make any allowances. It's dog-eat-dog. The California game's that."

At last I was in. A moment's thought, so as not to spoil the drift of her talk, then, "But why need it be quite so . . . ?"

Women are good at jumping to conclusions, even when other people haven't the faintest idea what they're talking about.

"Enormous is America's way. And it isn't necessarily corrupt. The sports percentages would still get slipped to some syndicate no matter who was playing the championship. Political nominations always have been fixed. Drug companies have done secret deals ever since they were quoted on Wall Street. Drugs arrive in tons, not ounces, so payola rolls on over all federal enforcement agencies. It's the American way to grab a piece of the action. A percentage of major-city real estate development always gets hived off . . ."

Antiques, business, labor movements, union dues, local politics, imports. I listened, wondering. Game? Stakes?

"I just wish it had stayed at that level for Denzie's sake. But ever since Moira's mad idea that he'd have a cast-iron presidential ticket, he's been like a crazy man. It was Moira's idea to add it to the stake."

"Shhh, love," I said. "Hold together a moment. Forget all this. You've an ally at last."

We lay embracing, langor and warmth stealing over us.

"Darling?" she said at last.

"Yes, love."

"Are there . . . are there different ways of making love?"

Sometimes, women don't expect uncertainty. They're positive we blokes know everything about sex. You lose credibility by showing hesitancy. It's one of the few times reflexes come to help. Even my brain went along this time. We answered jointly in the affirmative.

ORLY delivered me at Bethune's, by Seventy-fourth Street near Columbus Avenue. I grumbled because I was starving, and Anita's Chili Parlor exuded aromas that made me weak at the knees. Even if it was spelled wrong—America's got rotten spelling—we could give it a try. Orly wouldn't hear of it, hurried me in.

The place itself was another disappointment. The showroom was nearly bare, with a few Edwardian bits of furniture, a silver salver or two, a scatter of paintings that had yet to age into conviction, a couple of scientific instruments—a microscope, sextant, a couple of timepieces—of modern design. Fatty Jim Bethune came to greet us, cigar in pollution phase, waistcoat bristling pens.

"Lovejoy, huh? You're going to revitalize the antiques stake, huh?"

"How do." I put out a hand. He ignored it, shouted to a matronly assistant to take five, and wheezed into a captain's chair—fake, lacquered brass studs, railings set into coarse six-ply. We sat on a poor 1940s couch fraying in a desperate attempt at authenticity.

Orly gave me a warning glance. Whatever it was, I was in the California game now. Gina'd said so. Presumably just as much as this gentleman. We were all evidently sharing one stake.

"He doesn't know much about the game, Jim," Orly said.

"Then what the hell? Sheet, this ain't no nursery."

"He's a divvy, a scammer from the old country."

"Jees." Bethune wheezed, coughed, spat phlegm into a huge handkerchief. His hair flopped with every breath, side to side with metronomic regularity. I watched it, fascinated. "What you do, Lovejoy?"

"Do?"

"Jesus H. Christ." He stared. His eyes were rheumy close to, set small into putty features. "You think N'York's a pushover? That it?"

"Well, actually—"

"You listen up, dumbo." He leant forward to prod. "Jennie passes word, okay we got to. But you're shit here, right?"

The pause seemed long to me, but maybe it was infinitesimal. He took my silence as meekness. He was nearly right.

Ash fell onto his waistcoat. He looked shopsoiled. It crossed my mind that maybe Jim Bethune was less than superb at running the antiques side of things for the Aquilinas and their stake in the game. Maybe I was here as a stopgap? Catalyst?

"We raise our part of the stake, Lovejoy. From antiques. You heard antiques?" His flab oscillated with merriment, settled as the wheezes died. "We take a cut of selected prices from the auction houses. We're currently adding a national museum to our contributors—" more splutters of amusement—"they start contributing next week. In time for any little card-playing we might wanta do."

I waited for the jubilation to lessen. "How do you make them chip in?"

His eyes were beads through a smoke veil.

"This dumbo's going to raise our ante, Orly?"

Orly smiled weakly.

Bethune spoke quite kindly, as if he'd realized at last that I was no threat.

"We make a bomb threat against a museum, right? It's glad to pay a little, stop them bad old bombs. Same with auction houses. It's regular money."

"You accept payment how?"

His pleasantry evaporated. "That's no concern of yours, boy, and don't you—"

He stubbed his cigar, lit a fresh one from a humidor younger than himself. In an antiques warehouse? But I was all attention to this mastermind, and clearly listening with nothing less than total admiration.

"Pay? Okay. They see Bethune's gets antiques to the value of the protection money. I sell, and that forms the stake, see? It's simple, easy."

"That's amazing, Mr. Bethune!" I exclaimed. "Don't they go to the police?"

I felt Orly stir, as if he suspected pretense.

"Police, Lovejoy?" Bethune grinned, charred teeth sausaged in two rolls of pink blubber. "We got friends there."

I warned myself not to overdo it. "But suppose this museum doesn't pay up?"

He was amused at my naiveté. "Why, a little fire in their basement. Nothing serious."

"Marvelous, Mr. Bethune," I said, clearly thrilled. "Well, thank you for explaining. Is there anything you want me to do? I'm ready to help."

He smirked at the very thought. "Not yet, Lovejoy. I'll be sure and let you know."

"Orly. Anything else to add?" I asked meekly.

He was puzzled, but a little wary. "No. Jim's covered it all."

I rose, smiled, said thanks. "Then I'd better report in. Can I use your phone, Mr. Bethune?"

There was one on the wall nearby. I rang the number, got the girl with the mechanical voice.

"Lovejoy. Urgent for Mrs. Aquilina, please."

Waiting to be connected, I smiled at Bethune, who was telling Orly about some joker who'd wanted to negotiate a reduction in the protection fee. Fatty was very, very relieved I'd proved such a mug.

"Gina? Lovejoy. I've just finished with Mr. Bethune. Yes, Orly's here." I listened, nodding as she asked if everything was satisfactory. "Yes, definitely. Mr. Bethune's done a perfectly neat job. Pleasing himself. He's a dud. Replace him forthwith. Brains of a rocking horse."

The line was silent a moment. Gina asked, "Can he hear this?"

"Yes. Bethune's right here." I looked back, Bethune's complexion had gone muddy, his eyes currants in plaster. I gave attention to the phone. "Still there, love?"

"That was unwise, Lovejoy. You should have—"

"No orders in antiques, love. Anything else, I'll hear and obey. This cret's ripping you off. He's taking a double cut, first on the levy, then on the antiques' selling price. He's hiving."

"Hiving?"

"Taking a toll on every transaction. Your income's less than half what it should be. Before you ask, no, he's not told me the figures."

"What action do you recommend, Lovejoy?"

"Do I get paid this time?"

She got the joke. "No. You're being well paid—in dollars. Jennie's fixed your account today. You'll be pleasantly surprised."

"However much, it's second best." Into her gentle laugh I said, "Bethune? Save him. Demote to second adviser."

"But Orly has other duties. So who'll be first?"

"Me."

"I might have guessed." She hesitated. "One thing, Lovejoy. After what you said, you've got to raise the income for our stake in the California game. You understand? Whatever Bethune raised, you must double."

My throat was suddenly dry. Maybe Sophie had taken more out of me than I'd realized. "I understand."

"I'll send immediate help, in case." A pretty hesitation, then, "Good luck, Lovejoy."

I hung up. "Right, lads," I told the pair cheerfully. "Let's get down to it. Jim, you're sacked. Okay?"

They'd both risen, appalled. The antique dealer was gazing across at the windows, the low-grade antiques, as his world imploded. Orly was motionless. He was an irritation, this one.

"Gina's sending a team along. Here, Orly. Do you reckon that Anita's place does takeaways? Hop across and bring some grub. I'm starving."

He moved toward the phone. Enemies nark me, especially as I'd done nothing to make him my foe. "No, Orly. Bring it yourself. Plenty of them bread things. And be quick about it—or I'll tell teacher."

Orly was white. He swallowed, exhaled long and steadily. The effort to walk out of the door was superhuman, but he did it. Thoughtfully I watched him go. Funny, that. It raised the question of whether Gina was in league with the private scam Orly was running, or whether he was in it only with Fatty Bethune. But I'd peeped from Mrs. Van Cordlant's kitchen, and seen Bethune and Denzie Brandau paying her a clandestine visit, which raised the question of whether . . . My head ached.

"Jim," I said quietly to the fat man. "A quick word."

A limo slid to a stop outside, illegal parking. Tye Dee and three Suits alighted, came in. I waved. "Wotcher, Tye. Can you have a quick shufti round, see the doors are locked, and bring the staff? That means everybody, okay?" I was beginning to like this okay at the end of everything. It was sort of inviting, friendly. Tye scattered his people. A neat dapper bloke entered carrying a briefcase. I sighed. Accountants were arriving.

"The office, please. Impound all files, get them in some sort of order, okay?"

"Right." He beckoned a clone and a secretary to follow.

"Right, Jim," I said quietly. "Tell all. Including the private thing you've got going with You-Know-Who, okay?" I nodded to the street, terse and cryptic to show I wasn't bluffing even if I was. "Orly'll be back in a minute. It's as long as you've got."

I was in a hurry to find Magda.

15

THE Benidormo had slipped into almost total decay. The desk man had crumpled into dust the instant his telly cooled. The phone was layered in rime. I once saw a sea village flooded on the neap tide. This foyer looked like the aftermath without marine life stirring beneath the tatty carpet. Nobody about. For reassurance I went back to peer into the street, shivered, went upstairs to my room wondering if the world had vanished without me. Eerily, a western saga was shooting off to no Zole. For once I was glad to hear a rhythmic pounding from Magda's room.

Ten minutes, then the bloke left. Magda's abuse was crisper than before, more desperate in a way I found hideous. She followed him along the corridor yelling invective. His growled reply was inaudible. I gave her a few moments' grace, tapped on the door. It flung open.

"Who the sheet . . .? Lovejoy! You're . . ."

"Here," I said. "Hello, Magda."

Her hair was embattled, her face marked. Derelict is as derelict does, where a woman's appearance is concerned. I used to think women were barmy, forever at mirrors with paints. I now admit they're infallibly right about makeup. In fact I'd go so far as to say that cosmetics are essential, the thicker and gaudier the better. You can't have too much, though women of course think the opposite, being wrong again.

She looked ninety, haggard, death on sticks.

"In yours, Lovejoy. Not here."

She doused the telly, did that swish of hair and sat on the edge of the bed. The lazy hotel swine hadn't made it. How many nights had it been since I'd last slept there?

"He beat you up?"

"A couple since." She had a sort of defiance, as if she expected me to whale into her too. Odd, because I'm never really narked with people, not often.

"How are you managing, Magda?"

"Not as good as you, Lovejoy. Fancy suiting, handmade shoes. Your lady's a spender."

"How's Zole?"

"Okay. He brung good two days."

"Stolen stuff?"

Magda lit a cigarette. She was spoiling for a fight. Her clothes were ragbag, shoes on the welts and soiled. When a woman's lipstick gets ragged at the edges, it's all up.

"Lovejoy, you stupid fucka, listen up. That set's here as a signal, see? Zole brings his loot when it's off, stays away when it's on. I'm getting rubbed off the street out there. Girls team up when hooker bookers move in." She was trembling, smoking in drags, pluming the blue aside from a twisted mouth. "You're just too stupid, okay?" She dabbed at her hair, surrendered.

One thing I'm bad at is knowing what to say when a bird weeps. I wish we'd been taught things like this at school, instead of calcium chloride and the Corn Laws.

"When you didn't come back, Lovejoy, I thought they'd . . ."

Done for me? I had money to give her, but not straight off. I'm not as dim as all that.

"I need your help, Magda."

She looked up at me from the bed, disbelieving. "Help? Shag's all I do."

"I may be going somewhere." I paused too long. "Okay? I need somebody I can trust."

"Lovejoy. I got something to tell you—"

I shoved her down when she tried to stand. Give me a battered bone-weary prostitute, I'm as tough as they.

"I know about the phone calls to Tye, how much you were paid."

She was baffled. "Whyn't you beat me?"

"I have people for that now, love. They're better at it." Not much of a joke, but she calmed with a nonsmile. I didn't quite know how far to risk the little I knew. There's that Arabian saying, isn't there: Doubt your friend, sleep with your enemy.

"If I've guessed right, I'll be traveling out of New York, several places, in a hurry."

131

"Somebody after you?"

"No. But I'll need somebody around." The surprised understanding in her eyes made me speed through a denial. "Not a bird wanted on voyage. I need somebody close by to do the occasional job, keep contact, be at certain places."

"You want me? What about—"

"Take Zole. I'll pay you, and fares."

She was casting about the space just as Fat Jim Bethune had.

"Outa N'York? I never been . . ."

"You'll need clothes, Magda." I'm always wary about telling women things about their gear. "Though your frock's pretty, er, smart, love, it might, er . . ."

"I'm in fuckin' *rags*, Lovejoy." She ran a finger across her cheek against wetness. "Is this up real, Lovejoy?"

I pulled out a small wad. Bethune's money, until I'd given harsh orders to the accountant.

"Dress Zole reasonable, nothing way out. And don't take any lip from him. He's coming. I'll need him for a couple of specific theft jobs. Okay?"

She looked. "How d'you know I won't blow the money?"

"I trust you. Don't show yourselves in your new stuff, or somebody'll guess. Be here every even hour from midday tomorrow, twelve o'clock, two o'clock. Understand? Ready to go."

"Lovejoy, I'm scared." She still hadn't put the money away, but her pocket was torn and she'd left her handbag in her room. "I'm not . . . so good at reliable."

She was scared? I nearly did clout her one when she said that. I drew slow breath. "Magda. This is your frigging country, not mine. You've got to look after me, okay? You just remember I'm the one who's got to be looked after, not selfish cows like you."

She appraised me, nodding slowly. Age was slowly fading into youth. A glim of a smile nearly showed.

"You're right about that, Lovejoy. Deedy."

Different woman, same opinion. "First job's to collect something from the airport." I passed her a piece of paper with a flight number. In the safety of Zole's absence I'd dared a phone call to Easy Boyson, who'd been going mad.

"It's a stiff envelope. You'll have to pay out of that money. Bring it with you."

We said a number of okays, some doubtful. She headed for a mirror. I left then.

THE cocktail party I was made to attend could have been better placed. I mean, New York's galleries and museums are famous. Think how superb a splash in some prestigious museum would be, with antiques and paintings all around so you needn't see people swallowing oysters and stabbing each other. Instead, you could respond to the melodious chimes of a Wedgwood jasper, a Blake drawing, see the brilliant leaves tumble on a Sisley canvas.

But it was a posh hotel. We swigged, noshed the groaning buffet, and everybody talked. The people were all there from the boat, including Moira, Commissioner Kilmer, Denzie and Sophie—the former paying little attention to Moira except when their looks accidentally lingered. Good old Melodie Van Cordlant was there, meaningful with glances and arm squeezes. Jennie was with everyone, curt except with Nicko, on whom she fawned. Orly clung to Gina, talking loudly and occupying her every moment. Berto Gordino, lawyer of this parish, came with Kelly Palumba, for whom Epsilon the showbiz magnate competed in shrill tones. Kelly looked a million quid. Long might it last, I thought. Monsignor O'Cody was last to come. Jim Bethune was at the far end of the room, now in his Sunday best, being spoken to by Tye Dee in an undertone. Hey ho, I thought with sympathy.

"Canapes, sir?"

"Ta, Chanel. Home team playing today, eh?"

I was the only one eating. All the rest were swilling at other troughs.

Chanel checked we weren't overheard, said, "Always is the home team, Lovejoy. You gotta believe it."

Mr. Granger called out that all guests were invited through into the conference salon, where drinks would be available. I complained that I'd only just started, but there was a concerted rush for the double doors. I grabbed a load of rolls, cheese, some slabs of egg-looking thing, while

Blanche hurriedly loaded up more for me. No pasties, and biscuits are New York's lack—mind you, they'd only have tons of cinnamon in. I was last into the long room.

Places were marked, as for a wedding reception. Kelly had started giggling, was being shushed by Epsilon and Berto Gordino. I found my name card between those of Orly and Gina.

Nicko appeared, with Jennie, took the position of authority.

"Jim Bethune sends his apologies, friends." He had one small piece of paper before him, served up by Jennie. "Lovejoy's taking his place from now on."

"Is that legit, Nicko?" Denzie Brandau asked easily, smiling round the table. "First I heard of it."

"It is, Denzie." Nicko seemed oblivious to the sudden silence. "Any questions?"

"Where exactly does Lovejoy take over from Jim?" Charlie Sarpi asked. I wondered how he managed his moustache. Sophie prevented herself from giving him the bent eye just in time. Gina was watching her across the phony mahogany.

"Right away, Charlie. Every level."

"Look, Nicko." Denzie did that politician's shift to indicate exasperation. It consists of obliquely arranging his trunk, plonking a hand firmly on the table, arm outstretched, and crossing his legs. "Who *is* this Lovejoy? I mean, where's the beef?"

"Lovejoy'll double the antiques stake, Denzie. There's the beef."

A ripple of interest ran round the table. Monsignor O'Cody peered down at me, specs gleaming.

"How'll he do that, Nicko?" Commissioner Kilmer barked. It was honestly that, a sharp yap, grossly out of keeping with his tall bulk. I don't know what he'd been like as a young bobby, but even aging as he was he put the fear of God in me.

The silence meant me. I was eating my grub, which I'd made into rolls. I can't resist anything in bread. I hurried the mouthful, swallowed.

"Lovejoy?" Nicko said.

"No, thanks."

The silence now meant ???

"What the hell's that mean, Nicko?"

"Stay calm, J.J." Nicko let me swallow, come up for air. "Lovejoy. You must bring in double what Jim Bethune did. Do you know how much that is?"

"Yes, Nicko."

His hands opened expressively. He was so patient, but getting quieter. Any minute those dark lasers he used for eyes might actually swivel onto me and sear the inside of my skull. I didn't want that.

"Are your methods so secret they can't be divulged?"

"Nicko." I shoved my tray away, showing my sincerity. "I'm out of my depth here. Oh, I'll get the gelt."

Nicko's gaze charred nearer, less than a yard from my right shoulder. Even Gina leaned away. "With help?"

"Yes. I'll need two helpers, fulltime." Before anybody could cut in, I started my spiel. "See, I don't know who's on our side, Nicko. I know you are. And Gina. And I think Jennie. But these other ladies and gentlemen I don't even know. I don't know what the stake is to be—everything I cull from antiques? And for what?" I tried to spread my hands like Nicko but it didn't work and I felt a prat, so put them away. "This game, Nicko. Tell me who's got a right to know, and I'll come clean about my methods, every detail."

"The game in Manhattan is finished, Lovejoy." Nicko looked at Jennie, got an imperceptible assent. "On the *Gina*. Remember?"

"I was behind the bar, Nicko."

"He's stupid," Commissioner J.J. Kilmer barked.

Nicko nearly smiled, leaned forward. "Let's hope you're not this stupid about old furniture, Lovejoy. The game. We're the players, Lovejoy. At first, we play against each other here in Manhattan. The stakes are based on personal . . . wealth." Now he did smile. I wished he hadn't. "It's up to each player to raise his or her stake. Nobody is allowed to default. The stakes can come from anywhere."

"Tell him," Jennie put in. It sounded a question but wasn't.

"If a player were to bring personal cash, Lovejoy, we'd be limited to however much he or she could withdraw from

135

a bank account, right? So we accept promissory notes. Then the sum waged can be relatively huge."

Jennie took over. "Very damaging, Lovejoy, in a city where any major withdrawal is noticed by Manhattan's wallet watchers." She held the pause, waited for my nod.

"And you can bet next year's takings?"

Jennie smiled. "You got it, Lovejoy. If the bet's mega dollar, and based on certain illegal practices—"

"Not that word, please," from Berto Gordino in anguish. "From selected activities, Lovejoy."

Once a lawyer, I thought.

"—Why, it's easy to handle. Suppose a police commissioner were to bet fifty percent of the police hack and lost, okay? He'd simply raise his hack. That's the stake."

I looked round the table. Bullion prices would be lifted fractionally to provide the losing margin if Melodie lost. Hadn't she said something about Monsignor O'Cody fiddling the diocesan funds? Politics was Denzie Brandau's wager—presumably he peddled influence in the time-honored way, for a price. Charlie Sarpi was a drugs man, Kelly Palumba the real estate queen, Epsilon the showbiz hacker . . .

"If the game's over, what're we all here for?"

"Because you lost, Lovejoy."

"I what?"

Nicko smiled. His eyes were miles off now, thank God. "Everybody here pays their losses into the kitty. That kitty's the stake when we get to L.A. For the California game."

"Thus getting a share in the New York wager." Jennie was dying to spiel out a load of figures. I could tell.

"Which I shall bet for us all in—"

"—In the California game," I said. "All New York? One bet?"

"He makes it sound unfair," J.J. said, inventing the wheel with his first-ever try at irony. People chuckled.

Melodie intervened, dear thing. "You see, Lovejoy, we gamble to see who wins here. In New York, see? In Florida, why, they're doing the same thing. Then there's four bets come from the Midwest, six from California, one from Washington . . ."

"The game itself's held yearly, Lovejoy. Each bet's the

product of sectored interests." Nicko shrugged. "It's up to each to get the best possible finance behind them. The bigger the stake, the bigger the win."

"What's the game? Cards? Roulette?"

Nicko chuckled, hailstones on tin. "The entire loot of the nation, Lovejoy."

"For twelve months," Jennie amended. "Shared among us, in proportion as staked. The game on the *Gina* was to decide who plays in L.A. And the total stake."

I drew breath to ask my one remaining question, but Orly was already sniggering. "Except you, Lovejoy," he said. "You're the one here with no share. Yet."

"Methods, Lovejoy?" Nicko could afford to look all cool. He'd won megamillions. Except now he had to gamble it for higher stakes still.

"I said double Bethune's stake," I reminded him calmly. "I meant quadruple."

He tilted his head Jennie's way as if interrogatingly. "It's in ten days, Lovejoy. Nobody could possibly hack so many millions from antiques in so few days."

"Anybody lend me an aeroplane, please?" I asked, rising. "And I'll need a bank account—paying-in purposes only."

"A moment, Lovejoy," Gina said, but I twisted my hand free.

"I can hear them clearing away the grub out there. I'm starving." I gave a bright smile down the lines of faces. "Can I get anybody anything?"

I just caught Blanche and Chanel wheeling the last trayfuls out, thoughtless cows. They only laughed when I ballocked them about it. You'd think women'd learn, wouldn't you? It's a wonder that I'm so patient. I warned them that one day I'd lose my temper altogether, but they only laughed all the more. It's no good trying to tell women off. They're like infants, only laugh and think you're daft.

Somebody inside had come to a decision by the time I returned with my tray. Nicko promised a private jet, two goons, a secretary, and license to travel.

Nobody mentioned chains, but they'd be there, they'd be there.

16

JENNIE was efficiency itself, I'll give her that.

Thirty lasses came, mostly skilled, beautiful, drivingly ambitious. I picked a small timid bird called Prudence, in specs, clumsy, dressed plain. No wonder the U.S. excels. I didn't know a hundred words per minute was humanly possible. They all knew computers and could start instantly. I was worn out, told Prudence to start in twenty minutes.

"You'll never regret this, Lovejoy," she told me with solemnity. "This is my greatest opportunity, traveling secretary. I've always been a halfway girl, y'know? Sort of nearly getting there—"

"Prudence," I said. "Rule one: not much talk."

"You got it, Lovejoy."

We were alone in the foyer of the Pennsylvania. "There's another thing, Prudence. I'll need certain, er, commercial tasks done in great secrecy. They'll fall to you."

She was over the moon. "Economic espionage!" she whispered. "Lovejoy, rely on Prudence!"

I was to remember that, later.

MY team assembled at Pennsylvania Station. Tye was along, of course, monolithically, saying nothing. I'd told him not to come armed, and he'd agreed. I didn't believe him. He needed a secret howitzer. I had a first real look at Prudence in action: today with obvious contact lenses a foot deep and extraordinary flying elbows, as if protecting her files. I'd slimmed my team down to just us, was now having misgivings about my wisdom.

"Prudence," I said wearily as she scattered her files all over the coffee shop for the umpteenth time.

"Sorry, Lovejoy." She retrieved them.

Jim Bethune arrived, gave Tye the bent eye.

"I don't believe this," he said. "Us? Up the stake in the 'cking *game?*"

Travelers were pouring past. Touts were touting. We were scrunged up at a small table, at least those of us not dropping folders. The coffee was dire, first bad quaff in this wonderful land.

"Which museum were you milking, Jim?" If he had any thoughts of undermining my position, now was the time to disillusion him.

"Lovejoy," he said, confidence swelling, "this is between you and me, right? I don't discuss business in shitholes."

"Tye," I said evenly, "get rid of him."

Tye rose, hauled him upright.

"Wait a minute, Lovejoy. I don't mean—"

I gave him my saddest. "Jim. You've blown your one chance. Good-bye, and good luck."

He clawed desperately to stay by the table as Tye started leaning toward the exit. A boy with a white forage cap by the popcorn stand edged nervously into the walkway.

"You can't do this, Lovejoy! Metropolitan Museum of Art. Bickmore's the boss . . ."

Tye walked him out, returned. Bethune stood outside staring in, kid at a toffee shop window perishing of neglect.

"Right, team. Prudence, you come with me. Tye, you also, but act like a chauffeur or a private assistant, okay? Jim's to be brought in once I've got going."

"We need him?" Tye asked, surprised.

"Essential. Let's go."

On the way to the street I told Prudence to phone Bickmore and get an immediate appointment; subject: security.

THE Metropolitan Museum of Art claims to be the largest in the western hemisphere. It's right, but I'm not too sure about the arts bit. Don't misunderstand me. It's got tons of genuine art. It's also got tons of stuff that is hard to classify. I can't come to grips with a massive cube with a grandiose title. I allow that it's art, but not my sort. I need the big stone block to tell me something about the bloke whose name's on the caption, and it doesn't. That off my chest, I admit that any place with 3.3 million works of art truly is a wonder.

Bethune waited nervously by the information desk while Prudence scurried on ahead, Tye patiently scooping up her dropped papers. I spoke harshly with Jim. It was difficult moving, because of the Madonna and Child. The terra-cotta was set in a nook by the stairs at the end of the enormous hall. Blue and white glaze is often a giveaway, as here. It bonged like a cathedral bell into me. I believed the Andrea Della Robbia label—it was his uncle Luca who enameled glazes this color onto terra-cotta. I'd seen pictures of it, loved it for years. Who hasn't? But to see it in the flesh . . .

"Lovejoy? Mr. Bickmore's waiting."

Prudence scampered alongside, shoes clacking. "Are you all right, Lovejoy? You look—"

"Never heard of hay fever?" I told the silly cow, then felt sorry when she fumbled in her handbag for medicaments.

The office was grand. Bickmore was a tall, arid man of the old school. He had a knack of being willowy, so he could peer over his bifocals. I'm used to the worm's eye view. And I've been put down by every trick in the book. I smiled, shook his hand, sat as Prudence's files cascaded around.

"Prudence's been with me a long time, Mr. Bickmore," I said. "The only polymath in my corporation."

"You're not American." He was broad smiles. "What museum is your favorite back home?"

We chatted a while about the British Museum, a few others, just enough to prove I was on intimate terms with their layout. I supplied him with a card citing me at Nicko's office address, and was in no doubt he'd checked before letting us in.

"It's a matter of security, Mr. Bickmore," I said pleasantly. "Yours, not mine."

His split-level specs sloped disapproval. "You're not selling, Lovejoy?"

"I'm not. You are. We bought tickets," I added, smiling to show no hard feelings.

"Think of it as a suggested donation, Lovejoy."

"Always makes fees seem easier, Mr. Bickmore."

"Security," Bickmore said coldly. "If it's a matter of—"

"Of the protection money you were going to pay." I let the silence solidify. I'd warned Prudence not to be shocked. She was scribbling it all down, pen flying.

Bickmore gave orders to an intercom, rose and closed an intervening door.

"Protection money?"

"Prudence? Get Mr. Dee in, please. And Mr. Bethune." Bickmore watched Tye and the dealer enter.

"Mr. Bethune? Tell Mr. Bickmore, please."

Fatty spoke, face wooden. "It came to my notice that the Met was being oppressed by protection racketeers. I've paid for you, and will continue to do so."

"For the foreseeable future," I finished for him irritably. Give me strength. The silly sod had only two lines to learn, and he'd ballsed them up.

"Why would you do that, Mr. Bethune?"

"Lovejoy persuaded me by his reputation, Mr. Bickmore."

"Thank you, Bethune," I said. The pillock's delivery had been putrid. Tye left with him.

"Well, I'm very, very grateful, Lovejoy!" Bickmore said slowly. He waited, Prudence's pen zoomed, I waited.

He was a shrewd old administrator. He cleared his throat. "This makes a considerable difference to our finances this coming year, Lovejoy. I shall make out a report to the trustees. The board of regulators will be eager to express . . ."

His speech dried. I was shaking my head. "I, er, influenced Bethune to show my good intentions, Mr. Bickmore. I'm eager to see your museum survive. I can't have this lovely—" I coughed; there's a limit to falsehood—"this hotchpotch of a building damaged. Millions of customers come every year. Some might get injured."

He looked from me to Prudence. "But it is protection? You're after money?"

"No, Mr. Bickmore. I'm after painless money."

There was a plan of the building, floor by floor, occupying one entire wall. I crossed to it, trying to seem sure of myself. I guessed Prudence was coming along from the crash of tumbling clipboards.

"You've got the Rokeman Primitive Museum incorporated here, Mr. Bickmore?" I nodded. "All those Benin heads, Nigerian sculptures, tribal items. Fantastic, eh?"

"Lovejoy. If you're making some sort of threat . . ."

I turned away, knocking into Prudence, who was just then rising from having picked up her things. What the hell had she brought all that stuff *for*, for God's sake?

"There are threats and threats, Mr. Bickmore." He was a secret smoker. I recognized his wandering hand, edging under stress toward his waistcoat pocket's rectangular bulge. "Think of a threat that brings money in."

His hand halted. Maybe lessening tension.

"A profitable, ah, threat?"

"Plus a percentage of it to someone else."

He thought for quite a time. I looked at the plans, flicking idly through catalogs and yearbooks.

"Lovejoy," he said finally, fingers tipping together. "This scheme, to increase our finances. Is it the sort of scheme that could be announced to the media?"

"Media's a must, Mr. Bickmore," I advised gravely, and his face wrinkled into a guarded smile.

"Can you explain the details, please?" he asked. "Coffee?"

THERE are skeletons in every cupboard. The Met Museum has them a-plenty.

Just like the British Museum—which has bought fakes, duds, phonies, wasting millions in its time—most museums have spent fortunes on fraud. I'm not condemning them, because crime's as close to my heart as it is to museum curators'. The Met is a prime "lifter," as the trade says—that is, a big official repository of antiques, any sort, which it will buy from illicit sources.

I reminded Bickmore of this in detail, until he suggested we send Prudence out for a rest. I declined.

"And what *is* an illicit source, Mr. Bickmore?" I continued earnestly. "The Elgin Marbles were purchased in good faith, proper legitimate bills of sale and everything."

"True, true!" He was delighted to find common ground in international law.

"So your Veracruz figures—especially that fifteenth-century Standard Bearer, and the one they call The Smiler—really *should* be here." Pause. "*I* think, Mr. Bickmore. And those Ecuador and Peru vessels too—incidentally, are they really Chavin period? Though I'll bet your Peru gold mask's really a Chimu, right?"

"What are you saying, Lovejoy?" His voice had gone thick. Mine does that.

I leaned forward confidentially. "Supposing one of those nations' ambassadors started a row at the United Nations . . ."

He bristled. "Lovejoy. I will not countenance any return of any of our legitimate—"

"Or illegitimate? Like that Maya series of tomb artifacts you bought three years ago?" I wasn't disclosing confidences. Every day brings fresh tales of important scams like the grave-robbers of Italy, the poor old Mayas, the threadbare Aztecs. Civilization spreads at exactly the pace of tomb-raiders.

"I deny every insinuation, Lovejoy!"

"Sit down, mate. Think a minute." He subsided slowly. I could hear his gray cells starting up with a whirr. "A series of articles in some Latin American newspaper, raising all hell about the national treasures you've got here. Their national treasures. Or in an Accra daily, with African politicians complaining of neocolonial exploitation. Get the idea?"

"No." He spoke only for Prudence's pen.

"Let me explain. World headlines yell it's those bad old Yanks again, nicking antiques. The world loves shouting this slogan."

"So?"

"So you issue a denial—the same one you used over the Tairona Columbia items, the Kwoma New Guinea ethnics. Isn't it a bit odd incidentally to have those near the North American exhibits?" He didn't answer. I smiled now, home and dry. "You raise the admission fee—okay, recommended donation—to that gallery. Cloak it in mystique. You have a special guard, get local volunteers on oh-so-terribly vital vigilante duties, maybe even restrict the numbers of visitors." I spoke over his shocked gasp. "You sell a certificate that they've seen it on the Great Dispute Day. Do I have to spell it all out?"

He removed his glasses, possibly for the first time since birth. "Nothing creates interest like an argument."

"Wrong—like a *patriotic* argument." I watched his smile begin, slowly extend, eliminating wrinkles. "You're the patriot who takes on the might of . . . well, pick a country."

"There's one thing, Lovejoy. No ambassador has criticized us to the United Nations, not for three years."

"Not for two years, six months, and seventeen days, Mr. Bickmore." I smiled and stood, extending a hand. "I honestly do think another's about due any day now."

He came with me to the door. "We haven't cleared things up, Lovejoy."

"We have," I said. "Six times what Bethune canceled."

He spluttered, reeled. "Six times?"

"It's simple. You up your special ticket. Respond to the news splash, you'll not know what to do with the money."

His only grief was the thought of a fraction of the income slipping through his sticky administrator's fingers. "But that's an impossible fee, Lovejoy!"

"Not a fee, Mr. Bickmore. Think of it as a suggested donation. Ready, Prudence?"

BY THE end of the day I was worn out. We'd done over half a dozen museums, all official places with superb antiques, paintings, furniture, stuff I'd have given my life to halt at and adore. But that was the point: My life was the stake.

It's called a "trilling" in the trade. That is, you introduce a kind of pressure from a third person—nation, ambassador, whatever you can think up—and shove it onto a second person. You yourself are the third person that makes up the prile. The problem is, you're inextricably linked, bonded for life in a trilling. It's not just a once-off, some deal you set up and close tomorrow and it's goodnight dworlink at the door. Oh, no. A trilling's everything but a marriage, though there's even less love, would you believe. The one important factor different from all other con tricks is that big trillings need big organization. And even little ones sometimes do. Our U.K. trillings occur in London, Newcastle, and Brighton. I've only been in two in my time, and was lucky to get out of both.

We did trillings on the Brooklyn Museum, the American Numismatic Society Museum, two modern art galleries where I drove a harsh bargain because I was feeling bolshie and Prudence and I'd had a row because by then she'd got the bit between her teeth and was geeing me along like a bloody tired nag. Plus the Museum of Broadcasting Arts off Fifth Avenue at East Fifty-third Street, where I drove one harder still on account of I blame them for time-wasting. Oh, and the natural history place. That was a particular difficulty I'll tell you about, in case you ever do a trilling.

You vary the trilling, of course. The threat of an international lawsuit wouldn't work with a natural history place, at least not much. But I had little compunction, what with the American Museum of Natural History standing on Columbus Avenue, Central Park West, and being the size of London. It chills my spine. I mean, stuffed animals are all very well, but the poor things should have been left alone, and I'm not big on dinosaurs even if 2.8 million New Yorkers see them every single year.

It's a question of tactics. I had to raise the great Disease Scare Tactic on this occasion, telling the gentle Mrs. Beekman after an hour's jockeying that she would soon hear a clamor that would close her museum, possibly for good, if she didn't accede to my humble request for a small fraction of the ticket takings. She was a harsh bargainer. I was practically wrung out by repeating my gilded threats under her vociferous cross-examination.

I told her, "Our London churches are excavating their crypts all over the city. They have devoted doctors to check there's no diseases itching to pop out and grapple with the populace. Understand?"

"London had its problems in the seventeenth century," she said primly. "So long ago, wasn't it?"

Okay, so she knew that diseases fade away. "The public doesn't know that, lady. And what with AIDS, series of unknown viruses yet to be announced . . ."

My clincher was promising to have specimen newspapers delivered to her next morning, carrying banner headlines announcing Contagious Disease Risks at Museum of Natural History, adding regretfully that it might be difficult to prevent them falling into the wrong hands. I also promised that she'd be saved the bother of legal claims filed against her museum. She tried the police threat. I asked her to phone Commissioner J.J. Kilmer and talk the matter over with him.

She surrendered eventually, guaranteeing a payment of fifty cents on the dollar. I guaranteed a bonus: Her request for staff increases the following year would be given favorable mention in high places. I wouldn't pass that on to Denzie Brandau, of course, because I was lying. She'd really put me through it. I'd tell Jennie to pay a fraction of each Natural History installment into a numbered bank account in, say, Philadelphia. In Mrs. Beekman's name, of course. Safety does no harm.

Trilling ploys are not necessarily animose. You can have quite friendly gambits. Like the Bickmore one. I mean, that would bring money pouring in over the transom. We'd get a share, but so what? A plus is a plus is a plus. The numismatists—loony obsessionals the world over—were a pleasure to deal with, because I could faithfully promise a major find of certain hammered silver coins, right here in New York State! The bloke was really delighted, because the carrot (there's always got to be a carrot in a trilling) was that the hoard would be mainly the sort his main foe collected.

"Fall in value of your pal's collection?" I guessed.

"He might be inclined to sell," he replied evenly.

"Good heavens," I said just as evenly. "Whereupon you'd buy them, the day before the coins were revealed as counterfeit?"

He fell about at that, me laughing with him.

"I'll see the publicity's done right," I promised. "Fancy some early English hammered silver coins, soon to be discovered at Roanoke? Only, I've got some maniacs back home who'd be really keen to have a regular thing going . . ."

See what I mean? Some antiques people are a pleasure to do business with.

THAT evening I totted up the sums fleecing in soon, and found I'd bettered Jim's by a clear six-fold. It took me two hours on the phone with Prudence close by reading her notes in the hotel at Pennsylvania Station where Jennie had booked us. I fixed all the frayed edges, the outstanding threats and promises, settled the transfers, formed up a method of checking on the payments with Gina's accountants, and had the contributors listed at Jennie's.

Prudence was paid. She was flushed, exulting.

"You know, Lovejoy," she said, transported. "I'm on a high! I'm flying! The girls back at the agency would never believe me."

"Will never, Prudence," I warned. "Confidentiality. Besides—"

"Yes?" she breathed.

I thought, what the hell. I might never get out of this. "Would you care to stay for supper, Prudence?"

"Supper? Oh, yes!"

It's the one way to guarantee silence. As guarantees go.

17

FOUR o'clock in the morning I sent Prudence home—pedantically reporting the fact on the phone to a somnolent Tye, to show scrupulous observance of the syndicate's rules. He was narked, but it gave me the chance to give Prudence instructions about collecting an envelope from a certain international airline. I gave her the flight number.

"I'm depending on you, darling," I told her wide eyes. "It's life or death. Bring it when I send for you."

"Oh, Lovejoy! Nobody's ever depended on me!"

I tried to look disturbed, exalted. I was knackered. "I love you, darling, okay?" But that didn't sound quite right. There's more to okays than meets the ear.

That was two incoming envelopes, Prudence and Magda. I rang the syndicate number.

"Morning, Gina. Lovejoy. I'm leaving New York this morning on the jet. What guards do I have?"

She made the plumping noises of a woman rudely wakened, tried to unthicken her voice into day.

"Tye'll decide. Where to?"

"I'll be hacking the New York auction houses in very few days from now. Meantime, I'm flying to six different states."

"You've already raised the necessary sum, Lovejoy?"

"You might need an edge, love." I left space for her to explain why now suddenly we needed less money, but she said nothing. Well, suffering women have a right to privacy. "My list's at reception."

"No," she said quickly. "Courier it to me. Now."

Christ, I thought. She's in greater difficulties than I'd guessed. I streaked to my room, wrote out a list of addresses culled from the public library, and gave it to the motorcycle maniac. Ten minutes flat.

A word about hotel night staff. They love things to do. I gave them five minutes to settle down, then remembered something very vital, and made them get a second courier. I sent him to the Benidormo with a note to Magda, to hurtle back with her signature as proof. I tipped them, said both couriers should go on the one bill, please, for simplicity's sake. That way, I'd be the only person who knew about Magda and Zole tagging along. Then I roused Tye and told him we were moving.

By nine o'clock we were in the air, heading south in slanting sunshine over the biggest, loveliest land God ever lowered to earth.

THE entourage included Tye and two bulky goons called Al and Shelt who sat with knees apart and literally ate nonstop, peanuts, tiny savories, crisps, popcorn. I'm making them sound friendly, but I'd never seen such menace in all my life. And a brisk stewardess, Ellie, all cold eyes and no repartee. The pilot Joker, his pal Smith, and that was us.

Is America superb, or isn't it? Its hotels can get couriers, any hour. A *pilot*, would you believe, accepts that business considerations are enough! It all seems so normal that you start wondering why the whole world can't be just the same. On the Continent you get the exhausted glance at the watch, vague assurance that maybe sometime ... In England the pilot—assuming you could speak to such a lordly technocrat—would ask what's so special about your business that it can't be changed to suit his convenience.

The coffee was superb, drinks were there, and I could have had a film shown if I'd wanted. A suitcase of clothing was provided, I learned.

So what was wrong?

I concentrated. I'd sent out for two books and nine magazines before breakfast. *And got them!* I wasn't sure how my plan would stand up to stress, but I was beginning to have an idea whose side I was on.

"Tye?" I said some time later. "Can I get a message sent to the ground?"

"Anywhere, ten seconds."

"Time the U.S. upped its performance," I said. "Joke, joke."

The lassie swished up, poised for duty. I sighed. There's

only a limited amount of efficiency a bloke can take. I put a brave face on it, and asked her to get a printout of Manhattan's auction dates, and anything she could muster on George F. Mortdex.

"And send word that we're arriving for prospective interview with him or his deputy, from London, please."

"What name are you going under, Lovejoy?" Tye asked.

"Mine," I said. "But we may not become friends."

He said nothing, but passed his goons a slow glance. They nodded. I swallowed. Maybe I'm unused to allies.

"Is THIS a ranch, Mr. Verbane?"

He beamed, walking ahead in his handmade tweeds, crocodile shoes. We followed his perfume trail.

"We use domicile hereabouts, Lovejoy. Virginia thinks the word ranch infra dig, y'know?"

He was effete, even bubbly.

The estate—all right, domicile—was not vast, certainly not much bigger than Rutlandshire. Noble trees, vast undulating fields with white fences and pale roads curling into the distance. It was beautiful countryside, which always gets me down. The house was the size of a hamlet. Civilization lurked within.

Swimming pool, tables on lawns, awning against the sunshine thank God, lovely white wood and orange tiles, ornate plasterwork in the porches. George F. Mortdex was worth a dollar or two.

Mr. Verbane offered me and Tye seats on a verandah where servants were waiting to fuss. He accepted a tartan shawl round his knees. I avoided Tye's sardonic look, smiled and said I'd rough it without a blanket.

"We don't often get unexpected visitors," Verbane said. "We're so remote from civilization."

A couple of gorgeous figures splashed in a pool nearby. Gardeners were trimming beyond. Grooms led horses along the river that incised the spreading lawn.

"I had hoped to see Mr. Mortdex himself."

Verbane sighed, all apology. "That's out of the question. He's so old now, always works alone. I have to manage all his personal affairs." He smiled, waved to the girls. "Though it's an absolute *slog*. Racing's such a terrible obligation. You've no idea."

"Responsibility's a killer," I agreed.

"That's so right!" he cried, his self-pity grabbing any passing sympathy. "I'm sometimes *drained*. How marvelous that you understand!"

"Like antique prices."

He smiled roguishly. "I knew it! You're an antique dealer!"

I smiled back. "Antique dealers give antiques a bad name. Like boozers give booze."

He passed glittering compliments to the waitresses over the drinks. He'd insisted on madeleines. I had a few, though cakes that little go nowhere and it was over an hour since we'd left the plane.

"I absolutely *adore* negotiating, Lovejoy!" He yoo-hooed to a sports car arriving at the stables. A lady in a yellow hat waved. I'd never seen such friendliness. I felt in a procession. "What'll we negotiate *about*?"

"Mr. Mortdex's collections," I said. "Their falling valuation—"

He sat up, focusing his attention.

"Falling? You're misinformed, Lovejoy. There isn't a collection that has withstood fluctuations better than Mr. Mortdex's. I select and buy, on an absolutely personal basis."

The tea was rotten cinnamon stuff. "I mean Wednesday."

He was a moment checking his mind. I knew he was desperate to dash indoors screaming for the computer, but he was perfect so couldn't be found wanting. Finally he swallowed pride, that costly commodity. "What happens next Wednesday?"

"Your statue gets impounded."

"Statue?" He tried indolence, then casual when that didn't work either. I'm all for facades, which are valuable things, but only when they're some use.

"Aphrodite. Fifth century B.C., that you bought in a secret deal three years ago. Wasn't it twenty million dollars? That English art dealer who lives not far from Bury Street in St. James's? Everybody was so pleased—except the Sicilians."

A lovely bird did her splash, rose laughing from the pool in nice symbolism, yoo-hooed, looked hard at us when Verbane ignored her.

"You're thinking of the J. Paul Getty Museum in Malibu, Lovejoy. They're the ones who bought Aphrodite."

"I heard," I said. I waved to the girl for him. She returned the salutation doubtfully. "Tye? Could you go down to the motor car, please? I think I've left that dictaphone thing."

"You be okay, Lovejoy?"

"I'll shout if I'm in danger."

We were alone. During the intermission Verbane summoned bourbon entombed in ice. He quaffed long, had another. I really envy these folk who can drink early in the day without getting a headache.

"I haven't any strong feelings, Mr. Verbane," I said honestly as I could. "Hoving's opinions about the Getty purchase aren't my concern. Though I wouldn't like to discount anything Hoving said, especially after he bought the St. Edmundsbury Cross."

"Are you claiming—?"

"Nothing. These rumors about a second Aphrodite being taken from Sicily and sold through London are the sort of rumors that shouldn't be resuscitated." I saw his brow clear a little. "Don't you agree?"

"Of course I do." He coughed, took a small white pill thing while I waited with the silent respect all medicines deserve.

"I deny having any Aphrodite, Lovejoy."

"Course. I'll support you, if anyone asks my opinion."

This scandal isn't quite a scandal, not as major art and antiques frauds/purchases/scams/sales go these days. It was just before the nineties that the Aphrodite row erupted. She's lovely, an ancient Greek marble and limestone masterpiece spirited—not too strong a word—into the harsh public glare that money provides for any valuable art form. The Getty people made honest inquiries of the Italian government, and bought. Then nasty old rumors began whispering to vigilant Italian police that Aphrodite was stolen. Aphrodite (her name actually means "lovely arse," incidentally, though the Romans called her Venus) is worth fighting for.

The battle continues, though the value's soared in the meantime.

The rumors I'd heard had mentioned a second Aphrodite from the same source. Possibly a fake, my contact had said on the phone two days back. Well, Verbane's delusions were no business of mine. His support was. The antique trade's maxim is: Sell support, never give.

"At a price, Lovejoy?"

"No. At a swap, Mr. Verbane."

"I don't trade that way. Mr. Mortdex hates it."

I could see Tye slowly heading back. I'd arranged a series of signals should I want him to take more time. I tried to flatten my hair reflexively. He instantly paused to watch the horses, now mounted and cantering. "You buy at auctions, Mr. Verbane."

"I heard about you, Lovejoy." No pansy mannerisms now. He was lighting a cigarette, cold as a frog. "Doing the rounds, protection racket in museums?"

"You've been misinformed. I made a sale, in antiques. If your informant told you differently, she's lying. Which should set you wondering why, eh?"

He'd stared when I implied his informant was a woman. It wasn't as wild a guess as all that. The second Aphrodite was supposed to have been "bought" by an American natural history team in search of lepidoptera near Palermo. Natural history, as in Mrs. Beekman. I calmed him. "Mrs. Beekman didn't tell me anything. I'm a lucky guesser."

"What do you offer, Lovejoy?"

"One percent of your last valuation, paid into an account I shall name. Thereafter, one percent of all your purchases or sales, same destination."

"And you'll do what in exchange?"

"I'll tell you of three high-buy fakes, international market."

He considered that. "How do you know this?"

"That's for sale. And their location. And who paid what."

"As *facts*?"

We settled finally. I declined his offer of a meal, though it hurt. By then he'd provided copies of the Mortdex Collection valuation. I promised him I'd have it checked by auditors who'd visit within the day, whereupon the naughty Mr. Verbane produced a different sheaf of printouts. Managers of private collections are the same the world over.

He stayed me as I made to leave, reminding me of the promise.

"Oh, yes. Antiques." I'd already worked out what he deserved. "The Khmer art sculptures, Southeast Asia. Remember the November sales?"

"Yes." He was a-quiver, almost as if he'd bought a sandstone Buddha. "I remember."

I bet you do, you poor sod, I thought. "Several were fake, Mr. Verbane. Can you believe the perfidy of such a famous auction house? Though I must admit that if I'd half a chance to loot that temple in Kampuchea, I'd have been tempted."

He licked his lips. A girl called an invitation to come and join them. He quietened her with a snarl.

"That sandstone thing's recent, made in Thailand. Mr. Sunkinueng who was Phnom Penh Museum curator—"

"But the reputation of Sotheby . . ." He was giddy. I'd have felt almost sorry for him, except I didn't.

"Reputations are made for breaking. That four-armed god sitting on a lion, from Angkor Wat, 1200 A.D. Bought by a famous American collector." I looked about at the lovely countryside. "Who lived hereabouts."

"Fake?" he whispered. His lips were blue.

"Modern fake," I said cheerfully.

"You said you'd tell me something I could . . ."

"Make on? Very well." I thought a bit, as if I hadn't already made up my mind. "You're rivals to the Getty Museum in California, right? Well, their male Kouros statue from Greece is said to be two thousand years old—by kind friends with a vested interest."

He brightened, as they all do at the grief of rivals. "But its attribution is doubtful?"

"Don't ask me. Ask Giuseppe Cellino—he'll tell you exactly how it was peddled round every antiques museum and gallery in the known world by a Swiss dealer for three years. He has all the addresses, times, dates. Don't say I sent you."

Smiles and grief were still competing on his face when we drove away.

"Lovejoy?" Tye said as our limo paused at the entrance of the imposing estate. "How much of all that was true?"

"All of it, Tye," I said sadly. "All."

He was driving, taking us carefully out into the two-laner. "Then how come these big experts don't know from fakes? That Sotheby Gallery place is supposed to be—"

"Tye," I said, watching the great house recede into the distance. "There's enough of us already in. Don't *you* start, okay?"

"Capeesh, boss."

At the airport while Tye and his goons saw to the plane, bags, paid off the saloon car, I phoned news of the hack to Gina. Then phoned Prudence to get moving. I never carry a watch, but checked the time and reckoned Magda and Zole should be about halfway to my next destination. It'd be risky for her, but that's what women are for.

18

WE WERE airborne in an hour. Joker and his ambling mate Smith cleared us for landing in Chicago by dusk. I felt I'd been traveling for years. Tye's two goons were still uncommunicative, the air hostess Ellie of amphibian responsiveness.

Tye still hadn't mentioned why one of our tame vigilantes hadn't traveled with us to Mr. Mortdex's ranch. Or why we'd been followed there and back by a separate saloon motor that kept vanishing and reappearing. It even changed its color once. I felt less friendly toward Tye now, because I was doing the business as well as anyone could, right?

"Tye," I said over a meal of surreal splendor—Ellie ignored compliments—"I have a secrecy problem."

He didn't quite stiffen, but he was expecting Lovejoy Deception Hour. "What things?" he asked. All his food came fried. I'd never met a bloke like him for demanding fried grub.

"It's between ourselves, okay?" I cleared my throat. "You know Prudence? She's flying to Chicago, should be there now. I told her to book us in, er, together."

He nodded, methodical with his fried burger slab thing, inch by square inch, regular as a metronome. His dining habits were admirable.

"So? She's secretary, right? Doing her job."

"No, Tye," I explained. "She and I, er . . . in Manhattan last night. I've said she should meet us. I'll need a little time for a special . . . conference."

"You 'n' her?" He swigged wine, not breaking his masticating rhythm. "You got it, Lovejoy." He paused. Three squares of burger accumulated on his plate. I realized he was laughing, possibly an all-time first. "S'long as I know you isn't going any place." Al and Shelt laughed along.

156

◆ ◆ ◆

I COULDN'T get the hang of all that water. There were even ships on the damned thing. I'd thought we were a million miles inland.

"Where are we, love?"

Prudence had a map out in a flash, dropping notes and pencils like a sower going forth to sow.

"The Great Lakes, Lovejoy."

I looked into the darkness. It was illuminated by a trillion lights, like a city of crystal on a gleaming shore. I shivered. Prudence squeaked I must be cold. I just caught her from upping the thermostat to critical. You've never met anything like the heat of an American hotel.

"You know what's wrong, Prudence? Your country's just too big, too beautiful, too everything."

"I'm glad you like it, Lovejoy. But we're a little short on history. I've heard of your lovely old buildings, traditions—"

I wanted to prove to Tye that we were ensconced in snuggery and up to no good. I chose my time carefully to open the envelope she'd collected from the airport. It contained the first of Easy Boyson's Sherlock forgeries, just the one page but pretty good. I was proud of him. I concealed it in my folder, told Prudence not to answer the door until I got back, and wore myself out descending the hotel stairs.

A taxi took me from the harborside to O'Hare International Airport. I was glad to see the end of all that water in the nondark dark. I'm only used to lakes you can see across.

Magda and Zole were waiting in a nosh bar. I was delighted to see them. Zole was having some sort of row with the manager over a gaming machine he claimed was rigged. Magda was pale and washed out. She looked smart in her new coat and shoes, matching accessories.

"I'm not used to this, Lovejoy. I done as you said."

"Well did, love." She'd never been out of New York before.

Zole came and smoldered, eyeing the one-arm bandits. "Hey, Lovejoy. All Chicago's fixed."

"Hey, Zole ma man," I said. He sneered, joined us. "You got a broad, Lovejoy? Or you aim t' be stickin' Magda?"

I'd almost forgotten how to have a headache without Zole around.

"Play the machines, Zole." I gave him all my change. He sauntered away, hands in his pockets, head on the swivel.

Magda passed me her envelope. I took it.

"Ta, love. This address is a theme park, whatever that is. There's a big exhibition of antiques in a barn. Houses, rooms done up like in the nineteenth century. When Zole steals the item I've written down, make sure he walks within a few feet of me, okay? On his way out. Stay with him, and don't steal anything yourself."

"Will we be all right, Lovejoy?" She hesitated, glanced toward the counter where Zole was having a heated exchange about the food prices. "Only, you heard about our fire?"

"Fire?" I went cold.

"The Benidormo. An hour after we left like you sent round, your room blew a firestorm. Ours went too. A couple's hurt bad. A man died in the stairwell, burned terrible."

"The hotel? My room?" No wonder she looked pale.

"I'm sheet scared, Lovejoy. Fires, guns. I had all that crap, y'know?"

"You won't be, love," I said, thinking of being followed at Mortdex's.

"I seen it on the news at the airport. Not Zole."

I passed her some money. "Love, any time you want to cut out, you can. But I still want your help. Book your flight soon as I leave. Tell Zole nothing except that I want him to steal the antique as a game, to—" I'd worked the phrase out—"to put the bite on somebody."

She nodded. She'd had her hair done. I said she looked pretty, which made her go hard and call me stupid.

Zole, tact personified, helped matters along by telling Magda she should lay me quick and we could get back to the Big Apple. I stopped Zole trying to filch a woman's handbag from a table as we left.

"Give my regards to Joe and, er, Gertrude," I said, bussing Magda a so long in the main concourse.

"You makin' them up, Lovejoy?" the little nerk demanded.

"Yes, Zole," I told him, to shut the little bugger up. We

exchanged no further information. The hotel stairs were a hell of a climb. Prudence welcomed me with relief. We made mutual smiles until sleep rewarded us with oblivion.

WE FLEW over Illinois in broad daylight, Iowa, into Omaha with me breathless at the spectacle. I thought, this nation had to invent theme parks? It's one great glorious kaleidoscope. Maybe paradise is already down here, and we're so busy moaning and grumbling that we can't believe our own eyes.

With Prudence primly distancing herself from me—I'd agreed to her stern warning that we should not behave as if there were Something Between Us—the flight map showed names I couldn't honestly believe in. Manchester and Cambridge and Dedham, I'd accept those. And Delhi and Persia and Macedonia I'd take on trust.

"But Hiawatha?" I asked Tye. "Peoria? Des Moines? Oskaloosa? Sioux City? Come on, mate. Who's making them up?"

Prudence's secretarial training came to the rescue. She had an hour's lecture on name-lore programmed deep within, and was still explaining why Skunk River was not a myth when we separated at the airport.

The helicopter seemed so small. I'd only ever been in one before, and that under atrocious circumstances. I still get the shakes, and was silent for the whole flight, a little over an hour. I always keep wondering why they don't strap a huge parachute to the bloody things, in case its whirring blades spin off.

We landed beyond a small town that called itself a city, and were driven through woodland and glades, emerging onto a cliffy outlook over a river. You'd call it splendid, if you like countryside. The greeting I got I'd have called splendid too, if I liked phony.

"Preston Gullenbenkian," the mighty orator intoned, fixing me with an intent beam. "I'm yours in the service of the Lord of Hosts."

"I'm Lovejoy, reverend," I said, feeling inadequate, like I'd met Wesley. "You received our—"

Gullenbenkian intoned reverently, as if I was a gospel,

"Your word was heard, Lovejoy. And acted upon." He paused, hand on his heart. "It's my way. I want you to know that."

We were outside a pile—as in vast unbelievable palace. I'd thought Blenheim was still in the U.K., but here was its isomer overlooking that panoramic view.

"The mighty Missouri, Lovejoy." He raised his eyes to heaven. "We must give thanks to the Lord for all His generosity." He dashed off a quick prayer.

I dither in the presence of holiness. He was a tall, sun-tanned man, the sort who always gets lead parts in westerns. But his gear was perfect, his teeth glittering, his skin oiled and shining.

"And it's simple Prez, Lovejoy," he resumed, leading me up the great straight drive. "Sure, I'm in holy orders. But that doesn't entitle a humble, ordinary man to seize on outmoded elitisms."

"That's good of you, Prez."

He shot me a glance, casually acknowledged several youngsters loitering about in a not-so-aimless manner. Lads and lasses, they were long-haired, in sunspecs. Two of them had rifles. Whatever he wasn't, Gullenbenkian was astute.

"Necessary, Lovejoy. Your people wait here."

"Tye, please. See your pal gets enough peanuts."

Tye and Al stood watching as the gospeler and I trod to the verandah. I daresay Tye had planted some sort of recording gadget on me this time, expecting this. Better if he had, so it wouldn't just be my word against anyone else's.

"What hospitality may I offer you, Lovejoy? Not often I audience somebody from your neck of the woods." He laughed, a practiced, all-embracing laugh. I'd always thought only monarchs and popes gave audiences.

"Nothing, thanks, Prez. I just came to talk."

"Talk how?" The interior echoed. Baronial wasn't the word. It would have done for a duke, a prince. It was brand new, the ceilings vaulted, the stained glass windows soaring, sweeping staircases curving upward to a high domed ceiling. It was splendor so garish I almost couldn't speak.

"A money offer, actually."

We passed through the hall and out into a closed courtyard. Three youngsters faded at our approach. A girl emerged, served a tray of drinks, retired. I wondered why they were all so scruffy.

The gospeler caught me looking after her and smiled.

"Not *my* devotees, you understand. The Lord's servants. They're wonderfully motivated in our service."

"Who's our?"

"The Lord's. And mine. Instruments of the Lord's intentions here upon earth. Six months only."

That old one. "What happens if they stay longer?"

He raised his eyebrows. Every hair on his head seemed mathematically inclined, devoted to giving proper service. Steel gray hair, bright of eye, gold watch clinking on his wrist.

"They don't. Many try, Lovejoy."

"No second helpings, then?"

"None. Much better for them to live here a while, restore their flagging energies, the better to leap again into battle."

He explained how each crusade into the major cities was organized, the thousand prosletyzers who preceded him. "We organize bands, marches, spectacular events."

"Show biz?"

"Got to be, Lovejoy. The Lord can't be made to hide."

We chuckled, such friends. "Which brings in revenue to build the Own Decree Crystal Dome?"

"Praise God, yes it does, Lovejoy. I'm pleased you've heard of our little enterprise."

"Cathedral, isn't it?"

"They're already calling it that?" He was delighted.

"I'm afraid I haven't seen your television show, Prez. I haven't been in the U.S. very long."

He snapped fingers. A serf darted out, to be sent for a timetable of his broadcasts. For somebody not quite God, he was an impressive simulation.

"Your money offer, Lovejoy," he reminded.

His lady—I'd seen photographs—joined us, bulbous and with the face of a doll. Disconcertingly, her voice was a shrill monotone. Her cosmetics were thickly troweled on, lips protuberant with lipstick, her eyes deep in cream, liner, receder, heightener, lowerer, brighteners. I thought she was lovely.

"Annalou, Lovejoy," God's sub belled melodiously. "Come to see our Deus Deistic Theme Park, perhaps worship a little, and make an offer."

"I'll be right glad to show you round, Lovejoy," Annalou said. "You be here for our broadcast?"

"Afraid not, Annalou. I've to be back in Manhattan within the day." I stuffed the program details in my pocket and we boarded a small electric car thing driven by a long-haired kulak called Glad Tidings.

Annalou explained while Prez dispensed papal blessings to bystanders. "Our devotees abandon all their trappings of the World Without while they sojourn here. Including their names."

And property, the articles said.

We drove slowly down a graveled drive through rose gardens, out into lawns and fountain courts where hymns played on chimes. Recordings of unseen orchestras piously serenaded us. People began to appear, wandering and smiling. It was like a film set, the people affluent, blissful, contentedly calling "Praise the Lord" as we passed. I'm not used to holiness on this—indeed any—scale. I felt unnerved. Annalou fondly took my hand.

"The place gets to you, Lovejoy, don't it? Peace divine."

"There's the theme center, Lovejoy."

Prez's voice was husky with pride. Turrets and towers formed a surround, for all the world resembling a child's wooden fort rimming an enormous glass dome.

We drove up among the thickening crowds of visitors. Prez was telling me it would be finished in two years' time, if investments kept coming.

"Investments?"

"Contributions are investments in holiness, Lovejoy. Joy repays joy!"

To my alarm they began singing a hymn. People all around joined in. I went red, feeling a duckegg, not knowing the words and feeling too stupid to join in even if I did.

We stopped at the main entrance. "Praise all goodness, friends!" Prez cried, shaking hands with anybody he could reach. People slapped backs, cried heavenly slogans. I nodded, tried to smile.

"Good be praised!" Annalou cried in her dreadful mono-tone, using her heavenly shape to wheedle a way through the crowd. I followed.

We were on a forecourt laid out with biblical scenes in mosaic, with tableaux showing prophetic events in grottos lining the route. Close to, the glass Deus Whatnot grew to huge dimensions.

"So far, the only entrance we use is the small southern one, cloistered against evil, of course, by our famous Exhibition of Eternity."

"It's in connection with that, Prez, that my financial—"

"A second's prayerful thought first, Lovejoy!" Prez intoned, hauling me toward the entrance. I understood: no money chat among devotees.

We paused before a waxwork tableau while he said a lengthy prayer. I stood respectfully, trapped by Annalou's pressing figure and Prez's athletic bulk. Visitors all about paused with us, praying along.

The entrance was done up like a church porch. "See that it's Jerusalem, Lovejoy? Isn't the symbolism just cute?"

"Great, Annalou." I wished she wouldn't crush my arm against herself so enthusiastically. Not in a church, even one like this. I was getting hot under the collar.

"Our Exhibition of Eternity reveals the splendor of God's own times, Lovejoy," Prez said in a blast of hallelujahs as the crowd unglued and we started in.

"The antiques?"

"Evidence of former times when Good walked the earth."

"I'm so moved," I said to Annalou. And I really was. I could have eaten her with a spoon. No wonder the contributions—well, investments—came rolling in with a bird like this fluttering her eyelashes on your television set.

"I can tell, Lovejoy," she whispered. If only it hadn't been in a monotone.

Somebody bumped against me, tripping me. I stumbled and would have fallen if Annalou hadn't been so close. Magda's angry face swam into my ken and vanished in a sea of devotees.

We had entered a kind of gloamy grotto. A waterfall cascaded before lights. Antiques were close. I felt a strong boom in my chest, and turned to see Zole ostentatiously swaggering out.

"Wait, Annalou!"

"Yes?" she breathed.

"You're sure all the antiques are in here?"

"Why, yes, Lovejoy!"

"There's one being carried out. By that little lad—"

She caught Glad Tidings, he pressed an alarm. Everybody froze. The hymns stopped. Lights bashed on. Devotees crowded in and marshaled us all along walls, whistles sounding outside. Annalou and Prez dragged me through the crowd out onto the forecourt.

"That way. I felt something really overpowering."

"Felt?" Prez pondered that, prayerfully I'm sure. I saw Zole with Magda heading for a public long-distance coach, walking with composure.

"I'll tell you who had it." I closed my eyes, swaying, overdoing things rather, but trying to keep in with the spirit of the place. Pretense is contagious.

"Freeze, everybody!"

Everybody stilled. Glad Tidings muttered that he should shake everybody down, where's the problem. I said to wait.

I stalked toward where Zole stood with Magda, opened my eyes, gave a quick wink at Zole. Magda was furious for some reason, but that's only a woman doing her thing.

"Hand it over, sonny, please."

I held out my hand to Zole, quickly adding as he drew breath for a spurt of insolence, "My name's Lovejoy. No harm will come to you, we promise."

"You sure?" he asked suspiciously, little sod.

"We promise in the name of Good, don't we, friends?" I chanted. "Forgiveness is all. Suffer little children to, er . . ." What the hell was it? "And we shall be, er, blessed," I ended a bit lamely.

"Here. It was just lying around."

Zole gave me a statuette. I almost dropped it in shock as the red-hot glow spread into me and the bells thundered in my soul. I'd never, ever seen anything like it. God, but it was lovely, lying there in my hand where it belonged.

It didn't look much, just a small hard-porcelain figure of Moses with his tablets inscribed in Hebrew. But it was Chinese, old as the hills, typical feeling and colors. They're not even imitated (yet, yet!) by porcelain fakers on the antiques marts (yet!), so you're almost certainly in possession of a wonderful find if you've got one at home. They're supposed to come in a set of six, various Old Testament characters—Joshua, Noah, that lot.

Weakly I passed it to Annalou, and pulled out a roll of money. This was props gelt, high-denomination notes drawn through Tye, to be returned in the plane. People gasped at the size of the roll. Ostentatiously I peeled one off, and gave it to Zole with a flourish.

"Here, sonny," I said loudly. "Your need is greater than mine, as the Lord sayeth." Or somebody. "Now, lady. Go and sin no more!"

"Praise the Lord!" somebody said mercifully.

"Amen!" I chirped. I was so moved I honestly felt tears.

Magda and Zole were ushered away, but I walked after them and beckoned a taxi forward from the car park line. I didn't want vengeful devotees inflicting an impromptu penance on them. I gave them what I hoped looked like a genuine blessing as they pulled out. Show over.

I turned, bumping into Annalou. Prez was talking in low tones to Glad Tidings and three other serfs. I dried my eyes.

"Lovejoy!" Annalou said, dropping her voice three notches and taking my arm. "You're so sweet!"

It's true. I am. I was thinking what could have happened to me if that Zole hadn't done his stuff.

"Good is in each of us, Annalou," I intoned. "Though I am the worst of His flock. Can I admit something to you, Annalou? It's this. I'm sore afflicted by lust—yes, even now, even as we were about to enter the temple of the, er, Deus." I'd forgotten the bloody name. God, it was a mess. "For you, love. I've never felt this way before, not even since I found the sacred Mildenhall Treasure, or that missing Rembrandt from Dulwich Art Gallery."

"Not since . . . ?" She took my arm. Her breast pressed against my quivering form. "For little me, Lovejoy? You felt carnal sinful desire . . . ?"

"I have to admit it, Annalou. The instant I saw you, I fell. I'm sure Satan sent me—"

"Shhh, Lovejoy." Prez was approaching. The three devotees were looking hard at me. She whispered, "Say nothing yet, Lovejoy. Until you and I've had a chance of a prayer together."

I composed myself and together we went into the Exhibition of Eternity. I paid the admission fee with a large denomination, and managed to look offended when the devotee offered me change.

Two hours later I was breathless and stunned.

Take any—for that matter every—art form, cram it into a partly finished glass building arranged as caves, crystal porticos and arches, alleys and terraces, all under one great luminescent ceiling. Add dancing fountains, glass chapels, and glowing altars rising musically from the ground. Add moving glass walls with portraits of bad, bad art ("Unfolding in eternal sequence!" gushed Annalou). Add automaton choirs, electrically powered with glutinous hymns pouring out from crannies everywhere, on stages that rose and sank. Add Eternal Damnation with a fire shooting from a bottomless pit where automated gremlins stoked furnaces and electronic groans put the fear of God in you. Search lights reamed away in dark corners—"Let there be lights!" Prez crowed ahead of us.

"The greatest scene of all, Lovejoy!" Annalou told me, more friendly than ever. "Real genuine people choirs are still the greatest pull!"

The RGP choristers sang, swaying delirious with joy. People clapped in time and rocked to and fro.

They were all dressed in cottas and cassocks, reds and whites and blacks. Microphones, those least sanctified instruments, dangled and amplified.

"A small choir, only a few folks come, see?"

"A big choir means a bigger crowd, more revenue?"

"You better believe it."

The Sanctum Antiquorum charged a special admission fee. You got a plenary indulgence on a Parchment of Prayer, for an extra fee. It looked like real parchment to me, which raised the unpleasant thought that some sheep somewhere had given one hundred percent.

"This is a genuine scale copy of the Vatican Museum's forum, Lovejoy!" Annalou claimed. "We're hoping to buy a church from your Wiltshire, complete with gravestones, and install it as an added attraction in a Cornice of Contemplation."

The antiques were a mixture of fake, fraud, and the genuine. Paintings, mainly Italian School, mid-eighteenth century, a couple of frescoes, walls from genuine old monasteries, arches and pillars from Germany, a couple of French cloisters. It was a marvelous show, but an impossible mishmash. Yet what's wrong with that?

Silver chalices, gold monstrances, rings claiming kinship with ancient bishops and saints, a chunk of everything vaguely religious was included. There was a hand-shaped left-handed tea-caddy spoon I particularly fell for—once used in Catholic services for shoveling incense into the thurible at High Mass. (Tip: Any collector will give his eyeteeth for a left-handed one of these, being so much rarer than the right-handed sort.) Madonnas abounded, statues bled and wept with artificial abandon. Crutches dangled from arches, testifying to spontaneous recovery from afflictions.

I'm not knocking all this, incidentally. Whatever your salvation depends on, go to it and good luck. Just don't ask me to subscribe to the magazine.

I spent too long gazing at the small sextet of ancient figures from China, one of which I'd rescued from Zole. Seeing them all together, I honestly wished I'd not bubbled the kid, but sent him back for the other five and waited in the getaway helicopter or something.

"Honey." Annalou squeezed my hand, having detected but misunderstood my sincerest form of emotion. "We can maybe work something out, okay? You and me?"

"It's love, you see," I explained thickly, gazing at the wonderful small porcelains. The Jesuits had these done in seventeenth-century Peking. I reached and touched them one by one, feeling the glow.

"I'll always remember them, Annalou," I told her truthfully. "They're what brought us together."

"Shhhh!"

A few more hymns and we made our melodious way out into the air. I was bog-eyed, and had to sit down beside an Inspiration for Invalids arbor. It faced a Garden of Eden, with a politely clad robot Adam taking perennial bites from a plastic apple while a demure Eve looked on in automated horror at a snake winding its way round and round a tree. I had to look away.

"I can see you're overcome, Lovejoy." Prez was with us. He'd had a space cleared for us by devotees, the invalids' wheelchairs and stretchers being moved on temporarily while we spoke.

"I hoped it wouldn't show, Prez."

They exchanged significant glances while I pretended to be superawed by the crystal building. It didn't take much effort.

"Lovejoy. Your financial offer . . . ?" He sat beside me, clapping his hand on my shoulder while Annalou pressed close. They were quite a team. "It's to do with your special gift, right? That was the most fascinating display of perception I've ever witnessed. Why, a gift like that, recognizing antiques by *sense*, why, that's a gift that must be used for Good. I feel we have a rightful claim on your services, Lovejoy."

I came to, smiled. "That's right, Prez. I came here to offer my gift in your service."

"How wonderful!" Annalou pressed my hand. "That means you'll be able to stay a while, rejoicing in prayer!"

"Afraid not, love. But I will provide a list of items that are fakes. In your exhibits, as they stand."

Silence. I admired the ghastly Deus building. "You deserve help, Prez. I was guided here by a higher power."

"Well, I feel that too." He was uncertain.

"Those saintly relics from Trier, the pottery on display by the Saints of Europe scenarios. They're fakes, Prez."

"They're . . . ?" He looked hard at Annalou. From the corner of my eye I caught her worried shrug.

"We'll get confirmation from Queen Mary College, London. They do it with physics somehow. Some mumbo jumbo called inductively coupled plasma emission spectrometry.

That'll show it, I'm sure. And that Roman glass from the Holy Land's all rubbish. They use spectrophotometry, I think, but we can give them a call—"

"Fakes?" Prez said faintly. He checked we weren't being overheard. "Lovejoy. You can't be right. Our foundation bought those items from the most reputable sources."

"You have my sympathy, Prez. And so has your lovely wife here." I dragged my eyes from his lovely wife and gave him my best soulful smile. "I feel your anguish. Here you are, having built up this great . . . er, thing. And now to realize you've spent a fortune of your income on worthless junk. It's a setback, Prez. I weep for you."

"Are you sure, Lovejoy, honey? About the fakes?"

"Shut up!" Prez snapped at her in an undertone. I tried to look startled. He smiled at me, abruptly back to holiness. "Lovejoy. The strain of this revelation's afflicted my soul. Are you sure?"

"Yes. That specimen of Egyptian grain from Jospeh of the multicolored coat fame is duff—er, false, Prez. Like the bowl it's in. I think these science people use something called electron spin resonance for that—"

"Lovejoy, we got to talk."

He signaled Glad Tidings and the custom golf truck. We drove to his private palace through crowds of adoring devotees, who cried their blessings down upon us. I felt a right prat, and a fraud, but that's par for my course. He gave few blessings on that return journey.

Deals are hard for me. I mean, I'd have loved to have called off the whole thing and scarpered, with those precious gleaming Jesuit porcelains as payment. But that would have left Magda and Zole, and Gina, and the California game looming a week away. And dead Bill. And Rose Hawkins. And me on the run from everyone on earth.

So I listened, was offered everything I wanted if only I'd join this heavenly pair and their labors. I was left alone with Annalou for a sordid set of promises while Prez ostentatiously conversed with his special bodyguard of devotees outside in plain view—allowing us time to reach some sort of conclusion, I surmised. I weakened, made promises to return, saying I'd use my services on their behalf all round the religious antiques markets of the world. She sulked, but brightened when I showed fear of my lust being recognized for the sinful thing it was. She slipped me an address in St. Louis where she had a private apartment for religious retreats. I pretended to be exalted, thrilled. Which of course I was.

Then it was Prez's turn while Annalou went somewhere. I insisted I simply had to write to all the authorities I knew about this terrible fraud that had been perpetrated on this holy enterprise, giving it maximum publicity for the sake of honesty and . . .

I got two point four percent of the investments in the theme park. I insisted on refusing the one percent of the admission fees to the church Exhibition of Eternity, and said it would be my personal contribution to the work. He watched me go, musing hard, as Glad Tidings walked me out to where Tye and his goon waited by the helicopter. I was wringing in sweat as we ascended into the heavens. See what religion does to you? It's catching.

19

THE risks in antiques fraud are relative. Other criminals risk the absolute. You've never heard of a fraudster involved in a shoot-out, of the "Come in and get me, copper!" sort. Or of some con artist needing helicopter gunships to bring him. No, we subtle-mongers do it with the smile, the promise, the hint. And we have one great ally: greed. And make no mistake. Greed is everywhere, like weather. You get varieties of it, from tempestuous to a benignity so tranquil you kind of forget that it's there. But it's never very far away, thank God. Wasn't there a European king, heavens preserve us, done for fiddling his investments the year before last? See what I mean?

Fraud is the daughter of greed.

Going, that second day in Louisiana, to the house of the famous collector Mr. D. Hirschman, it seemed to me that I hadn't needed to be lucky so far. In each case the marks' greed had bolstered my endeavors. Their greed had made them overreach—Mortdex's man Verbane was hiving off a share of the Mortdex millions for himself, so couldn't afford a whiff of scandal. Annalou, bless her, had succumbed to that greediest of impulses, the craving for more. She'd believed that her obvious charms would seduce me into helping her and Prez to cull still more ancient religious relics to drag in more susceptibles to the fold. Prez's greed had been more direct—let's shut this bum up, in a manner beneficial to all.

I defy anybody to answer this next question with a resounding negative: Have you ever been a fraud?

Think a moment before answering. That hair tint? That little white lie about being only twenty-four? Your height? Weight? Telling the doctor you honestly stuck to his rotten diet? And saying yes, you really stayed home every night your partner was away in Boston . . . ? Fraud. The church is

171

at it, governments, the U.N., Inland Revenue, emperors and monarchs. But there're some kinds of cons that are morally permitted, it seems. Like spying, like in wartime, like when Scotland Yard does a drugs stakeout and captures dope smugglers.

Fraud is a necessary part of our personality. No good complaining. We're all born con artists.

I would have had great hopes for Zole, if it hadn't been for that damned dog.

"WHY did you let him buy that mongrel, you silly cow?"

"He's a kid. It didn't cost. Where's the harm?"

"Whose was it?" I grabbed Zole by the throat. The dog growled threateningly so I let him go.

It was early evening. We were in a street filled with sound and ironmongery, scrolled iron balconies and music bands milling away in every doorway. I was having to shout to make myself heard.

"You little sod, you thieved it."

The dog Sherman was a small white Scotch terrier thing that had seen better days. It kept grinning at me, coming close, wanting an orgy of affection. It forgave easily.

"Lovejoy. That business at the Deus Deistic Theme Park. Did it work out okay?"

"I was worth more'n what you gave, Lovejoy," Zole claimed, cocky little swine. Just how much he'd been worth, for a few seconds while holding the porcelain figure, he'd never know.

"Magda." I addressed myself to her, forgetting the little psycho with the pooch. "I have an important visit to make. Did you find out about the Benidormo?"

She told me what she'd learned from the papers—I hadn't wanted to be seen by Tye et al. feverishly hunting through the dailies for evidence of a bomb outrage in my cooling bed. Unexplained, it seems. Arson, possibly some insurance scam, was being mooted. Ho hum.

"How long will this last, Lovejoy?"

My last phone talk with Gina had been that the California game would be at Revere Mount, five days hence. I'd wired facsimiles of the two Sherlock pages, posted them express, revealed they were fakes, told her what to look for as proof. She'd seemed pleased. So the Hawkins connection was broken, and Sophie Brandau would be as pleased as I. I still had the rest of the places to hack, then the Manhattan big two auctioneers, the hairiest problem of all. After that, I might be able to take it on the lam while they went to play their neffie game.

"Week, give or take, love."

"Then?" I went uncomfortable. "Happiness with that Annalou whore?"

"I dunno what. I can't plan."

Zole's dog peed on a lamp post. Nice that New Orleans still had lamp posts, though. Zole admired its effort.

"And us?"

Meaning her and Zole but excluding me, I hoped.

"I'll think of something, Magda. One thing." I hesitated, took advantage of Zole's preoccupation with Sherman. "You don't phone Tye any longer, do you?"

I shifted from foot to foot while she composed herself.

"Once, since we started out, Lovejoy." She added quickly, "I didn't tell him about the envelope, though."

"What's Tye promised you?"

She looked into the distance. Some parade was forming up, bands tuning up, people with banners and flowers. Everybody seemed to carry cornets and trombones. Colored dresses, floral scarves, a couple of floats surmounted by pretty lasses under arches of blossoms.

"He's said we might, well, get together." She looked at me, shrugged. "Some time, y'know how it is."

Smooth old Tye. I felt my loyalty evaporate, quick as sweat on a stone. I'd practically saved him on board the *Gina*. I'd been helpful all along, really. No more. And he knew I'd a helper trailing along, which meant Magda and Zole were now handicaps, no longer allies.

"You still going to phone him?"

"No. Course not."

I'd got rid of Tye by being so docile while waiting for Mr. Hirschman to fit me into his busy schedule, that Tye'd readily agreed to let me go alone to the collector's home. He was busy making arrangements with Prudence I'd asked

173

for in New York. For a second I thought to question Magda further, but gave in. She could tell me whatever she wanted anyway. I gave her money, told her we'd possibly be another day here. I wasn't sure. We'd meet at the waterfront. As we parted, something Zole did stuck in my mind. I grabbed him as he slipped something under Sherman's collar.

"What's that, you little tyke?"

"Lemme go, Lovejoy."

A knife, a shiv about eight inches blade, an etched horn handle. I showed it to Magda, thunderstruck. People in the street took no notice, too occupied watching the loud bands form in procession.

"Magda? This child's got a dagger! For God's sake, woman! What the hell are you thinking of?"

She shook her head wearily. "Don't sheet me, Lovejoy. We look out for each other best we can, okay?"

"No it's not okay!" I blazed. "He's still a—"

"Don't say it, Lovejoy!" Zole threatened, all aggression. Sherman growled. I growled back and it gave a canine sort of shrug and settled on its haunches to await the outcome. "I'm no kid! I already stuck three pimps tried to muscle—"

"You stay a kid until I tell you different, understand?"

I cast the knife into the harbor waters, and marched off in a fury.

"We in a strange town, Lovejoy!" he shouted after me. "We gotta carry, man! Or you done."

Ever get that feeling that you're suddenly the center of a world gone mad? It happens a lot around me.

"DAM, everybody calls me, Lovejoy," the collector said. "Would you believe Damski for a first name? Sort of goes with Hirschman, right?"

A humorous man, but laughing without a crack in his face. His dark eyes were humorless. I wondered if every high-fly collector has a facade of mirth, but then remembered Mr. Verbane.

The house was one of a terrace, a street actually as I know streets. A curved courtyard with shrubs in pots and trellises supporting climbing plants—wisterias, vines, bougainvilleas at a guess, though usually when I'm showing off with plant names women come and correct me. Wrought iron gates, pavements and garden patios seemed to be the New Orleans fashion.

We entered through french windows, a comfortable and masculine salon. Hirschman was impassive, rotating his whole body before sitting down, a Bavarian Victorian clockwork automaton. He was pudgy in each limb. Rings shone on his fat fingers. I recognized a pro.

"It's your collection, er, Dam." I could see no purpose in delay. "I've come for a proportion of the valuation."

"Protection, Lovejoy? You don't look the type."

"Not in the way you mean, Dam. Protection for your unbought, as well as the bought."

"But I finish up paying you, that it?"

"Yes."

"Anti-Semitic, huh?"

"Some of my best friends, et cetera."

"Never mind the boughts, Lovejoy. Them I got, a'ready. Tell me the unboughts. I never heard that scam before."

"The Kröller-Müller Museum in Holland," I said. He was too cool. I felt the humidity reach into my clothes and sweat start tickling.

"I heard of it." He lit a cigar like a bratwurst, admired his smoke.

"In that forest, by Arnhem. The robbery took two minutes—smash glass, rush twenty paces into the gallery, grab three Van Goghs, vanish. Remember it?"

He spread his hands, in mock appeasement. "How'd I remember, Lovejoy? You only just told me. Terrible, terrible."

"The police were there in a flash. The crooks were gone in half a flash. The museum still has two hundred and seventy-five works by Vincent, but . . ."

"The three have never been found?"

"Not so far, Dam."

"Why come to me, Lovejoy? I'm one of millions."

"You've companies in Japan, Dam. You've offices near the Mitsubishi Bank in Tokyo—the one lately held up by the Yakuza street gangs there."

"And they pulled the Kröller-Müller heist? That what you're saying?"

"No. They're the ones stole the Corots in France. Like the so-say Corot copy you later exhibited, saying you had it painted the same week, copied from photographs."

"You're alleging my copy's the genuine stolen Corot? I have certificates to prove—"

"I'm a divvy, Damski. Any test you like."

Which brought silence in on cue, amid smoke and the barking of a dog nearby. I'd been pleased to see the old-fashioned roadstones outside in the street. Tradition dies hard in New Orleans, it seems. I wondered if those marching bands were part of the same tradition. Dixieland? Wasn't that the stuff they played hereabouts? Or was that Nashville? I'm hopeless with music, though I sing in a choir in my home village.

"Eh?" He'd just said something momentous.

"I'm going to have you silenced, Lovejoy." He sounded friendly, thoughtful. "But first, I'm going to do you a favor. I'm going to explain why."

"Silenced?" I said stupidly.

"As in terminal." He was at pains to seem reasonable. "Do you know what I'd give for your power to divine, to divvy genuine from fake? Everything. Instead, that power is vouchsafed to an oaf like you. A drifter, on the make for a few miserable dollars."

"I'm not like that—"

"Instead, I lack totally that extraordinary power that you have in abundance. It isn't that which I find unforgivable. It's you. You, Lovejoy, are a gargoyle not to be tolerated. There's one point more."

I licked my lips, looked for escape.

"Don't worry. I've more sense than to execute you here, in my own home. I'll have it done before you leave the city, parts of which can become very fraught and dangerous."

"I'll call the police," I threatened feebly, wondering why I'd told Tye to stay away the only time I needed him.

"The other reason is, I've come from nothing, Lovejoy. I've risen by the exercise of my own brain, astuteness. Triumph of the will." He smirked at the aptness of the phrase. "Ironical, no? I'm not going to have you coming in here and taking my—*my*—possessions back into public ownership—

176

ownership of dolts and fools who couldn't look after them as they deserve to be looked after. They forfeited them. They deserved to. I tried the fools in Holland, the idiots in France, before the jury of my own mind. And found them guilty."

"So you transferred ownership?"

"And shall do more. Lovejoy. Without your assistance." He smiled beatifically, spent by the effort of revelation.

"You were the barrister for the defense, Lovejoy. You must pay the price for having lost the trial. Good-bye, Lovejoy. Start running."

Shakily I rose and went toward the patio, through the french windows, expecting gunshots any minute. Then the street, through the squeaking wrought iron gates, into music and flowers and people.

And the lowering dusk.

20

THE bar was a walk-in, more like a shop than anything. The windows were skimpily curtained. Lights were on, shedding gold onto the pavements. And the music was a delight—at least, I'd have thought so if I'd not been scared.

I'd chosen a seat where I could look out. Everybody in the place seemed to smoke. The band was into melodious action. The mugginess meant all doors stood ajar, all sounds mingling. I didn't want to miss Magda and Zole. Almost as if they were a lifeline.

That's the trouble with confidence tricks, especially the extortion kind. It's the Emperor's New Clothes—it only takes some nerk to point out that he's got none, and all barriers are down. I'd tried phoning the hotel, but Tye wasn't available. Prudence was inexplicably out.

First time on my own. Why now?

Anxious, I scanned the gathering dusk. What I'd seen as a harbor front was a river. America's rivers are so vast I can never tell if they're the sea or not.

New Orleans is built in a loop of the Mississippi, between it and a lake, I remembered from Prudence's maps (where *was* she for Christ's sake?). I could see ferries toing and froing to the south side. A few small power boats zipped around. A place on the front advertised boats for hire, but they were shutting up shop. The entire city isn't all that big, not for the U.S. Say, seven miles by four, with its Lake Pontchartrain only the size of an ocean. Across the Mississippi the land fritters away into swamps and islands. I'd seen it on our approach to Moisant International Airport. Nice for a holiday, not for escape. Except two men had been looking down at me from a balcony as I'd left Hirschman's courtyard, and I was already seeing at least one every few minutes among the people.

A cluster of tourists—so what was I?—went by, calling to each other. I went among them, walking toward the river as they went. A charter boat, Dixieland music stomping from an upper deck, with fairy lights and a spurt of water from the ship's side. The gangway was manned by two pretty lasses who wanted me to sign on for the voyage, or at least have a brochure.

"I'm waiting for my friends," I said.

They laughed. "Won't we do?" and all that. Any other time, I thought.

Then I saw him. It was one of the two men, no mistake. He was walking slowly along the front, staring into each cafe, bar, restaurant. I wasn't wrong. I looked about for his oppo, found him. A steady double act, one strolling into each honky-tonk, the other scanning the crowds. Methodical, gradually advancing, eliminating possibilities. Which meant ... Oh, Jesus. The other side too, from the ferry concourse. Two more, doing the same, just as anonymous, just as implacable, only they were in jeans and sneakers.

"Here, miss. I'll have one, please."

"Sure it's not three?" Mischievous with the smile. I could have thumped her.

"Eh?"

"Your friends."

Magda, Zole, and the dog Sherman arrived, all breathless.

"Ah, just in time!" I babbled. "Cancel the ticket."

I grabbed Magda's arm, pulled her across the road and into an alleyway, Zole expostulating.

"Where the hell've you been, you lazy bitch?" I gave her.

"Hey, stay cool, ma man," from Zole. I clipped his ear to shut him up.

"There's some people after me," I babbled, trying for calm and failing. "They're here, on the riverside. I want you to go and phone Tye now. Not tomorrow, not next week—*now*. Understand?"

Magda was so sad. She stood there, filled with sorrow. Sometimes women are so frigging useless. I almost knocked her down in my terror. It was bubbling up into my brain, blotting all thought.

"He checked everybody out, Lovejoy. You too. Gone. And Al and Shelt."

"Gone?" I stared at her. Al and Shelt, the peanut eaters?

A kitchen hand frightened me to death by suddenly bursting out of a raucous interior and rattling a dustbin into place. He slammed back inside. The alley darkened, the light extinguished. "Gone where?"

"Just gone, Lovejoy. Everybody."

"Didn't he say where?" I glanced toward the lights. The gleaming river looked a barrier now, not an escape. But Magda'd promised me she wouldn't phone him, and she had.

"Sheet," Zole said. He was carrying Sherman. The dog looked knackered. Why do they always gasp when they've done nowt?

"I had to come, Lovejoy, in case you . . ."

Fight or flight? Always the latter, for Lovejoy Antiques.

"Come on. We'll try to hire a boat and go . . ."

"Sheet, man," Zole was saying over and over. I realized why when I made to drag Magda toward the riverside lights. A man was standing against the glow, in silhouette. He was the one with a snappy hat, rakishly angled, and a suit of many stripes. I'd never seen such huge white cuffs, spats even.

"Mine," he told his left shoulder, and his mate faded away round the corner. "I say mine, man," he told over my head. The two sneakers-and-jeans were deep in the alley.

"Okay," one called, laughing. "But he looks real mean, okay?"

They emitted hoarse huh-huhs of laughter. I wanted the loo, a hang-glider, anything. We were left with our killer. I mean my.

"Okay, lady," the man said. He was about ten feet away when he finally stopped strolling forward. Where the frig was that kitchen hand now, when I wanted him? I could have dashed through the kitchen . . . "You and the kid take off."

"Magda," I pleaded weakly. I was quivering, my voice pathetic. I'm disgusting at the best of times.

"Come on, Sherman," Zole said, treacherous little traitorous bastard reneger, betrayer of a friend who'd helped the corrupt little sod.

Sherman. The dog. They're supposed to guard us, right?

"Kill," I said weakly to the stupid hound.

"You got it," Zole said.

I don't really know what happened next, only that Zole dropped Sherman to the ground as the man had reached into his jacket and pulled out a weapon. There was a crack, but near me, not near him. A second shot came from the man into the ground with fragments of stone pavement flying everywhere. Magda yelped, I whimpered, Sherman screeched, any mixture of the three. In that same millisec Zole had gone flying backward, spinning and hitting the ground. The man was sagging, slowly sinking to the ground, as if trying to pick something up at a party without being noticed much. He seemed preoccupied.

I picked Zole up, tears streaming down my face.

"Zole. I'm sorry. I thought he'd just do me—"

"Let me down, silly fucka," Zole said, wriggling. "Where's ma gun? I gotta finish the motha fucka—"

He escaped, searched for something on the ground. Sherman was howling, shivering worse than me. Magda was shouting, holding my arm, pulling, trying to get me to run past the kneeling man who had stilled, slumped ominously against the wall.

"Hang on," Zole was calling. "I gotta find ma gun an' finish him—"

Sherman howled and Magda screamed for Christ's sake to come on, the others'll be back. Zole was stumbling after, Sherman's lead round his legs, the mongrel howling and whining. And bleeding, I saw as we stumbled up the alley toward the street lights, from a scratch near its nose, presumably a splinter . . . And Zole was fiddling with a gun as he followed, grumbling at the thing. He shook it like a rattle, listened hard to its sound as he tried to work the trigger.

I snatched it off him and flung the thing into the alley. We ran toward the boat, the pretty girls waiting for the last trippers to climb aboard. We joined them. Thank God for New Orleans music. It deafens you to everything else. I paid, and though the girls looked at us a bit oddly, Magda was talking breathlessly to them and I was paying money over, and all was peace and light and safety as the boat pulled away from the mooring and we glided away up the lovely broad flowing Mississippi.

WATCHING the paddles turn water on a steamer is hypnotic, even a new and utterly phony side-paddler. The trippers seemed to be some sort of convention, fez hats with tassels and secret songs bawled into the universe. Beer flowed. Some other passengers were like us, normal and very, very glad to be there.

Normal? For that read abnormal.

I stood watching the shoreline. I had only a few dollars now. Rescued by a homicidal child, supported by a prostitute. And now leaned on by a dog that was still trembling with fright. The cut on its face was about a tenth of an inch, the worm.

Tye had gone. Prudence had gone. All right, Magda lied—she'd told me she wouldn't try to contact Tye. But she'd come to warn me.

Zole came, threw Sherman some unspeakable protein, and passed me a glass. I tasted gingerly. Wine.

"Hey, ma man. Whyn't you ball Magda? See, if you stick each other, we's team animals, right?"

I turned to inspect him, leaning over the glittering dark river. He was hardly out of nappies, and listen to his language.

"Where'd you get the automatic, Zole?"

"Bought it. Cheaper'n N'York."

"There could have been another accident. What if the safety catch hadn't been on?"

He snorted scorn. "Ain't no safeties on revolvers, Lovejoy. On automatics, sure. This wasn't no 'matic magna."

I scrutinized him. "You ever shoot anybody before, Zole?"

"Nope. 'Cept a numbers drek near East Forty-third one time." He showed a scar on his shoulder, pulling his shirt down for me to see. "Got cut bad bad, man. Dee bee recoil, y'know?"

He reached down and embraced Sherman, now wolfing the meat. Drinkers whooped by, yelling something about going fishing.

"Lovejoy? Tye comin' after us?"

That hadn't occurred to me. Leaving me to face Hirschman's hoodlums was one thing. But would Tye hunt me down? Zole saw clearer than I.

"Dunno, Zole."

"Then what's the plan, ma man?"

"Yes, Lovejoy. What's the plan?"

Magda. Another tour boat creamed out of the darkness with lights and music, paddle wheels splashing. People waved and shouted, and our lot waved and hollered. Zole took a bead on the bridge and went, "Pow-pow-pow!" I almost clipped his ear as correction but thought better of it.

"I'll tell you the story, love. See if you know."

Zole went and brought drinks for us both while I told my tale, every detail, including the phony scripts, how I'd tried to bring in a number of fake pages to prove to Gina I'd combed the kingdom for the Sherlock grailer. I explained that would expose Moira Hawkins as a fraud, so allowing Gina the chance to eliminate Moira from the gamesters. I spoke with grievance. I'd done well by Gina. And now Tye makes a mistake like this, almost gets me killed.

"Why, Lovejoy?" Magda asked when I'd done.

"He *dumb*, Magda," Zole said.

"Well, see, Magda, it's like this . . ." Like what? Nothing came to help. "It's complicated, see? It's raising millions from antiques and art—"

"So?" She lit a rare cigarette and smiled wryly when I moved to windward. "So why her people let you get killed when you raisin' so good?"

"Wastin' yo' time, Magda. He but *dumb*."

"Shut your face. Magda, I think she said something about . . ."

Magda shook her head slowly. "I'll say for her. She's got the hots for Denzie Brandau, right? Along comes Moira Hawkins with the big dig, the dream scheme. Dumb Denzie falls for Moira's play—that president crap—leaving Gina washing the coffee things. See? So she minds to wreck Moira Hawkins's gran' plan."

"But . . ." But that wouldn't explain Tye's failure to come and protect me from Damski Hirschman's goons, would it?

"Gina Aquilina gets your pages, like you sent. She has them tested. Sure, they're dud. She's got all the evidence she needs to confront Denzie Brandau and Moira Hawkins. So out goes Moira. And guess who that leaves to pick up Denzie's daisies?"

"So Gina withdraws Tye Dee . . . ?"

And the peanut eaters, and the plane from New Orleans. And the bank credits I was using. And Prudence. And the rest of my little circus. A dead man wouldn't need helpers. Yet I'd been successful. If Gina was sure that she and Nicko would win the California game, she'd be sure of snaffling Denzie Brandau as well, once he ditched the shadowy Moira. Plus his big run at the presidency, with Gina his first lady, perhaps after Sophie had bought some tragic but convenient accident?

"Lovejoy," Zole said. "How you *get* to grow old, ma man? I don't *believe* him, Magda."

I counted out my few dollars, watched by them both. "That's it. I'll understand if you cut and run."

"See how dumb he really is?"

"Stop talking, Zole," Magda said evenly. And the lad subsided. I couldn't believe it. Never listens to a word I say, but heeds her matter-of-fact shush. "I haven't got much more, Lovejoy."

Zole rebounded. "Me too."

Dog? Gun? Magda's expenses made more sense than any of mine.

"You got your list of places, Lovejoy. Maybe we try shaking them down?"

"No, Magda. I wrote them to Gina, places, dates, names, everything. If she's the one who marked me down . . ."

"You aren't thinking of California, Lovejoy?"

"We know where the game is, love. We know when, who'll be there. Fancy running for the rest of our lives?"

"Running's dumb, man," from Zole.

"Zole's right, love."

"Hey, Lovejoy! You'm learnin'!"

We went to join the party, Magda sitting close to me as we spent our last on drinks and food. The old saying is, your last bite lasts longest. It transpired that we were heading upriver on an all-night paddler party, destination Baton Rouge.

21

THE night was idyllic. What better way to spend a balmy warm night than sit on the deck of a pleasure steamer on this great river of midnight velvet, watching lights go dreamily by?

At least, it would have been, if I wasn't the quarry of hunters. If the little lad asleep on one of the boat's benches with his dog hadn't shot and possibly killed a man. If the prostitute who was his . . . what? Pal? Mother? I'd not asked . . . if she wasn't probably sick of the sight of me. I mean, before I'd hove into view her life was plain and ordinary, right? Well, not quite those, but certainly ordered. She'd hook a client, charge him the going rate, repeat the process, while Zole stole. Together, a living.

Then me. And Tye Dee, who makes her a spy. Next, they're running like hell because of me.

On the same deck, a sleepy trio of conventioneers were talking about fishing. Music wafted from the big saloon. Women laughed. Occasional shouts. The wheels shooshed and thumped. The warm night felt like heaven. Sweat trickled down my neck, but for once I didn't mind. Even Sherman looked content, having extracted maximum sympathy for his nose scratch from a hundred cooing women, crafty canine. He'd fed like a lord. And he snored.

The shore lights glided past. A couple of late boats strung with fairy lights heading downriver passed close enough for us to hear their music, see the dancers waving. Our drinkers and dancers crowded the rails calling good wishes. You can't help thinking how wrong preconceptions are, can you? I'd thought America was all plastic food, angry motorists, no history. Okay, I thought ruefully, people sometimes hunt you, but that was partly my fault—I should have run the instant Rose Hawkins spotted my lust for antiques.

The boat went junketing musically on under stars through

American velvet. No wonder the world and his wife wants to come. That notion finally set me thinking about the plight I was in, the road out. The California game. Because if I wasn't dead from Hirschman's goons and Gina's betrayal, I was still in.

By the time dawn shimmered into the eastern sky I'd got a plan of sorts. I'd need luck, a little money to start with. Plus a hell of a lot of other people's money to finish with.

BREAKFAST found me the money to start with, in the form of Magda. She looked surprisingly fresh and level of eye. The main cabin had magically become a dining room—musical still, the Dixieland players pleased as Punch with a captive audience. Zole stoked his boiler faster than me, almost.

"Lovejoy." Magda passed me a bulky serviette. "Don't unwrap it here."

"How much d'you get, Magda?" Zole demanded through a mouthful. "These dudes're good for plenty—"

Money. Magda had earned money. During the long exquisite night while I'd thought mystical thoughts, Magda had been . . . I cleared my throat.

"What's this, love?"

"We need money. We got none. I got some."

"He's but dumb." Zole fed Sherman a load of ham.

My headaches always try to tell me something. I'm too slow to realize things until afterward. I'd stopped eating, which, in a woman's presence, always bodes ill for me.

Magda picked at her food, the way they do. She was deadly serious. "They that serious, they'll know we're headed for Baton Rouge. They'll be waiting, see?"

Jesus. I'd not thought of that. I'd assumed it was just a matter of booking a flight.

"We separate, Magda." At least half of me was thinking. Without Magda, Zole, and a Scotch terrier I'd travel faster, maybe stand more of a chance. This was no time to feel guilt.

"Split up, Lovejoy? You on your own?" I don't think she'd ever smiled a wintry smile in her life. Every smile was warm with understanding. I'm not sure I liked it. "Without us you wouldn't be here."

They make you sound helpless, women. I was narked. "Look, Magda. I'm the one that matters. Let me tell you that a divvy's the rarest frigging creature on earth. Without me . . ." I tried again. "Without me, the whole . . ."

Hang on. Without me *what?*

Without me, the antiques staker would have still been old sticky-fingers, Fat Jim Bethune, the antiques stake maybe a tenth of what I'd made it.

Without me, Moira would have Denzie hooked on her daft Sherlock scam, and Gina and Sophie would both be in the lurch. Which was the opposite of what Gina wanted, if Magda's interpretation was right. Meanwhile, I had Busman as an ally, back in that warren. I'd never needed a library so badly.

"How long've we got, love?"

"The boat docks Baton Rouge at ten."

Difficult. Zole must have seen my face fall. He snickered. "He dumb."

"Call me that once again and I'll—"

"What, Lovejoy?" He noshed on, taunting. "You can't even—"

"We get off before Baton Rouge," Magda said. "Get a car. I've spoken with the man." Magda looked out at the gliding scenery. "There's a smaller place across the other side. He'll set us down in a boat."

Legit. I'd noticed the lifeboats in the davits, of course, had all sorts of mad plans brewing. She'd simply arranged it. I didn't need to ask how.

AN hour later we were on dry land, hired a car, and bowled north on U.S. 61. Magda drove while I slept with the dog sprawled over me. When I awoke, we'd passed Natchez, filled up at Vicksburg, and were coasting due east on U.S. 80 with intermissions for Sherman to have a pee.

"Magda," I said once. "Shall I drive a bit? I mean, you've not had much sleep . . ." I dried. "Where'll we stop?"

"Atlanta, Georgia."

I like the way Americans never say a name but what they make a doublet, Memphis, Tennessee and that.

"We've missed out a lot of places," I observed. "Why?"

"He but *dumb*," from Zole.

"Stop calling him that," Magda said before I could draw breath.

Zole looked across at her, and not a word. He gave me a look over his shoulder. Silence. We pulled into Atlanta on the main route 20, and found a smallish hotel equidistant between the state capitol, Cooks, and Emory University. Zole got me every newspaper and magazine under the sun, and I started reading like my life depended on it. Magda vanished, Zole vanished, the world vanished.

ANTIQUES are the norm of my life. For most others, it's time—like how did the Tokyo Exchange perform overnight, how will Wall Street do today. Yet even that isn't constant. I mean, time varies in America—now isn't now in New York if you're in New Orleans, and its different again in Los Angeles. Fashions are never the same two minutes together. This year's color's not tomorrow's. Governments roll over and die, and new bums come rioting in.

But antiques *are*. I'm told some mountaineers and astronauts share the same feeling: Whatever else happens, there's always Everest or Jupiter. Ambition rules us all, from dreamy starlet to maniac billionaires. But I see life against a backdrop of lovely things—furniture, paintings, jewelry, porcelains, candlesticks to Constables—that older folk made with the love of their hands and left to move us to tears with beauty.

Except everybody isn't the same. Some people would walk past the Mona Lisa without a glance. I used to know a woman like that. Used to sit up all night culling news of investment bonds, yet she had a Turner painting on her wall. Barmy.

My point is that everything valuable has its doppelganger, its fake counterpart. The general rule in antiques is, the pricier the antique, the more serious are the contenders for its throne. This means the fakes are taken more seriously.

And fakes are everywhere.

The list of fakes is enough to stop the average person getting out of bed in the morning. Aircraft parts, cardiac pacemakers, antibiotics for death-dealing infections, even blood transfusion equipment, vie with precious Old Masters, priceless jewels, documents, bonds, share certificates, family records. Everything's up for grabs. Equally so, too. Nothing is sacred to the faker. That children will die from the wrong drug doesn't matter a damn to fraudsters. Nor that helicopters will fall from the sky when some dud bolt shears in flight. Fraud is the achiever's religion.

By four in the morning I'd found the sort of man I was looking for. I put on the television news channel for an update. Quickly I decided I'd move in two stages. I made a transatlantic call to tell a retired Major Lister in Rutland exactly how I wanted him to have his photo taken. I told him exactly what to do and why. I wanted them at the office of a multibillionaire who was in deep trouble. Then I rested, asking to be roused at six o'clock.

Magda returned our car, and I spent three hours in the splendid public library while she and Zole rested. I'd been on tenterhooks in case either had got caught or didn't show up, or simply vanished, having decided they'd had enough of me as a nonpaying passenger. They should have done. I'd have ditched them if I'd had half a chance.

She booked us on different flights from Hartsfield Atlanta, she and Zole to Los Angeles, me to New York. It was an awkward leave-taking. She checked me over as if I were a child going to a new school: spotless shirt, briefcase, suit pressed, shoes glittering, tie sober yet crisp.

"Your hair never stay down, Lovejoy?"

"Not really." I was embarrassed. She'd gone to so much trouble.

"You know to get them to radio ahead?"

"Yes, ta. I've got the list, love."

"If you need something doing Lovejoy, remember you can hire. You're in Big A."

"I'm learning, Magda. And thanks. See you in L.A."

"Take care, honey."

I went red. I'd never been called honey before, not properly.

"And you, love. You too, Zole."

"Here, Lovejoy." He gave me what looked like a pencil case. I waved them through the gate, patting Sherman to show I wasn't scared and he was to guard them until we met up.

Heading for my boarding gate, I opened Zole's present. It was a throwing knife. I dropped the blood-curdling implement into the litter bin. The flight was on time in New York.

22

"I've heard of America." Major Lister had ogled the skyline all the way from the airport. He made the announcement as a concession to fashion. "Truly amazing."

We'd rehearsed his part until we were both word perfect. He had the photograph, silver framed, and a parchment citation, sealing wax, everything. I was really proud of the craftsman I'd sent him to.

"Vertigo ask much?" I worried uneasily.

"He says you still owe him. Some lady in Morton."

"I'll pay." She'd been keen to have a bonfire of all her possessions, in order to sell them. I'd fixed it for her, with a little bit of help from my friends. We call it a tinder job in the trade. (A tragic house fire loses you all your precious antiques, only it's fakes that get crisped, see? You sell the untraceable genuine antiques at some far-flung auction, and get the insurance as a bonus.) I'd taken three months to fake all her stuff. I'd worked like a dog. Vertigo had done three marvelous portraits.

"This gentleman expecting us, Lovejoy?"

"Aye. It may only be his assistants, but it'll be as useful."

Maynooth Tower was the great Thomas Maynooth's gift to the great city of New York—his phraseology, nobody else's. We gave John Lister's name, and were ushered up to the upper triplex where Maynooth's think tank never closed. Its beacons shone ceaselessly to inform the universe of Tommy Dynamite's unflagging zeal in quest of the American dream.

A smoothie of each sex welcomed us, with clones. Opulence ruled. I felt positively shoddy, but then I always do. John Lister's bearing carried him through, spick and span.

"This is Major Lister," I explained. "Rutland Orphanage. I called you earlier."

The lead lass shook hands with aggression-filled doubt. The others stood aloof with threat.

"We have no record of the appointment, Major Lister. Nor of a c ntribution f romM r Maynooth to your orphanage. Also, Mr. Maynooth's real busy right now and—"

"The citation, Wilkins," John commanded. I leapt to obey. "Miss, will you let me conduct the ceremony here? We fully comprehend. Mr. Maynooth's time is of the essence."

"Ceremony?" The clones swapped glances.

"Of thanks. I have a citation, and a small acknowledgment of Mr. Maynooth's generosity. It saved our orphanage."

Lister cleared his throat, conducted the head lady from behind her desk, produced the scroll.

"In the name of the Rutland Orphanage, of Maltan Lees, in testimony of the generosity of—"

"Hold it, please."

An anxious gent disappeared from the anteroom. We waited. It took two minutes, and we were ushered into an office as broad as the bridge of an ocean liner. The whole of Manhattan was spread out before us. We actually looked down on skyscrapers. My head swam.

The man at the desk rose. Fortyish, smooth and easy, with eyes that had once known humor, but no longer. Prematurely bald, with three rattails of hair slicked across his pate. It looked dafter than baldness, but even rich people are funny about hair. He'd run to fat, given half a calorie too many. He shook our hands. I deferred to Major Lister. We explained our purpose, Maynooth nodding and listening. Then he lit a cigar, took three rapid puffs, extinguished it with regret into an ashtray piled with enormous remnants of aborted smokes. He waved his aides out, and we were alone.

"Wilkins?" he asked me directly. I was standing near Lister's chair.

"That's me."

He said no more for quite a few minutes. During them he extracted and read the citation. Then he examined the photograph, carefully perusing their dates on the reverse.

"What do you get out of this, Wilkins?" he asked eventually. His calm was a delight to see. I glowed with admiration of America and all her great businessmen. Hardly a single clue, and he susses out every nuance of the baffling problem instantly. Great.

"A contribution from others, Mr. Maynooth."

"You putting me on?"

"No, Mr. Maynooth."

He swung his chair, practicing, perhaps never having done it before. He wasn't in show business, this genius.

"Nothing would be easier for me than to call in the photographers, pics with you presenting the scroll. The publicity would do me a barrel of favors, I can tell you." He eyed me.

He laughed mirthlessly, quoted, "Maynooth Marches into Bimbo Limbo." That, and his wealth, was why I'd chosen him. A pious ex-seminarian suddenly exposed as a fund funster with a secret taste for sexual acrobatics was too good to miss.

He stayed my comment with a hand, did his nonsmoking smoke trick, gazed longingly into the ashtray.

"Bastard doctors," he said. I agreed, nodding with conviction. "I'm subjected to the most scurrilous attacks, lawsuits, abuse, since my, uh, personal philosophy became public. It's a feeding frenzy. Every moral vigilante group on the east coast's after my blood."

He tapped with a pencil, snapped it, dropped it anywhere. He hadn't looked away from me.

"Major Lister's orphanage is legit, right?"

"Correct, Mr. Maynooth."

"How much did I donate?" he asked wrily.

I went red. I'd forgotten what I'd said for Vertigo to put on the scroll. "I think twenty thousand."

"The columns'll claim it's a put-up, by my own publicity people."

"They'd be proved wrong by hard independent evidence, Mr. Maynooth. Major Lister's certificate acknowledges receipt of your generosity a year ago, before any opprobrium."

He mused, "This out of the goodness of your heart?"

His mind was too slick to flannel. "Not really. If it doesn't work, I'll try something else. Somewhere else. Don't worry. We'll reveal nothing. Nobody knows we're here. Major Lister here'll vouch for me."

Silence for a moment, while he grew angry with something out of view. "You know what those bastards are doing right now? Running a 'cking *cartoon* about me! 'Brother Tommy's Toon Time.' I'm suing, but . . ."

"My mate's come a long way," I said to soothe him. I didn't want him mad. "Might as well call in your tame city clickers and get your cent's worth, eh?"

"Twenty thousand's nothing. You can have it anyway. The morality brigades are opposing my casino, threatening to close me even in N'York!"

"Could they?" I was interested.

"They can damn well slow me down. This is America."

"They'll not close you, Mr. Maynooth. Not after what happens next."

I waited while he reran the words. "This is the bite, huh? The bite that costs nothing?"

Honestly, I felt quite sorry for him. Nobody likes to have their genital activities plastered over every tabloid and screen, to the howls of enemies.

"You need to prove anew that you can organize your businesses and casinos in a law-abiding manner." I felt eloquence effervescing with the glee of fraud. "Difficult when the moral battalions beseige Maynooth Tower. It has to be major evidence."

"Like what? I've got every security agency in the country on my payrolls and it's not enough."

"Parts of New York are a mess, Mr. Maynooth. Your Taxi and Limo Commission alone tries four hundred taxi-driver offenders a day for assault and abuse of passengers. The killings, muggings, the crime—"

"Gimme a break. It's not my fault."

"Supposing you halted all crime in one area for a whole twenty-four hours? Call it a Law Day."

"That's dumb talk, Wilkins. We got police. They try and fail." He was the sort of bloke I suppose women fall for, in the prime of life but in a cleft stick. His affair had suffered more mud-slinging than Richard III. He gave in when I said nothing. "You know they were tipping me as a presidential nominee?"

"There'll be one fewer of those in a couple of days, Mr. Maynooth. Work out what you'll say to the cameras. You'll be shyly conceding that you're a secret benefactor, and an anticrime potentate. You'll contribute this gesture as good will to this great city of yours. Clear your path almost immediately."

He was still sour about other nominees. "They got that punch-drunk Texan as sellingest contender. And that shifty bastard Brandau. I could lose them any day of the week."

"I'll lose you Brandau this week, Mr. Maynooth."

We talked seriously then, with John Lister's head turning like a Wimbledon regular's between us. It took a little over an hour. Mr. Maynooth gave the orphanage a donation way above his previous year's mythical donation, following which his minions were summoned to round up the media photographers. I quietly faded. They could do without my picture.

As John left for the airport, dollars winging ahead of him to Rutland, I went to see Busman, to ask a favor and start negotiating a price for Thomas Maynooth's new invention, a piece of peace in Manhattan. I needed success now.

THERE'S that theory of success, isn't there—confidence makes you win. Lose heart, and you've lost no matter how big your army.

I took a taxi over to Eighth Avenue, and walked into the terminal. It was getting on for six, the day drawing in. Maybe it was tiredness, maybe from being away from antiques so long, but I was so really down. At the terminal I had a quick coffee while I wondered what I'd do if I failed with Busman. Should I try to see Sophie? But maybe she too thought I was dead. Or Gina? Too risky—I'd have a fatal visit from Tye. Rose? At least she was innocent of all the mayhem. I'd maybe look her up when it was over.

Nothing for it. I was uneasy, spinning out the coffee because it felt safer. I felt unshaven, soiled, tired, almost doomed from dispirit. I went into the maelstrom of travelers to seek Busman.

A small cluster of youths marauding on the outskirts of a passenger group seemed the most promising. I went up to them and said Busman had sent for me. They didn't mug me, just directed me into the concrete warren. I plodded down, feeling the loneliest figure on earth.

The atmosphere had gone, somehow. I walked the tunnels, asking loudly at every molestation for Busman, telling I was sent for, that Busman wanted to see me. Whatever the previous impression I'd had of this subterranean dump, now it was sickly, sordid. The mystique had gone. What had seemed a strange pervading smell had become a fetid stench. The walls were smeared offal slabs. The perverts and prostitutes mauling in corners, the junkies rubbing blood-stained sleeves, the muggers brawling over thieved wallets had once seemed exotic derangements. Now they were a mess of degradation. I ploughed on, saying loudly I was to see Busman and Trazz.

A Flash Harry emerged from nowhere, came along with me the last few airless corridors, telling me stories of problems they'd had with police lately. I said sure and yeah.

The big control place was shoddier than I remembered, strewn with waste paper, more crowded, more smoke and screens but now a dungeonlike tomb. Busman was there, hearty and welcoming. Trazz came creaking up aslant, doing a laugh of surprise, tsss-tssss.

"Lovejoy, ain't it? You made it back to the Apple."

"Hello, Trazz." I gave Busman my hand. He took it with more of a practiced lean than he had once before. A politician's grip now, but still friendly. "Wotcher, Busman."

"You been away, Lovejoy."

"Bit of a holiday."

We did some word sparring. He unbent a little more, laughing properly and telling me stories of his activities in the terminal. I eased too, thinking I was just tired, imagining things. Trazz went to check some of the screens' scrutineers.

"Busman. I came with a proposition."

"I thought, Lovejoy." The big man beamed. "I can't agree outright. Gotta warn you."

"I understand. Could you stifle all the crime here, for twenty-four hours?"

He fanned himself showily in astonishment. We were at his desk. No phones, I noticed. Everybody else seemed to have several. I gave him time to work it out. Slowly he shook his head, regret uppermost.

"You askin' me to throw a fortune, Lovejoy? Ma money

comes in steady, fourteen scams. In N'York scams is business. Halt business, ma people suffer."

"Suffer how, Busman?"

"No money, that's how. They pay breath, make deals, pay the vig on loans, up cuts, things you never even heard of, Lovejoy. They gotta work, or I displeased." He chuckled.

"If they didn't work a day, Busman. Got free paid instead?"

He whistled, thinking fast. "You know how much that'd cost, boah?"

He'd never called me boy before. It had an alien sound. "The protection for a block of real estate's a tenth of the annual rent. A ten million dollar rental, they pay some syndicate a million?"

"Right." He swung in his chair, finally put his feet up, like great boats. "I get five cents on every took dollar, Lovejoy."

"That, then. Plus what your others'd need?"

"This real ? he asked, figuring as he went.

"Depends on the price, Busman. The man might well be the big P before long."

He called Trazz. They talked out of earshot, made phone calls, got a girl to work a computer for a while. Then he returned, giving me his new and disturbing beam.

"You got it, Lovejoy. Midnight to midnight, in three hours."

"From now?" That shook me. I hadn't realized it would happen so fast. I took the paper on which the girl had written the sum, seven figures. I gulped, nodded, said the deal was probably on.

We shook. I was to phone a number in a few minutes. I was given the same Flash Harry guide, and left.

But something then worried me more than it should. As I turned, I saw in a big-screen console angled near Busman's desk a strange reflection move. It was Busman's head, swiveling as he looked at Trazz. He gave a shrug and a nod combined, turning his palm upward, thumb out. An odd gesture, it seemed out of character, macabre. Yet when I turned to wave good-bye from the door, Busman was beaming in my general direction and gave me a wave. Trazz, shuffling and angled, grinned after me with the grin of a cadaver. I didn't shiver. I walked away from my friends, just managing not to break into a run.

The escort got me safely to the street. I phoned Mr. Maynooth, said it was on, how and where the money should be paid, and rang off.

Then I really did scarper, like a bat from hell, into the New York night, not really knowing who was after me but traveling at speed in case I found out.

23

THERE'S a vital difference between being a tourist and being in your own town. That difference is a bed, nothing more, nothing less.

A tourist has nothing, because even the bed, loo, water tap, is rented by the minute. Laying your head down is at somebody else's behest. But if it's your own pad, you can tell everybody else to clear off and shut the door on the blighters. The difference is tourist tiredness, that state of utter weariness where you get taken for every penny, when you buy stupid things, when con merchants come out to play on the bones of the gullible. Exhaustion's a grim mutagen. Even the smartest tourist eventually begins trading dollars for dimes, hard currency for zlotniks.

This was me. I was worn out. Not physically, but my instincts were a dud battery.

Friends come in useful about now. But Magda and Zole I'd sent into exile. Bill had died on these very streets. Busman had agreed to a deal, which was likely to start working soon, but somehow I felt under threat. I realized what was bothering me. That gesture I'd seen reflected was the one he'd used before, when telling Trazz to hit Charlie Sarpi's transgressors. I know finality when I see it. It's different from dismissal. That there'd been an element of regret in Busman's manner didn't allay my fear.

I was in theaterland, none yet loosed, so the nosh bars and stalls weren't crowded. I found a darker place to sit and stoke up with grub. I've been hunted before, and know that food and loos lend alacrity. I kept an eye out for enemies, and thought.

Fredo's bar might still be open, but so what? Josephus, Della, Fredo, Lil, Jonie—what was I to them? A fly-by-night, that's what. And I'd flown. That too is the American way, zoom off to a better take. I didn't know where any of them lived, either.

Sophie Brandau, the one I was really drawn to? Her husband wasn't likely to welcome me. Melodie Van Cordlant might, but I suspected she was too embroiled among the gamesters for me to fling myself on her mercy. Fatty Jim Bethune? I'd done him a favor, but he wouldn't regard it as such. Orly hated me. Nicko? Jennie? Two unknowables. Was there refuge among the lower orders, like Blanche? Not while she and Tye were shacking up, there wasn't. Rose and the Hawkins family? But Moira was Denzie Brandau's busty lusty. Rose ran silent and deep. Maybe she hated me too. Chanel was out.

Which left Prudence, erstwhile lover, Miss Reliability. And I knew her address.

The bus took me some of the way. I walked from Lexington, turning left at the little supermarket into East Thirty-sixth, and found Prudence's impossible surname on the Apt 6B voice box. I had the sense to disguise my voice, trying for nasality and a Central Europe accent. The squeak answered with Prudence's inflexion.

"Passel serviss foor, uh . . ."

"Be right down," she said, careful girl.

I flitted down the slope as far as the Third Avenue corner, and stood hunched. I could see into the well-lit porch. Tye Dee came to the glass vestibule, cautious and slow, looking obliquely, then did a rapid step to stare uphill. The stress was unmistakable. I saw his head rotate, a deliberate scan of the tall terraced houses opposite. I didn't move. A displaced shadow points better than a flashlight. Tye's bulk withdrew. I waited, leaning on the corner, and was right. A full minute later, his head came slowly into view, did its pan, then vanished. And so did I.

SOKOLOWSKY was in the phone book. I had the sense not to bother, instead got a taxi to Perry Street, and walked. The street was more like a street than any I'd yet seen, every house accessible, no transparent double doors manned by vigilantes, local cafes and nosh bars on the go even at this late hour.

The old man was suspicious when I buzzed. I said who I was, but for old time's sake did the lurk-and-lour trick in case he too had a battalion of goons, then trotted forward and up his steps just before he closed the world out.

"Evening, Mr. Sokolosky. Lovejoy."

The corridor behind him was feebly lit. He nodded, reluctantly admitted me. He arranged complicated chains on the outer door.

"You're hard to remove, Lovejoy. Like my Aunt Esther's lemon tea. Carpets it stained stayed stained." He shuffled ahead, turning out lights as he went. "She's staining Heaven's carpets with her tea. You come when the water's off. Can you explain it? Manhattan an island you can spit across, without water twice a week? You give money. For what? For them not to give you water?"

"Mhhh."

We shuffled inside. An iron expanding gate blocked the stairs.

"You wonder why I've a gate across the stairs? I'll tell you why I've a gate across the stairs."

"No, honest. I wasn't."

"I'll tell you anyhow, because you're wondering. I've a gate across the stairs because they break in. People who know nothing break in. Like weather. Always there." He paused, took my arm at the entrance of a small cluttered room, shoved me as though I was inert until I could move no further and had to flop into a chair. "Technology we got like Africa's got drought. We teach the young miracles my grandfather wouldn't believe. For what? So they can learn nothing. Instead of a job, they break in and steal what they can reach. It's life. Who says life isn't terrible?"

"Thanks for letting me in, Mr. Sokolowsky."

He creaked into a chair. "Visitors who come through the door I can live with. You'll have some tea. It's Russian style, so the glass burns your fingers. You know anything Russian doesn't? It's life."

I nodded thanks, unsure whether it was an act. I knew he was an alert jeweler, who saw much and spoke little.

He poured hot water through tea leaves in a sieve, added a slice of lemon, heaped sugar in, stirred, kept the spoon. I felt my eyelids drooping. It was all so peaceful, so innocent. He raised the kettle to remind me of the scandalous water problems, shrugged in his shawl, gently went, "Scheesh!" and painstakingly set about bringing some thick apple cake thing.

The room had a bar fire. Books lined the walls. A globe and worn rugs lent a medieval air. It could have been any century, except for his electric kettle and the water problems.

"You wondering why I have only one table lamp?"

"No, no."

"You have a question nobody answers, that's suffering. So I'll tell you. I have only one table lamp because electric's had it good too long. I could afford two, three, a dozen. Count the lights in this house. I could have them on every minute every day, but why should I? The electric company's better than the water company? Don't insult my intelligence, Lovejoy. Eat. You've a way to go."

"Thanks, Mr. Sokolowsky." It was good, a sort of thick apple pie. Was it the famous strudel they mention in pictures?

"You got killed in New Orleans, Lovejoy. I for one don't believe it. I didn't then, I don't now." He spoke with a grandfather's comforting gravity, everything debatable whatever the evidence of your senses.

"No. I made it." Somebody had reported I'd got topped. Hirschman wouldn't have, so it must have been the goons themselves. Perhaps they'd have copped it from their bosses if they'd reported a failure? To them I was only a stranger passing through, my killing a job to be paid for and forgotten.

"I thought as much." He was in a rocking chair. He plucked occasionally at his shawl, the habit of age. "You see this street, Lovejoy? The notices, what they write?"

"There were lots of posters—"

"And such posters," he said severely. "You read them? Karate lessons? Chinese contemplation? Gays, lesbians? Macrobiotic cooking? This is civilization they learn Chinese think, can't think American a'ready?"

"Well, I suppose change is everywhere—"

"Run, Lovejoy," the old man said sadly. "Run."

202

I'd lost the thread. "Eh?" He'd just been talking about cooking.

"Run." He reached and closed the book on his small table. "Lovejoy. They'll know you're alive sooner or later. My advice is run, run till you've no need. Then you can stop. It's life. I'm telling you because I know."

"I don't know what I'm running from, Mr. Sokolowsky."

He removed his spectacles, replaced them. "That's something I don't know, Lovejoy."

"Run where?" He knew I was honestly asking.

"My advice isn't good, Lovejoy. So tell me what you've done since you didn't die."

More or less, I told. He poured more tea, holding up his kettle to condemn the water company. I worried it was all some delaying tactic to keep me here while he secretly signaled Tye and Al and Shelt.

"The California game's a legend, Lovejoy," he said at last. "I've lived a lifetime and can tell you legends are nothing but trouble. Like New York's water supply," he interposed bitterly. "Legends you've got to handle like bombs. Cover them up, hide from their effects. The rest of the time, ignore them. But their fame spreads. People want to walk with legends. See the problem?"

"Publicity would prevent the California game."

He sighed as only old Sokolowskys can sigh.

"You're teaching me, Lovejoy? Oy vey. You know so much, you're running from you don't know with nothing in a strange land?"

"I apologize."

"No hard feelings. Manners I remember." I had a sudden image of him elsewhere, fumbling for a fire tiger to poke some nonexistent fire. "The California game's the biggest and most illegal. Take a fraction of every business in America, that's the stake. It's always simple faro—you know faro? Your win, my win. Nothing simpler, the one game nobody can cheat, no skill required."

"Faro?" I'd had visions of some exotic protracted gambling game lasting through nights of smoke and drinks.

"One card's chosen as marker. Everybody sees it. You deal a new deck into two separate piles, one your win pile, one your loser. Whichever pile the marker card falls into, so you've won or lost."

"Is it worth it?" I'd heard of the great poker championship in Las Vegas, with fans saving a lifetime to enter. "You might as well do it by phone."

"It's a secure way of passing power, Lovejoy. Handing over power's where all trouble starts."

"Whoever wins gets the hacks?"

"And decides who can play next time. Nicko won last year." His gaze was the saddest gaze I'd ever seen. "This hurts me to say, Lovejoy. Go from here. I have to phone or they kill me. I'll give you time. But go now."

I thought I'd misheard, reluctantly decided I hadn't. I finished my tea, thanked him.

"You need a loan, Lovejoy, speak this side of the door."

"No, thanks." I paused in the dimly lit corridor. "If you were me, where would you go until daylight?"

"There's all-nighters. Tell jokes until dawn. Here in America there's so much to laugh at." His expression was sobriety itself.

"Thanks, Mr. Sokolowsky. Maybe there'll be a time . . ."

"Maybe, Lovejoy," he agreed, and I was out and on my own.

THAT night I walked, was accosted intermittently by figures and shapes that frightened me. I lurked in all-night diners where I could, ducked out when the going got rough. One seemed to specialize in brawls. Eventually I risked a taxi, got dropped off where comedians talked jokes into a hang of smoke over tables populated by an audience who never laughed. The worst was, those comedians were the best I'd ever heard. It broke what was left of my heart.

Came dawn. I decided I'd risk visiting Mr. Sokolowsky to check the details of the game. I went by subway, riskily joining the first commuters of the day, a lighting at Christopher Street on the Broadway–Seventh Avenue line. I felt like death warmed up, as my gran used to say.

The view from the end of the old jeweler's street kept me moving on. Ambulances and police and fire engines wahwah about New York every hour God sends, so I'd not sussed the significance of a team tearing past as I'd headed that way. But outside a small crowd had gathered, and a covered shape was being gurneyed into an ambulance. I didn't look back.

A suspicious mind like mine might conclude that old Sokolowsky had told his masters that I'd called. They'd possibly hunted, failed to find me, and exacted the ultimate forfeit. My mouth was dry. I was tired, lost.

But antiques beckoned. I went into a huge commercial building that claimed to be the center of world trade. I believed it. I submitted to a professional shave, which started me imagining gangsters bursting in to do a routine assassination, had a headwash (exhausting), manicure (embarrassing), and shoeshine (most embarrassing of all).

The tonsorialist, he said he was, talked ceaselessly, praising Tommy Maynooth's brilliant innovation—a midnight-to-midnight Law Day, which was the talk of the town because it seemed to be working. Grand Central to Tenth, West Thirty-fourth to Forty-eighth, not a single mugging or killing yet, a whole ten hours!

I did my best with the accent. "Who's this Maynooth genius?"

"Here." He showed me a morning paper a foot thick, Maynooth being honored by one Major J. Lister. "Tommy Maynooth maintains this foreign orphanage. He's mad the papers found out."

Good-hearted, and modest with it. "He should get the nomination."

I left, into Manhattan sunshine. I felt prepared. Let me die among antiques.

24

PLAYING antiques auction houses against each other is the ultimate. It's the dealer's fandango. Sooner or later we all skip the light fantastic, to their tune. The Big Two skip fastest of all.

I'd chosen Mangold, of Geneva, London, Paris, Monaco, and everywhere else where money lurks. Nicko's people—I supposed Tye Dee, Al, Shelt—would be watching Sotheby's and Christie's, because the plan I'd formed with Gina included those. Mangold's wasn't big. I'd chosen it from many. The reason was its forthcoming lawsuit against the Big Pigs, as dealers call them.

I simply got a hire car—you can get these in America—and drove there in splendor. Remembering Oscar Wilde's essential for the con trick, I smiled constantly, trying for an aura of wealth. I was Mr. Dulane, of Geneva and London. I was also a lawyer. The head man saw me with all the readiness of the smaller company under threat.

We shook hands, some more amiably than others. I apologized to Simon Mangold for my appearance, claimed jet lag and airports. He said it gets everybody.

"You're the son of the founder?"

"Dad died last year."

His attitude announced that he was going to go down fighting. But that only tells everybody you're going down anyway. It must be something about the antiques that does it, makes bravery ridiculous. We were in a paneled office, nothing old in it except a couple of beautiful Chelsea porcelains that warmed my soul. Here was a man who loved antiques, but whose love was the doom of his firm.

"That's when your troubles started, I hear, Mr. Mangold."

"It's in the papers," he said bluntly.

"The Bigs are nothing if not acquisitive." I went all sympathetic. "I'm here to give you information that may help you."

He digested this. No fool he. "Give?"

"Give. As in donate. If you like the gift, I'll suggest a course of action that will benefit us both. If you don't, you're free to use the information for nothing."

That fazed him. He excavated with a toothpick, examined his palms for buried treasure, stroked the surface of his desk. I watched, marveling. We just ask to be researched by sociologists.

"That clear-cut?" When I nodded, he asked to see my business card. I shook my head, said I was traveling light.

"Would you hang on a second, Mr. Dulane?"

"Not that either," I said, varying my smile to show no hard feelings. "Your secretary can check the International Business Directory; you won't find us. I haven't much time." I was narked and shut him up. Hell, it was my prezzie. People want jam on it.

"I've chosen your auction houses, Mr. Mangold, because my information will damage your competitors, please my principals, and enable you to survive. Ready?"

His mind clicked round. The large auction houses were trying to launch a closed shop, effectively eliminating Mangold's from the antiques market. They'd both tried to buy him out for years. The price for survival was to vanish into either of the Big Two. Mangold's was suing, despairingly trusting the law courts. Which showed how desperate he was.

"What if I ignore your information? Or simply use it free?"

With some people doubt's an industry. It was a long way to L.A., and time was running out.

"Mr. P. Silnow's the missing third man in the Northampton scandal," I said. "The Roman silver hoard was valued at sixty-seven million dollars soon after its discovery. Cheap at the price. Silnow is the chairman of a famous firm in Fifth Avenue and London, et cetera. Currently they're trying to force you into a partnership you don't want."

He pressed a buzzer, spoke into an intercom. "Get Mr. Feldstein and send for Mortimant—"

"Unbuzz your lawyers, Mr. Mangold, or I pretend you've misunderstood and you'll look a prat."

He hesitated, a lifetime's habit, reluctantly concurred.

"And the recorder, please." I held out my hand for the tape. He tried telling me it erased automatically, but I didn't continue until he'd lifted the tape from his drawer and placed it on my palm. I continued with my true story.

"Everybody knows the story. How the English lord bought the fourteen ancient Roman silvers, illegally acquired via Lebanon from Yugoslavia. All in contravention of UNESCO's embargo on smuggled antiques. The British Antique Dealers Association's 1984 Code was also broken. No wonder Christie's was furious!" I smiled pleasantly, all Edward G. Robinson. "They hate to be confused with archrivals, right?"

"Sure." He was weighing me up. "You have evidence?"

"Who needs evidence?" I asked in all seriousness. "Mudslinging auctioneers don't." I held the delay, then said, "Do they, Mr. Mangold?"

"This information, properly used, could seriously damage even a firm as famous as, say, Sotheby's. Or Christie's."

He meant improperly, but I let it pass.

"True. Like that terrible Louvre Affair, eh?"

"The Louvre Affair?"

"Spelled as in Poussin, Mr. Mangold. May I refresh your memory by quoting, 'The Louvre stopped at nothing in its effort to swindle honest people . . .'?"

Once upon a twenty-five years ago, a Nicolas Poussin painting of 1628 was auctioned by a French engineer. The auctioneers paid him a measly 200 quid for it, offhandedly telling the owner it was an el cheapo Bologna school effort. The engineer was sad, of course—but even sadder when the papers blazoned news of the Louvre's fabulous discovery of (surprise surprise!) his selfsame *Olympos* painting! Except it was now rare, authentic, and priceless . . .

As Mangold feverishly tried to keep up, wondering about possible links with his rivals, I listed others for him where the Louvre and other galleries had misbehaved.

"A really malicious person could remember that terrible episode where a certain poor convent sued the Louvre— which had just paid half a million for that famous Lorenzo Lotto masterpiece, the one the Catholic nunnery had just sold for seventy measly dollars, on certain auctioneers' advice." I tutted, doing a lot of head-wagging to show how I deplored all this. "Fair profit's fair profit, Mr. Mangold. But that's too many percents for me. And I'll bet the papers'll think the same, if you happen to refresh their memories."

He licked his lips. I'd got him, on his own lifeline.

"There are links between famous auction houses and auctioneers who arrange first sales, Mr. Mangold. The pattern's there. It's up to you to bring them to the public's attention. Viciously, savagely. The public understands ruthless greed, but likes to deplore it in others." I heaved a sigh, in memory of poor old Sokolowsky. "I just can't help feeling sad over that forthcoming announcement of lawsuits that will be brought against Sotheby's of New York." I stood, smiled. "Well, thanks for your time, Mr. Mangold—"

He quivered like a greyhound hearing the hare. "Lawsuits?"

I sat. "Didn't you hear? Well, I hate to be the bearer of really bad news, but it's just that the antiques dealers in the U.K. are fed up. So're the ones on the Continent. Tomorrow there'll be a media salvo about chandelier bidding, from the Antique Internationalers, in London."

He thought that one through. "But any A.I. member who made that protest would . . ."

"Be driven into the ground by the biggies? Course it would. But it'll happen, sure as God sends Sunday. Unless you don't want it to."

"You wouldn't link Mangold's with an outrageous—"

"Never. We've got somebody else, who'll do it for a fee. It's all fixed."

He subsided, said slowly, "That will inflict irrevocable damage on them. Immediate."

Not so outrageous after all. We both thought over the history of recent doubts. They centered on what the trade now calls "Bond borrowing," and please note the capital.

It came to light when Van Gogh's painting *Irises* went up at a Sotheby's auction. (Incidentally, why is it always poor old Vincent who catches the bad glad? It's high time some other poor sod had to go.) A mere $53.9 million won the hammer, as we say, for brave Aussie Mr. Bond. Everybody was thrilled, especially auctioneers everywhere. And why?

Because prices were through the roof, and so was their commission. The trouble was, half the gelt was borrowed. Guess who from? Why, the auctioneers themselves!

The world outcry was followed by instant explanations, that the world's top auction houses hadn't deliberately intended to drive up the prices of art works by a secret loan, that Sotheby's policies would change, et yawnsome cetera. Worst of all, the art market went gaga.

"Art dealers began to ask if the Museum of Modern Art would have paid so high for the next Van Gogh, if Picasso's self-portrait would have touched forty-eight million, all that jazz."

"Names?"

I passed him a list of the international dealers who'd complained to the press.

"You'll combine your diatribe with all sorts of veiled accusations of complicity, naturally. You'll ask why Thyssen paid over fourteen million sterling, at Sotheby's, for a painting he already half owned. You'll scream outrage when the A.I. hullabaloo is raised tomorrow about big auctioneers allowing the new relay bid—you know the old trick: Joe nods to Betty who winks at Fred who scratches his nose so Jean waves to the auctioneer. You'll holler, Is this fair? and all that. You know how to yell, I'm sure."

"Mangold's has been the subject of abuse from—"

"Sure, sure." My tone was cold. Asking for sympathy, and him an auctioneer. "False high estimates: 'anticipatory valuation' to the trade. That too will be complained about. New legislation will be demanded from the Europeans, and Parliament. Quote Turner's *Seascape-Folkestone*— the whole trade knows about that. And cite the different values given to different museums for the same painting." I pretended to think a while, though I'd already decided. "That Cuyp painting simply couldn't be officially worth only three million sterling in Wales, and twice that in Edinburgh, right? Here's a list of suggestions for your press handout, with details and dates. Some you'll already find in your clippings file. Others are my own . . . imaginings." I smiled. Even he cracked his face a little. "I'm hoping you'll dish the obvious dirt, Mr.

Mangold, like telling the world that all those awful hundred-thousand-dollar Utrillos are fakes."

"Three full pages, Mr. Dulane?" He read rapidly, looking for his own name, relaxed when it wasn't there.

"I was pushed for time."

He did smile then. "Who'll be making the protest to the Antique Internationalers?"

I sighed at the memory of what it would be costing me when young Masterson, Eton and Oxford, suaved to his feet and delivered the speech in Brussels. I'd be paying for the rest of my life, if I lived that long.

"An interested party, Mr. Mangold," I said mournfully. "Here's your bill. Just get me secretly to Los Angeles, at maximum speed. Add pocket money, and we're quits."

He folded the lists away. "When your man has raised Cain in Brussels, Parliament, the European Commission—"

"Now, or I cancel." I stood, the better to run.

He moved even faster, clambering his desk to wring my hands. "It's a deal," he said.

"Plus the phone call." He unwrung, as if hearing me demand that secret four percent discount on commission that they allow antique dealers, as a bribe. I explained. "The call I'll make very soon, from L.A., asking you to agree that you'll donate to me one hundredth of the joint Sotheby-Christie Impressionist sale prices."

He gaped. "That'll be a fortune! Mangold's could never afford—"

"Mangold's will," I promised. "Because the Rail Pensions Fund can't risk scandal. Play your cards, and they'll switch the sale to you. Surely you can afford one percent of their gelt?"

Tears filled his eyes. "If that comes to pass, Mr. Dulane," he said huskily, "I'll give you two percent."

His mind was orgasming at the thought of failures and suicides among his rivals. I was pleased. I'd hate to see auctioneers mellow. Keep progress at bay, I always say. You know where you are with sin.

25

MANGOLD did an efficient job. No ostentation, just sent his secretary to conduct me along miles of tortuous corridors. We came out through a shopping mall where a hired saloon waited. A private plane from a small airport beyond Little Ferry, and I had time to think and hope and be relieved the fliers weren't Joker and Smith.

The loveliness whizzing below brought tears to my eyes, seeing it all being wasted because I was zooming to fabulous California and probable demise. I was heartbroken with pity for Lovejoy Antiques Inc.'s stupidity. So I wallowed and planned, and finally decided I'd better be ready for anything, or else.

Which brings me to a little place called Los Angeles.

ONE thing you have to admit about East Anglia is that its villages have centers. Each town has a middle. Every city has an area that definitely is bullseye. Like an idiot, I'd assumed Los Angeles would be similar. I'd actually told Magda and Zole to meet at the railway station, six o'clock every night until I showed up. I'd stay at some hotel "near the town center." I remembered using the phrase.

Lovejoy, he dumb. Brains of a yeti.

For Los Angeles is a tangle of cities, towns, areas, coasts, harbors, suburbs, all by the veritable dozen. I stared down disbelievingly as the massive spread grew beneath us. Strings of motorways wound through cities strewn about the globe's surface, motorcars streaming along umpteen-lane highways that melded, parted, and emptied themselves into the misty distance where still more cities sprawled. I'd seen rivers of traffic before, never floods.

Just as I thought I'd identified L.A.'s town center, it was supplanted by another. And another.

Shakily I asked the air lass what this place was. She looked brightly out of the window.

"That's old L.A.," she said fondly. "Great, huh? We'll be landing at one of the airports shortly."

Get it? *One* of the airports? I shrank, didn't want to disembark. I was already lost. I'd thought Los Angeles was a seaside resort. Instead it was a universe.

We landed at a smaller airport near Glendale. It was as big as most countries, and took six minutes to slot me into a car. I laid low, occasionally peering out. The world was rushing, whizzing to God knows where. The driver was a Turk, who talked of baseball for the twenty or so miles.

"YOU look like I feel, Lovejoy."

I'd never been so glad to see anyone as Magda and Zole. He'd acquired a skateboard, blew gum between cryptic aphorisms, still swiveled like a periscope poking up from Nautilus. Magda looked what my old gran called Sunday shod, meaning respectable on the surface but don't take too much on trust. Her clothes were bright, her face rested into a youth.

"This place scares me, love."

We were in a self-service near the station. She had found it, said it was safe.

"I've already seen two people mugged. In broad daylight." I waited for this to take effect. Magda shrugged, Zole blew a bubble. "And some of the . . . girls seem as young as, well, Zole here. One solicited me on a tricycle."

"I'll take you round Hollywood and Vine. Some of them blocks beyond Sunset Boulevard you wouldn't believe, Lovejoy. Two of your friends get themselves happy there."

"They did?" I asked uneasily.

"Al and Shelt. That Kelly Palumba and her sheet."

"She dumb. Her man pays dumb dollar."

"Epsilon," Magda translated. "Buys for her. She's stoned."

"Magda." It was hard to start, even after a few goes. "Look, love. I'm really grateful . . ."

I hate saying things like this, especially to a bird, because they're inclined to feel they have a right to you more than they have a right, if you follow. But when Magda and Zole had come into the station I'd almost fainted with relief. And when she told me she'd done as I'd asked I almost filled up.

"I found Revere Mount, Lovejoy. It's Malibu."

The self-service place was enormous. Two women in studs and black leather were jeering by the till, men round them whooping and cheering at sallies. A weathered, frayed old man was slumped at a table, head on his hands. Outside it was almost dark, traffic glaring and snorting for headway. Nobody seemed to be watching us.

"For the game?"

"Uh huh. They staying every which way, Pasadena, Long Beach, Santa Monica."

But Al and Shelt were Tye Dee's two special goons. And Magda'd mentioned them practically with her hello. Which raised the small question of how she'd done so well.

"Where are the Aquilinas?"

"Beverly Hills. They got a house, a battalion of friends." She told me an address in impossible numbers.

"You've done marvelously, love."

Zole happened to be listening, picked up a vibe of doubt. He'd been strolling among tables, picking leftovers from plates. Habit of a lifetime, I supposed. There's an old Polish millionaire I know in London does the same. Collects priceless porcelain, but once was a POW. "Cost us plenny in calls, Lovejoy," he put in. "And she done favors for free with a agency man, Boyle Heights."

"Zole," Magda said in her special tone. He shrugged, resumed his scavenge. "It's known, Lovejoy. Society gossip on TV, convention talk."

"They know to arrange what's said, love. They own everything I've ever heard of. Can you give me names?"

"It was easy at first. That Palumba broad'd been on the movies once, turkeyed out. She was in the papers. Finding the hotel, getting to know waiters, the lounge hustlers, pretending I was looking for a sister." She half smiled, grimaced slightly to warn there was no way to postpone bad news. "It's tomorrow, Lovejoy. Big place. Movie people use it, studios, syndicates, you name it. Night, ten o'clock."

"Where are you staying?" I'm pathetic sometimes. Had I never been in a strange city before? I sounded like a kid trying to join her team, let me play or I'll tell.

She hesitated. "I got to pay this guy, Lovejoy. Another time?"

"Fine," I said, my best smile on. "Look after Zole, eh?"

She shrugged. "It's what I do, Lovejoy."

We agreed to part without thinking further, the station to be our meeting place, day after next. After that would be straw guessing. I tried to find something warm and grateful to say. She seemed to wait in expectation, finally collected Zole. We parted. She didn't wish me luck. And with Zole on hand she'd not need any.

I remember her squaring up to walk to the taxi rank. Loveliness is sometimes in the eye of the beholder. Sometimes it's just better than beauty, and that's that.

I REGISTERED at a downtown hotel that had an armed night guard on the door. I gave complicated instructions about being roused the instant my missing luggage arrived from some mythical but erratic airline, and slept fitfully dreaming of gamblers with knives for fingers.

The sun dawned me on streets gaunt without people. The area seemed oddly vacant, a studio oddly empty. Windows seemed shuttered from perversity rather than need. The few shops that opened were scored with graffiti, abusive and delirious. L.A. clocked early didn't look a going concern. It looked raddled, sickening for something, yet feverishly determined to conquer. The walls of buildings were pockmarked, as if firing squads had lately been about their business. Vacant ground wore skeletalized cars lying lopsided with one cheek into the ground. I walked enough to be pervaded by the sense of Los Angeles, which is action deflected beyond control, omnipotence revealing its secret neuroses. Then I went and earned the reproaches of the desk clerk for having actually walked instead of traveling by gunship, and booked out, ostensibly for the airport.

Working out my gelt, I had enough left to put me in some sort of social order, and to get me to Revere Mount Mansions. Time was already spinning L.A. faster than I wanted. Revere Mount was a play on words—wasn't he the patriot who'd ridden to warn of an invasion? More importantly, he was a fabulous silversmith whose work I've always admired. It seemed an omen. Then.

26

REVERE Mount Mansions deserved the plural. I was glad of two things: I didn't have to storm it, and that I'd decided to suss it out before night fell.

It stood back from a cliff edge that overlooked a multilane highway flooded with headlights. A road nosed the Malibu hillside as if trying to find contour lines among the bushes. Why was the land so dry? Colored lights arched over the gateway proclaiming that Revere Mount Mansions was Heaven's Gift To California. Close to, it looked as if the paint wasn't yet dry.

Not that I got close to straightaway. Nor did I lurk in the undergrowth. I'd stayed away seeking middle-class mediocrity until the day began to wane, then prepared for action. I spent hours being toured round Movie City. I ogled studio sets, saw where the great directors had shot this movie and fought that mogul. On a normal day I'd have been thrilled. Now, I just kept asking the time and judging how long it would take to reach Malibu. People kept giving me brochures or begging. I've never seen so many people asking to have their clipboard signed in support of some cause or other.

We passed it on a coach trip. In mid-afternoon sunshine it was brilliant, a Samarkand of a place, El Dorado, with golden towers Camelot would have been proud of. Peacocks fanned their tails among the laid gardens. Small pagodas and summerhouses dotted the walks among lakes and waterfalls. The coach guide was in raptures.

"The gardens alone took a quarter of a million tons of stone, fifteen thousand plants and bushes . . ."

People photographed, darted from one side of the coach to the other, called for the driver to pause because the sunshine was catching somebody's lens wrong. The guide even said that it was currently a focus of a huge all-American convention of charity associations, and L.A. was especially honored yet once more folks to be the site of might . . .

I honored Revere Mount by seeing how far it stood from the road—half a mile. The cliff seemed pretty sheer. When finally the hillside ran out of patience and recovered its slope, the drop was sudden until barricades landscaped some sort of surety for the traffic on the teeming highway below. If I'd been the roadbuilder I'd have gone round, only the opposite side ended in close wooded screes. Distantly, glints of water showed. The hills astonished me by their height and dusty brown dryness.

Men stood by the gateway. They wore livery, but garments do not hinder truth. Smart, vigilant in constant communication. There were seven, taking turns to leap forward to direct drivers along one of the three roads through the ornamental gardens. The main building had more verandahs than a castle, more windows than any Vatican. Outlying smaller places were presumably the kind of separate motel buildings America has perfected. Then the driver called he was behind schedule and we drove on across bridges beneath which no rivers ran, to lose the view among dense cloying trees.

I'D HAD the shakes ever since reaching America. I couldn't remember a single hour when I'd been quiet, at peace. I'd always had to be running out of the firing line, working out where I was, what the hell I ought to be doing to survive. Maybe that's what folk meant by the American Way? It certainly was Magda's view of her world, and Zole's opinion of his. Things here weren't immutable. What today forbids, tomorrow might make compulsory. Today might hang you, and tomorrow sanctify. But even with dusk rushing the hills into night I couldn't find it in my heart to scold America. Why? Because love is the same, after all. The lady sloshes you with her handbag one day, and the next day pulls you, moaning.

Eight o'clock, I went over my words, trying to spot unexpecteds.

Nine, I phoned the reception at Revere Mount. I tried to sound as if I were delayed by impossible inefficiency somewhere, bullied over the girl's routines, said to get urgent word to the gate supervisor, make sure I wasn't delayed because I'd barely make it before the game. Then I rang off, sweating. It could have been the sticky heat that drenched my palms, but wasn't.

Sometimes—in love, war, gambling, any sort of risk—time is paramount, no pun intended.

Half past nine I was out on the pavement watching taxis. The third driver looked as if he knew the area and could get a move on. I flopped into the cab and told him Revere Mount Mansions fast.

He drove like a maniac. I would have been frightened to death, but was there already.

I'D WORKED out my phraseology, tersely gave it the gatemen.

"Point me to the game. I'm late, a'ready."

Two barred the way. A third approached, stooped to examine all occupants. I noticed the lights were clever. However a car was positioned, light entered from every direction.

"Evening, sir. I think we have a full complement."

"You think wrong."

A list was consulted. "Have you a number, sir?"

"Alhambra one-four-zero, for Christ's sake. Lovejoy the name. Nicko called it yet? Sheet, I oughta seen Gina and Tye Dee before now—"

"It's here." The man glanced at the others, flicked open a thick wallet of photographs, checked one against me, nodded, spoke to the cabbie. "Up the main drag, left, big square annex on your right. Don't deviate."

"Got it."

Two minutes, and I was trying to look casual at the entrance of Revere, having my photograph checked and re-checked, moving into affluent aromas and ascending a staircase out of *Elizabeth and Essex* with showbiz music accompanying the hubbub of talk.

My scheme included washing hands, smiling at the staff and giving them joke time. Easy to make a show of haste without actually hurrying.

It was one minute to ten when I reached the main gathering. I knew I was going to be the only one not wearing a dinner jacket, and I was right.

I waited, admiring the chandeliers—modern gunge—and the wealthy woe school of dross decor, the sort to impress. There must have been some three hundred people glitzing away, every shade and shape God made. I stood on the landing, ducking and weaving at one side of the entrance as if anxiously looking for my party.

"Lost, sir?" a flunky asked.

I grinned. "The game's my home, man. Alhambra one-four-zero my number."

"Alhambra? They're all up front, by the dais. You just made it. Here come the announcements now."

Nicko was tapping the microphone, Gina—not Jennie—gorgeous beside him. I kept still beside the entrance. There were plenty of people, milling, snatching last-minute drinks, plying others. Excitement was in the air. A band was fading with slight rattles, clashes, trying for their enemy, silence.

"Ladies and gentlemen—friends all!" Nicko's voice had octaved echoes and an afterwhine. "Welcome to the nineteenth California game!"

People whooped, applauded, crowded closer round the dais. I could see Jennie, Melodie, Epsilon, Monsignor O'Cody, the commissioner, and Denzie. No Moira, no Kelly Palumba. Charlie Sarpi was there, but less good-humored than the rest. And astonishing me by his presence, tanking on booze and twice his natural hue of grue, Fatty Jim Bethune of antiques fame.

"We are gathered here—" Nicko paused for the shrill screams of laughter as Monsignor O'Cody waved to acknowledge the applause—"as guests of the Californians, for which our eternal gratitude."

Applause, whistles, yells, jokes. Nicko stayed the congratulatory riot. He was a consummate crowd-handler. Should have been a politician, I thought wryly. My heart was thumping, blood shushing my ears.

"As last year's winners, we poverty-stricken New Yorkers will—"

Pandemonium, ladies stamping the floor and screeching, their men howling affable insults.

"—Will lead. All sectors have already nominated their players. Observers in the galleries as usual, please. Ladies and gentlemen—the game's on! Go go go!"

The elegant throng crushed the far exits. Two, beside the central dais. I hung back, finding my mark. They were an intense, less than jubilant, cluster of half a dozen who didn't scrum forward with quite the same rapture. I strolled up, grabbed a wine from a side counter, but only after checking that the half-dozen wall bars were free of Manhattan familiars.

"Don't you Californians praise your traffic to me ever again!" I exclaimed, grinning at a woman shut into a mass of emerald slab silk. Her jewelry was dazzling, but not antique.

"Had difficulty?" She wasn't into the group discussion. I'd seen her eagerness to roam. Women love a party because excitement rules within bounds that they can change any time. "We're Florida, incidentally. Jane Elsmeer."

"Raising the ante?" I chuckled, took a swig. "Tell your friends to throw in the towel. Lovejoy's the name."

"Hi. You're confident." Her eyelashes batted. I nearly had to lean into the wind they created.

"You're exquisite, but I fear for your bank balance." We were all drifting down the room as the crush lessened and the crowd thinned through the exits. "We got over twenty times our last year's gelt." I smiled into her astonishment. "That do you?" I took her arm. "Jane, honey. I'll see you don't starve, okay? Come to Lovejoy. Nicko's got my number." I chuckled, squeezed her hand.

"Twenty?" She glanced over to her people, still debating. "Is that possible?"

I said soulfully, "With eyes like yours, Jane, I'll let you hear more any time."

Her hand held me back. "No stake's more than double, is it? I didn't really listen to the announcement, but—"

"Difference between two and twenty's zero, right?" I laughed. Ushers were begging us tardies to move into the game arena. "Twenty, God's truth. See you in there, Jane."

I strolled down the emptying salon, nodding and saying hi to barmen and generally being a pest. I hoped I'd done enough.

In a mirror I saw Jane Elsmeer talking to her Florida

syndicate. They were shooting looks my way. I did my act with another glass, and was almost last in. But not quite last. One of the Floridans hung back even more, and made sure he was standing immediately behind me at the last second, as the doors closed on the gloaming of the game.

AN AQUARIUM. Not really, but like that.

We, the watching crowd, were rimmed round a glass-enclosed balcony. Down below, a boarded arena with one great central table covered in green baize. It was oddly reminiscent of a snooker championship, except with the audience arranged in sloping crystal. We were in semidarkness. The arena below was brilliantly lit.

Our gallery ran the full circumference. It was difficult to see the faces of the crowd, though I searched among them for the Manhattan lot. Glad of the gloom, I edged along, casual pace by casual pace. Happier still to see the avid concentration of everybody staring down into the game arena.

It was cleverer than I realized at first. The table's wide surface could be seen from every position in the gallery.

Below, Nicko was chatting to three blokes, all as important, all as cool. Power emanated from their stances. One was so fat he should have been a joke. Except for his stillness you'd have passed him over without a thought. But creatures aren't stationary. Nature says move, a sign of life. So we fidget, shuffle, cough in church, look round when the movie hits a dull stretch, try not to yawn when our loved one's going on and on about her damned row with that parking attendant.

Except this bloke stood. You could have drawn round him in a gale, he was so static. Which is another way of saying he was a hunter. Fat, okay. Nobody taking much notice of him, okay too. But he was the frightener. The man.

"Okay everybody!" Nicko's voice on some concealed intercom made me jump a mile. Everybody else started buzzing with expectation. "Here's Vermilio!"

The crowd applauded, which was a bit daft, seeing the arena people couldn't hear us, though we could hear them. The immense rotund man spoke into a microphone, a surprisingly high voice.

"The successful stakers are the following teams: Alhambra of New York, automatic entrants as last year's winner."

The crowd fell silent. I saw a couple of birds near me cross their fingers. We'd all gone quiet. Nobody strolling or pairing off now.

"Renaissance from Chicago. The New Miners from Houston, Texas—is that name for real? Will somebody ask Harry? The Strollers, Philadelphia. The Governers, Washington D.C. . . ."

Ten groups had bought places. The names were greeted with stifled exclamations, cries quickly shushed by others hanging on Vermilio's every syllable. I was enthralled. Somebody nearby was sobbing, whispering about an appeal, third year lockout and—

". . . and last the Dawnbusters of Hawaii!"

Hubbub rose. People congratulated people. Some dissolved in relief. Women squealed more ecstasy than the men. Down in the lit arena Vermilio handed over to a bloke in a plum tuxedo, who began to intone lists of figures for each of the teams Vermilio had announced. Nobody took much notice, though I saw the Florida folk, Jane Elsmeer among them, frozen at one of the panes, staring down with a terrible intensity. I eyed the signed exits, hoping I could make it if it came to a dash.

"The grand total staked on this year's game is the highest ever." The plum-coated bloke raised his pitch by way of bliss, surely the accountant. "It is two point oh nine times last year's in absolute dollars, ladies and gentlemen!"

The applause was general and heartfelt. I applauded along, smiling absently. People were muttering with some urgency near Jane Elsmeer. I edged nearer the window, apologizing to a lady whose scarlet sheath dress lacked only a Canterbury cross in gold—even a Regency copy of the Anglo-Saxon would have done.

"You get in?" she asked.

I tore my eyes from her dress. "Oh, I'm an Alhambran," I said. "I upped our stake twentyfold. I like your dress, love. Have you thought of combining it with a simpler brooch? I know those Cartiers are fashionable, but a genuine antique—"

She had to amputate herself from this guff with a low

222

excuse, whispered something to her man. I caught, ". . . the Aquilinas, right?" before she smiled, returned to collect more admiration.

The talk round the Floridans was causing some attention. "Are you particularly interested in old jewelry?" she asked, taking hold with a gamekeeper's grip.

"My life's first and only lovelust," I told her pleasantly. "Though if I'd met you earlier I'd revise my career moves. Hardly any woman can wear genuine antique gems, love. It's a delight to find one who has the class."

Not true, of course. Antique jewelry draws any woman's glory. God knows why they buy expensive modern crud, when antique decoratives are cheaper. It always amazes me.

He saw me. Across the arena, in through the sloping tinted glass opposite, Fatty Jim Bethune saw me. The growing noise, now practically arguments, round the Floridans was attracting attention. It had attracted his.

I waved, smiling. No good shouting round the balcony, but the arena lighting struck upward, picking those faces nearest the glass.

"It's him," Jane Elsmeer was saying, closing. She had a woman's second dearest wish, total attention. People were following.

"Hello, Jane," I said. "Do you get to play?"

"Lovejoy. Upped by twenty. He told me."

"At least that," I said modestly. "Though I can't claim to be in on the totalizations finalizationwise—"

And that was that. My feet hardly touched the ground.

THE room felt like a medieval Inquisition chamber. Some houses, even rooms, have an aura as if evil intentions were ingrained by a malevolent hand. In fact, it was to guard against such forces that ancient builders buried holy relics— and sometimes the architect—in the walls. Still done today, except we make polite social occasions of laying the foundation stone.

The man Vermilio watched me come. He was standing by a desk. He was the only bloke I'd ever seen not use a desk for extra authority. The plum-tuxedo accountant was beside him. Nicko was there, staring ominously past me.

Plus a line of goons standing along the paneled walling. Everybody looked at me.

"Lovejoy, huh?"

"Yes." I advanced, smiling, hand outstretched. "I don't believe I've had the—"

I was stopped by a gesture. "No games, Lovejoy. Talk."

"What about?" I waited, asked Nicko anxiously, "Nothing wrong, Nicko, is there? I did everything you said."

"Mr. Vermilio wants that you tell him what you told the Elsmeer broad." The plum-tuxedo man said the words with an accountant's terrible pedantry. People come, people go, accounts go on for ever.

"Mrs. Elsmeer? We were talking about the game. She said she hoped they'd get in, their stake was special. I said ours was twenty times up on last year's, so we were sure to play."

"Twenty." Vermilio sounded like asking for a gun. "Coats?"

"Nicko declared a little over twice last year's stake for his Alhambra team, Vermilio." Coats might well be an exploited nickname, heady stuff for an accountant. Except maybe he wasn't just an accountant.

"I can explain, Vermilio, Coats." Nicko spread his hands in appeasement. "This guy's new in. We employed him to see if he could increase the contribution from antiques. He failed." He smiled, calm personified. "We got Jim Bethune back instead."

"But Nicko," I exclaimed, indignant. "Mr. Bethune's figures were less than a twentieth of—"

"He's a blusterer, Vermilio," Nicko said. "We had to give him a try. But he couldn't deliver."

"I got the concession from Mangold's auctioneers like I promised, Nicko!" Nicko tried to interrupt, but Vermilio silenced him by a look. "The percentage from Mortdex. God, Nicko. The hack from Louisiana alone is over three times what you had from all the art markets last year! The hacks from Maynooth, Gullenbenkian, bring it at least to eighteen times Bethune's figures—"

"He's insane, Vermilio. It can't be done."

Nicko was green. His eyes did their laser trick directly

into me. I didn't care. I was suddenly immune. Once a threat is diluted, it might as well go all the way.

"Let's hear it."

Vermilio stayed on his feet. Coats called in several tuxedo people from outside. They sat around me in a circle to listen. I was made to talk. The line of goons against the paneling didn't move. Nicko stood beside Vermilio while I spoke quietly to show I wasn't a madman.

"I was working in a bar," I began. "I fancied a few antique items worn by a customer. Her sister noticed my interest, guessed I was able to recognize genuine antiques by instinct. It's called being a divvy. Nicko Aquilina came to hear of me, took me on his payroll. I investigated Jim Bethune's antiques firm in Manhattan. It was a front for fraud—"

"Fraud's essential in the California game, Lovejoy." Coats, in reprimand. I didn't respond. Let him dig my trench for me. "All our stakes are hacks."

"It's not fraud," I said quietly. "It's fair, legit legal."

Coats was irritated, challenged on his own ground.

"You heard the announcement. Washington stakes an extra half billion this year, hacked from the Irish illegal immigrant levy. Houston, Texas, cuts in the same from the environment lobby. Hawaii brings in a new billion from glass pipes—very promising, now ice-crack's on the mainland here. Chicago's brought another half billion from Pentagon hacks—"

"Dull, dull," somebody muttered. "What's new? It shoulda been new."

"Like fuckin' Philly, uh?" somebody in a gaudy polka dot bow tie shot back. The listeners brightened. I did, with the realization I was relatively small fry among this lot. "Still workin' the fuckin' Panama Bahama dirty dollar shunt? Jeech!"

"Atlanta's new," a smooth smiler put in conversationally. "Except a World Soccer Cup stadium hack only works one time. Once the stadium's been built all over the fuckin' place, that's it, though maybe next time—"

"Lovejoy?" from Vermilio.

They shut up. I was back in the limelight. "Mine isn't fraud. It's legit." My attempt at snappy speech was pathetic.

"Your antiques hack is legitimate?" Coats looked for help.

"Ring Mangold. Ask him if he's agreed to chip in a percentage of the shifted auctions. Nothing illegal there, by any country's laws. Check Gullenbenkian. It's legit. Check that Maynooth's input's legal. Ask Verbane if the Mortdex contribution's legal or not." I waxed indignant, almost believing me myself. "That's what I told Nicko, didn't I, Nicko? And Jennie. Ask Tye Dee. He'll tell you. He was with me all through when I arranged them. He's got witnesses. I've a list of hotels, room reservations."

I was moving about, pleading for antiques now, not for me.

"The trouble is, people like you come to think of antiques as a commodity. They're not. They're people, the best things on earth. Can't you see that, played right, the antiques world can chip in as much as the rest of an entire stake? Nicko'll tell you. I worked it all out for him weeks ago—"

"A legit hack?" Coats almost reeled. "There's no such thing." He looked at the Atlanta man, appealed, "The World Cup building program—the hack was twelve percent of total. Massive!"

"I don't like the word hack," I protested. "Or fraud."

Vermilio pondered massively. "Check his numbers," he said. "Nicko? He's right, you're wrong, okay?"

"Sure."

"It looks like the Alhambra stakers tried it on," Coats the accountant said. "Risking less'n they hacked. Should they lose, they keep mosta the hack. If they win, then nice for them."

Vermilio smiled, like a mountain parting to show worse mountains in the interior. "Compensation," he announced. "A bet. Nicko's on the line. He wins, he keeps his ass. He loses . . ."

The meeting dissolved in whoops and an exchange of bets. I looked at Nicko, but received nothing. He knew only what I knew. I was pouring sweat too, and the air-conditioning was at maximum chill.

FARO'S said to be the oldest card game ever.

You pick a card, and chuck away the rest of that pack. Then you take a new pack, and deal into two piles. If the

226

matching card falls into one pile, you win. If in the other, you lose.

Money, usually. Life, in Nicko's case.

The Alhambra crowd assembled in silence away from the exit signs, when finally the galleries were crowded and rumors had settled into a steady hum of hatred. I'd tried to say hi there to Jane Elsmeer, but she'd managed nothing more than a reflex twitch of the lips. I'd even smiled at the scarlet lady to no avail.

"Play ball!" somebody called. I wish they'd warned us. I came slowly down to the deep russet pile, heart banging enough to shake me.

"The Alhambra syndicate, first. Nicko Aquilina plays."

A girl was at the green, placing decks of cards. People were examining them, all watched by Vermilio and Coats. The scrutineers nodded, talking as if everything was normal.

"We go first, eh?" I asked a man craning next to me.

"You an Alhambra?" He asked through the artificial dusk, staring. "Good luck."

Why did I need luck, for heaven's sake? I'd done the decent thing, revealed the truth about my scams, told Vermilio how everything worked when I was asked. No. It was Nicko, Gina, the rest who were for the high jump if Nicko lost. Tough luck. But I'd soon be out of here . . . wouldn't I? Vermilio had said Nicko, not me.

Suddenly I wanted Nicko to win. Not because my throat was slate dry, no. And honestly not because I felt faint at the thought of the terrible crime that would be committed on him if he didn't win. But we'd been, if not quite friends, sort of acquaintances who'd done each other no real harm, and I'd quite enjoyed my stay in America after all, lovely country and everything—

"Ten of diamonds is Alhambra's card."

Nicko placed the card face up for all us watchers to see. Coats nodded to the girl, who slowly started dealing her pack, one card to her left, another to her right. People murmured. I swallowed, trying tiptoes to see over heads. Word had spread that more hinged on this result than mere money, crime.

"Your win," she said. Jack of clubs.

"My win." Three of hearts.

"Your win." Ace of spades, to a swell of talk swiftly muted. People near me made superstitious gestures.

"My win." A four, clubs.

Fingers sometimes do their own thing. Mine were trying hard to grasp hold of my palms, hoping for a heavenly ladder.

"Your win. Game over!"

The babble erupted, me whimpering what was it, who'd won, was it—?

"Lucky," the man grinned with gold teeth at me. I could have throttled him.

The crowd relaxed, talking, betting, swapping predictions. I pressed through to glimpse Nicko stepping back, taking his place in the line-up as the next player stepped up. God, but he was cool, that Nicko. I saw Gina's expression across the arena fishbowl. Waxen, a million years old. Where was Sophie Brandau? I'd not seen her since I'd arrived. And Kelly Palumba, lucky in her addiction to be out of this. Monsignor O'Cody was gray, talking intently with three grave suited men, explaining his innocence in everything, the way of all religious leaders.

"Philadelphia to play. Frank Valera the nominee."

We—Nicko, I mean—were safe for the rest of this round. I didn't listen. All I wanted now was for the rest to lose first round, and Nicko'd be clear. I went to ask for a drink. The door goon wouldn't let me out until the whole first round had been played all through. Then he allowed me into the grand salon, where a good-humored barkeep poured me lemonade, asking if I'd won much so far. They all wished me luck as I reentered. The pillocks thought it was routine gambling.

Start of the second round. I asked people in the semidarkness who was still in, got told to shush. Nicko was just stepping up to pluck the marker card, as the girl's new pack was shuffled in. We—no, *he*—wanted the seven of spades this time.

He made it with only five cards remaining. I collapsed with relief. He had the cool to smile at Vermilio as he withdrew without a wobble. I was almost fainting with fear, my suspicion hardening that maybe Nicko's fate would also be mine. I wanted to ask the man with the gold teeth why he'd called me lucky. It was Nicko who was up for the chop, wasn't it?

People were whispering all round the gallery now. There's something about terror that stimulates. The women were panting, the men steaming with heat. Passion was king. The place felt humid, as tropical outside as in. Hands were moving. Suggestions were being whispered. I heard some woman groan a soft "Oh *God*," pure desire. A lecher's dream. It happens in cockfights, some sudden lust blamming your mind from nowhere.

By taking hold of people I learned that four had lost in the first round. I stood as if stunned. Gina's face had gone. Instead, Fatty Jim Bethune's stared down beside that of Monsignor O'Cody. His lips were moving. A prayer, even? I was tempted to walk round the glass gallery, stand with them, maybe ask Gina where was Sophie, decided I didn't want to be with a load of losers, and stood shaking while the cards were shuffled. I wanted the dealer girl, now a lovely dark lass who'd removed all her rings, to fall down in a palsy, anything to stop the cards coming.

Six remaining for the second round. Two more lost while I watched and had to forfeit their stakes. People had calculators out, clicking and tapping, in that terrible tide of whispering, the heat impossible.

"Third round," the caller announced. "Alhambra, Nicko Aquilina."

The door was just closing. I made it to the salon, asked for some grub, went to the kitchen, following its noises.

My voice had almost gone. I was drenched, sopping and unwholesome, wet running down my nape, my thatch of hair plastered down Twenties style. A bloke suffering from supernourishment among the trays and gleaming steel surfaces shouted for assistants, and I was brought a plate of genuine American food, meaning it was bigger than me. I asked could I sit in the air, and they let me through.

It was coolish out on the kitchen step. I sat, noshing. Nicko was up there in the game, his awful stare now no use. Everything hinged on the turn of a card his way. Or not. I looked out into the night. Sophie, Rose Hawkins, that sister of hers. The ambitions of Sophie's husband Denzie, consummate politician. And the reason they—okay, so Hirschman gave the word—tried to have me killed in New Orleans. And Bill's death. Sokolowsky. And the hotel fire. And upstairs in that enclosed arena of green baize Nicko was even now winning. Or losing. What was the statistical chance, one in four? Racing punters say there's no way to win above two to one.

Behind me the kitchen clattered in its steam. Hideous places, kitchens. The kitchen had gas. Gas from cylinders. I left my plate, stepped out. Two dogs loped by, black and straining. I called a hi to the dog handler.

"Lovely animals," I called.

"Bastards," he grunted, jerking and pulling.

God, but dogs can look malevolent. A muted roar wafted out into the night. I almost collapsed. Nicko's win, or loss? The card could fall only one way, no in-between.

Cylinders. I'd nothing to light anything with, and they were huge great things, shining with dull reflections from the floodlights of the Revere's facade. It was eerie, a waiting film set. Movie memories. I shook. Maybe I was coming down with something. Worse, maybe I wasn't, and reality was knifing my soul.

Another guard walked by, coated in red plaid, a hunter's nebbed cap showing for a second against the lake's distant gleam, his boots scuffing gravel. I called a hi there, got a grunt as he passed. Maybe I'd sounded drunk enough. I'd tried.

Seven cylinders, two already tubed into the wall below the noisy kitchen's half-open windows. Each cylinder had a pale panel, presumably warning of calamities that could ensue if you didn't watch out. I've always been frightened of these damned things. I once saw an accident at school. A cylinder had fallen sideways, being unloaded from a lorry, the valve striking against a curb and popping off a hundred feet into the air. The oxygen cylinder had shooshed along the ground like a torpedo, smashing through the school wall, miraculously missing us little pests standing frozen to the spot. Nobody had been injured. We'd thought it wonderful, especially as the white-faced science teacher sent us all home for the day.

If Nicko'd lost, they'd come looking for me. I reached, unscrewed each of the two connecting nuts until I could hear an ugly hissing sound from the valve. I wanted a long, slow leak. I went along the row of cylinders and did the same. It's gambling people who are supposed to like fear. I'm not one. My arms were almost uncontrollable by the time I'd done the last. I stood there, legs trembling. Was this liquid gas fuel lighter than air once it vaporized? Did it just float up, to give some future astronaut a fright when he lit his fag in the stratosphere? Or did it sink low and lie on the ground like a marsh miasma? I'd vaguely heard that was what frightened our ancients, when marsh gases lit spontaneously, their sinister blue flames flickering along the roadside swamps and scaring travelers to death. If the latter, I was standing here being gassed, risking being blown to blazes. A stray spark from the kitchen window could set the gas ball off.

I returned the chef's plate, said it was the best nosh I'd had since my wedding, and scarpered back to the salon.

To see a few men and women emerging for a smoke and a drink. They stayed clustered by the doors to the gallery, not to miss the call.

"It's the last play," a woman told me when I asked. "Nicko Aquilina's on the line this time. He and L.A. are left in."

She was drooling, kept taking my arm. Everybody was thrilled, breathing fast, loving it.

"It's thrilling, hon," she told me huskily. "Know what I mean?"

"Sure do," I said. I lit her cigarette for her. "I'm so excited I just can't tell. You here with somebody? I'm Lovejoy."

"My husband." She hid her scorn so only most of it showed. Her head inclined and her lips thinned. "I'm Elise Shepherd." A suave man, cuffs glittering with diamond links. Ramon Navarro from some old black-and-whiter. Odd how many here were lookalikes of the famous. Something in the California air?

There was something else in the air.

"Pity," I said quietly, squeezing her arm. "Elise, love. I've watched you since I arrived." I made sure Ramon Navarro was making headway with a slender bird sequined in turquoise.

"You have?" She squeezed my arm, glancing, weighing opportunities. Somebody caught her rapid scan, waved. She hallooed, trilled fingers.

"Is there nowhere we could go for the last round and . . . ?"

"Yes?" Her tongue idled along her upper lip.

"And enjoy each other's company?"

"God, no. I might be able to . . . no, that wouldn't work. Barney'd miss me, the bastard."

An announcer called the restart. I kept hold of her, desperately needing camouflage. She interpreted my fright as passionate desire, which it was.

"There's a corridor around the gallery," she said quickly, as we all began to move and talk rose excitedly. Some silly old sod told me this was the most exciting time he'd ever experienced. I could have hit him.

"Where, for Christ's sake?" I could have clouted her too. A smile flitted across her mouth. "You're a tiger, hon. Door to the right. We could hear the calls from out there, while . . ."

"See you there. Hurry, darling."

The goon standing at the gallery entrance had seen me talking with the woman. I winked. He raised his eyebrows, knowing the score. I walked through the corridor door, leaving the gallery entrance.

The corridor was empty. Wide, dark maroon velvet walls, gilded statues with lamps simulating old torches in frosted glass. Pathetic. Twice the price of genuine antique lanterns. Designers are unbelievable. I walked slowly down the corridor, counting steps, hearing the faint hubbub inside. The corridor curved round the gallery. Windows, closed against the thick night's slushy aromatic air, were seried round the curved walls. Ornate, with alcoves every ten yards, plush double seats trying to look Regency.

Except there was a goon, standing there against an inner wall. And another beyond him. They'd thought of everything, our Malibu hosts. I walked, nodding as I passed the first. The second was twenty yards further on.

Hurry Elise, you lazy cow. Where the hell was she?

She was coming to meet me at a trot, somehow having escaped from her husband the other way. I grabbed her, nodded to the goon with a feeble smile. He turned away, walked deliberately back toward the door I'd come through. I crushed her close, squeezing the life out of her, pulling her along the corridor.

"Wait! Here—"

"No, er," I gasped, trying to rush and reveal deep heart-felt passion. What the hell was her name? "We must have . . . I can't wait, darling."

"This one!"

She tried slowing into another alcove. Luckily it was occu-pied, a couple twisting sinuously to synchronized gasps. I hauled her, whisper-babbling. A goon turned aside, arms folded. God knows what they were used to.

"Last round, folks!" The announcer's echo made me whimper.

"Here, darling?"

"Yes, yes!" I flung her down and clawed feverishly at her bodice. Why the hell are their clothes so complicated? You'd think they'd go for simplicity. You can get scarred for life. "I can't wait, er . . ." Name? Esme, Ellen? "Darling."

Directly below us, faint clashes of the kitchen. If I'd had any sense I'd have counted the windows along that side to make absolutely sure, but maybe the dog handlers would have stopped me.

We overtook passion on the outward run, me ripping at her, shoving the dress off her shoulders and scrabbling at her thighs. The more uncontrollable my sheer lust, the more authentic my presence out here in the corridor while the idiot of an announcer called for silence.

"Alhambra's card, the jack of hearts!"

My mouth was everywhere on Esme, only occasionally meeting hers as we mangled and mauled.

"Don't mark me, Lovejoy, for God's sake, honey, no, no—"

"Darling," I gasped, sprawling over Ella, almost forgetting

233

why I was there in the storm of frenzy. There was no doubt she was gorgeous, a million times more wondrous than any woman I'd ever—

"Alhambra win!"

Thanks, heaven, I remembered to say as Emma and I sank into that mutual torment, giving hurt and receiving it, wrestling to deny and abuse. She was openly weeping with delight, mouthing crudities, emitting a guttural chugging cough as we— "Alhambra lose ... Alhambra win ..."

Win, Nicko, I thought. At least, I would have thought that if I wasn't sinking below consciousness as Elsa dragged me in and down and out into space and bliss was enveloping—

"Alhambra lose. Jack of hearts, and Alhambra lose ..."

Eh? I slammed into Esta, listened to that reaching hum that followed me, calling desperately for my mind to realize, and *do* something. I dragged away from Elena with a long wail of deprivation, scrabbled for my jacket, which some stupid pillock had cast aside, fumbled, yanked out the cigarette lighter that I'd stuck in the right-hand pocket after lighting the bird's cigarette, and hopped with my pants round my ankles across the corridor toward the window, whimpering with fright and seeing Elsa's thunderstruck face gaping after.

You can't open a window with your pants down, nor trying to pull them up. You can't kick, either. I had my jacket. I wrapped it round my arm, averted my face and slammed the window glass, feeling something maybe give in my elbow. I felt the muggy night air wash in.

"What the—?" somebody along the curved corridor called.

The lighter was a gas thing. I pressed, got light, spun the control for tallest flame, tried to look out and down as a goon hurtled at me, lobbed the thing out onto the cylinders below.

Heat slammed the world, spinning it round. Odd, but all a brain remembers is clatter, clatter, when you find it hard to think what on earth could be clattering, when fire is shooting with a terrible tearing noise and a whole side of a building comes apart with a low screaming sound.

234

I remember thinking I should have maybe warned Emelda, at least told her what I was planning, but that's typical for me, because by then something prickly was cramming itself into my face and people were screaming about fire, and a great golden shape was mushrooming out of the darkness nearby as a building crumbled and the hillside spread light and flame as a beacon for the world.

27

YOUR mind plays tricks. I can see myself running, scrambling up when I fell among vegetation, hauling myself along on all fours when the terrain suddenly let me down. It was some old serial I'd seen when little, funny man at antics to make laughter. Except this one was bleeding, clothes anywhere. And it was me.

Finally laying himself down, spent and stunned, among rocks with a curtain of flames ascending the hillside, something from a biblical epic now, roaring with a terrible grandeur and a massive building's turrets silhouetted against the orange-scarlet. So many colors, so much to see, if only the man's eyes could see. They couldn't quite focus. And people were screaming and shouts coming closer among scrub. And, oddest of all, whole trees suddenly exploding like they'd been fragged by grenades as the heat reached them and their romantic perfumes caused the night to quiver in a death thrill as they sucked the flames into each burst of spark.

And the wahwahs, flicking their reds and yellows and blues in feeble simile while the mountainside erupted in roars and the fire moved through the vegetation like savage ascending lava.

The helicopters came, and police, and lights shone from the sky throughout the land, and it was all fireworks and spacecraft and people jumping down.

In one last feeble frame, me looking down from some great flying thing onto the forecourt of that great place, where uniformed people, very like police, were taking orders from a dapper figure standing there in the mayhem and disorder as vehicles and helicopters moved stately all about him, the center of that swirl. Except it couldn't be him, because he was surely dead, wasn't he? He'd lost the game. And in any case he was the instigator of the crimes, and the deaths. Hadn't he ordered two people killed, not counting me? And I sank and let the frigging world get on with it. I should have stayed with Irena, and left things alone, let them take their course. Or maybe I ought to have run back in for her after the explosion? Better to have stayed making love, even if it was on that fake antique banquette.

At least I'd have finished something.

"MR. SHAMOON? Joe?"

Somebody was tapping my face, like nurses do when you're coming round from the anesthetic, the swine.

A policeman was sitting by the bedside. Mine. Why mine?

"Statement time, Joe."

He had a brewer's goiter, the beer belly hauled in by an ineffectual belt hung about with firearms and ominous leatherette cases. All that blubber was presumably paid for. But why is adiposity threatening in uniform? A thin geezer would have seemed friendlier.

"Eh?" Who was Joe? I wasn't up to discussing people yet. I watched the cop. He chewed, more threat. A nurse swept in, swept out. Should be paid by the mile.

"Where were you when the fire started at the Revere, Joe?"

"The fire?" I was Joe?

My mind cranked slowly into gear. A hospital of some kind. Should I recover, or stay slightly delirious? I've been concussed before now. This didn't feel quite the same.

"I remember a fire," I said slowly. It seemed to take years to get the words out. "A sort of blast, people running, screaming, helicopter, fire up a hillside . . ."

"You got it, Joe." He seemed pleased, told a hand recorder the time, place, date. "What were you doing at Revere Mount?"

Not what you think, officer. "Waiting for the boss. Some sort of charity . . ."

"Uh huh. You see the fire start?"

"No. I was with a . . . I think there was a broad."

"Okay, Joe. I'll be back."

He left. Joe lay wondering why he wasn't Lovejoy.

The jacket? It was surely mine, the one I'd grabbed up. Or was it? The neighboring alcove had held the moaning couple. They'd been further into reality than Ellen and me. I couldn't quite remember if the bloke had shed his jacket. But I could recollect how I'd had to shuffle obliquely across the corridor to the window, snatching up a jacket as I'd hopped, trying to haul up my pants with one hand while . . .

Good old Joe Shamoon. Hope he made it. Or maybe he was still back there, into bliss?

I slumbered, woke and had a drink. Orange juice.

When I woke it was night. I clambered erect, steadied my dizziness against the wall, checked I wasn't bleeping from any wires into one of their infernal machines or being dripped into.

There was a light switch. I put it on, stared at myself in the mirror. Yes, Lovejoy all right. For a fleeting second I'd had a horrid vision of seeing some other bloke's face, as on corny telly reruns. I looked almost a picture of health.

My clothes were in a small wall cupboard, but no sign of any wallet. I brooded and dozed until dawn, then got hold of the first nurse I could and asked for my valuables, please. She brought them quickly, openly assuming I wanted to arrange payment for hospitalization. I almost choked on that, but it seems to be their system.

"Sure this is mine?" I checked shrewdly.

"Positive, Joe."

Still Shamoon. I had Joe's wallet, billfold of money, credit cards with signatures, two sets of keys, driver's license, spectacles. I didn't need the specs, but took them anyhow, and two checkbooks. Joe did all right for himself. I wondered what Mrs. Joe Shamoon was like. Maybe I could finish what naughty old Joe had started so vigorously, when I found the addresses. The two addresses were in L.A. Both had phone numbers.

With many a groan and wheeze, I asked the desk girl to hold the completion papers steady while I signed my credit-card gelt over to the hospital. The sum made me gasp, but I disguised it as a sudden twinge. I sent down for new casual clothes, billing it up to good old Joe Shamoon.

Then I left hospital, after a health check with the registrar. They called him a resident intern, as if he were an old-age prisoner. Funny language. He said I'd got off okay, but prescribed a ton of pills for me. I put them in a dustbin as I left.

One thing, I bet Joe Shamoon was having a hell of a time if he was trying to get treatment on Lovejoy's credit in there.

"What's the joke?" the taxi driver asked, surly.

"I just got better in hospital," I said.

"That's a joke?" He snickered. "Hell, L.A.'s the joke, man."

REDONDO Beach was the second of the two addresses. It was a low condominium block alongside the seafront road. Joggers were scooping their feet the way they do when finally the taxi dropped me by the sand. Sunshades and the weirdest collection of parasols adorned the coast in numbers I'd never seen before.

I tried dialing both of Joe's homes, in case he should answer and I'd get myself arrested. Also, I was suddenly more worried about turning up, a strange husband for an alarmed wife, maybe a set of babes all wondering who the new geezer was. No answers.

One thing about California, you can wait on a beachside without giving rise to suspicion. It's what the ocean's for. I sat in a line of reminiscing geriatrics from the Bronx and New Jersey and Brooklyn all saying how they'd like to go back but who the hell wanted snow, and better to get mugged occasionally in sunshine than in an alley filled with ice and falling masonry, huh? Some, especially the old birds, had reflectors shooting hot sunshine up from below under their chins. They wore false white paper noses and a ton of cream. They all agreed retirement was great. I said I could see that, listened until the guard in the condominium block got up from his stool under the awning and went inside. I said so long to my gang and quickly entered, fiddling with the keys, then climbing to the third floor.

The doorbell brought nobody. I worked the three keys— no flies on Joe Shamoon—and let my breath out slowly as no dogs, pets, families came forward with fast-fade grins.

It was a small place, as America goes. Two bedrooms, a

kitchen, a living space with a view of the seafront, and quite a pleasant small balcony with chairs bleaching contentedly in the sunshine.

And Nicko.

Behind me the outer door opened gently, letting the verandah curtains waft out, then closed sibilantly. Tye Dee and his goons, doubtless. I was suddenly so tired. All for nowt, my exertions of last night—or the night before last? I'd lost a day somewhere.

"Wotcher, Nicko."

He laid aside his book, Moss's *The Pleasures of Deception* I noticed with curiosity. He nodded, painstakingly lit a pipe. I watched, the old craving coming as always. I once gave a pipe up, still hanker after the ritual. The swine drew in, pocketed his pouch, stubbed the bowl, did the whole, what did they say hereabouts, enchilada?

"Wotcher, Lovejoy." He managed it, with the vicious shark grin of a born killer. "We gotta change words."

"What's the point?" I couldn't help being bitter. I should have taken my chance, let the pig die instead of blowing the damned building to smithereens. Served him right, the murdering—

"You got work to do for us, Lovejoy. Antiques."

Well, maybe his killer's grin was friendly.

"Eh?" I might spin the talk out and make a dash for it, hide out somewhere among my geriatric pals on the waterfront.

"We had no idea about antiques, art, that kinda stuff, being the scale you showed." He leaned forward, the pipe smoke driving me mad. "Deal, Lovejoy?"

"Deal, Nicko."

"You work for us three months, okay? Then you go."

His features were affable, but knowing. What a pleasant bloke, I thought after quick revision.

"Hang on." I dredged up a score of suspicion. "How'd you know where to find me?"

"We planted Joe Shamoon's stuff on you. Easy. Poor Joe's in surgery. He'll make it—until his wife learns the circumstances of his, uh, accident."

In some helicopter. I remembered being lifted, flying, people cutting my clothes, lights swirling.

"Nicko." My head was aching. I'd had no rest except for hospital, and their idea of quiet's to clash cymbals all bloody night. "Who's this we?" He'd just been slain by the game syndicates for losing. I'd heard it called, while Esmerelda and I'd been making smiles. Optimism's not got staying power like pessimism.

He waited, smiling at the people behind me. "Got it?" he asked at last.

"Gina?" I said.

She came round, smiling, sat across from me with the sun-filled verandah window playing her advantage. She looked good enough to eat with honey, except you wouldn't need the honey.

"Gina." I made it a nonquestion.

"In one, Lovejoy. Well, in a couple hundred, give or take."

"You're police? Or crooks who turned coats?"

"You got it. Federal switchers. We got watchdogs, so we play ball." He was wondering what I'd guessed. I helped him.

"Why'd you pull Tye and the hoods, let me get killed?"

"You did too good, Lovejoy. We want control of money routes, not new shark routes everywhere."

So I was to be part of their control. At least I'd be alive. Except that wasn't enough.

"It started with drugs pure and simple, Lovejoy."

"Not pure, not simple." Gina was gentler but more implacable. "Ice, heroin for the postcrack sinks, anything to double on, at any cost."

"The Drug Enforcement Agency started us in, Lovejoy. The game was dominated by them and the junk bonders and savings-loan defrauders. It used to be little old currency swappers."

"Days of innocence," Gina said. She could arrest me any day.

"You showed us a new line, Lovejoy." Nicko went slowly to the window, gestured for somebody to come, but take their time. "Though we'd learned plenty of other new lines. Property, hacks on harbors, airports, commodities, information tapping, computer miking, show biz, religious flakes, lotsa old stuff. You showed us the power of antiques." He turned, curious. "How come we didn't see it before you came, Lovejoy?"

"You trusted reputations, Nicko. Like famous auction houses—you think the great Fake exhibition at the British Museum could have come about without them? Or that Echt Vals Real Fake Exhibition a decade ago in Amsterdam? Or that terrorists aren't a part of the antiques game, robbing simply to sell or ransom. You should read about Istanbul's go-betweens." My tone was growing bitter, hating the way antiques get it every time, treated like dirt except when money gets quoted.

"We don't miss much, Lovejoy," Gina said.

I rounded on her. Somehow I was standing. "Much you know, you stupid bitch. You miss the nose on your face. Can't you see that in antiques there's *no such thing as theft*? Oh, there's fraud all right, tricks a-plenty. But theft? Antiques laugh at it."

"Prove you weren't just a lucky bastard, Lovejoy!" Nicko was pointing at me.

"Shall I?" I yelled, in fury now it was all falling into place. "Shall I, you legalized murdering sods, the pair of you? Shall I? Seeing you let poor old Sokolowsky get crisped just to stay in with the syndicate? Shall I? Seeing you let Bill get run down for the same reason? Seeing you were willing to have me shot down, when they missed burning me in the Benidormo hotel blaze?"

He backed down, with an effort. "Some things have to be, Lovejoy. It's a war we're in. People get killed in wars."

"Aye, you murderous pig, but not always the right ones." I was so mad I couldn't see for a sec, just stood there shaking. Magda and Zole could have died in that alley. Worse, so could I. Just like that Tony off the *Gina*, during my introduction to the whole rotten business. I just didn't know who was right or wrong anymore. Both sides played as dirty. I was so frigging tired, worn out.

"I'll tell you," I said dully. "Think back. That Gardner

Museum theft in Boston—what was it, quarter of a billion, yesterday's giveaway prices? They stole Vermeer, Rembrandt, ultimate antiques. Tot up the thefts of antiques for that and the previous four years, it comes to four billion, yesterday dollars."

"And there's no such thing as theft?" Nicko scoffed. The curtains wafted out. This time I didn't hear the snick of the latch. I was past caring.

"You think you've proved me wrong? The Japanese Yakuza, the Mafia, all the terrorists and extortionists in the world know different. Heard of such a thing as the statute of limitations? Most countries have one. Time has a habit of passing. In a couple of years Monet's *Impression Sunrise*, stolen from the Marmottan Museum, Paris, will emerge. The thieves can market the damned thing, immune by law. It's legal now anyway—Japan's statute of limitations is only two years."

Gina asked, "Hasn't it been recovered?"

I stared. I honestly don't believe these people. "Aye, love. *Fourteen times!* Each time's the one true genuine one." I explained to ease their perplexity. "You see, love, once a special unique porcelain, bronze, ancient vase, piece of one-off furniture, painting, is stolen, there's very little to go on to tell if what's being offered for ransom is the one true original. Or a fake."

"They do that?"

"The *Mona Lisa* was stolen in 1911. Half a dozen fakes were sold for underhand fortunes—until the genuine one walked in, years later. It's routine.

"Ninety-five percent don't even get recaptured. Ransom's a cool ten percent of value. Your own Foundation of Art Research admits that only one-twentieth ever come home anyway." I smiled, hoping it was as wintry as Nicko's. "But then the statute declares the robbers immune, and out they come. If there's any hassle, they simply add some small blemish— slightly change a hue of the sky in one corner, enlarge the canvas perhaps. You law people make me frigging laugh. You think because an antique's catalogued somewhere that nobody'll buy?"

"But they will?"

"Give me the money and a month, mister. I'll buy you any antique or art work stolen in the past two decades."

"What about the ones heisted before that?"

"Advertise. Orly and Jennie'll tell you. It's quite legal." I turned, made way for them to enter the conversation. "Antiques are the one currency that survives inflation, flood, financial panic."

"Or fund laundering?" Jennie asked.

"Ideal. It's all the better—you don't have to give the artists their cut. They've already starved to death yonks ago."

"No moral sheet, Lovejoy," Orly said. He still hated me.

I turned, gave him my bent eye. "I hated you less when you were only a murderous crook, Orly." I shook my head at Nicko. "No thanks, Nicko. No deal. Do your own dirty work."

"He's the one, all right," Nicko said. "Book him."

28

"YOU got that, Lovejoy?"

"Aye, love. Off pat."

"Your story of what happened after the explosion?"

"I found myself running over the hillside away from the fire. Got a lift, hid out at a filling station in El Segundo. Stole money and clothes from a motorist who stayed over."

Jennie had worked with me the full twenty-four hours.

"And where are you heading?"

"For Manhattan. I'll stay with Melodie Van Cordlant on Madison. If not her, then with Mrs. Brandau. Should I check Jim Bethune out?"

"Bethune died in the fire."

Another. I didn't sigh, just nodded and quoted the contact numbers Jennie'd drilled into me.

"Good, Lovejoy. You've got it. Contact in emergencies."

So they'd come and save me? Like they did Bill? Like Sokolowsky? Tony?

"You'll take over the antiques place, tie in with Busman like you did. Peel off the auctioneers, same as you suggested. Then you'll big-buck buy, establish the chain of selling through the international art market . . ."

I went along, listening to her gunge. Loony tunes, for a bloke like me. I'm the one who thrills to a single Chelsea porcelain figurine sold over a nosh bar counter in a Suffolk village. This scale of things was money madness, coin crazy. I only felt right at a village jumble sale, with one woman whose eyes I could safely look at, playing that most ancient of all games.

"Sure, Jennie," I said most sincerely. "Exact. I got it exact." God. I almost sounded right.

"You establish contact first from here. They're still in L.A. We got their numbers, okay?" She passed me a typed list. They were all there. Sophie, Melodie, Kelly Palumba,

Moira Hawkins. I was into a winner here—as long as I loved what I was to do. "You arrange to meet them here, play them along. They're in separate hotels."

"Gimme the phone, hon."

Jennie frowned. "Try to keep that Limey talk, okay? It kinda pleases, y'know?"

"Very well, love."

I spoke to Melodie, Kelly, and Sophie Brandau in that order. Melodie was over the moon, thrilled I should be desperate to check she wasn't injured in the fire.

"I've been worried sick, Melodie doorling," I said, almost starting tears at my deep sincerity. "How soon can I see you, sweetheart?"

"Come right away, Lovejoy! We can have dinner, and—"

"I've very little money, honey."

"What's a dollar?" she screamed softly. I swore I was on my way, and dialed Kelly.

She was more difficult.

"Is that goon Epsilon with you, Palumba?" I demanded. "If so I hang up."

"Yes, but don't," she said, thinking with a woman's natural alacrity when deceiving by phone. "It's my financial adviser, Eppie. I have to see him tonight. You go to the premiere, I'll follow on, okay?"

We fixed for eightish, her place.

Sophie was circumspect, very Grace Kelly, polite and distant.

"You weren't at the Revere, love," I accused. "I wouldn't have gone if I'd known you weren't going to come. Though it's marvelous that you didn't. I'd have been frantic you might have been hurt."

"Denzie?" I heard her call. "A woman's guild wants me to speak on political family life tonight. Will that be . . . ?"

"Nine o'clock, Sophie Brandau," I told Jennie curtly. "Pencil her in. Any more?"

"No, Lovejoy." Her mouth was set into severe disapproval, squared. "Go whenever you must."

"Can I get a lift?"

"Cab it, Lovejoy. You've enough. Expenses."

"So I have!" I said brightly. "See you back at the precinct house." We'd arranged weekly reports to begin with.

I got a taxi from the rank six blocks along. I walked in the fading sunlight, which slanted across the boulevard from the lovely western horizon. You don't get horizons like those in California for colors. I strolled, looking out for muggers, sidestepping rogue joggers, watching for falling meteorites. I was learning American vigilance.

"Where to?"

It seemed an age since I'd been elsewhere, in the East, telling a Chinese cabbie to take me to America, fast as he liked. I watched the lovely curved shore line recede as we turned inland and joined the flood of traffic. God knows where everybody was going, but they were all shifting apace.

The central station wasn't quite so crowded.

TWENTY minutes to six when I reached there. I'd hung about as distantly as possible—not difficult in such a whopping place. I had coffee for ease of lurking, and stayed off center until I saw them.

In she came, cool and swinging, being eyeballed and ogled as she entered. Zole was with her, yo-yo zipping to everyone's annoyance, Sherman trotting.

It was a hard choice to make, really, for somebody like me. I'm my own worst enemy, always have been. The choice is always made for you, my old gran used to say. You think you choose, until you see what there is. Then you find it's all done, choice out of the window and your feet hurrying the way they would have anyway.

The trouble was, Magda wasn't going to be easy to bid farewell. She was a typical woman, sticking to your mind like glue just when you wanted to be away out of the starting block like a gazelle. Her and her idiot criminal maniacal treacherous little kid who shot people and thought it right just because it was me going to get gunned down. A cool Bonnie and Clyde couple, except once she'd told me about how she would send Zole to school and he'd be a great doctor, lawyer, a real educated man full growed, able to look anybody in the eye.

Nothing for it. I had to go. This was the moment to accost her, say good-bye, it was fine while it lasted, thanks for everything. She was looking at her watch, pacing. Zole was off somewhere. He'd abandoned his skateboard, was down to walking. Though I noticed he'd been carrying a trannie, to annoy everybody within earshot.

I cleared my throat, rehearsing my time-to-say-so-long speech. I'd the words all off pat, just as I'd decided in the taxi across town. I walked toward her, among the passengers heading for the barrier.

There was no decision to make, not really, not when you thought of it. Luxury, endless love, lusting my paradisical way from penthouse to penthouse, one lovely rich woman to another, panting and groping, ecstatic with delirious lovely wealth flowing my way, and every solid dollar legit as I took a massive percentage for my trouble. That was life. A dream.

"Hello, love."

She spun, gladness in her eyes.

"Oh, Lovejoy! You came! I was start'n to think maybe—"

"Where the hell's that little pillock?" I said, moving her toward the train. "Less than ten minutes to go and you let him wander off. Why do you never take any notice of what I say? Silly cow."

"Don't you start on me, Lovejoy. Not after what I've been through, waiting and worryin'—"

"Hey, man! Time you showed—"

I clipped the little sod's ear. "Where the hell've you been? I've been waiting this past half hour—"

"Hey, Magda," the little cret complained. "Can't we ditch Lovejoy? Only, I gonna get real mean he does that one more time—"

"Shut it, pillock. And turn that damned thing off." I gave Magda the three tickets I'd bought. "Come on."

"Kansas City?" Magda was clipping along in her red shoes. "Why Kansas City, Lovejoy? You never told we goin' there. I got bags packed back in the hotel—"

"You shut it, Magda. I'm sick of people asking me things." How the hell did I know why Kansas City? It was just that I recognized the name from the list of places by

248

the ticket office. "I don't even know where the bloody place is. Does Sherman travel free?"

"Lovejoy, he dumb, Magda."

We boarded the train, impossibly high off the ground like all American trains. I was telling her how I'd teach her a few essentials about antiques, get her started in a small shop. It's the easiest thing in the world to find one little good antique, then another . . .

Magda was smiling as we took seats. "Thanks, Lovejoy. Even if it is only sorta temporary. Know what? I thought you'd left without us."

I settled back as the train began to move. First thing was to make her start apologizing profusely for her terrible wicked doubt of my sterling character. Then we'd have to take it from there.

"I see, love," I said, hurt and quiet. "It's always me that's treacherous, is it? When I've risked everything to get here just to make sure you'd be safe, and Zole get somewhere settled—"

"No, honey. Hush. I'm sorry, darlin'. Me and my big mouth. I'd no right to say them things, Lovejoy . . ."

Okay, I thought, and wondered if there was a good dining car on the damned thing. Sherman snored on me, and we rolled eastward out of L.A.

FOR THE BEST IN PAPERBACKS, LOOK FOR THE

In every corner of the world, on every subject under the sun, Penguin represents quality and variety—the very best in publishing today.

For complete information about books available from Penguin—including Pelicans, Puffins, Peregrines, and Penguin Classics—and how to order them, write to us at the appropriate address below. Please note that for copyright reasons the selection of books varies from country to country.

In the United Kingdom: For a complete list of books available from Penguin in the U.K., please write to *Dept E.P., Penguin Books Ltd, Harmondsworth, Middlesex, UB7 0DA.*

In the United States: For a complete list of books available from Penguin in the U.S., please write to *Dept BA, Penguin, Box 120, Bergenfield, New Jersey 07621-0120.*

In Canada: For a complete list of books available from Penguin in Canada, please write to *Penguin Books Canada Ltd, 10 Alcorn Avenue, Suite 300, Toronto, Ontario, Canada M4V 3B2.*

In Australia: For a complete list of books available from Penguin in Australia, please write to the *Marketing Department, Penguin Books Ltd, P.O. Box 257, Ringwood, Victoria 3134.*

In New Zealand: For a complete list of books available from Penguin in New Zealand, please write to the *Marketing Department, Penguin Books (NZ) Ltd, Private Bag, Takapuna, Auckland 9.*

In India: For a complete list of books available from Penguin, please write to *Penguin Overseas Ltd, 706 Eros Apartments, 56 Nehru Place, New Delhi, 110019.*

In Holland: For a complete list of books available from Penguin in Holland, please write to *Penguin Books Nederland B.V., Postbus 195, NL-1380AD Weesp, Netherlands.*

In Germany: For a complete list of books available from Penguin, please write to *Penguin Books Ltd, Friedrichstrasse 10-12, D-6000 Frankfurt Main 1, Federal Republic of Germany.*

In Spain: For a complete list of books available from Penguin in Spain, please write to *Longman, Penguin España, Calle San Nicolas 15, E-28013 Madrid, Spain.*

In Japan: For a complete list of books available from Penguin in Japan, please write to *Longman Penguin Japan Co Ltd, Yamaguchi Building, 2-12-9 Kanda Jimbocho, Chiyoda-Ku, Tokyo 101, Japan.*